THE NECROMANCER'S

DRAGON

The North Sea
RUNEFELL
MIRRORHOLD
The Mustang Mountains
Whiteheart Trading Co.
ALFHEIM
Xyaxon's Shrine
Moonridge
The Ankoku Pass
RHUMBEK
HINTERLANDS
Diamond in the Rough Co.
Ulrich's Shrine
Gold Shard Mines
Shadowgreen Grove
Silver Creek Mines
Fractured Hills Mineshaft
The White Plains
Summerfall
Lake Peril
Graywinter
Starsong
The Grand Exchange
Azrael's Shrine
The Heartland Mines
The Opal River
Heaven's Tear
NUVAK
Purewater Fishery
Helshire Village
Blackheart Village
TO SNOWHAVEN
The Black Bog Forrest
Sunfang
The Aurora Peaks
MTS.
RIDGELAND
Starlight Railroad
Darkhollow Mines
WINTERGUARD
Dark Blood Hold
THE DRAGON'S
Ghost Lake
HEARTLAND
Azure Basin
ARMAGEDDON
1576 ED, Gwelion Sagine, Cartographer
Mount Blackrock
The Turquoise Ocean

THE NECROMANCER'S DRAGON

Book 1 in the Armageddon Trilogy

C.D. MULLER

Lunar Wolf Press

To Richard,

We never got the chance to say goodbye.

CONTENTS

CHAPTER 1: THE GIRL AND THE DRAGON

Nervous—dreadfully nervous Gromm and Beck Steelmane had been. As brothers and Flying Officers of Her Imperial Majesty's Air Force of Dragon Riders, they and their dragon, Vulcan, had barely escaped with their lives, escorting their precious cargo to Helshire Village: an unconscious young girl and a stolen dragon egg.

Gromm was the muscle of the two due to his size and bulk compared to Beck's leaner frame. The two donned silver-streaked armor, their boots shaped like dragon talons. Despite their many physical differences, they shared the same brown hair and blue eyes, connecting them as brothers. Vulcan, a solid red dragon the size of two houses with scales as jagged and sharp as obsidian, had been their partner for many years, the three sharing more than twenty years of combat experience.

The Imperial Air Force was a branch of the military that engaged in battle and other duties on the backs of dragons where only men could serve. Since the alliance made with the dragons nearly one thousand fourteen hundred years ago, the Council—a group of thirteen powerful elders gifted in magic led by Vidar Helios—learned from the One Hundred Years' War that dragons could be used as weapons of catastrophic destruction. Thus, the Council established the Force and prohibited unauthorized riders and handlers unless they served the Imperial army. Though dragons were rumored to be reincarnations of the Divines themselves, Vidar and the Council trapped them in chains to control their Divine fearing nature.

Yet, dragons weren't the only creatures being restrained; Empress Aryl Aurora, an elven maiden most fair, ruled Armageddon's empire alone after losing her husband over two hundred years ago. Since then, the land had been under hers and the Council's rule. However, Vidar feared Her Imperial Majesty succumbing to madness after the death of her husband, thus creating a political struggle. Because of this, the Council had been questioning her leadership and seizing to take control of the Empire.

They arrived at Helshire Village on the third evening, a dainty settlement with no connections to magic, as the locals didn't wish to be involved in anything strange or mysterious. Yet, it was the perfect hiding place away from the Lich who had been pursuing the dragon riders for stealing the girl and the dragon egg from him.

Known and feared as the most powerful undead necromancer among man, elf, and dwarf kind, the Lich claimed Death's throne in Oblivion before manifesting himself within the mortal realm; the underworld suffered from his ten-thousand-year sovereignty. His actual name —no one would dare speak it as it brought bad luck and misfortune. Gromm and Beck grew anxious when recalling his cultists, known as the Obsidian Order, clad in eerie silver masks and midnight blue robes chasing them from Mount Blackrock, the Lich's lair.

Blackrock's volcanic peak occupied the border of Mirrorhold and Armageddon, the fortress polluted with thick smog writhing around the obsidian castle, swirling with dark magic tainting the atmosphere. Massive like a city capital, the black magma citadel pierced the heavens with spiked towers.

As Vulcan landed gracefully before a secluded, cozy home that flaunted a stone pathway weaving through a lovely, well-kept garden, his ruby eyes fixed unblinkingly like two red moons on a man who suddenly appeared beneath the dimly lit lamppost standing guard. Gromm and Beck flinched, as they assumed the stranger appeared in a plume of smoke; he donned a long, red regal jacket with gilt trimmings and a golden waist buckle to match. The man's raven-feathered textured hair swept past his pointed ears, but his face hid behind a black and white mask. Their mysterious greeter moved more swiftly than any human could, as to be expected of an elf. Whoever he was, this stranger helped save them from the Lich and met them at the village at Divine's speed.

Though Gromm was taller than his brother, this man towered over him, peering through a fearsome mask that made the brothers quiver in their boots. One half was painted black, contrasting a flaring white design around the eye fading towards the edge, and the other side displayed the same pattern but reversed colors. Emblazoned upon the forehead was a black fox head; Gromm gasped upon recognizing it immediately: the symbol Varathka Gundisalvus—a brilliant war general and writer—used during the One Hundred Years' War.

After the battle, Gundisalvus was charged with treason, endangering the Empire for failing to disclose information about a secret weapon the Lich sought, ultimately starting the war. It was a powerful sword called Ragnarok with abilities to destroy and create worlds. After all, Xyaxon, the Divine of life and creation whose sovereignty claimed the spirit realm of Niflheim, blessed it himself. He was often portrayed as a lion made of fire, though his proper form remained unknown to mortals. The second Divine, Death, the Shepherd of Souls—whose actual name was stricken from history after losing Oblivion's throne to the Lich—was a draconic beast with seven heads and ten horns. Ulrich—whose real name couldn't be enunciated by mortal tongue—the third Divine of war, destruction, and technology, roamed the physical world as a giant emerald dragon. Together, the three Divines maintained balance and peace.

Vulcan swung his massive head around, snarling through clamped fangs at the regally dressed stranger, but Gromm spoke softly to calm his nerves. Being the brave-hearted hero he was, Beck jumped into his partner's arms; grumbling over his brother's foolishness, Gromm immediately dropped him. Yet, the elf man turned a deaf ear to their bickering as he approached the dragon's saddle fit to carry a crew of twenty bodies and quizzically looked at the unconscious young girl and satchel hiding the dragon egg.

Uttering his prayers to all three Divines, Beck cautiously stood up, shaking until Gromm placed a heavy hand on his shoulder, keeping him grounded. "W-who do we owe this pleasure?"

The mysterious stranger finally acknowledged the two after satisfying his curiosity and approached Gromm instead, deeming him the stronger brother. "Phantom Dust." They cringed at his stoic tone, but he raised his hand in peace. "You have no reason to fear me, for you and I stand on the same side. I am here to ensure the completion of your task." Phantom Dust paused when he took note of the girl's near-death state, and his eyes shimmered behind the mask. If the brothers saw, they withheld their opinions.

The young lady was a lovely maiden approaching adulthood; her long, chocolate-brown hair flowed across her thin and frail body. Dressed in only tattered rags, her dirtied and hair-covered copper-hued face still radiated with beauty; she was a gorgeous creature that lit up this dark and damp corner. Etched into her left hand was a strange symbol: a crescent shape drawn into a circle.

"What in Oblivion is that?" Beck asked, pointing at the girl's hand, but his question reached deaf ears.

Before either Gromm or Beck could argue, the man snatched the bag with the dragon egg and held it close to his chest before gesturing towards the house. "Gromm, carry the girl. Chaliss is waiting for us. Come along."

Baffled by how he knew their names, the brothers understood that Phantom Dust knew the mysterious girl, but he neither explained how nor why, and it would be improper to pry. Instead, they unloaded the saddle in silence, grateful for their moment of respite after their nearly botched mission.

As they and Vulcan stood in the middle of the sleeping settlement, a woman appeared to them, a tall, thin, and beautiful maiden. Her raven black hair was long enough to be tucked away into her leather belt, her green dress accentuating her amber eyes. Her name was Chaliss Branwen.

Without offering the men a single word, she held out her hand and pointed at them. Gromm and Beck caught each other's gazes before Chaliss said in a calm and serene voice: "Follow me inside. It's not safe out here." Dust and the two brothers nodded as she led the way. "Loki alerted me of your arrival."

"That damn fox," Gromm grumbled.

Chaliss shared in his resentment, and at the sound of his name, a brilliant orange fox about the size of a small dog ran from the front door to greet them. "Loki, at your service." The fox bowed. His mastery of their language didn't faze Dust and the brothers, as Loki was a shapeshifter, but he was only limited to three forms he could take: aside from his fox visage, he could only transform into a little girl, a raven, and an older man, using his powers when deemed necessary. The fox was only loyal to Her Imperial Majesty.

Gromm moaned, but Beck gave the fox a firm nod to acknowledge his greeting before following Chaliss inside. Her house was welcoming from the opened door to the wide hallway; gas lamps flickered like candles in the rooms, and upon the wall in the parlor was a small black and white photograph of Chaliss with her son, Rahim Branwen. The brothers' stomachs rumbled when they saw a cauldron filled with beef stew sitting over the open fire pit in the kitchen, the delicious smell teasing their nostrils. Dust, however, remained stoic and unbothered as usual.

They followed Chaliss into an empty bedroom devoid of all furniture but a freshly made twin-sized bed; a lovely window graced with a flowerpot filled with evening primroses, their golden petals gleaming like fine jewelry. Ensuring the girl was comfortable upon the fresh sheets, the five exchanged proper introductions and reaffirmed they served the same side, Gromm and Beck regaled Chaliss and Loki of their almost failed mission until Phantom Dust saved them from their deadly predicament: nearly being swallowed alive by a massive wyvern several times Vulcan's size.

"As a Chain Master," Dust began, "I can easily take down a dragon on my own."

Gromm said, "Because you're the only bloody Chain Master in Armageddon. Only one man has ever learnt the art, but your actual name eludes us."

"It's best to keep it that way."

Finally, Beck asked, once they finished their tale, "Who is the girl, and why did the Lich want her and the dragon egg?" He leaned towards his brother and whispered, "What do you reckon the Lich was going to do to them, Gromm?"

"Oh, blast it all, you nitwit." Gromm lifted his massive hand and slammed it against his brother's head, "What do you think he would do, invite them to a tea party? No, he would kill her and probably raise the hatchling for his own." They ignored Dust shifting uncomfortably in his spot as he tightened his grip around the concealed dragon egg.

"Blimey, I'm sorry. After all the things that necromancer and his bloody followers have done…it's astounding why we had to rescue them."

Dust bowed to the girl but kept his silence; Gromm crossed his arms over his broad chest but reached into the sack he carried and pulled out a rolled parchment. "Orders are orders, and I would never cross the Empress. Besides," he leaned close to Beck, "with that Phantom Dust fellow watching us, I wouldn't dare. Odd gent, but someone I wouldn't cross, that's for damn sure."

"Shh," Beck pressed a finger to his lips, but Dust didn't react; instead, he swept the girl's hair away from her delicate face.

When he finally spoke, however, the tense atmosphere only further steeped the room: "The Council isn't to know about the outcome of your mission. Only report what you must but see to it that Vidar and the others do not know this girl's name or of the egg's existence."

"*We* don't even know the girl's name, but Vidar will ask—"

Beck was wholly interrupted when Dust's head spun around. "I will not repeat myself: if word got out about her and the dragon egg and why the Lich captured them in the first place, the Council will be involved, and only the Divines know what will happen then. What is discussed here remains here."

"I could only imagine if word got out about her and the dragon. The two would become legends worthy of Divine praise," Chaliss added, and she bit her cheek; Gromm and Beck were left wondering what secrets followed the mysterious child and dragon, as Chaliss seemed to know more than they did. When Dust glared at her, Chaliss recoiled. "Forgive me. Would you like for me to make some tea?"

She used this as an excuse to leave once everyone agreed and calmed her blazing thoughts as she prepared and served earl grey with lemon and sugar, cheese crumpets, and biscuits. Even Loki indulged a little. Gromm covered his mouth with a napkin upon finishing his tea. "That tyke from the photograph—your son, I take it?"

Chaliss nodded and faced Dust. "Rahim is aware that we will have an addition to our household for the time being. The poor dear may stay for however long she needs a home."

Though Chaliss, Dust, and Loki agreed, Gromm and Beck still exhibited some reluctance to this plan in withholding information from the Council. "Won't those old coots figure it out? You can't hide the two forever. What if the dragon hatches?" Gromm snarled and grumbled when Chaliss couldn't give him an answer.

Dust snorted as he finally set down the satchel on the bed; the leather slid down, revealing a large, beautiful but jagged, oval-shaped stone about a foot long. The eggshell itself looked to be encrusted with rubies and topazes, the colors mixing like a burning flame. Never seeing a dragon egg quite like this, the brothers crept closer for a better look, Dust immediately handed it to Chaliss after tying it back in the pouch, protecting the forbidden treasure. "From Silver's calculations and the shell beginning to harden, I fear that may be soon. Keep it safe and hidden for now until we can figure out what to do later," he warned, "Soon, I'll ask Silver to come for it when everything settles. Let no one know you have it."

Once Chaliss agreed and left with the precious paragon, Beck nibbled on his crumpet like a mouse with a piece of cheese. "It would be treason if we got caught."

"This is a very precarious situation indeed, but we won't as long as you do exactly as I say," Dust declared, "Only report what you must, but no more. Your orders are directly from Her Imperial Majesty."

Gromm cleared his throat and clapped his hands together. "Then, we have no business staying here, and Vulcan is giving us an earful. We may as well return to Alfheim for a much-needed holiday."

After the Steelmane brothers said their farewells to Dust, he turned and looked at the girl once more before taking his leave. "May the Divines watch over you and the dragon, Selena Liongod."

CHAPTER 2: THOR

Nearly a week had passed since sixteen-year-old Selena Liongod, a lovely young maiden blossoming into womanhood with sun-kissed copper skin, had awoken from her near-death-like stupor. Yet, the village remained unchanged regardless of welcoming its newest resident. What baffled Chaliss and Rahim the most was that she had no memory of who she was or why the Lich captured her, to begin with.

Not too thrilled about the idea of having an older adopted sibling, Rahim teased and bullied Selena for the mark she bore on her left hand. It took him almost a month to adjust, but Rahim finally made amends for his terrible behavior, and the pair were like brother and sister once they declared a truce.

Selena was intelligent for her age, always caught somewhere in the house with a book open in her lap. Subjects mattered not, whether they were about Armageddon's history, different magics, or mathematics—Selena considered each tome a piece of hidden treasure. If she didn't have a book ready, Rahim trapped her in a card game or a round of chess. He may have been the one to teach her the game rules, but Selena always won.

Just as the sun crept through her window, Selena awoke with a jolt from another dream she had about the legendary sword, Ragnarok. Lately, Xyaxon's famous weapon was her new topic of interest, so it came as no surprise that it often haunted her thoughts. However, there was also a dragon egg that Chaliss kept hidden in the storage room, its shell beginning to crack.

It didn't take long for Rahim's voice to rattle down the hall as she got up; her eyes lazily scanned the opened book about Ragnarok sitting on her bedside dresser, and Selena remembered she fell asleep reading again.

Rahim stormed up the stairs and pounded on her bedroom door. "This isn't the time to sleep. Mum is coming back from town soon to make breakfast."

Rubbing her eyes, Selena slowly opened the door when he wouldn't give up, her long hair tangled in knots. "It's too early for this."

"Rubbish." His eyes landed on the book cover, and he cringed; unlike her, Rahim loathed books. "No wonder why you're so tired. You spent the night reading again," he saw the cover, "What's this about Ragnarok? It's just a myth."

"I beg to differ. Like Varathka Gundisalvus, Genesis Altessa believes and has proof of its existence."

Rahim drew a blank expression. "Genesis who?"

"The scholar who studied dragons and discovered magic over sixteen thousand years ago—"

"Right, I believe I've heard you prattle on about your secret love before." Selena's face burned, and when she denied his accusations and explained Genesis died long ago, Rahim added, "Dead men won't break your heart. Besides, you shouldn't worry so much about reading; it's not important."

"It is to me."

He groaned. "I thought all women talked about marriage and finding a good husband with prospects."

Face still flustered, Selena looked down. "Now you're just ridiculous. I may be sixteen, but that doesn't mean I'm supposed to find a husband. Besides, I wouldn't make a good wife. I'm not pretty enough."

Rahim rolled his eyes. "Here we go again—I don't want to hear this." The two stopped when the door clicked open downstairs, and Chaliss called their names. Eyes gleaming like a candle's flame, Rahim excused himself to bother his mother instead.

Selena sighed at Rahim's point; women who developed an interest in reading were ignored or sometimes shunned and ridiculed in public. However, this did not stop her from enjoying her hobbies.

She inspected herself in the full-body mirror, running her fingers through her long and wavy chocolate-brown hair. She was thin—too thin, compared to most girls and women in the village. The only physical feature she liked about herself was her sea-green eyes. Yet, seeing her left palm bearing the symbol, Selena sighed as she wrapped it in a piece of cloth, her same routine every time she left the house. Much like her memories, the mark was foreign to her. Chaliss was at a loss whenever Selena asked; she tried researching the matter before, but every book she believed had the answer led to a dead end. "Why would anyone want someone like me as a wife? I'm too different, but I suppose it could be a good thing."

Books from her collection cluttered her desk on top of a large world map listing different continents. One landmass read Armageddon, their Empire. Because of Armageddon's proximity to the far north, the continent was always icy—even their summer months could expect some snowfall. Runefell was another connecting landmass to the east; Mirrorhold, the size of the two combined, was their western neighbor. Blackstar, however, floated in isolation south in the ocean.

Armageddon comprised four powerful kingdoms, each with its capital. Alfheim was the city of the elves in the Fire Kingdom, while Rhumbek belonged to the dwarves in the Earth Kingdom. Nuvak, primarily humans, was in the Air Kingdom, and Snowhaven—home to a primitive mix of races—was a large group of isles within the Water Kingdom. The only route to reach the remote capital would be to sail through the harsh, icy waters of the unforgiving Turquoise Ocean.

Their settlement, Helshire Village, stood alone on the outskirts of the Fire Kingdom province. The Dragon's Heartland, a massive forest surrounding their home, stretched across the most southwestern part of the continent, with the Ridgeland Mountains securing the border to Mirrorhold. South was the Black Bog Forest that few ventured through; legends of bizarre creatures were enough to keep even the bravest men away.

Thinking about how Rahim would pester Chaliss, Selena said to herself, "Hopefully *Matu* won't be in a foul mood." '*Matu*' meant 'caretaker' in the Elven Language as a term of endearment. It was not a common language to use: most of it was forgotten and lost to the ages.

As she ventured downstairs, the windows caught three massive shadows drifting over their nestled village: black dragons soared above, carrying vessels that Selena assumed to have war supplies. Her Imperial Majesty's Air Force was in disarray, gathering soldiers and rationing meat; Alfheim was preparing for war, as the Council feared a surprise attack from the Lich.

Rahim had already beaten her to the kitchen, bouncing in his spot as Chaliss—after putting away the food she bought—dished fried eggs, bacon, tomatoes, and mushrooms with tea and, for Rahim's request, coffee.

Their breakfast began the same way: Rahim still lightheartedly teasing Selena for always reading instead of learning how to cook like, in his words, "A proper housewife should."

Before Chaliss could scold him, Selena reached over and pinched his ear. "I don't want to be a housewife," she declared, "I want to do as I please, even if all I'm ever good at is reading."

Rahim was about to argue, but one look from Chaliss was enough to make him swallow his words. "That's enough from you."

In between sips of coffee, Rahim cautiously chose his following words. "Yes, you can do whatever you please as you rave like a lunatic about Ragnarok." He laughed.

"Ragnarok? Are you still reading about that?" Chaliss asked.

Selena's face turned red as Chaliss avoided any topics about the ancient sword as much as possible. She believed that the stories only brought terrible luck; in her opinion, magic was taboo. "A sword created by Xyaxon—the most powerful weapon in the world," Rahim exclaimed, "Find it, so we can use it to fight against Venexus." Selena shuddered at hearing the Lich's real name; she prayed never to encounter that necromancer again. Yet, Rahim wouldn't drop the uncomfortable subject as he shoveled the last of his eggs into his mouth. "He used to be a powerful sorcerer from Oblivion, and now he's come to our world."

"We will not talk about this anymore," Chaliss snapped, "any mention of demons or liches is enough to bring bad luck, and we don't need any more of that here in this household." Her voice was sharp and stern, enough to make Rahim and Selena recoil.

"I'm sorry, mum."

"After breakfast, I need you two to start your chores."

Although Selena was always interested in learning about magic, everyone in Helshire wasn't exactly keen on the art. Only magic users were born with the gift of manipulating the energies, and those with the aptitude would travel and study with Alfheim's scholars, perfecting their craft. Even then, it took years to master any single element. Selena always wondered if she was ever born with a gift like that, but just like her past, she may never know. Instead, she dreamt of the possibility.

Rahim groaned, but he and Selena cleared the table when they finished eating and began washing dishes. Yet, when Chaliss left the room, he asked, "What will you do with that sword? Are you going to use it to kill the Lich?"

Confused and bemused, Selena squinted at him. "Why would I do that?"

"Because he's evil. He kills people and forces their souls to join his legion of the undead." Rahim held his hands above his head and curled his fingers like claws.

Her attempts at reassuring herself that Rahim was lying failed. "That's not true."

"He left Oblivion to take over the world."

"Stop it."

"It's true." His fun ending, Rahim sighed. "So, what are you going to do with Ragnarok?"

"Nothing. I just wanted to know more about it."

Rahim laughed. "You're never going to find the damn thing. Soon, you'll start raving like a madman like Gundisalvus."

"He may have been insane, but I believe he knew what he was doing."

"But he was still mental. He got himself locked up in Mortemholdt after the war ended because he was a lunatic." When Selena turned a deaf ear to his ramblings, Rahim tapped her shoulder and pointed out the kitchen window. "Look. Do you know that house across the street? That was his, and I know it's haunted. I bet his ghost is there."

Selena raised a brow. "Now you're just making up stories."

"I swear by the Divines. I've walked by it a few times, and I've heard moans and groans." Rahim imitated the noises, and Selena threw her washcloth at him. The two stopped when another pair of large, red dragons sailed gracefully over their house. "Imagine riding on the backs of one of those," Rahim said in awe.

"I had a dream about a dragon egg before," Selena said, "and it was getting close to hatching. It looked like the one *Matu* keeps hidden in the locked storage room."

"You just keep getting weirder," Rahim said, shuddering. In his opinion, strange occurrences plagued their household since Selena's arrival, though he failed to elaborate whenever Selena asked him to provide an example. As far as she was concerned, Helshire Village was almost the same as it had been before she came.

However, what Selena wouldn't admit was that the dragon egg called to her. She had snuck into Chaliss' room on several occasions while she and Rahim were away to look at it, its ruby and topaz-encrusted shell dazzling and alluring. Selena made it a habit to talk to it as if the egg was a sentient being; on her last visit, she placed her hand upon the shell, feeling a small heartbeat, full of life. It mattered not that women weren't allowed to become dragon riders—the Council couldn't order Selena to stop dreaming.

"Would it not be famous to ride a dragon?" Selena asked herself when Rahim was out of earshot.

The following days passed uncomfortably, as Selena's dreams surrounding the dragon egg grew with her increasing anxiety. Perhaps Chaliss sensed the upcoming hatching day, as she spent a great deal of time inspecting the egg, going as far as sleeping and eating beside it. Selena couldn't imagine what Chaliss would do if the dragon hatched, as Vidar and the Council would immediately take the hatchling away as soon as they receive word. However, the morning Selena awoke from her latest dream announcing the first cracks beginning to show, Chaliss was in hysterics before rushing to the storage room.

Selena and Rahim at once followed and watched as Chaliss placed down a special cushion, and gingerly set the shaking egg upon it. It stopped moving briefly but cracked more seriously when Selena stepped forward; a clawed tip wing poked out, chip-tipped nose and talons scrabbling through the cracked rubies and topazes.

The hatchling would soon discover a new world through a slow awakening, one different from its accustomed darkness filled with blurred patterns and colors. Selena saw fresh, amber-colored eyes brighten as the dragon's pupils dilated from the sudden seeping light welcoming the new creature; the glistening crimson dragonet's triangular head popped out, and suddenly, the two halves of its shell flung apart.

The slimy interior of the egg trailed behind the red dragon whelpling as it clawed and crawled its way across the scattered pieces on the pillow, leaving a path of slime and blood. Sniffing and flickering its sleek tail, the dragon unfolded its five-spined golden wings like a lady's fan, phalanges delicate and thin, the texture like parchment. Specks of purple, red, and yellow ovals dabbed the trailing edges of both of its wings; its stomach burned a gilded glow, magnifying the hue of its sparkling amber eyes. Its newborn hide gleamed like polished rubies crafted by the world's finest jewelers.

The dragonet's face donned a formidable bone mask with two horns upon its head curving inward like a crown, and three tiny horns adorned its jawline. A long forked red tongue slithered from between its small but sharp fangs to taste the fresh air for the first time.

Selena herself was impressed and awestruck; she had never seen a hatchling before, let alone witnessed the birth of one. She, nor Chaliss and Rahim, did not have the knowledge to identify the breed. Perhaps it was a rare one, for his coloration and physical features were unlike any dragon they had seen from both sides. The hatchling was large, almost the size of a large dog. Although Selena and Rahim watched in amazement, Chaliss was very pale when she stepped and knelt towards the creature.

However, the hatchling grew bored and impatient with its newfound audience and busied itself cleaning off the bits of shell and slime from its glorious hide. Selena swallowed hard when she remembered that dragons obeyed no command. She wondered what would happen if the dragon refused to listen and accept a new rider.

The dragonet reared its head back, ember sparks igniting from its nostrils as it unfurled its already large wings. Chaliss immediately recoiled as it stood upon its haunches to examine its surroundings more closely, and when it turned to explore the storage room, Rahim took a few steps back. Before Selena could react, the dragon came past her and sat up to look at her inquisitively.

Its eyelids clicked as it blinked at her, its slit-pupiled eyes blazing into hers. Her spine suddenly turned cold when she heard a resounding rumble echo in her mind, the same noises it made deep in its chest. Her skin prickled, and her neck hair stood on end when a guttural, yet intelligible voice pierced her thoughts, but a voice clear as crystal chimed through her subconscious: **Selena.**

Her face grew white as if she had seen a ghost. "P-pardon me?" Based on Rahim's and Chaliss' expressions, Selena knew she was the only one who heard it. While she was questioning her sanity, the dragon fixated its slits set against its golden eyes upon her, and that was when she realized—

Rahim's voice shattered her trance. "What are you playing at?"

Chaliss kept opening her mouth, wanting to speak but no words came forth; a murmur of shock went around the room from the unfortunate turn of events, but the dragonet paid no attention to what would be a dire situation.

It—no, a he, for the voice was masculine—reexamined Selena, only pausing to stretch out his muscles and wings before scratching the back of his neck. The deep voice returned to her thoughts: **Are you afraid?**

From her books, she had read that dragons absorbed knowledge about this universe through dreams and visions while still in the shell. Though it came as no surprise that he learned how to speak, Selena never imagined talking to a dragon. "N-no, not at all," she said, still pale, "Do you have a name?"

"Selena, you ought to leave this room now before it's too late," Chaliss said.

However, her warning went unheard, as the dragon approached Selena. Already, his head reached her chest while he snaked his neck around her body. **Thor.**

Her throat turned dry when she met the dragon's smoldering stare, still ignoring Chaliss and Rahim. "S-so it's t-true. Y-you're the one speaking, then."

The cold answer crept through her thoughts. **Yes.**

"A-and what does 'Thor' mean?"

My name. When she couldn't give the dragon an answer, he repeated, **My name is Thor.**

Dragons only bonded and communicated through telepathy with those they deemed worthy. When the dragon was ready to make the connection, it could take weeks or even months before establishing the initial link. Once they made the bond, the two were together forever. *Truly remarkable,* Selena thought.

Thor stood on his hind legs, and his snout touched her nose. **I can hear you.**

Quivering in both fear and awe, she met his unblinking gaze. "You can hear and read my thoughts?"

Yes. Selena's heart throbbed in her throat, and the dragon released a series of chirps like a cat. **I trust you.**

It's a pleasure to meet you, Thor.

Time froze as the two were locked in a gaze, and the world stopped spinning during their silent communion. He lifted his claws to her face, but his ivory daggers were gentle against her soft skin. **Selena Liongod.**

Chaliss didn't have a choice; a dragon and rider couldn't be separated. Upon Thor's immediate request, Chaliss brought a tub of fresh-butchered pork. He was a messy eater, scattering blood and bits of flesh across the floor and his hide. Since it was made clear that Thor chose her as his rider, Selena took on the chore to clean away the bloody meal from his red diamond-cut scales. He exhibited great pleasure in being wiped down and appreciatively rubbed his head against Selena's side like a cat happy to see its owner.

The newly formed pair settled in Selena's room, with Thor tucking his head into her lap and falling asleep. Selena couldn't help but smile as she ran her fingers across his jeweled hide, careful not to stir him from his slumber. He didn't wake until later that afternoon, and Thor asked many questions about the world; Selena taught him the basics to the best of her ability, such as the alphabet and the calendar system. When Thor demonstrated his reading skill, Selena wrote out the twelve months while enunciating each word. *Mortas, the first month, then Varinth.*

Thor sniffed her hand while she continued. **Korvas,** he read the third.

Selena nodded and smiled. *Azniine, Turnadas, Xol, Solvryn—*

Arelion, Goldfire, Stardusk—

Astar and Moonstar.

He asked her to read to him during their time together continuously, and her initial discomfort at sharing their mental link washed away. Instead, she was filled with wonder and enjoyed their conversations, despite Thor's limited vocabulary.

During supper and evening tea, Selena presented Chaliss and Rahim with Thor's recent developments. Thor, meanwhile, gnawed at a leftover bone in front of the fireplace, ignoring their conversation. Yet, his scales shimmered from Chaliss praising his growth and intellect.

"I thought you were acting like a raving lunatic this morning." Rahim devoured the last of the scones when Selena finished. "But now imagine being a dragon rider."

Selena involuntarily smiled and Thor chirped, but Chaliss was the only one who didn't share their sentiments. Instead, she whispered, "I pray the Council won't find out."

After they were excused for the night, Thor made himself comfortable at the edge of her bed, wrapping himself within his coils. Selena joined him with an offer to read a story about powerful dragons within the Mythic Flight—guardians of their elements who fought bravely in the One Hundred Years' War. Throughout her tale, Thor inched his way towards her, the gleam from his ruby scales sparkling in her eyes. He climbed up her crossed legs and sniffed her face like a cat when inspecting its owner. His appearance never bothered her; despite Chaliss and Rahim admitting that his form frightened them, Selena found Thor fascinating and beautiful. Dragons, she knew, were to be feared and were nearly as powerful as the Divines themselves.

Too bad that the Council uses them for war, Selena thought, and Thor snorted in agreement. She closed her book and sighed when Rahim's earlier comments about the necromancer crept upon her. "I hope the Lich won't bother us. I wish I knew why he wanted us in the first place." Her eyes darted to the mark on her hand. *The Lich could be why I can't remember anything, and maybe I have this.*

Thor's snarls caught her off guard. At first, she thought her dragon was angry with her, but Thor rushed over to hide in her lap. **Undead murderer!**

What are you talking about?

The Lich. That necromancer. Murderer!

It felt like a pair of hands were upon her throat. Thor seemed to know what the Lich was capable of, but why didn't that necromancer kill her when he had the chance? *Do you know why the Lich wanted us?*

Thor immediately growled through clamped fangs and dug his claws into her blankets, creating ripped punctures through the fabric. **That murdering necromancer!**

What does he want?

Only shadow and darkness.

Her skin crawled with goosebumps, but she quelled her dragon's boiling wrath through gentle reassurances, and the two gave in to their creeping stupor. Even as Thor drifted into dreamland, he muttered the same word repeatedly that rang into her fading subconscious: **Ragnarok.**

CHAPTER 3: BENEATH THE STARRY SKIES

Meaningful conversations between her and Thor filled the following days; it was fantastic to indulge in speech with another intellectual. By week's end, Thor's academic exchange was on par with a scholar's; his intelligence and curiosity astounded her. No matter how far apart the two were, Selena and Thor could still communicate clearly.

Yet, Thor never did explain what he meant by his ramblings about the Lich, and Selena feared to ask him. Instead, she did her best to keep up with his growing appetite and spurts, for he threatened to eat Chaliss out of house and home.

While fitting her knapsack on her way out the door that late morning, Thor interrupted her troubled thoughts as he trotted behind her, tail swishing with every step he made. **Please wait for me. You know I can't run that fast.**

Selena spun around, inspecting his size, concluding that Thor had officially outgrown the pack she used to hide him when in town. Unfurling his wings that were now long enough to wrap her, Thor jumped and glided to where she stood. His triangular-shaped head—matching her head size—met her shoulders upon stretching out his long neck; Thor's talons looked like curled daggers ready to tear his prey to shreds. The sunlight lanced through his smoldering wings like stained glass, casting orange, yellow, red, and purple flecks across the ground.

Before he could take another step down the pathway, Selena ushered him back inside. *I'm afraid you're too big to hide in my pack.*

Thor peeked around her and let out a tiny wail, sweeping his tail across the floor. **But I always go with you.**

I promise to return soon with food.
Now you're bribing me to stay.
Never.

Thor immediately spun around and sneezed, letting loose a few wild embers that scorched the corners of Chaliss' carpet; Selena quickly stamped them out before offering him a deal. *After I buy more books, I promise you will have me all to yourself for the remainder of today. Deal?*

He wrinkled his nose and stuck out his slippery forked tongue but sighed. **Fine. Deal, but you will return soon, yes?**

Of course.

Despite Thor's objections as she stepped further out of the house, he remained still.

Luckily, their house was far enough away from where Thor's brief appearance went unnoticed; the small settlement nestled between two hills remained slightly protected against the cold weather, as was expected at the end of Varinth. The locals began their day-to-day routines, oblivious to the train rattling in the distance, meeting the small stop outside their hometown.

Locomotives were primarily used for transporting goods between the kingdoms, while a small number were for transportation that the rich could only afford.

The bustling village made her feel warm in their cold world; Selena knew most of the locals by name. Most were cordial, always asking her about how Chaliss and Rahim fared, though they scowled when she spoke of her hobbies. Yet, Selena was happy enough, and her life in the village itself was all she knew, but it wasn't full of rainbows and butterflies: nightmares tormented her every evening. Her torpor of madness often replayed the murder of a mysterious man or her possible past abuse and defilement from the Lich, whose evil knew no bounds. However, Selena was always relieved to wake up with Thor nestled beside her, as he knew how to quell her night terrors.

A small circle of stalls camped in the middle of town, displaying various goods, such as fresh vegetables, cured meats, and jewelry. Selena met with the local butcher, Odin, while he was in the middle of ordering one of his sons to hunt in the Black Bog. "Oi, I haven't seen you about in some time." Noticing his lack of supplies, Odin sighed, sharing in her disappointment. "This food ration is killing me, but I still have some to sell ya."

Selena looked at the near barren shops in dismay. "Do you believe that the Lich will attack?"

"Vidar and the Council wouldn't extend this effort if they didn't feel that the Empire was in danger. If ya ask me, I think the Lich is recruiting those horrible creatures from Runefell to join his army. Bloody Orcs. I hope never to see those foul, ugly things near my home. I'll lop its head off and mount it on my wall if I ever come across one." Just hearing Odin talk about Orcs made Selena's skin crawl. She had never seen one before, and she hoped she would never have to; they were barbarians who enjoyed killing without remorse.

He and Selena concluded their business exchange, and she eyed the other stalls before two familiar brothers interrupted her with loud conversation. She hadn't seen Gromm and Beck Steelmane since she was rescued. "I'm not sure what we're gonna do," Gromm growled while shaking his head. "We're already low on supplies. We ought to make one last stop before reaching Alfheim."

Beck agreed but stopped and waved Selena down to join their company. "It's good to see you out and about. It's been, what, almost two months? How have you and the hatchling been getting along?" Beck flinched when Gromm held up his big hand to smack him for a slip of the tongue. "Err, sorry."

Amused, Selena adjusted her knapsack and looked over her shoulder when Thor poked at her thoughts, snickering in amusement. "I'm browsing through, as usual."

Still trying to find the ancient sword, Thor teased, and jested her about falling in love with Genesis Altessa, and her face burned.

Gromm cleared his throat, interrupting her conversation with Thor. "I have something for you." He dug through his pockets and pulled out a flask. "I think you will need this," he whispered so that only Selena could hear, "it's oil for your dragon's scales to keep them from chafing and drying out. People would start to question if a young lady like yourself was trying to buy some. The Council is shipping most of it to Alfheim and Rhumbek for war preparations, but this should last you for a while."

"Thank you very much."

After receiving the gift, the two brothers began bickering once again. Bemused and fascinated, Selena watched Gromm and Beck walk away, wholly ignoring her. However, Thor was still curious about Ragnarok, and said, **I don't know why you're stuck on the old sword when it probably doesn't exist.**

That's not true. Gundisalvus had proof.

He had a touch of lunacy. He was a madman, claiming he knew where it was but kept babbling about utter nonsense.

I still believe he knew something, and I will eventually find out. Selena hastened to the merchant—named Arthur—she wanted to visit from Thor's urging. She ignored the strange stares and glances from the villagers, but she couldn't turn a deaf ear to the snide comments about how "it's not right for a woman to read," and "watch, she'll start getting ideas."

However, if Arthur frowned upon her hobbies, he reserved judgment and always gave her a warm welcome. Upon seeing her approach his stall, he pulled out a few specific books for her. "After you asked me last week, I finally have the biography of Gundisalvus. It's a little more expensive, but I can lower the price since you're one of my regulars." Agreeing to two gold pieces instead of five, Selena concluded her transaction and rushed back to the house with her purchases.

She returned to Thor impatiently waiting by the front door, in the same position. **It's about time, my dear.**

Even if I had arrived earlier, you still wouldn't have been satisfied.

Thor snorted and pushed her towards the kitchen with a slight nudge of his muzzle. Selena set the wrapped beef next to the breadbasket on the table and offered Thor a few scraps as a peace offering.

As Thor gobbled up his treat, Selena heard Chaliss yelling Rahim's name; he dashed downstairs, running his fingers through his tangled dark brown hair to undo his mother's work in fixing it. When his and Selena's eyes met, Rahim placed his fingers to his lips. "Shh. If mum asks where I'm at, tell her you don't know."

There was a crease in Selena's brow as she grabbed a piece of bread, and Rahim disappeared out the door before she could ask what he meant, and Chaliss stormed down the wooden steps moments later. Her long black hair swept behind her with every stride she took. "Thank you for doing some shopping. Where did Rahim go?"

"Dunno. What happened?"

"All I did was try to fix his hair, and he ran away from me. I wish Rahim were more mature like you."

Selena knew that time again: Chaliss was getting ready to send Rahim to his Uncle Rowan's house. First, as a threat, Rahim ultimately knew he was going regardless. However, at his old age, Rowan was insane, still believing he was a spy for Her Imperial Majesty after thirty years of retirement. Rahim was, unfortunately, a victim often caught in Rowan's traps specifically set to test his ingenuity and cleverness.

After putting away her new book, Selena kept her promise; she and Thor took their usual positions behind Chaliss' house near the Black Bog Forest, the perfect hiding place for her companion. Thor's eyes whipped over to a couple of rats scurrying by; he came to a crouch with his sight glued upon a single rodent and pounced upon his prey, his ivory talons dyed with its blood. Selena felt a little sick and turned away. To her relief, Thor should now have no issues hunting for himself. Yet, she recalled the lack of supplies and game, and Selena grew worried that Thor would eventually run out of food if war preparations continued.

The two sat down on a circular patch of grass surrounded by dead trees, with Thor wrapping his tail and wings around her. The pair watched the metal-hued clouds sail across the heavens, and Selena took solace in their serenity.

Thor snaked his head around, pointing his nose heavenward. **I want to go up there.**

What do you mean?

Thor unfurled his wings, gaze still fixated on the drifting clouds. **When I learn how to fly, I want to soar through those clouds. I would love to take you with me.** Her legs suddenly became like lead as she focused skyward. Though she dreamt of riding on a dragon, Selena almost lost her bearings from the thought of being airborne. However, she couldn't bring herself to voice her fears without possibly offending her companion.

The two remained in their tranquility for hours before Selena realized she had to leave. Thor was already asleep, his perfectly cut ruby scales kissed by the late afternoon sun, making him look like a gleaming pile of treasure. Thor stirred and awoke when she shifted, stretching out his claws while yawning. **May we read together tonight?**

I promise that we will. For now, I'm going inside.

When she stood up, Thor eyed his surroundings, curious about what adventures lay beyond the trees. **I want to stay out here and see if I can find any more—what do you call them?**

Rats.

Yes, rats. I want to hunt more rats.

After supper, Selena kept her promise to Thor, and she shared her new book with him before bedtime. The world grew quiet, and all seemed right during their time spent together. However, she couldn't shake away the feeling that she was being watched, and her skin prickled.

Flipping through Gundisalvus' biography, she eventually came across his family tree and found the name 'Marceline' near his, listing her as his daughter. After reading the paragraph underneath, Marceline was only fifteen years old when she died. "Cause of death unknown," Selena read aloud, "she was found with internal bleeding during her last performance."

Interesting, Thor said. Eventually, Selena found an old declaration printed on a page, proclaiming news about the dreaded senior war general. After suffering from madness and depression, Gundisalvus tried committing suicide by drinking himself to death. However, he disappeared after his release from Mortemholdt prison; the mystery intrigued her. Thor lowered his head and nuzzled her arm. **I wonder what became of him.**

I wish I knew.

Hours flew by, and Selena returned inside when the sky blackened with storm clouds. Thor, however, remained intrigued by the forest and made it his life's mission to inspect every stone and tree he came across. Selena had never seen such curiosity from an extraordinary creature. Before returning to her room, she watched as Thor remained relentless in his endeavor of climbing up the tree branches and practicing flying. Several times he would hover before he was forced to land; she eagerly waited for the day that he would learn to fly and soar through heaven's plumed spires. When he was satisfied with his progress, Thor curled up on the ground and drifted to sleep, ensconced within his coils; the dim moonlight made him gleam like a pile of gold.

"I wonder what he dreams about."

Her steps quickened through the house and up the stairs when the sudden flashes of lightning made her skin crawl, and she felt the house tremble from the thunder. Selena dove in her bed and grew buried in the sea of covers, protecting herself from the terrible sound. It took her a while to find sleep, but eventually, she drifted into the realm of dreams:

Selena stood in the darkness, but her eyes stung from the sudden bright light that lit a stage; sitting beside her was a rugged-looking man. His clothes reeked with alcohol, his face pale and rough with blue-grey eyes filled with emptiness and despair. He had a piece of parchment in his lap with notes jotted all over it.

A piano waited on the stage for the young, beautiful maiden emerging from behind a nearby curtain. Her long, white dress made her look like a ghost; pearls adorned her tied-up bun.

She placed her hands upon the keys and played a couple of beautiful notes that rang through Selena's ears like the bells of a cathedral, and she began singing.

Selena did not know how long she had sat there, but the music bewitched her.

Then—

An ear-piercing sound shattered her ears. The man beside her stood up and screamed while rushing towards the stage. The young woman convulsed on the floor as blood poured from her mouth, her gown dyed crimson.

"No, Marceline…someone, anyone, help my daughter. Please help…."

Like an oil-spilt canvas, her vision grew suddenly dark, and Selena soon found herself standing in Helshire Village near where her house would be with the sound of footsteps running from behind her. She whipped around and gasped when she saw the man she recognized as Gundisalvus run through her as if she were a spectral spirit. Not long after, a dreadful creature emerged from the shadows—a monstrous black snake with a red crest mounted on its forehead and a large scar running through its left eye. Astride the creature was an eerie figure draped in shadow.

A slight sound escaped Selena's mouth, but she had no urge to move; the creature slithered by as if she did not *exist. Yet, her vision vanished, and the scene reappeared like drizzled ink on parchment: she stood in front of the running man once more, leaning against his old brick house, sodden and breathless. He held a scroll but stuffed it away in his cloak, his arm bleeding uncontrollably.*

    The snake suddenly appeared from behind the house, but Gundisalvus rushed across the dirt road, clutching his chest. It was too late: the snake lunged forward with lightning-fast attacks and snapped its fangs into his side before recoiling back. Gundisalvus wailed out with pain as he fell and trembled in the dirt while the venom took its toll. The snake's handler jumped down and strolled over with no remorse; the figure pulled out a revolver and pointed the barrel between the dying man's eyes, stoic and silent.

    Gundisalvus spat to the ground. "The Divines help my poor soul." The unspoken figure kicked him in the sides and stomach before leaving him in his crimson puddle.

    Her vision faded but focused once more; the unfortunate war general limped through an old cave, stripped of all but a stone table and a leather-bound journal lying over a paper-piled mess. The apparition of Gundisalvus stumbled and fell in one seat, his trembling hands grabbing the journal and writing what would be his final words. "I wait for Death. I feel hungry and tired—so very tired of running. The venom is taking its toll on me, and I fear this being the end. My secret goes with me to my grave: it rests beneath the starry skies. I hear Death coming."

Selena jolted awake. Her heart raced and sweat beaded her forehead. Lightning flashed across the sky, and she saw shadows of claws stretching across her walls, ready to snatch her at a moment's notice. Her ears rang from her own heart's fast ticking, beating sound. She opened her mouth to scream, but no sound came out. The lightning cracked across the sky, and the dark talons disappeared.

She immediately snatched her blankets and dove underneath her bed. The thunder rumbling outside made her quiver; someone was there, watching every move she made. Her paranoia grew as she tightened her grip on her sheets to keep herself covered.

However, her nerves eased slightly when Thor's soothing voice chased away the squall in her mind: **Why are you afraid of thunder and lightning? It can't hurt you inside.**

It's hard to explain as I've always been afraid of.... Her thoughts faded into Oblivion.

Humans have irrational fears over weird things.

Are you afraid of anything?

Dragons have no fear. Although she had her doubts, she still wished she wasn't so much of a coward. As the night wore on, the storm eventually subsided; when Selena told Thor of her nightmares, he didn't reply at first. **Come outside,** he finally said. After ensuring the storm had passed, Selena grabbed towels before joining Thor near the tree, his illuminating scales and burning amber eyes greatly contrasting the darkness. When she vented about her phobia of thunder and lightning, Thor looked down at his claws, contemplating, and said, **I hope this isn't a coincidence, but I felt a dark presence nearby last night.** Thor paused when he saw her horrified expression; her face turned pale when she thought of the shadow claws reaching for her.

I'm afraid, she admitted, *that there is a monster following me, us.*

Thor broke into low growls. **Now I understand why you're afraid of thunder and lightning. Next time, I will chase those shadow monsters away.**

CHAPTER 4: THE VAMPIRE AND THE DRAGON

The same nightmares preyed upon her over the next month, repeating the unusual phrase, but Selena did her best at distracting herself by tending to her growing dragon. Now the size of a large warhorse, she had to be careful around his weaponed claws, as they were sharp enough to slice someone clean in half. His five-spined bat-like wings could wrap around a huge tree and still overlap. Luckily, despite the food ration, he always found plenty of deer and elk to satisfy his ever-increasing hunger, as hunters weren't brave enough to venture far.

Rahim had the unfortunate displeasure of being sent to his Uncle Rowan's house. Two weeks earlier before the carriage arrived, he made a huge fuss in going, but Chaliss remained relentless. "If you send me there, I'll die," he argued, but he didn't have a choice. However, Selena's company was far from bleak; dragons were considered the most intelligent creatures ever to walk the face of the earth, and Selena was honored to witness Thor's intellectual growth. His mind was like a yearning child's, absorbing all he could. Day after day, Selena read him books on history and literature, mathematics, and physics.

The smell of the early morning dew was welcoming as Selena juggled her books while making her way to Thor's hidden and self-made sanctuary. A small jar of oil was in her pocket with a washcloth hanging out. From Chaliss' borrowed texts written by Genesis, as hatchlings grew fast, their hide needed to be oiled at least once a week to prevent scales from drying or cracking. It had been about a week since the last coat, and Selena knew it was time for another polish.

Thor patiently waited for her arrival, and as Selena moved closer, his tail swept up more rock and dirt, anxiously waiting to have his scales cleaned. Selena sat down on the tree stump beside him and set down her books with the jar and washcloth, and Thor stood up and stretched. He looked forward to the weekly polishing because he loved showing off his gemstone scales. It didn't take much oil; just a dab from the end of the washcloth was enough for his head and neck alone. Selena enjoyed watching his hide glisten like perfectly cut diamonds as she went over the jagged edges. She felt like a jeweler polishing gemstones as she carefully wiped down his body.

After about a half hour, she stepped back and took in her handiwork. Thor was one of the most beautiful dragons she ever got to behold; she couldn't wait until he was as large as the others so that she could fully appreciate his majesty. Chittering, Thor snaked his head around and sniffed his glistening hide. **Thank you.**

You look dazzling. Selena wiped her hands off on the clean side of her washcloth before setting it and the jar aside and grabbing the book she brought with her. *Did you want me to read this? It's about alchemy.*

That sounds delightful. Thor exerted extreme caution as he laid down next to her, not wanting to dirty his freshly cleaned scales; he couldn't help but fuss over his appearance despite Selena's assurance that he was fine.

She opened the book and began reading the research notes like a textbook from scholars. Never had she seen such complex formulas and concepts, but Thor understood what she read, and soon, she did too. Together, they learned that the basic principle behind alchemy was that it required an equal exchange to create something else entirely. For instance, if Selena wanted to, she could make gold from an ordinary piece of metal or craft an elixir to cure all diseases.

Selena read that there were different schools of magic, such as alteration that specialized in creating wards or healing magic that relied on water. It was fascinating; all magic revolved around the four elements: air, water, earth, and fire. However, there was a brief mention of a fifth element, but the book didn't detail it.

Thor's eyes widened in delight. **Something about spirit energy, I reckon.**

Selena flipped through the pages but stopped when Thor arched his neck over her and sniffed the air. She marked the page she left off and set the book down. *What is it?*

Thor got up to circle their tree and began digging in the ground with his paws. Unearthing a crystallized rock, he pushed it over to Selena's feet with his snout, his eyes flickering red. **I saw this glittering in the ground beside you. It's beautiful and shiny, whatever it is.**

Selena went to pick up the rock that he dug up. She examined it in the fading sunlight, admiring the shimmering rainbows reflecting across the ground. *I believe that this is quartz.*

Are there more like this?

Selena looked from the rock to her dragon, realizing that Thor was fascinated with shiny objects other than his gemstone scales. *More gems are prettier and more valuable than this. I wish I had the money to get you all the gold and treasure in the world. I'm sorry to say that I am poor.*

He recoiled. **Oh.**

But we can keep this, as it's pretty enough. Selena placed the rock near his spot, smiling, hoping it made Thor feel better.

I would like that very much. He opened his maw, and plumes of smoke erupted from the back of his throat. Selena was always amazed by the physiology of dragons; in her previous book, she and Thor learned they had two sacs with holes inside their mouths near the back of their throats. One produced a flammable gas while the other created sulfuric acid, which mixed before the dragon breathed fire. Yet, Thor remained oblivious to Selena's silent adoration. **Will you read some more for me?**

As she reached for the next tome, her eyes caught a white blur flickering through the tree branches. Thor saw it too, his smoldering gaze fixated on the direction it disappeared. *What was that?*

She heard a low rumble coming from the back of Thor's throat as he unfolded his wings and bared his fangs. **Someone is spying on us. Do you want me to find out what it was?**

No. It might be nothing, but I'll check it out.

Oh no, you will not.

I'll be fine.

No! Thor immediately reached over with a protective arm and herded her close to his chest, snaking his head in every direction while snarling. **I will not allow anything to happen to you.**

Your behavior is entirely unwarranted. When trying to pry herself away from Thor's grasp, he tightened his arm muscles until she couldn't breathe. Eventually, he released his grip upon her pleas to not be crushed. *I will only be gone for a moment, but I promise to return.*

Only if I can go with you.

There will be no need. Besides, I don't want to risk someone from the village seeing you.

I wouldn't give a damn if it meant your life was in danger.

It won't be.

Through gentle reassurances, Thor eventually agreed, but he still wasn't happy. **If anyone or anything attacks you, I will rip them to shreds.**

After putting her book away, Selena marched towards where she had seen the white blur and wandered through the trees, leaving Thor and their cozy home behind.

The sun was high in the sky, the heat seeping through the forest's greensward. Her earth green shirt and mud-brown skirt tore from the sticks and twigs reaching her from the bushes. The dirt turned into mud, her boots slipping away into the slippery slope.

Yet, she paused when her ears pricked to the sound of crunching leaves behind her; a warm hum buzzed overhead, like a swarm of bees drawn to a flower's sweet nectar, and she heard a voice like auditory honey. "Hello there."

Selena twirled around, and her heart stopped to see a young man approaching, donned in a white cloak tied by an azure chain draped across his chest, accentuated by his golden belt. Three long teal-tipped feathers held by his shoulder's circle pin caught the sun's gleam. Though Selena was a petite young lady, this man towered over her; she attempted to look at his face, but his dress hood draped his head in shadow.

"Uh, hello." Her voice nearly failed to escape her dry throat; their awkward exchange increased her pending anxiety.

The man's voice carried an aristocratic air as if she were speaking with a scholar from Alfheim. "It's such a lovely day for a stroll. Wouldn't you agree?"

"Forgive me, but I don't believe we've been formerly acquainted. Who are you?"

The young man pointed at himself. "Me? No one in particular." Selena raised a perplexed brow to his nonchalant mannerisms; he lifted his hood. The man brushed his fingers through his long snow-white hair burning like a white flame, gleaming with iridescence in the sun. Selena found herself drawn to his piercing ice-blue eyes hiding behind a pair of spectacles perched on the bridge of his nose. He was young; Selena guessed he was close to about her age. He bowed. "Oh, where are my manners? My name is Silver. What is yours?"

She curtsied in return. "Selena Liongod."

"It is a pleasure to make your acquaintance, Miss Liongod."

"Err, likewise," Selena hesitated. Assuming he was the white blur she and Thor saw, her investigation ended. "I don't mean to sound rude, but it is getting late. I should return home."

Before she could kneel and turn away, Silver reached out and grabbed her left hand. Selena gasped from his sudden cold and soft touch. "No, wait. Please." Silver's face burned like fire as he looked down, and his eyes squinted at the mark peeking from the cloth. Selena yanked her hand away from his, and Silver stepped back, looking ashamed for his sudden rash behavior. "I humbly apologize, my dear."

Selena wasn't sure if she was angry or embarrassed. Either way, her red face gave it away as she held her hand away from prying eyes. "Apology accepted, but I think you were following me earlier. Please tell me why you're here."

"Me? Oh, nothing. I was merely enjoying a wonderful afternoon stroll through this forest until I stumbled upon you and your wonderful companion. I had to get a close-up view of your dragon." Silver grinned ear to ear.

Her heart was close to bursting from her chest to know someone else saw Thor; she feared Silver would report them to the Council. "Y-you must be mistaken."

"Nonsense. Pretend like I was never here. I swear I won't say anything—I know how bothersome it is dealing with Vidar and the Council."

Can I trust this stranger? Regardless, Selena relaxed her shoulders. "Thank you, but I really must be going. It was nice meeting you, Silver. Farewell." She excused herself, and as she began her trek, Silver clasped his hands behind his back and followed her. "Why are you following me?"

"I'm not. It just so happens that we are traveling the same path together." Another vast grin appeared on his face, brightening the darkening forest.

"I don't see how that's possible, as I'm returning home."

"But you came from that direction. You're heading deeper into the forest, my dear." Silver pointed oppositely. To Selena's astonishment, she realized he was right, for the Black Bog had suddenly grown thicker. Her unfamiliar environment sent a chill down her spine. "I'm only here because I'm looking for someone. Perhaps you've seen him?" Silver bent over and placed his hand above the ground. "He's about this tall, with brown and orange fur. He talks a lot, goes by the name of Locky, Looki, Mooki, or something like that."

"I've never seen nor met anyone like that." Selena knew only of Loki and thought that Silver was referring to him. However, she didn't trust him enough to share their possible mutual acquaintance.

"Well, he's typically a fox. Have you seen any foxes around here?"

"Why are you looking for a fox?"

"It's a rather confusing story. If you wish, I shall tell you whenever we have the chance." He deeply bowed after casting another grin.

"Perhaps another time. Thank you for your riveting tale, but I have been away long enough." She curtsied and spun around on the balls of her heels back in the right direction but paused when she saw a black blur —no, a man dressed in all dark clothing—dash towards Silver.

"There you are, you son of a—" His sentence cut off as he smashed into Silver, and the two rolled into the ditch nearby. Selena heard swear words echoing through the forest, and out of fear for Silver's safety, she crept closer to see him lying on the ground with a thick boot upon his head.

The man in black hoisted a coffin-shaped case larger than him strapped over his back; he had it set against a nearby tree trunk. A white stripe parted his jet-black hair, intensely contrasting a scarlet cloth wrapped around his neck and stuffed into a black collared gentleman's shirt. Yet, he looked like a wild man with no concern to follow a formal dress code: shirt untucked with dirtied black breeches. Even his chiseled face needed a clean shave.

His wrath matched the sun's heat. "Dammit, you're such a pain to track down during the day."

Silver wrapped his hand around the man's boot and pushed it away. "Then why don't you take your nap in that coffin?"

The man hissed through his teeth and put more pressure on his foot. "D has been on my ass because of your *escapade*."

Silver laughed. "What Phantom Dust doesn't know, Kain, won't hurt him."

"But he *does* know," Kain growled and swore, "you arrogant brat. Sometimes I want to crush that little skull of yours."

Selena immediately thought Kain was going to kill him. *There's no time to find help.* She called out for Thor, but it felt like there was a mental block, wholly leaving her in solitude. Her first time alone with her thoughts unnerved her; the desperation to run and hide crept behind her. The world was suddenly too quiet there.

Dismissing her crippling anxiety, she grabbed a nearby giant stick; in a pitiful rescue attempt, she ran over and hit Kain with her brittle weapon. When she slammed it over his back, it broke in half with a loud crack, and much to her dismay, Kain didn't flinch; instead, he laughed at her failure. "So, the little princess does have some fight in her." He turned to face her but kept his boot on Silver's head. Selena gasped when she saw his fangs and bleeding crimson eyes. *He's a vampire.* "All right. I'll bite." A malicious sneer played upon his lips. "You'd make a good snack."

Thor, where are you? Selena trembled with her broken weapon, frozen solid to the ground as Kain loomed over her with one hand reaching for her neck.

However, he paused mid-stretch when Silver muttered an indistinguishable word under his breath. The puzzled Kain slowly lifted his boot from Silver's pressed face. "I'm sorry, what?"

"Dragon!" Silver's voice pierced the forest's veil.

As if on cue, a large shadow drifted over the three, and the trees bent to the sudden strong gale threatening to tear the forest asunder. A black dragon with musty and putrid scales polluting the sky flew above the opening of trees, its rotting hide corroded and mottled. Sludge dripped from its curled talons and along its pudgy face, devoid of horn ornaments save for the two long curls upon its crown. Instead, its frill lining the jawline flared and trembled when it unleashed a thundering roar that made the trees quiver. Selena would have believed the creature to be ill if it weren't in mid-flight; it flew as true as any other dragon she'd seen.

Its two large claw-tipped wings slashed through the air. Saddled over the dragon's back were three riders donned in silver dragon-head-shaped masks and dark blue robes trickled in steel buckles and trimmings. When the mottled drake looked down to see Silver, Kain, and Selena, it roared once more and dove after them, claws and fangs ready, but its pupiled-slits fixated on Selena as its primary target. It opened its mouth and reared for an attack, black fire boiling from its maw.

Just as the dragon was about to strike with a breath of fiery destruction, Kain rushed past Selena and grabbed the beast by its gaping jaws with his bare hands. In retaliation, the first rider raised his hands and began casting lightning bolts in Kain's direction while the other two pulled out loaded guns. Yet, their attacks were interrupted by the dragon's sudden jerks and thrusts to break free from Kain's hold.

Selena backed away while Silver hurried to his feet; he grabbed her arm and forced her to run with him away from the attack. She peered over her shoulder when they left Kain behind to deal with their unwanted guests. "But wait, what about—?"

"Not to worry, my dear." Silver led her to an enormous fan of bushes ahead, pushing her into the turf before joining himself. Only upon seeing her concerned expression did he grin; Selena couldn't understand how he could remain so calm. "Oh, don't worry. Everything will be fine. Here, take a look for yourself." He nodded towards the scene, and Selena sheepishly poked her head out of their hidden sward.

Through the strain of his muscles, Kain slightly fixed his footing for a better grip on the dragon's maw. His black fingernails were like claws as he chucked the drake's head to the ground while yelling, "You overgrown lizard," and tossing its body around like a rag doll, throwing the three riders off the saddle.

"Leave the dragon and find her," one commanded through his silver bone mask.

Kain moved to the side of the dragon's neck with his fangs bared and dug them through its putrid scales, drawing boiling black blood. A dark aura emanated from Kain as he sapped the energy from the poor creature, the body eroding to the bone. Selena shook and trembled in fear; no matter how dreadful the scene was, she could not tear her gaze away.

Kain jerked his head back after feeding off the dragon's corpse and laughed when the handlers pulled out blood-colored blades. "Your head will look good mounted on a stake, vampire."

While Kain kept the first rider busy, the other two headed towards Silver's and Selena's hiding spot. However, before the mysterious enemies could reach them, Silver jolted to his feet and jumped out. "I wouldn't go in there if I were you," he sang.

Ignoring Silver's taunts, the first robed man announced to his companion, "Find her. The Dark Master wants her blood."

The Dark Master? The only one who came to mind was possibly the Lich himself, and Selena assumed their new acquaintances were his devout followers.

Silver said coolly, "I'm sorry to say that you'll be walking away empty-handed. You can explain that to your *master*." Words fired like bullets. While Selena cowered in the corner, she watched the two minions rush in after Silver. However, he danced around them, avoiding their attacks with his hands behind his back. "I don't think you two are trying hard enough."

The two attackers stopped, looked at each other, and nodded. One of them immediately vanished while the other confronted Silver directly, whose expression immediately changed as he took a defensive stance instead. The cultist hissed. "The Obsidian Order is eternal. Even if you defeat us, more will come."

Silver growled and immediately pulled out two enchanted swords hidden in the sleeves of his jacket, beheading his attacker with one swift movement. The corpse burst into flames as it collapsed, and the head rolled away. Although she was amazed by the magic, Selena didn't have time to admire his skills; she felt a sudden jerk of her arm and the cold touch of metal pressed into her throat.

The assassin growled in her ear. "If you attempt to move or speak, I will kill you right where you stand. Now, lead me to the Dark Master's dragon."

She swallowed hard, knowing that he would kill her either way. She locked gazes with Kain, whose eyes widened as he swore under his breath and rushed forward to face the third robed man; before his adversary could react, Kain grabbed the cultist's shoulders and sank his fangs into the man's neck, draining him in seconds.

The surviving zealot forced Selena to stand as he dragged her back into the trees, sneaking away from Kain and Silver. She kicked and struggled to pry her arm free, but her assassin sunk his blade deeper into her skin. A feeling of grim and despair washed over her, and she wished she had listened to Thor in the first place.

However, Silver's voice echoed from the trees. "You know, I don't appreciate the death threats made to Miss Liongod, especially for someone of her stature. You and the rest of your commoner filth *Order* have no right to stand near her." Selena and her captor looked up to see Silver walking from the grove on a nearby hill, his gleaming swords ready for another fight.

The cultist laughed as he cautiously circled Silver with Selena still bound. "Commoner filth? We are the loyal subjects to the Dark Master."

Silver twitched, but his gaze shifted to Kain, who ripped off a fang from the dragon skeleton with a loud snap, holding in between his fingers like a throwing knife, and chucked it at the distracted robed man in the back of the neck. Time froze before the assassin loosened his hold, and Selena hurried to Silver's side when the minion lowered his dagger and dropped limply to the ground.

Kain casually walked over with his hands in his pockets and rolled the body over with his foot, forcing the rider to look at him. The man was paralyzed from the neck down, but his eyes looked upon the vampire with fear. "At least I get to crush someone's skull today."

Selena looked away as Kain's massive boot lingered over the frozen face and dropped against the man's skull, the bones crunching into the ground. Kain then turned towards the two with his hands still tucked away, blood dripping from his face and clothes. Selena quivered when he approached close. Yet, he paused and said coolly, "You know, you should be a little more grateful to the person who just saved your life, child."

Selena struggled to speak. "T-thank you."

Kain, however, remained unmoved by her trembling fear. "Do you even know who they were?"

"N-no."

"Oh great, you still don't remember a damn thing, do you?"

"There's no reason to insult me when I don't even remember who *I* am." She immediately withdrew her remark when Kain's crimson eyes regained their earlier bloodlust, but he held his temper in check.

Instead, he pointed at the corpses. "Those masked monsters are part of the Obsidian Order—stay away from them. They're demons bound by oaths and pacts made with the Lich and have formed a cult dedicated to him. His word is their law, and right now, that necromancer wants you dead for taking his dragon. More will be out looking for you."

"*His* dragon? It's not my fault Thor chose me over that monster. Thor will not have him." When Kain only grunted, Selena asked, "Why does the Lich want Thor?"

Before Kain could answer, Silver interrupted. "Are you done scaring her for the day? Don't you have something to report to D?"

"Yes, I do. Walk her home. Do something right for once, but going forward, we must stick to the plan." Kain gritted his teeth and swore under his breath. "Now that the blasted Order know they're here, we don't have a choice but to intervene. Make sure Chaliss knows." He sauntered away to grab his coffin case, and he vanished through the trees in a plume of smoke and shadow, leaving Selena confused how he knew of her caretaker; it was possible Chaliss knew of him and Silver, too.

Silver spat at the ground where Kain previously stood, but he sighed. "I'm certain Chaliss is worried about you." Selena nodded. He winced upon seeing the minor cuts near her neck when helping her to her feet. "Let me look at that." Silver lifted her chin to better look at her nicks, and her eyes locked with his for a moment. "When we return, I'll give you an elixir to help that heal faster."

Selena couldn't help but fall victim to her fascination over Silver's and Kain's use of magic. Although her village considered it taboo, she was intrigued and consumed with a burning desire to know more. "Thank you for saving me. Both you and Kain were brilliant."

"Why, thank you." Silver took pride in her compliment. "You know, I would be honored to show you." Selena's eyes lit up from the offer. "Scholars and mages in Dragonspire have mastered the elemental arts; their doors are always open to those with the willingness to learn."

"But what if I wasn't born with the gift?"

"You'll never know unless you try."

His tempting offer made Selena want to say yes right then and there, but what would Chaliss think? Not only that, but she was still skeptical about Silver's intentions. Yes, he saved her life, but she wondered if there was a hidden motive such as wanting to kill her himself. *If that were true, then why would he rescue me? No, that wouldn't make sense.*

The only way to know for sure was to pry information from him, as he and Kain knew who she was and why the Lich had abducted her and Thor's egg in the first place. She chose her questions one at a time without appearing insulting; upon further inquiry over Kain's relationship, Silver explained, "Kain Vanguard is a captain of the Shadow Templars. Don't worry; he's on our side. If you ever get into trouble, he will always be there to help, and so will I."

"Who are the Shadow Templars?"

"They're a secret group of vampire assassins in contract with Her Imperial Majesty, and they serve only the imperial family. The Council is oblivious to their existence." Confused, Selena couldn't understand how a vampire could be out during the day. "Not for very long, as the sunlight makes him gravely ill, but it can't kill him. That's why he always carries his coffin if he needs to hide during the day." Silver bellowed in laughter. "It'll be difficult to kill him. You would have to chop off his head, mount it on a wooden stake, and leave it outside as the sun rises. If you can even get close enough to the bastard, good luck to you."

"With his strength, I couldn't imagine anyone has gotten close to killing him." She paused. "Who is Phantom Dust?"

There was a furrow in Silver's brow as he scrunched his nose, regretting the following words coming from his mouth. "He's our *boss* who prefers to go by D."

Growing more impatient for information, Selena couldn't help but fire out, "But you and Kain still hadn't answered my earlier question. Why did the Lich want Thor and me? I don't understand."

Silver abruptly stopped and said: "There is a lot that I'm not allowed to tell you. My dear, I wish I could. All I can say now is that he needs you both."

"Why?"

"I'm not allowed to—" his voice abruptly cut off. Selena noticed that his lips twisted and locked, but through a few moments of mumbles and groans, he could finally speak again, followed by loud curses. "That's the reason."

Selena looked at him with grave concern. "Should I be worried about this and you?"

"What? No, no, no—not at all. You'll learn soon enough when deemed appropriate." Noticing how Selena remained unconvinced and unhappy with her unanswered questions, Silver cleared his throat and changed the subject. "We should be almost back."

The forest suddenly became familiar, and Chaliss' house appeared through the trees; her link with Thor re-established itself, and she felt at ease once more. A ruby shimmer dashed from her tree, and Thor galloped to the two, only stopping with wings extended, and he growled in between clamped serrated fangs. **At last. What happened to you?** He reared his head back, but Silver raised his hand in peaceful surrender before reassuring Selena's safe return. Still snarling, Thor snaked his head around, examining her before returning Silver's smugness with a growl. **Who is he?**

He's the white blur we saw earlier, but he's a friend. Selena still wasn't sure what to call him, but his intentions at least seemed worthy enough. As Silver led her to the back door, Thor bombarded her with many questions regarding her sudden disappearance and their severed connection. Selena's only explanation to the latter was that the dark magic following the Obsidian Order was somehow responsible for their isolation.

Yet, the pair were interrupted when Chaliss opened the door, and her eyes widened. "You?" Her response confirmed Selena's suspicions; she knew them after all. "W-what are you doing here? What happened?"

Silver grinned and readjusted his spectacles. "I promise all is well at the moment, but I must warn you: he knows they're here."

Chaliss looked at Selena and Thor, swallowing hard. "Allow me some time—"

"I'm afraid we've run out of time." Silver bit his bottom lip before meeting Selena's confused gaze. "The Order found them, and now it's a matter of days or weeks before the Lich himself makes his grand appearance."

Thor suddenly growled and snarled from the news, and Selena's face turned white as if she had seen a ghost. "What are we to do?" she asked.

Chaliss sucked in her cheeks and beckoned them inside; Thor, however, was too big to fit in her house. Instead, he laid his head through the door, snorting, his slitted eyes fixated on Silver like a hawk eyeing its prey. "I need to call for Rahim's return before we're to leave—oh, by the Divines, I shouldn't have sent him to his uncle's."

"You didn't know, though I must advise that he'll be safe there in the meantime."

"He'll never forgive me. Pray give me a few days to prepare and get him home safely before we must leave."

Silver pinched the bridge of his nose, but eventually decided. "Fine. You have three days to prepare, but D, Kain, and I will intervene if anything happens before then."

"Agreed."

When Chaliss went outside to fetch a carriage for Rahim, Silver led Selena to her room; he pulled out a vial filled with red liquid from his pockets. "Here, I believe I owe you this. Apply it to your neck with a cloth, and it will heal by nightfall."

Before Silver could leave, Thor nudged Selena's thoughts. **He has a familiar scent. I want to know who he is and if we can rely on him.**

Silver remained calm when Selena repeated Thor's words. "You can't. Just know you two are safe."

"Chaliss seems to know and trust you. Who are you?"

Silver's face widened with a smug grin. "Let's say that I'm a very old friend."

CHAPTER 5: THE STORM

Shortly after Silver left and she applied the ointment given to her, Selena made sure to enlighten Thor with the tale during their brief separation before he deemed himself satisfied; meanwhile, Chaliss confirmed that Rahim should return by late afternoon tomorrow. Yet, Selena couldn't help but ask how she and Silver were acquainted. Chaliss had served Selena her green tea with honey, as was her usual request, before finally answering, "He's the henchman of Her Imperial Majesty. Don't always trust everything he says."

"Why is that?"

"He's a very unpleasant fellow. Silver despises being around others and speaks ill of anyone he meets."

Selena refused to believe that after meeting him, but she instead asked, "Do you know Kain as well?"

Chaliss bit her bottom lip. "I've only heard about him, but I've never met him."

"How are you familiar with Silver?"

"Only that we serve a common ally. Silver tends to keep to himself, and I didn't think it was important to mention him."

"What about the Lich?"

Her question made Chaliss turn pale. "Other than he's a powerful necromancer."

Selena shook her head. "No, not that. Do you know why the Lich wanted anything to do with Thor and me?"

"Where are you getting all these questions from?" Chaliss sighed when she noticed that she couldn't redirect Selena's curiosity. "I'm not sure. He usually remains secluded in his lair made of molten fire in Mount Blackrock. It's a dreadful place that suspends high above the land near the border of Mirrorhold and Armageddon. It only brings death. Her Imperial Majesty never told me why you or Thor would ever be important to the Lich, and it's probably best that way."

After finishing, Chaliss went straight to packing their supplies, no longer willing to answer Selena's questions. She sighed and returned to her room as the sun dipped over the horizon, feeling defeated. Her uneasiness drew Thor's attention from his evening hunt. **Will you be all right?**

I'll be fine. Thank you, but I know Chaliss is hiding something from me.

Thor growled. **I should be large enough to fly us away from here.**

A cold shiver ran down her spine. *Perhaps not yet.*

Thor groaned, but Selena ignored his complaints as she worked through the evening packing her bags. She reached up to touch her neck and noticed the wounds completely healed before she finished, and she fell into slumber, ready to embrace the ongoing nightmares.

After an evening of waking up nearly every hour, Selena awoke with dark circles around her eyes. Even as she got dressed, the same phrase echoed throughout her thoughts: *It rests beneath the starry skies.*

Thor was as confused as she was, but he suggested, **Perhaps it has to do with Ragnarok.**

After sharing breakfast with Chaliss, she grabbed her books, but as soon as she stepped outside to meet with Thor, Selena suddenly heard chirping noises squeaking behind their tree. She and Thor exchanged glances before circling the trunk, and the pair found a young black dragon sniffing the nearby ground. Selena eyed it suspiciously. *What is a baby dragon doing around here? Where is their handler?*

I don't know. Intrigued, Thor began pawing at the dirt, and the youngling paused, tail twitching before mimicking his behavior. **I think they want to play.**

He immediately dashed from his spot despite Selena's objections, and she cursed under her breath. The black dragon stopped and backed away when Thor charged forward. The slightly smaller intruder fanned out its wings five-spined wings dabbed in purple and red oval specs, its smooth and shiny onyx scales polished like a snake's hide. Two small horns adorning its head curved forward and down, its ivory claws clicking against the hard ground with each stride, tail swishing back and forth. The black dragon bobbed its head up and down and made the same chirping noise again. Thor mimicked its behavior. **He wants to play.**

Selena looked around. *Where is his handler?*

He's a feral dragon, and he's been observing us since we first came out here.

Intrigued, Selena watched with interest as the two dragons wrestled around in the dirt, wondering if they had a language all their own, but from what she witnessed, they only communicated through different sounds and body language. She sat down by their tree while the dragons played tag and read to herself. After a few hours of this, they made their way to her side and laid down beside her. Although reluctant at first, the black dragon eventually allowed her to pet his head.

The black dragon vanished through the trees only when the sun began setting, releasing a series of chirps and clicks as a form of goodbye. Happy to have made a new friend, Thor rubbed his head into Selena's shoulder. **He said that it was nice to meet us.**

Does he plan on coming back?

I don't know. The feral hatchling seemed like he was off in a great hurry.

A day passed since meeting the whelpling, and Thor occasionally wandered around to see if he could find his new friend again with no avail. Selena comforted him as best as she could. *I'm not sure if he will come back. They're wild dragons, after all.*

I know, but that was fun to have a little playmate.

You'll meet other dragons.

Yet, Thor's growth didn't slow; over the next two days, while waiting for Rahim to return from his uncle's, he became suitable to carry a group of five fully grown men. As if to commemorate his sudden spurt, Selena watched as he wholly unfurled his new, massive wings and launched himself heavenward, his ruby scales but a gleam in the blazing sun.

Throughout the new day, Selena remained by his side and watched Thor's multiple flights as he circled the trees, his wings summoning a devastating gale storm threatening to render the forest bare. **I want you to fly with me,** he declared.

Maybe not yet.

As Thor landed upon his haunches, wings still unfolded, he snorted. **Soon, I will leave you no choice, and I will not see you ride another dragon. If we're to leave here, flying would be much faster.**

Before Selena could answer, Rahim's voice interrupted her train of thought; he finally returned, but Rahim sounded exhausted. "There you are. Oh, by the three Divines, I am so sore." He shuffled outside and stood in awe of Thor's massive growth. While Rahim praised his size, the magnificent Thor couldn't help but hum and chitter with glee.

While asking about Rahim's visit, Selena debated whether she should enlighten him of her adventures but ultimately decided to wait until he fully rested before sharing her tale. Instead, she asked, "What happened to you?"

Rahim sighed. "That old git is insane. The entire time I was there, he bombarded me with these ridiculous puzzles. Some days, he would take me into the middle of the forest and told me if I wanted supper, I would have to make it back before nightfall. Those two weeks were like being trapped in Oblivion."

Selena could not help but snicker. Meanwhile, Thor swept his tail across the dirt, but his laughter bellowed in the back of her mind. Yet, Rahim ignored their behavior. "I spent about one-third of my trip hanging upside down from trees, stuck in his ridiculous traps. The rest was me praying to come back home. Also, no offense, but he can't cook to save his life. But I heard some interesting stories from the war: a prophecy was made over a hundred years ago by three Oracle triplets, the fortune-tellers who serve the imperial family."

Thor clicked his nails against the rocks. **How odd and fascinating.**

I wonder if they could tell us more about ourselves if we had the chance of meeting them.

Trying to learn the future would be folly. We are masters of our own fate.

Rahim was ignorant of their conversation as he continued: "I don't know if it's true or not, but he told me that the prophecy predicted that a person born of a dragon will be the savior of Armageddon."

Thor snaked his head around Selena's shoulder, humming. **Someone born of a dragon. Hmm.**

What are you thinking?

For some reason, that sounds familiar to me, but I don't know why.

Selena squinted at Rahim. "How is that even possible?"

"I don't know, and I can't trust what that mental oaf says anymore. His stories are more entertaining if anything." He stretched and yawned. "Mum told me something happened and that we're to leave soon. What's going on?"

Selena's mind buzzing, she asked for his company to join her into town so she could answer him and look for a book to research the ridiculous fable, half-believing it to be a myth. Yet, Thor reassuring he heard that somewhere before made her think otherwise and that perhaps it wasn't as far-fetched as initially thought. He pestered and pleaded to fly them into the town square, but Selena refused. *You mustn't be seen, remember?*

Impatient as always, Thor snarled. **I hate hiding. What should I do once I grow to the size of a mountain?**

Do dragons get that big?

Why shouldn't we? Eventually, the village will have no choice but to acknowledge me.

I'm afraid they may have already when you began your flying lessons.

Just hurry back, or I will fly you away myself.

Heeding Thor's warning with extreme caution as he would make good on his promise, Selena and Rahim hurried into the town square towards Arthur's bookstall and asked him for any books about the story regarding the fabled dragon-born. Through Arthur apologizing profusely for being unable to answer her questions, the two made small talk about the great library in Alfheim and that it may have what she sought. "I've also heard stories that a brilliant dragon runs the library. Listen to me prattle on about dragons running libraries. What next?"

Returning to the house empty-handed, Selena finally answered Rahim's questions as best as she could. However, she left out her meeting Silver and Kain, as she wasn't sure how Rahim would take the news that vampires were real. Before Rahim could interject, Selena saw Her Imperial Majesty's messenger, Loki the fox, running about the yard as if he had lost something. "What are you doing here?"

The fox immediately paused and bowed before her. "Oh, I beg your pardon, Miss Liongod. I was merely looking for Chaliss. Have you seen her?"

"She was in the kitchen last."

Selena opened the door and invited Loki inside before Rahim groaned and went to his room to sleep, grumbling before trudging up the stairs, "I'll ask again later."

She sighed, but seeing Loki reminded her of Silver. When she was sure Rahim was out of earshot, Selena said, "By the way, someone was looking for you, a man dressed in white who goes by the name of Silver."

It looked as though the fur on Loki's face changed color as if he had aged a few years. The fox took a step back and hid his tail between his legs. "No, you never saw me."

Judging by his reaction, Selena figured that the two were acquainted but that Loki did not want to see him for some reason. "What's wrong?"

"Silver is always so mean, always chasing me and wanting to eat me for some reason." Bemused and entertained, Selena spun around, and Loki's ears perked up when Chaliss walked downstairs, and the fox rushed over like a happy dog upon the return of its owner.

Chaliss immediately paused amidst walking towards Rahim's room, completely and wholly shocked. "What brings you here?"

"I must speak with you alone. Miss Liongod, if you please."

"Of course. I'll take my leave." Selena made her way up the stairs, but when Loki and Chaliss resumed their conversation, she stopped and leaned against the wall to eavesdrop.

However, Thor's voice interrupted her task. **What's happening?**

I'll find out soon.

When he thought he and Chaliss were alone, Loki asked, "Has she regained her memory?"

"No. It might be better that way, and at least she's happy here."

"I hope you realize everything is growing worse, and the Lich is mobilizing his army, ready to storm through Alfheim at any moment."

"I'm aware of the fact, Loki. The Order has already made its grand appearance, and those demons have revealed themselves spectacularly." When Loki didn't reply, Chaliss added, "The Empress is fully aware, isn't she?"

"Y-you never mentioned this. At this rate, we should invite them over for tea."

Chaliss' tone changed, and Selena knew she was irritated by Loki's attitude. "In fact, we must leave by tomorrow or else we may see the Lich soon. Now, if you don't mind, I have other matters that need my attention."

"Oh no, don't look so down. I find it much easier to deal with a grim situation with a smile rather than frowning, for your face might fall off. Or is that just a human thing?"

"You're nearly as bad as Silver."

A small squeak escaped Loki's mouth, but he regained his relaxed posture. "I must tease as it's been a while since we've talked about anything." Loki put his paw up and summoned a roll of parchment floating in mid-air. "This is very terrible timing, but Vidar sent me to deliver this."

Chaliss immediately snatched it from the air and read it with haste. "Terrible timing indeed. Why does Vidar want to visit all the sudden? I swear, the Divines have a cruel sense of humor." There was a brief pause. "Do you think he suspects Thor's existence?"

Loki scratched his ear with his hind leg. "Regardless of if he does or doesn't, I recommend keeping him hidden, and you will act as if nothing has changed." He paused and sighed. "I must also advise you to wait until after meeting with Vidar before evacuating. He cannot suspect anything is amiss."

"Could you deliver that message to D for me?"

"Of course."

Selena heard enough; she quietly tip-toed down the stairs when Chaliss and Loki went out the front door and bolted out the back. Thor was curled around their tree, but he opened one eye as she approached. Upon seeing her pale expression, he went quiet at first before stretching out his neck, and he looked heavenward. **The storm is coming.**

They spent the rest of the day and the next in anticipation over Vidar's arrival. Selena had never seen Chaliss look so uneasy before; she and Rahim had to remain in their rooms and stay away, and Thor agreed to remain grounded and hidden in the forest. When she had the chance, Selena did her best to explain the situation. Though Rahim was empathetic, he couldn't help but groan: "Now, I really want to know who and what you are if you're drawing this much attention."

"I wish I knew."

D must have received Chaliss' message, as Silver and Kain hadn't arrived on the promised day. On the day of Vidar's scheduled visit, Chaliss busied herself by cooking for her important guest, preparing a whole roasted pig on a spit with mounds of potatoes and other delectable side dishes. "She never cooks like that for us." Rahim mumbled from the cracks of his door. Selena shushed him, but he was right. Chaliss always said they were too poor to buy much from the market, but how could she afford a whole pig for Vidar? When Chaliss finished, she carried her dishes to the clean guestroom she had prepared, displaying the pig in the middle of the dining table as the centerpiece, garnished with rosemary sprigs, and drizzled with a honey sauce.

The clock chimed six in the evening. Chaliss flinched but darted out to get herself ready before the visitor arrived. When the coast was clear, Rahim declared, "Come on; let's sneak in and find out what's going on. Vidar will be here any minute." Rahim dashed from his room, grabbed Selena, and pulled her down the hallway to the prepared apartment. He was cautious when opening the door, his eyes scanning the long, wooden table displayed with food and wine. A tall, oak wardrobe sat in the corner; Selena smiled, for it was the perfect hiding place for them both.

She and Rahim rushed over and shoved themselves inside, concealing themselves behind the hanging clothes, pushing and squirming to make room. The wardrobe made a little noise with every movement they made, until they closed the door. She peeked through the small crack at the door, but Rahim pushed her a little. "I think I hear them coming."

Selena put her fingers to her lips; they watched and waited until they heard heavy footsteps, and the door swung open. Chaliss walked in first, followed by a plump man and a third follower concealed in a dark red cloak with rune symbols etched along the sleeves and edges. Selena assumed the plump man to be Vidar Helios, a stout half-elf. In his black suit, he blended in with the shadows. His ghostly white shoulder-length hair contrasted his slightly darker skin tone; not nearly as dark as hers, but his companion's ghastly pale complexion significantly differed. She couldn't tell the color of Vidar's eyes or if they had any color; they looked strikingly white, set ablaze by his hair.

Vidar took his seat in one chair at the end of the table while Chaliss and the other guest sat down beside him. He pulled out a handkerchief and wiped the sweat off his forehead before accepting the wine glass Chaliss poured for him. "Thank you, my dear," he said. Chaliss offered it to her other guest, but he refused. Selena's mouth watered a little when she watched the plump man and his companion eat; Chaliss, on the other hand, did not. Vidar wiped his face with a napkin. "Where is the young lady now?"

"She's in bed."

"Good. Has she said anything about her name or who she is?" When Chaliss denied all, Vidar cleared his throat. "That's such a pity but also quite vexing." Selena shifted a little, suspecting that Chaliss only lied to protect her.

She attempted to change the subject. "Yes, but she's been doing well since her arrival. We are honored that you and Ashur took the time to come all this way."

Vidar waved his hand after wiping the pork grease from his face. "It is no trouble at all. We were returning to Alfheim after enforcing the draft for all young men who are of age to fight."

Chaliss looked as though she had seen a ghost. "Rahim isn't sixteen yet—"

Vidar cut her off with a wave of his hand. "We know; that's why he never received any orders from the Council." Rahim and Selena exchanged glances. While Chaliss and Vidar were engaged in conversation, the third companion, Ashur, remained quiet, his hidden face locked on his plate and wine. However, Vidar continued. "We are on the brink of war. The Lich plans on retaliating after we sent our Flying Officers Beck and Gromm Steelmane to rescue that young girl. We made a mistake in fulfilling Her Majesty's request, and we cannot allow this to happen again."

Rahim whispered in Selena's ear, "I don't like where he's going with this."

The tense atmosphere steeped while Chaliss contemplated Vidar's meaning; she cleared her throat after setting her wine down. "I am certain the Lich would have attacked regardless."

"I'm sorry, Chaliss. We cannot focus on assumptions, but rather what's happening now and the consequences of our recent decisions."

"I understand, but—"

"Which is why the Council has reached its decision: we have arranged transportation to relocate the girl come tomorrow morning."

Selena felt as if Vidar struck her in the face, and Chaliss' eyes burned with fury from the announcement. "Relocate her where? What does the Council plan on doing with her?"

"We will escort her to Alfheim, but you must understand that this is for the sake of the Empire, and therefore, we cannot disclose any other information—it's classified."

Selena's heart sounded like a ticking clock ringing in her ears. Rahim turned and met her horrified expression; he understood the severity of her situation where she could be a victim of possible experiments, questioning, and the Divines know what else.

Chaliss continued pleading. "The Council must reconsider. She is a wonderful and sweet child. Why in the Divine's name would you do this to her?"

"In the long run, this will keep her safe. It's decided."

"I can take care of her here just fine. Please, there must be another way."

Vidar's eyes flickered with murderous intent, but he regained his genial facade. "We understand, but you must see it from our perspective. We spent money and resources rescuing this girl, all on Her Imperial Majesty's request. We want to know why we risked so much to save this child who doesn't even know who she is, and neither do we. Even the Empress is at a loss, yet she was the one who asked us for our help. Now, we must act. We will be back in the morning." Vidar took another sip of his wine before standing up from the table. "Thank you for dinner."

He and his companion left the room after Chaliss ruefully opened the door, but her eyes landed on the wardrobe. Selena gasped; Chaliss knew she and Rahim were hiding and eavesdropping. Instead of calling them out, she left the apartment with the two gentlemen, leaving Selena and Rahim alone with their swirling thoughts.

CHAPTER 6: THE GRAND EXCHANGE

The storm clouds billowed that evening, and Selena squirmed through her covers as the thunder echoed and the rain tapped on her windowpane. Frightened and confused, she didn't know what to do. Thor asked her how dinner went with Vidar, but Selena couldn't answer, and he understood the Council had ill plans surrounding their uncertain future. Yet, he shared in her confusion on their next course of action.

Suddenly, an idea came to her that would allow her and Thor to be safe from both the Council and the Lich, but it would be awful to pull off. "I'm sorry, *Matu.*" Selena sprung up and went towards her dresser drawers for her scissors and hand cloth to hide her mark. After wrapping her palm and walking to the mirror, she grabbed pieces of her long hair and began cutting. Tears trickled down her cheeks as she worked her way around her whole head, and when finished, her hair was just below her ears.

Near her pile of clothes on the floor was a thick, long piece of cloth she grabbed next. She took off her shirt and tightly wrapped the fabric around her chest to hold and hide her developing bosom. When satisfied to see her flattened chest, she tip-toed into Rahim's room and searched through his packed bags. To her delight, she found new apparel with a loose fit, perfect at concealing her curves. She knew Rahim was a sound sleeper and wouldn't have noticed the missing clothing.

She stopped when she saw a small, tied leather pouch filled with coins at the bottom of his pack. Fighting against her good nature, she took it. "Forgive me, Rahim."

After ensuring she had all she needed and was adequately dressed, she tip-toed out the back of the house with her large pack she put together the day before. Lightning flashed once more, and she saw Thor stir in his spot; unable to fight her fear, every roar from the thunder was enough to make her pause and shake until the sound passed.

When she relaxed, Thor was already upon her, blazing amber eyes fixed on her like two glowing full moons. **I almost didn't recognize you. What in Oblivion have you done to yourself?**

Selena reached into the top of her pack and pulled out Rahim's black bandit cap to wear, and she held up a rolled map, explaining her gut-wrenching plan: *If we're to remain together, we must join the Imperial Air Force. They can't separate us if we're soldiers and if I'm disguised as a boy, and the Lich will leave the village alone.*

Are you mad? We'll be walking straight into the lion's den. He sighed when Selena agreed, but she explained Alfheim would be the last place the Council would look to find her. **Do you think they'll blindly accept us as recruits?**

I'm still working it out. She paused and felt her chest tighten. *When we leave, the Lich and his Order will follow us. That way,* Matu *wouldn't need to worry anymore. I don't want to endanger her or Rahim.*

How would they know we left the village?

I don't know, but if the Lich found us before, I suspect he will recognize we're no longer here. When positioning her bag on Thor's back, her heart stopped when Rahim's voice boomed like the thunder still rumbling overhead. "You can't expect to leave me behind." He trotted with his packed luggage slung over his shoulder. "I heard you rummaging through my room earlier; I couldn't sleep after hearing what that pompous oaf said about you. I can help you two escape, and mum should be safe from that loathsome necromancer."

Defeated and undone, Selena knew it was folly to deny her plans. "This will be extremely dangerous, and I don't want to see you getting hurt on our account."

"Let me come with you. I don't want to deal with mum after you leave. If I stayed, I wouldn't hear the end of it."

"Wouldn't *Matu* be angry with you?"

"Oh yes, she'll be mad. But she can't be mad at me if I'm not here. Besides, I'm the only one who knows how to read a map, and I have a compass. You need me if you are trying to get anywhere."

Selena sighed, knowing that he was right. "All right. We'll stop and rest upon reaching the Grand Exchange."

While he and Selena positioned and tied their bags down near the base of Thor's neck, Rahim asked, "Have you thought your plan through?" Rahim's face turned pale when she reiterated her idea. "You're mad. That's where they were going to take you in the first place. We'll be right underneath the Council's nose."

"And yet, it'll be the safest place to be. I don't think Thor and I have a choice now."

Rahim opened his mouth to refute her argument but stopped when he saw her point. "Fine. I'll help you two get to Alfheim, but I hope you're right."

Thor scooped the two with his claws and helped them settle upon his back, with Rahim in front. As he wholly unfurled his fresh wings and shook away the raindrops, Selena pleaded, *We're not ready to fly yet.* **It would be so much faster than running.**

The lightning cracked the black sky directly overhead, and Selena cowered into his neck. *Please.*

Thor recoiled in shame for being too pushy and reconsidered her request. **Very well, my dear. I shall wait until you're ready.**

Selena breathed slightly easier. *I believe I would be once we get you into a harness first.*

Of course. Selena could feel his muscles tighten under her legs, and Thor broke into a full gallop. Rahim quickly wrapped his arms around the dragon's thick neck, the rough diamond-cut scales slightly digging into their legs. Although Thor's neck spikes were still short, Rahim kept banging his head against their sides with every movement made. Selena held onto Rahim's waist as Thor ran through the Black Bog Forest and away from the only home she had known.

The merciless rain cut across their faces like daggers; Selena peered over her shoulder at the vanishing house and whispered, "Forgive us, *Matu.*"

*****

Armageddon swirled into a deep slumber under the charcoal blanket, the land pierced by the relentless icy storm that had finally ceased. A large group of about fifty horsemen from the Obsidian Order made their way to the nestled Helshire Village, a sense of gloom lingering over their presence. However, a raven perched on a tree branch a overlooking the horse riders; still as a statue, it watched, anticipating what these intruders intended to do.

Their formation stood firm against the billowing dust cloud swirling around the horde. The riders remained focused on the sleeping hovel and ignored an enormous golden dragon gliding downward behind them. The dragon's weight from the landing made the earth shake and quiver under their feet. With uneasiness, the horses stamped into the ground and neighed as they struggled to move away, but the riders kept their mounts in place.

Even in the thick of night, the majestic, golden dragon shined like a polished sword, its silver wings christened by the frigid water droplets. It stood the size of a large house—a saddle built to carry about twenty passengers strapped to its smooth back and chest. A single rider upon the dragon directed his companion around the group of men until they reached a cliff overlooking the town.

The massive horde split and made a path for the gold and silver dragon. It moved forward with poise and grace, but it crouched near the edge like a mighty hunter eyeing its prey. Its rider, a young man who looked as if he just became of age, sniffed the air, and an evil grin played upon his crusty lips. His deep blue eyes scanned the village, the crescent-shaped scar running through his right eye wrinkling from the furrow in his brow. His raven black hair flowed behind him from the growing gale. Through the mental link he shared with his dragon, the young man ordered: *Burn it down, Doragon.*

The golden dragon growled through his serrated fangs and unfolded his massive wings. The horses backed away as Doragon launched heavenward, his tail slithering across the ground like a snake before being completely airborne. As if on cue, the horse riders followed the dragon towards the nearest building. Doragon reached the village within seconds, and as he and his rider approached the old, haunted house, the golden dragon reared his head back like a snake ready to strike and unleashed a torrent of fire that obliterated the structure in one pass. The explosion made the village tremble, and within moments, the panicked and dismayed residents burst forth from their houses. As they saw Doragon circling above and spitting his fiery destruction, the villagers fled in every direction in hopes of avoiding incineration.

The horse riders soon arrived at the chaotic party of death and flames, using magic and weapons to strike down every innocent. Their massive steeds would stampede through the stragglers, crushing flesh and bone with their giant hooves. High-pitched screams pierced the air as the Obsidian Order rampaged through the dusty street, pulling out their concealed firearms and shooting at the fleeing denizens, who dropped dead like flies. Those gifted with magic summoned a barrage of attacks: fire, electricity, ice, shadow, all intertwined in destructive harmony that brought the village into a cataclysm.

The watchful raven rushed from its perch and made haste towards Chaliss' home while avoiding the dragon's fire. Doragon circled back and belched another deadly conflagration that consumed a row of dwellings in a single breath. The horse riders evaded Doragon's attack as not to get caught in the smoldering inferno, as no force or ward could protect one against a creature of the Divines, as dragons were the ultimate source of magic.

The fire swept across the trees and made its way closer to the house with each passing second. The blackbird darted through the opened window and shape-shifted into its fox form after landing on the floor. Loki snarled as the house rumbled from the dragon's wrath, and another wave of flames scorched the Black Bog Forest.

"Chaliss, where are you?" Loki growled through his clamped fangs and rushed out of the room, believing the worst. To his relief, the fox saw her rush to Selena's and Rahim's room. As panic rushed through her, Chaliss threw the doors open and screamed when she saw the two were not there. She hurried down the hallway with tears spilling from her eyes until Loki caught up to her. "I must get you to safety."

Chaliss trembled and shook her head. "I need to find Selena and Rahim. I won't leave them behind. I can't —"

"No time." The air grew thick with smoke that seeped through the cracks of the doors and windows. The flames from the forest inched closer. "This way." Loki led her towards the front door.

Just as he and Chaliss escaped, Doragon made another pass with a blast of flames pouring from his open maw. The fire spread from rooftop to rooftop, catching all in its path ablaze. The fire consumed and decimated the row containing Chaliss' home, leaving a trail of smoldering ashes and debris. Chaliss froze in her tracks as she watched her home crumble. All the color drained from her face, and she almost collapsed when she feared the worst.

Loki growled and pawed at her legs. "I watched Selena and Rahim flee the village with Thor. They will be safe, but soon you won't be."

It took every ounce of her strength to pick herself back up, but Loki's news rang through Chaliss' ears like bells from a cathedral. Her mind snapped back into reality when he continued pestering her into following him to a safe location. The horse riders had already moved towards the other end of the village, but they left a trail of corpses and blood.

Loki and Chaliss hid within the shadows and snuck out of the village, avoiding the inferno wall leaving a scorched scar. As they reached a safe distance far enough away from Doragon and the Obsidian Order, the two watched the settlement burn as it screamed its requiem.

*****

The trio traveled through the night without a single word. Rahim constantly sighed and looked back through the trees but gave her a smile and a thumbs up when Selena checked on him. When the sun rose on the second day, the Grand Exchange was in sight: the largest marketplace in all of Armageddon, where those from the other kingdoms could exchange goods and conduct business.

Selena was paralyzed in shock at the blitz of noise, music, colors, and people upon arriving. She saw many of the kingdom's inhabitants everywhere she turned, selling whatever elaborate merchandise one could imagine. Carts upon carts, filled with precious products, rolled up the cobblestone road, and their owners asked whoever passed by if they wanted to buy—lines of shops and buildings strung on both sides of the alleys like a string of jewels.

An older woman with many necklaces around her neck came up to Selena, offering a piece of jewelry with beautiful stones of various colors. "Made from precious dragon eggshells," she said and pointed to a beautiful, gilded stone pendant, "this one is from the Imperial Goldscale egg—rare in Armageddon. Get your dragon shell necklaces at half price." The woman stormed over to a half-giant wearing an overcoat further down the road.

Avoiding being suffocated by the greedy merchants, Selena backed up a little and accidentally bumped into a grumpy dwarf who barely stood to her chest; he slammed his shoulder against hers. "Watch where yer goin'."

"I weaved this sweater from pure unicorn hair. Only four hundred and ninety-five pieces of gold."

"Dragonhide gloves," another merchant shouted, "Get your dragonhide gloves. Handy protection when brewing potions."

"Dragon scale earrings from the Blackland Steelwings of the Black Bog swamps."

Thor was careful with every step he took, but to his surprise, everyone swiftly moved out his way without interrupting business; yet no one in the Grand Exchange seemed bothered by his presence. *Dragons must be a common sight here*, Selena thought.

Rahim's head spun as he looked at all the shops. "I've been here a few times when I was younger. Occasionally mum wanted rare jewelry. We should be fine here, and dragons come through the Grand Exchange all the time. It's almost like a checkpoint for the riders." He pointed over at one building off in the distance. "I think if I remember correctly, that's the black market. You can find illegal dragon eggs for sale, potions, rare enchanted equipment, and who knows what else."

According to Rahim's explanation, the empty and decrepit building looked like it was out of business, but shady customers waltzed to the back door. Still, the shop owner didn't allow anyone inside but promptly delivered their requested merchandise. "The black market is right here in the Grand Exchange?" Selena asked, "If they sell illegal items, why are they out in the open?"

"There's something weird about that shop. One day it's there, and the next, it's gone. I'm not exactly sure how it works, but it's nicknamed 'The Vanishing Snake.'"

"Why 'The Vanishing Snake?'"

"Because it's a sneaky-looking shop, like a snake." Although Selena herself was not into illegal retail, that didn't stop her curiosity and the desire to check the validity of the rumors; however, she wasn't sure how a shop could 'vanish.'

Through Rahim's direction, Thor carried the two towards a black building shaped like a dragon with its head on the ground, the mouth serving as the entrance. Its wings stretched to the sky and nestled the shop within its protective barrier. The dragon's eyes were windows, smoke steaming out the pupils and pouring into the night sky. "The Black Pub. We can stay there for a while, and ahem." Rahim held out his hand as if expecting a token or a gift.

"What? Oh," She flushed in embarrassment when relinquishing his pouch of coins. "I'm sorry."

Rahim dangled it in her face, the sound of crinkling coins rattling her ears. "What's done is done, but if you steal from me again—" His threat was wholly disrupted when Thor swung his head around and growled in Rahim's face; Thor was no longer the size of a small dog, and Rahim zipped his mouth shut when a dragon nearly the size of two horses threatened to strike him down.

As the locals walked in and out of the dragon's mouth entrance, the torches' fire outside changed colors and shapes. It transformed into a dragon flying off, then a young woman who bowed and did funny little tricks; children gathered to watch the blazing show. Rows of different-sized stalls fit to house a dragon lined behind the Black Pub. After allowing Selena and Rahim to dismount and grab their bags, Thor inspected his soon-to-be new quarters, only to be shooed away by the groundkeeper. Rahim immediately intervened and offered the man a few gold pieces for Thor's new space. Suspicious, the man bit and tested the coins before nodding and pointing out an open stall; six total and a sleeping green dragon occupied the one at the very end. Its large harness leaned against the wooden posts, the dragon's emerald scales shimmering from a fresh coat of oil.

As Thor made himself comfortable in the one closest to the Black Pub, he snorted while inspecting his new housing accommodations. **Although I'm glad to sleep under a proper roof, this looks more fitting for a horse than a dragon.**

I wish I could build you a castle fit for a king. Will you be all right for the time being until we leave for Alfheim?

It would be unfair for me to say otherwise.

Selena felt a twinge of guilt. *You shouldn't have to compromise, but I'm not sure what else we can do right now. Alfheim should offer better arrangements.*

Thor flickered his tail and exhaled a plume of smoke. **In the meantime, while we're here, you should practice your new voice. You still sound like a lady.**

Selena gave him a strange look as he laughed, but she knew he was right. *I don't know what I'm getting myself into.*

Nor do I, but it is fun to poke at you. At least no one from the Council will recognize you.

They don't know what I look like, let alone my name. I'm so grateful for that advantage. After ensuring Thor was as comfortable as possible, Selena offered the groundskeeper an extra piece to add a coat of oil to his hide in the morning. Grumbling at first, he couldn't pass up the offer and promised to have Thor gleaming like a shiny new penny before instructing Thor on where he could hunt; his eyes flickering crimson, Thor stretched out his wings and launched over the stalls towards the designated sheep pen and plucked his two catches for the evening, one dangling from each foreclaw. Selena assumed they were raised as fodder for the passing soldier's dragons.

After being satisfied by Thor's temporary conditions, she followed Rahim inside the inn. The Black

Pub contained four different floors: the first held the bar and restaurant, while the remaining three had other rooms available for rent. Selena's eyes studied the sturdy pinewood foundation of the building, unleashing a strong scent of pine needles perfuming the air. In front was a black granite statue of the Xyaxon as a fire lion, perched on a pedestal hanging above the roaring fireplace. The flames from the hearth danced in the air, casting shadows along the wall.

The two were greeted by a long alcoholic display of different liquors, with windows showing the cooks preparing meals from inside the kitchen; patrons occupied every seat at the bar table, bothering the four servers mixing drinks. Thick glass tables lined the other side of the bar and eatery, large enough to seat five customers at once. Windows donned midnight blue curtains made of authentic unicorn hair—the softest substance on earth, augmenting the night sky with a trail of diamond stars painted across the ceiling.

After speaking with one of the servers, Rahim gave him a few coins and received a small piece of paper wrapped around a brass key. "I got us a room. Follow me."

The second door on the left was theirs; their clean apartment was simple yet matching in eloquence from the first floor. The night sky painting and the midnight blue tapestries were a constant theme used throughout the Black Pub. The queen-sized bed dressed in a blue and white quilt made Selena's eyes droop; she was ready to dive into the sea of sheets and pillows.

Yet, Rahim beat her to it and collapsed on the mattress through moans and groans. "I'm not moving unless we've been captured by either the Lich or the Council." He laughed but stopped when Selena wasn't amused.

"We're criminals."

"I've gotten into worse situations."

Selena raised a brow as she quizzically studied him. "That doesn't make any sense, although you've probably almost talked Vidar to death."

He snorted when Selena enjoyed her quip. "Regardless, we'll have to get you enrolled in the Force. It shouldn't be too hard—go up to Vidar and say you already have a dragon and that you two wanted to do the right thing by enlisting, and bam—you and Thor will be soldiers in no time."

"Are you sure it's that easy?"

"How hard could it be? There's a draft going on —you heard Vidar say so himself."

"Will we need official paperwork with orders or —?"

"That's what the Vanishing Snake is for: I'll check with them before sunset. Your papers will look so authentic that we'll easily fool Vidar and the Council." Rahim smiled at his cleverness.

"Are you sure?"

"Have I ever been wrong?" When Selena gave him a menacing glare, he waved his hands in defense. "Please don't answer that. This plan will work, I guarantee it, but first, we need to find you a new name." Selena began pacing back and forth with her hand to her chin, and Rahim grinned. "How about a name that means fire? Or what about 'Fire?'" Rahim recoiled when Selena gave him a disapproving glare at his suggestions. "Or you could go by 'Sapphire.'"

"That sounds like a woman's name."

"I don't hear you coming up with any ideas. Also, while you're thinking of one, you need to work on your voice because you still sound like a lady."

"But I am a lady." Face flustering, she grumbled, "Thor said the same."

Rahim slapped his forehead and bit his cheeks as his nostrils flared in agitation. "Focus because you need to start acting like a man." Before Selena could properly conjure up a new name to complete her guise, Rahim suddenly jumped up and clutched his stomach. "While you do that, I'm getting some food because my stomach is starting to eat itself." He then dashed out of the room before Selena could get in another word.

She continued pacing before plopping on the bed. "I'm terrible with names." Her mind raced to the different books she had read, and she thought of the first soldiers who joined the Force two hundred years prior; one name, Andric, stood out to her. As if to humor Rahim, Andric meant 'fire;' Selena couldn't help but chuckle.

At least I didn't have to worry about finding a name for you.

I already identified myself before hatching. Though we're connected, I didn't want another mortal to name me. Upon hearing Selena's thoughts on using Andric as a new alias, Thor gave his approval. **That sounds nice, although I think it's strange that you humans have another following it—a 'last name' or a 'surname.'**

Thank you, and it's a little more than that.

I don't understand why your kind needs more than one name.

It's because surnames can trace back to those you're related to.

Thor paused, and asked, **What about yours then? Does 'Liongod' connect to anything?**

There are no records of that name anywhere, sadly. What about dragons?

I see. Humans are fascinating, but we dragons are unique in our own right and don't need to be labeled with several names to distinguish ourselves from another.

But wouldn't you still like to see where you came from?

Maybe, but I couldn't care either way about my lineage. If anything, I wish I knew what breed I was.

Hopefully we'll find out when we arrive in Alfheim. The Council or any of the higher-ranked officers would be able to identify your nature. Selena pulled out some paper with a fountain pen and an inkwell to write it down. "Andric Liongod. I like the sound of that name. Yes, I'll be Andric Liongod."

I like it. I think it suits your alter ego.

I pray that wasn't sarcasm.

Not at all. I only hope Vidar and the rest of the Council won't see past your disguise.

They've never seen me, and they don't even know my real name. Liongod would still be safe to use.

When Rahim returned with food, enthusiastic that Selena fashioned herself a new identity, he took her paper and folded it in his pocket. "Okay, you will be Andric Liongod. You just turned sixteen and received your orders for the draft. You have a dragon because you saved his life, and now he's indebted to you, and you two agreed to serve the Empire and Her Imperial Majesty."

Selena nodded and grinned. "This might work."

"I will return soon." He nodded to the plate he brought with sliced bread and cheeses before excusing himself to take care of the forgery.

After Thor assured her he finished gorging his sheep, Selena grabbed a few pieces of bread and cheese before rushing outside to join him at his stall. As the sun dipped over the horizon, the large groups of traders and customers disappeared into their shops and inns for the rest of the evening, leaving the Grand Exchange completely desolate and nearly abandoned.

When Selena approached, Thor was busy picking his claws clean, but he stopped and wrapped his tail around her, pushing her close until she collapsed on his arm. She noticed the green dragon had left its stall with the harness missing.

Thor eyed the previously occupied spot and twittered. **He left with his rider shortly after you and Rahim went inside. His name was Aster, and his rider was Mr. Kingsleigh. The two were very polite, but they were at a loss as to my breed.**

Was that why you brought up surnames and dragon breeds earlier?

Thor looked dismally at his claws and shifted his weight. **The conversation made me wonder, but Mr. Kingsleigh assured me the scholars at Dragonspire could help if the Council could not.** When she reiterated Rahim's task, Thor chittered and hummed in delight. **I believe this will work, and Vidar still doesn't know I exist.**

Since no one else can hear our thoughts, you can refer to me however you wish.

Very well then, Andric.

You're not funny.

Thor's tongue slithered out and brushed against her cheek. **I can be from time to time. If anyone asks, we are on our way to the Force. That way, no one will question or report us to the Council.**

Aye. She sighed while reminiscing their lazy book-filled afternoons. *When we have more time, I would like to read together again.*

Yes, please. That would be delightful, and you could practice using your new voice.

Selena cleared her throat. "Like this?" Thor smirked. "I'm working on it."

You don't have to overdo it. Try maybe Rahim's tone? His doesn't sound too deep compared to yours.

She cleared her throat again and attempted to match how Rahim sounded. "How does this sound?"

That's better. You should be fine.

Selena leaned up against Thor's stomach and slid to the ground. Guilty as she was for abandoning Chaliss without a note or message, she prayed Chaliss would forgive her and Thor; as for Rahim's sudden involvement, though it was his choice, Selena was now responsible for his wellbeing.

Thor shifted his body and wrapped her within his coiled tail; his wings draped over her like a heated blanket, and her eyes grew heavy. The torpor she struggled against nearly prevented her eyes from catching a white dove flying overhead; its ice-blue eyes fell onto her as she finally yielded to the evening's cold embrace.

When morning came, Selena excused herself from Thor; she ordered a small bowl of fruit with salted pork before dragging her feet back to her room to get appropriately dressed. As a stranger greeted her in the dining area, Selena reminded herself to sound like Rahim when responding and used the story she and Thor rehearsed. She cleared her throat and said in her new voice: "We are on our way to Alfheim."

"Aye, I hear ya'll be preparing for war."

"I'm afraid so. I was recently called for the draft and will be reporting for duty by the end of this week."

Selena politely excused herself from the conversation but relaxed when he had bought her story.

Upon returning to the apartment, Rahim was impatiently waiting to deliver news of his success. "I found a professional forger, and they agreed to do it for twenty-five gold pieces. Your papers will be ready by tonight." He ruefully checked his pouch of coins. "We don't have a lot of money left, so we need to wisely spend what we've got. We will need provisions for the trip to Alfheim."

"If need be, Thor could hunt for himself and us." The two agreed to start shopping for non-perishable supplies that morning, such as salted pork, jerky, and jars of pickled vegetables—much to Rahim's disdain. After washing off the dirt and donning fresh apparel, she and Rahim trekked outside. The shining sun lanced through the cloud-covered heavens. Like the day before, the streets felt like a maze; Selena attempted to avoid social interaction.

The thundering noise was interrupted by a blue dragon making its flight overhead; its enormous wingspan engulfed the sky, draping the sun in shadow. Its head and back were decorated with many horns, save for its neck base. The brilliant, smooth metal-plated azure hide caught the light like a sword's glimmer, casting blue and purple specks across the buildings. Its sapphire eyes gazed downward at her a moment before resuming course.

"Take this and get what you think we will need." Rahim handed her a few coins.

Selena nodded. "I will meet you back at the inn in one hour." The two then went to do their separate shopping. As Selena searched through the stalls and stores, two people caught her eye as they broke from the crowd. One was a tall woman wearing a black cowl and a dark, green skirt sweeping over her leather boots. Her companion was a young boy near Selena's age, his closely-cropped sandy hair and brown eyes the same as Rahim's. The boy rolled the sleeves of his black shirt above his wrists, but he didn't extend the effort to fix his boot with the untied lace. He and the woman marched to the Vanishing Snake, and Selena, through great curiosity, followed them.

As she approached the black market's secret entrance, Selena choked on the smell of incense that perfumed the building. The purple walls and black ceiling matched the thick, velvet cloth that replaced the back door. A massive bookshelf containing many dragons and wizard figurines sat on display; on top was a crystal ball with a set of tarot cards next to it. A glass countertop lined up against one side, presenting a rainbow of exotic potions for sale. Further back was a warehouse of taboo merchandise, including illegal dragon eggs of different breeds.

The woman hissed at the boy, ordering him to wait outside, and approached the display, asking to see two secret elixirs. The merchant, a gypsy woman, searched through her cupboards and set out random potions requested.

Ignoring Selena, the boy walked right past her and sat outside on the steps, propping his head up with his hands. Intrigued, she walked over and asked, "Pardon me. I hope not to sound rude or intrusive, but who is that woman with you, and what kind of potions is she looking for?"

The boy was startled to hear her voice; he flinched, and his head spun around upon realizing she was there. "That woman is my sister, Medusa. I'm not sure what she's looking for, but you can guess considering...." His voice trailed off as he nodded to the shop.

"I understand," though Selena still couldn't fathom what anyone would hope to find inside.

He squinted at her as if he were studying an unusual specimen. "I don't think I've ever seen you around here before. What's your name?"

"S… err, Andric. Andric Liongod at your service." She bowed, thanking the Divines for catching her mistake early.

Luckily the boy hadn't noticed her near mishap. "Pleasure to meet you, Andric. My name is Myrrdin. Is this your first time here?" Selena nodded; Myrrdin stood up and dusted the dirt off his black breeches and pointed to different buildings, giving her a quick tour; first, Selena saw a dwarf busy hammering a piece of metal on an anvil. "As a blacksmith, he'll make you any weapon out of any metal if you have the right amount of gold. And the store next to it sells dragon hide, which is very rare. It's stronger than any leather, and I heard the dwarf blacksmiths use it to craft armor the dragon riders wear." To her dismay, she saw neither stall nor shop that sold books. When she asked, Myrrdin said, "Patrons don't come here to buy books, as most people don't like reading—except for the elves."

"The elves aren't the only ones who enjoy reading."

"Err, probably not, but most folks don't care for that." Myrrdin took a step back as he looked at her bewilderedly.

Selena held her tongue when she realized she snapped at him. "I'm sorry, I didn't mean that."

"No worries, all water under the bridge. If you enjoy reading so much, you will love the library in Alfheim. I live there in the Garden District." Upon further inquiry, Selena learned that Alfheim was divided into seven. "Why are you heading to Alfheim, if you don't mind me asking?"

"It's official business with the Council."

"I see. Were you drafted?"

"Aye."

"I reckon you probably just became of age then. I still have another year to go before the Council can legally take me." Myrrdin laughed.

"Hopefully, by then, this war will be over."

The two were interrupted when Medusa called for Myrrdin's prompt return. "I must go, as my sister is a very impatient woman. It was nice meeting you, Andric Liongod."

"Likewise." Selena waved him farewell.

He smiled and joined Medusa by the shop's steps. Before they walked away, Medusa glared at her, a frosty stare that sent chills down her spine. Selena felt the wind brush against her ears, and she heard a snake hissing nearby. Yet, as she whipped around to find the sound's source, Myrrdin and Medusa had vanished into the crowd.

CHAPTER 7: FLIGHT AND FRIGHT

She returned with a pack of pork jerky and a small oil container for Thor and found that Rahim had already beaten her back to the inn. After counting their combined inventory, Selena excused herself and joined Thor as he gobbled up his breakfast to the sheep's bones. The groundkeeper kept his word, and Thor's hide glistened from his morning coat; even the bits of meat and blood slipped off his scales like smooth glass.

When Selena approached, Thor whipped around, his smoldering eyes fixated on her. **You won't believe this, but earlier I felt this strange dark presence, but it disappeared as quickly as it came.**

Selena spun on her heels as if attempting to find what Thor was referring to, but thankfully, nobody seemed amiss; the locals and patrons carried on business as usual, and Thor assured that whatever the feeling was, it passed. He licked off the blood and gore staining his maw, but he paused and began snarling; Thor's slight throaty rumble grew to a loud growl.

Selena paused mid-step, and Thor sprung to all fours and urged her around to the front of the building. Her heart pounded against her chest, and she wondered if the dark presence had returned. *My dear?*

Someone's coming.

The two blended in with the crowd—Thor crouched behind a building across the street—and Selena watched two mysterious men pass by the dragon stalls. Yet, they remained close to the trees bordering the Grand Exchange, and although draped in shadow, Selena recognized them from the Obsidian Order.

The first said in an icy voice, "We must find her before it's too late."

"The Dark Master already noted her presence somewhere in the Grand Exchange. She must have escaped before we started the fire." The second laughed. "Helshire Village is nothing but rubble and ash."

"He needs her blood. Oh, the things he will do to her. Do you think he will gut her like a pig?"

"Her screams would be such sweet music."

"Let's keep looking, brother." They disappeared back into the trees, leaving Selena trembling and wondering how they tracked her down.

Thor's snarls and growls partnered with the growing streams of ember flowing from his flaring nostrils; the locals immediately avoided his fiery wrath, quickening their steps. While Selena was caught pondering over the dreadful and devastating news, Thor clawed at the ground, pulling heaps of dirt and rock, head hung low as his breaths grew heavy. **Blood and shadow....**

Thor, what's wrong?

Her dragon snaked his head up to meet her gaze, and upon seeing her concerned expression, Thor added: **You must think me mad. I feel like I know, and yet, I don't know.**

No, not at all. I'm just worried. But Thor....
Selena's thoughts escaped her when recalling the men's awful words. Her heart shattered like glass when he couldn't offer any comfort, and her eyes glossed over like a frozen lake. *Matu.*

My dear, I'm so sorry. You must tell Rahim.

Devastated, Selena fell to her knees. *If Rahim finds out that the Order destroyed his home and killed his mother, it'll ruin him, and he will probably blame me.*

You can't keep hiding that from him. If he blames you, then—

Then what?

I don't know. If Rahim does, let him.

Needing much convincing from Thor to deliver the grave news, Selena's steps felt heavy with each stride she made back to her room, her feet like lead. She found Rahim with a large plate of biscuits and crumpets, stuffing his face. It always amazed her that this bottomless pit somehow maintained his lean frame. "Can't talk, still hungry."

Selena tried to find the right way to say it, but Thor's words rang within her head. **Be careful. I don't know how well he will take the news about the fire.**

When he saw the look on her face, Rahim stopped. "Is something the matter?" Selena looked down at her feet as tears swelled behind her eyes. Her thoughts immediately raced to Chaliss, and she suddenly felt sick. With Thor's help, as she found the courage to utter the dreadful words, Rahim's face turned pale, and his breaths quickened. "What about mum? Is she okay?"

Selena's throat swelled. "I-I don't know for sure." Rahim spun around on his feet to hide his emotions, but he couldn't hold back his flowing tears. He cradled his head in his hands and fell to his knees. Selena approached him and placed a hand on his shoulder. "It's possible she escaped." Rahim shrugged her away; he shuffled over, swung the door open, and left without another word. She watched him disappear down the hallway, and she feared the worst.

That night, Selena lay awake in her bed, tossing and turning under the weight of the world. Her dread grew with every passing second. No longer having a home to return to and everyone she knew and loved was gone made her feel like her head was underwater. Rahim still hadn't come back; she would have to look for him if he didn't show by morning.

Only Thor's voice shattered the ensuing darkness: **Please join me. I wish you wouldn't tear yourself apart.**

But it's all my fault. I abandoned our home and let this happen.

How did you expect to stop them if you stayed? How would you have known this was going to happen?

I don't know.

Come here.

Sighing, she donned her cloak and grabbed a lantern sitting on her bedside table before going outside. Thor looked upon her with contentment as she trudged to his quarters. **That's better. At least now you can be here with me.**

She shook her head. *You should have seen the way Rahim reacted and how angry he got before he left. He just stormed out without saying a word.*

Thor raised a wing and wrapped it around her. **Rahim will come back. Let him be angry, but now you're the only family he has left aside from his terrible uncle.**

She wiped away her tears and laid her head back over his massive forearm. *I ran away and abandoned them.*

If you stayed, you would have died along with them.

I'm a coward, and I turned my back on them.

I think it was meant to be, and we will avenge the fallen with a dragon's wrath. Besides, how do you know that Chaliss didn't escape? She may still be alive. Selena didn't answer, and Thor added, **You suffered a great loss, but you need to let yourself heal and learn to forgive yourself.**

But what if I can't?

Then you will keep tormenting yourself until the past destroys you.

Selena set her lantern down as Thor extended a comforting wing and herded her close to his breast. He was the only one who could chase away the darkness threatening to swallow her whole, and for some reason, the desire to take him up on his flying offer crept upon her. She examined his wings and ran her fingertips across his jagged gemstone hide; it worried her that Thor still didn't have a harness like the riders in the Force, and she didn't want to hurt herself or fall off without being properly strapped down.

Yet, Thor snaked his head around and nudged her shoulder as he read her thoughts. **Did you want to fly with me?**

I would be lying if I said I didn't.

Chittering and purring, Thor stood up without warning and unfurled his wings as he stepped forth from his stall. Selena abruptly fell back from his sudden movements, and she quickly regretted the idea.

Then, my dear, let's conquer the sky together.

What?

You heard me. It's finally time for you to fly with me.

Her arms and legs shook as she approached; Thor scooped her in his talons and carried her to his back within his clawed cage. As she slowly wrapped her arms around his neck, Selena watched in great anticipation as Thor slowly expanded his wings, tail twitching, and leg muscles contracting. His back claws curled into the ground as he prepared for take-off, and Selena's head buzzed as he suddenly launched himself skyward in one leap.

Her stomach sank as Thor made his steep climb, the whoosh of his wings putting more distance between them and the ground. The Grand Exchange swirled beneath the pair as Thor spiraled towards the twinkling heavens and the crescent moon taunting them to come closer; Selena's eyes followed the line where the earth met the sky, and she felt like she was drifting in Niflheim's eternal cosmos.

As Thor made his sudden twists and turns, Selena was nearly bucked off, but she held on tightly to his horns. His wings pounded hard against her legs, and she felt his gemstone hide digging into her inner thighs as the turbulence threatened to toss her overboard.

Don't let go.

I'm trying.

Praying to the Divines, wishing Thor was in a harness, Selena tightly grasped his horns and the larger scales jutting from his neck; she pulled away when they dug into her palms, and her hands bled. Amidst her distraction, she lost her footing and slid partly off his back.

Don't you dare. Hold on. As Thor slowed down and held out a claw to grab her, Selena continued slipping, dangling on one side while doing her best to keep a grip. Eventually, he paused mid-flight, hovering, and extended his arm to push her back in place. **You're ridiculous.**

I told you I'm trying.

When satisfied Selena was safe, he resumed his aerial course over the White Plains towards the Mustang Mountains, and, without warning, he made a steep dive. Selena squinted as the cold air slapped her face and pierced her burning legs; her insides floated from the sudden drop.

As she looked beneath her feet to see how small their world looked from heaven's view, Thor unexpectedly jerked right and flew through a small cloud. Selena screamed and slid off his back once again.

You're absurd. I told you to hold on.

I'm slipping—

Hold on. Before Thor could help her again, Selena lost her grip and slid off, falling into the abyss below. Thor came to an abrupt stop and dove after her. Selena could not find the strength to scream as her lungs collapsed. The fall was so fast and sudden that all she could do was look out towards the horizon as the scenery dropped before her eyes; for that moment, it felt surreal and almost peaceful.

Thor zipped underneath her and held out his claws; she snapped out of her trance as she landed hard in his paws and, while trembling and shaking, immediately grabbed his curled nails to keep herself grounded and steady, but she couldn't find the strength to stand. Tightly wrapping his talons to ensure her protection, Thor brought her up to his face and nuzzled his clawed enclosure. **My dear, are you all right?**

Selena reached out from his paws and touched his nose. *I'm fine. I-I just—*

Thor sniffed her injured palm, and his eyes flickered a shade of grey when he noticed the blood on her hands and legs. **I won't hurt you again.**

We need to get you a proper saddle. Her eyes froze, and her head spun when she saw her legs; Selena nearly fainted as it reminded her of when she first blossomed into womanhood shortly after her rescue.

Thor's wings thrashed as he turned himself around in mid-hover and flew back towards the Black Pub. Their silent trip to the inn added to the tense atmosphere, though Selena did her best to reassure him he wasn't to blame. *I wanted to fly with you too, but we were just ill-prepared.*

As he landed by the front door and opened his claws, Selena stumbled through the tavern's entrance, with Thor watching her like a hawk. She propped herself against the edge of the bar table, and from the corner of her eye, she saw a blur of white rush down the stairs, followed by cries of anguish.

"Is that you, Rahim?" Selena then collapsed.

CHAPTER 8: TO BE A DRAGON

After her draining first flight with Thor, she faded in and out of consciousness. The blur of white was Silver; without warning, he scooped her up in his arms with ease and carried her up the stairs.

Rahim had returned after Thor took off and was currently tugging on Silver's jacket, asking him loads of questions about who he was and what happened. Silver, however, ignored his pests and demanded towels to lay on the bed. Only upon noticing Selena's battered legs did Rahim finally oblige, but he still grumbled, "I would like to know who in the Divine's name you are."

"Me? No one you should concern yourself with, my good sir." Silver's cold tone rattled Rahim further, but he did what was asked, and Silver laid Selena down on the bed. Before she wholly slipped into slumber, Silver pulled out another vial with the same red concoction upon their first meeting and applied the remedy to her wounds with a single drop. Her legs and hands immediately cooled, and her skin began repairing itself; the blood pouring down her legs returned to the opened sores, and her legs stitched themselves back together.

She instantly felt the strength of a dragon return to her limbs, and Selena wanted to jolt from her bed, but Silver asked her to rest for now. "Thank you for helping me, but what are you doing here?"

"My dear, we couldn't wait too much longer after Vidar's little visit. When I heard you were in the Grand Exchange, I tried to stop and warn you before you and Thor flew away." Though Selena assumed it was because he, Kain, and Dust were watching over her per Her Imperial Majesty's orders, Rahim remained in the dark regarding her new allies, as he was with his uncle. His questions came like fired bullets without giving Selena a chance to answer, but Silver continued ignoring him and asked, "What happened to you and your hair? Why are you dressed like a boy?"

Rahim flailed. "No, don't answer that. How did you recognize her?" He then pointed at her with an accusing finger. "Who is he, and how does he know you?" As Selena recounted their first meeting, Rahim's jaw dropped to the floor. "You're blooming joking."

"No," Silver and Selena said simultaneously, and the two laughed.

Rahim stared at Silver with wide eyes and pointed at him. "I don't trust this twat. There's something wrong with him."

Silver sucked in his cheeks and pointed at Rahim through his fuming expression. "I beg your pardon. I believe there's something wrong with you. Y-your eyes are too close together."

Rahim became a little self-conscious as he touched his face. "No, they're not."

Satisfying his humor, Silver offered to buy a new saddle for Thor to prevent future accidents. Yet, Rahim convinced himself that somehow Silver was behind the incident; when Rahim accused him of Selena's current state, she clarified the actual cause. "Thor felt bad about it."

Rahim's eyes widened in wonder. "You two flew together for the first time?"

"Yes, but that's not the point. Silver is only trying to help."

Rahim raised his hands in the air and began pacing at the foot of the bed. Meanwhile, Silver stuck his tongue out until Selena gave him a smoldering glare. Luckily, Rahim didn't see. "I don't trust anyone, especially since those damned asses from the Order and whatnot are wandering about."

Now drained from Silver's and Rahim's bickering, Selena finally mustered the strength and answered Silver's earlier questions regarding her current appearance. Yet, he cut her justification short. "Ah, I see. No need to explain anything else; I completely understand."

Selena and Rahim exchanged glances, and he muttered, "He's ridiculous," but Selena slapped his shoulder and demanded, "Where were you all this time? You've been gone for hours."

"I'm sorry, I didn't mean—"

"Don't make me worry like that again."

Silver cleared his throat, interrupting them both with the offer to teach Selena how to use magic in self-defense in the off chance of running into the Order again. Rahim rolled his eyes when Selena heartily accepted, and Silver began rambling. "It will prove invaluable to the Force, and sneaking in disguised as a young boy is risky. I want to help."

Before Selena could express her gratitude, Rahim barked in her place, turning a blind eye to her disapproving glares. "She doesn't need to learn magic tricks. And besides, what makes you think we want your help?"

"She will need to have some knowledge of magic to get into the Force and have proper behavior. It's required."

As Silver gloated through his smug grin and crossed arms, Rahim's face burned with rage. "I can show her how to act like a boy myself."

"Ah, but your mannerisms will probably get her kicked out. I at least know the proper social etiquette that will impress *any* member of the Council."

While Rahim grumbled inappropriate remarks under his breath, Selena jolted up—much to Silver's disdain—and attempted to play the peacekeeper role by positioning herself in between him and Silver. "That's enough. Rahim, I shouldn't have to ask you to be proper. Silver, I ask you to be more considerate given the circumstances." Thor's chuckle chimed across her thoughts; he thought this was amusing.

"I'm sorry, I didn't mean to make things worse." Silver's eyes darted between the two, and he leaned in. "Why? Are you and Rahim—?"

"What? Oh, no. He's like my brother." Selena shivered from the notion, as she never thought of Rahim in that way.

Rahim pointed at the pompous Silver, who remained oblivious. "Does he always act weird?"

Selena sighed and asked to be left alone for the remainder of the evening; Silver and Rahim ruefully left the room before glaring at each other, their expressions enough to ignite sparks. She peeked open one eye before poking at Thor's somber strands of thought; he withdrew. Selena was worried, as this wasn't like him. *Silver offered to buy you a new harness.*

She felt him perk up a little. **Did he now? That was nice of him.** Thor hesitated before asking, **How are you feeling?**

Selena maintained her soothing voice. *You did nothing wrong, my dear.*

It's my sworn duty to protect you: you are my rider and handler. How are we supposed to fly together if I put you in danger?

I promise we will do better once Silver helps us.

Good.

The tone in his voice perked up, and her heart soared to hear him happy once more. Content to have lifted his spirits, she drifted off to slumber; yet, she felt a peculiar, unpleasant presence nearby, the same horrible aura back from the village. Her dreams told stories about Ragnarok and the phrase whispering within her subconscious: *it rests beneath the starry skies.*

When she awoke in the early afternoon, the remedy completely healed her body with no scarring. Selena was willing to stock up on whatever miracle elixir he used for the future, or perhaps she could learn how to brew the potion herself.

After dressing and tying her bootlaces, Selena put on her cap and headed out to meet with Thor, who kept pestering her to see his new saddle. Upon seeing the massive harness propped against his stall, Selena understood Thor's enthusiasm; the new leather was large enough to carry a small crew of five grown men. Emblazoned upon the front buckle was a giant polished ruby identical to the hue of his dazzling scales, courtesy of Silver. Thor explained the harness was originally gem-less, but Silver took it upon himself to craft a lovely stone fit for a dragon. **I finally have a treasure to call mine.**

His radiant face matched the new gleaming ruby and grazed his claws against it before being interrupted by Rahim, who wasted no effort in revealing how much of a fraud Silver was. "Where did you get all of your money?"

Silver waved his finger. "There are things that are best left unknown in this world; money is one of them."

"But where do you get it?"

"If you must know, I make it out of thin air."

Rahim crinkled his nose as if he caught a scent most foul. "You must think I'm stupid."

"Of course not. I *know* it."

Thor clicked his claws against the rocks in amusement while Selena laughed. At the sound of her voice, Silver spun sharply on his heels with a massive grin on his face. "Ah, my dear Selena, you found my gift. I hope that you and Thor love it. It was the best they had, but I still wanted to add my modifications." He excused himself from Rahim and bowed upon approaching her. "How are you feeling?"

Examining him with a quizzical brow, she wondered at his reference to the endearing, 'my dear;' Thor was the only one who referred to her as such, and this wasn't the first time Silver used it. "I'm quite well, thank you. Thor and I love your gift, but please refer to me as Andric Liongod onward."

Silver clapped, amused and thrilled. "Ah, you've already created an alternate identity for yourself."

"Andric is supposed to report to Alfheim by the end of the week." Rahim pulled out the forged papers from his pockets, and without warning, Silver snatched them away. "You tosser, we need those."

Yet, Silver read them in eager haste. "Clever; I don't think Vidar will notice. Either that or they won't care one way or another. They're hurting for recruits, from what I hear."

Silver didn't oppose when Rahim grabbed the documents back; instead, he smirked when Rahim sternly said, "This is between Andric and Vidar."

"Yes, Rahim," Selena then took her turn and seized her fake orders, "between Vidar and me."

Rahim muttered under his breath. "I worked hard finding a professional forger."

Though Selena praised his competence, Silver distracted her with lessons on saddling a dragon properly. Meanwhile, Rahim leaned against a nearby tree, arms over his chest, glaring at them as he blew raspberries at her new mentor; Selena turned a blind eye to Rahim's childish behavior.

Silver gave his instruction as he pointed at Thor's different sides and angles, and Thor followed through in helping position the harness. Although uncomfortable at first, he was willing to grow accustomed to the straps, especially after seeing his new gemstone shine from his breast. However, when Silver mentioned the reins and bit —a long, metal rod attached to the leather straps at both ends to be placed in a dragon's mouth—Thor stuck out his tongue and backed his head away, snarling and growling. Selena and Silver stepped back from his sudden vehemence. **I'm not a horse, and I refuse to be treated like one.**

Selena bit her lip and suddenly felt ashamed for assuming that he would accept this unjust treatment. *You're right. You are a dragon of higher might and intelligence than us mortals.* As much as she attempted to make him laugh, she still meant every word behind her compliment.

Thor seemed pleased, but he recoiled. **I still want you to be safe.**

Squinting at the bit, Selena had an idea: she snatched it from Silver, and while unwrapping the leather pieces from the rod, she explained: *I will never treat you like a horse, but if I can tie these securely to your horns, I can still hold on without making you feel uncomfortable. Is this agreeable?*

Of course. Please, by all means. Thor's eyes turned sharp when he caught Silver in his vision and lowered his head down for Selena. **I will see to it that Silver knows better in the future.**

I'm sure he meant no ill will by it. Selena couldn't help but snicker, but deep down, she hoped Thor had no malicious intentions.

"Ah, I see what you're doing. Allow me to help too." After apologizing to Thor for his lack of better judgment, Silver rushed over and securely helped her loop the straps around. His wrath now appeased Thor hummed in between the beats of his dancing tail. After tying them down, Silver grabbed the separate pieces and, with both hands holding them together, he twisted the straps, molding them into one long rope looped between Thor's two large side horns with magic. After giving it a few tugs, the leather held.

Satisfied, Selena said, *This alteration works perfectly for me, but what about you?*

Thor shook his head, and his chitters vibrated from his neck. **A perfect accommodation, my dear.** After ensuring the harness was securely fastened, Thor gave it a few good shakes as he unfurled and folded his wings several times before Silver deemed it satisfactory.

Rahim snorted with his arms crossed. "How come you know so much about dragons?"

"I've done a lot more research than you can imagine." The smug Silver turned away and asked Selena to try out the new saddle for herself. With Thor's helping arm, Selena clambered onboard the spacious seat, feet catching the belt straps used to hold riders and luggage in place. The handler's bench was at the base of his neck;

Selena took her position and gripped the newly melded reins.

Silver, however, backed away with Rahim and the two watched in awe as Thor unfolded his enveloping wings like a lady's fan, and through a flicker of his tail, his haunches tightened for the upcoming spring. Memories of their first flight flashed through her mind repeatedly, and Thor seized his second chance to impress Selena with the liberties of being a dragon.

Thor flung himself skyward in one massive leap, his long crimson tail slithering behind him off the earth like a snake. She felt the adrenaline rush as Thor soared higher with every passing second. Her fingers wrapped around the reins, her body sank with the sudden climb in elevation; the wind crashed against her face and pierced her eyes like tiny daggers.

As the Grand Exchange disappeared beneath them, Thor steadied himself along the peaking horizon where the world and the sky met in an eternal line. The new harness was perfect, and Selena enjoyed a view that only the Divines could witness.

The pair enjoyed their moment of solace among the weeping heavens before Thor tucked his wings and brought himself into a nosedive. The world spiraled before them, and the two were soon on a collision course for one of the buildings.

Selena nearly lost her bearings until Thor zipped right on by with quick precision, and he unfolded his wings once more. She flinched and dug her face into her hands until Thor began encouraging her. **Look around you.**

She forced her eyes open, facing her initial fear, looking with curiosity as they soared towards the throat of the world. Thor flew without a bump or jolt; Selena's grip loosened from the reins as she relaxed.

You and I will conquer the heavens, and the Divines themselves will fear us.

Your fire will devour Niflheim.

She looked down at her feet and watched as the ground swirled beneath her. Thor swept his wings again, gaining altitude, and he made another turn towards the White Plains, stretching as far as the eye could see. She slowly released her grip from the straps, embracing Thor's sudden acceleration as he continued outward. Selena stretched out her arms and looked around without fear, feeling like she was on top of the world.

As happy as a bird swinging in the air, when Selena cried out in joy, Thor laughed at her. **Now you understand this is what it means to be a dragon.**

He jerked, and Selena fell forward; she snatched the reins and dug her feet into the pile of belts and carabiners. Yet their moment of serenity and bliss halted when she heard a low growl. *What's wrong?*

Look over there.

He leveled himself in the air and hid in the shadows of the clouds. Selena looked out to where Thor mentioned and noticed a group of horseback riders gliding across the plains and heading towards the Grand Exchange with urgent purpose.

The Order. The very mention of the demonic cultists left an awful taste in her mouth.

Shall we go in and take care of them ourselves?

No. We need to get back and warn Silver and Rahim.

Thor grunted but didn't argue. Selena tried to enjoy every moment of their flight back, but the Order pursuing them left a disdain feeling in the pit of her stomach; she wanted to vomit.

Landing upon his haunches first, Thor scooped Selena off the saddle and placed her down gently. She stretched out her legs as Rahim met with her with open arms. "That was brilliant. How was it this time?"

"It was spectacular. You should try it sometime." Rahim exhibited more reluctance than she did, but he smiled all the same.

Silver strolled over, clapping in applause. "You and Thor were brilliant, my dear. I daresay you were born to fly." Selena smiled, but it faded as she delivered the dreadful news. Rahim's face burned like it was on fire as he desperately wanted to avenge his mother, but he held his tongue. When Selena finished, Silver's face turned ghastly white. "How far away were they?"

"I'd assume they'll reach us by nightfall on horseback." Upon coming to the horrifying realization that the Obsidian Order knew hers and Thor's whereabouts, the group decided that the time to leave was now if they were to make it to Alfheim.

CHAPTER 9: THE TEACHER

The trio, with pell-mell preparations, worked through the remaining afternoon to ensure they packed the necessities for the upcoming and hasty trip. Thor's saddle was nearly loaded and ready, but much to Rahim's disdain, Silver spent a few extra minutes teaching Selena a few customary polite gestures, but she feared it might not be enough.

Soon convinced their initial plan to be folly, she didn't want to be punished nor lose Thor. *What if the Council saw through our disguise and didn't accept us into the ranks?*

One step at a time, my dear one. Instead, imagine what awaits us in the grand elven city. As much as she looked forward to the city's wonders, she couldn't control her restless behavior.

While in the middle of finishing packing her bags, her heart stopped when footsteps tapped the floors outside her door, and there was a gentle knock. "My dear, are you decent?" Selena rushed over to let Silver inside. "Rahim and I are ready to leave whenever you are."

"Yes." Her throat turned dry and scratchy. "What will happen if the Council refuses to let me and Thor join?"

"No matter what, you will not be alone," Silver reassured her, "just march straight to Vidar and keep begging him until he changes his mind."

"I doubt his mind would be easy to change." Selena smiled a little, feeling more at ease. She held her hands together and bowed. "Thank you."

Silver returned the same gesture, but they were interrupted when her thoughts rattled and echoed with Thor's sudden roars and growls. Unable to answer her, she rushed past Silver towards the window overlooking the dragon stalls; to her dismay, she saw four heavily armed zealots cornering Thor by his quarters.

His fury boiled like the building flames ready to erupt from the back of his throat, but Thor couldn't control a steady stream; instead, he unleashed a series of wild embers catching the trees and wooden stakes holding the foundation of the stalls.

Before Selena could explain to Silver their sudden troubles, she rushed out the door just as Rahim busted inside, breathless and pointing to the window. "We kind of have a problem." Agitated by his horrible timing, Selena pushed past and disappeared down the sleeping corridor to help save Thor.

"Liongod, wait." Silver called out as he ran out after her, leaving the dumbfounded Rahim.

"Really? Is it now my job to carry the bags?" He mumbled as he grabbed Selena's belongings and followed them outside.

Their series of unfortunate events involving the Order seemed unending; Selena met with the horrifying scene of Thor fighting back, swiping his claws at his surrounding captors, but another would inch forward with a gun and sword ready. The Lich's followers avoided casting magic at Thor, as dragons were impervious, but melee weapons still posed a threat. Flickering flames plumed from his clamped fangs as Thor snarled and growled, ready to unleash a devastating torrential inferno, but he could only muster a weak and unsteady flow that barely singed the ground. Instead, Thor roared through serrated teeth as his enemies drew close as if to intimidate them more.

However, one broke from the group as he noticed Selena's presence—she assumed him to be the leader—and pointed at Thor. "Capture the dragon but leave her to me." He was the only one without the mask, and though his face was shrouded in shadow, Selena quivered from his crescent-shaped scar over his right eye piercing the darkened veil.

As Silver caught up with her, he and Selena bolted forward, but the leader waved his hands, summoning large waves and blasts of fire. Before Selena could react, Silver positioned himself in between the attack and her; he held his hands together and created a sphere of arcane energy, protecting them from the blast as their orb pulsated with veins of purple lightning.

While the Order was distracted by Silver's magic, Thor used this to his advantage; he knocked their attackers down with one swipe of his tail before hurrying over to Selena, extinguishing the tickling embers waiting to escape his maw.

Silver whipped his head around with his hands still out, holding their arcane shield steady. "Quickly, both you and Rahim leave with Thor, now."

While Thor urged her to follow Silver's advice, Selena remained reluctant to leave him behind. "What about you?"

"Don't worry about me. I'll follow you when the coast is clear." There wasn't time to argue nor question Silver, as the Order made haste to surround Thor; even the leader, locked in his eternal struggle against Selena's new ally, frantically shouted orders not to let them escape.

Thor swept his tail, swiped his claws at the relentless attackers, and called for her when the path was clear. **We need to move, now.**

Selena rushed from Silver's barrier, and Thor plucked her from the ground, hastily placing her upon his readied harness. Yet, Rahim still lagged, but she soon heard his grumbling complaints as he stumbled outside with her prepared bag. "I'm just the bag guy. I didn't ask for this *magic*." Thor snatched the whining Rahim through his sudden screams and dropped him near his and Silver's packs strapped in the corner. "On second thought, I'm not ready to fly—"

Not giving him a choice, Thor tightened his leg muscles, and, with the stretch of his wings, he took off to the sky as the others swarmed. Rahim screamed as they flew higher, gripped the harness's edge, and fumbled through the loose straps to belt himself within the seat.

The leader yelled incomprehensible orders as he pointed at the fleeing dragon. As his three associates attempted to get into position with loaded guns, Silver broke his shield and dug his hands into the ground. The earth rumbled and liquefied beneath his opponents, and, with one swift movement of his hands, the swirling sand swallowed the cultists.

Snarling and hissing through his teeth, the leader contorted his arms to take a puppet master's stance. He summoned a black hole in the air, and hands made of shadow emerged, lunging and grabbing for Thor. Upon Selena's and Rahim's observations of the strange magic, Thor roared as he spiraled skyward, attempting to put more distance between them and the shadow hands; he dodged the first but couldn't avoid the second as it wrapped itself around his hind paw.

Silver dashed to the leader and snatched his hand as the dark magic pulled Thor back. Before the zealot could pry away, Silver's palm grew imbued in an orb of light, and both the portal and shadow hands vanished in a plume of smoke.

To his relief, Thor hovered momentarily mid-air, shaking his legs to ensure the rest of the black magic was gone and zipped along his course towards the White Plains. Much to Selena's surprise, Rahim was the one who leaned over the edge and said, "Thank you, all-powerful Silver."

Selena looked back with regret as they left Silver behind with the enemy: the two remained locked in an awkward stare down before the leader spun around and disappeared through the shadows. Satisfied, Silver then vanished in a cloud of smoke like the aftermath of a lightning strike.

As the trio soared higher, the back of Selena's neck crawled with goosebumps when she saw glowing yellow eyes with slits locked on Thor; Selena and Rahim heard a low growl, followed by a row of sharp fangs strikingly white against the contrast of the darkness. Only then did Selena realize it was another dragon. Thor flapped his wings harder to speed away, as his kin was perhaps twice, or even thrice, his size, but the dragon withdrew back into the shadows, abandoning the pursuit.

However, Thor didn't ease his wing beats; he flew as fast as he could until evening passed and morning came. The sun's bright, vibrant morning colors adorned the heavens, reflecting shimmering specks of red and purple across Thor's gleaming scales and golden underbelly. After Selena assured him they weren't being chased, Thor finally slowed his flaps to maintain a more leisurely pace, but he was already exhausted.

While Rahim busied himself looking over the map, Selena encouraged Thor to land and rest for his benefit, giving Silver a chance to catch up, but she wasn't sure how that would be possible against a dragon's speed. *He is full of surprises.*

Thor declined and persisted, determined to make a non-stop flight straight for Alfheim but eventually admitted his waning strength and searched for hills to hide behind. The beautiful, green lands stretched as far as they could see, flowing like ocean waves. The glistening Raging River could be spotted from a distance, weaving through the Hinterlands, running its entire course to rendezvous with the Turquoise Ocean.

Selena stroked Thor's neck. *Thank the Divines that dragon didn't give chase.*

As much as it pained Thor to admit, he eventually said, **Did you see the size of its fangs? I could only imagine how long its claws are.**

Selena felt a twinge of jealousy from the sound of his voice. *Yours will be larger than that dragon's one day.*

Twittering, Selena felt a deep rumble vibrate through his chest, but they continued onward in silence. As it became high noon, Thor grew too weary, straining his wings until his muscles burned. Thor eventually snapped when Selena begged and pleaded to land. **If we keep taking breaks, we may never reach Alfheim in time. I could carry you two all the way there without—**

You're staggering, and soon, you will push yourself too far. Thor snorted, making another sudden jerk that knocked the compass off Rahim's lap. *Aside from resting your wings, we need to give Silver a chance to catch up. Please?*

He released a few moans and groans in reply and finally made his descent when he found hills appropriate to hide the three; Selena knew she wounded his pride, but she would instead ask for his forgiveness later after earning a good amount of rest.

Upon landing, Thor helped his two passengers to the ground and stretched out his wings before collapsing; their hiding space set deep within the lush valley, the grassy plains whistling a gentle melody carried in the chilly wind. After Selena and Rahim unbuckled Thor's harness and unpacked their bags, the two stretched their legs; Thor rolled around, scratching his back and neck as his scales breathed in the fresh air for the first time in almost a full day. While Selena busied herself in re-oiling his scales to prevent saddle chaffing, she expressed concern over Silver's wellbeing and his no-show.

Rahim scowled in disgust. "He'll be fine. Why do you care about him so much?" Selena failed to answer, and Rahim bellowed in laughter. "You can't be serious."

She finished polishing Thor's back, and he chittered in delight as he examined her handiwork and gave his approval. "I'm afraid I—"

"What will your beloved Genesis think?" Fuming, Selena slugged Rahim's shoulder, yet she couldn't hide her burning embarrassment.

The teasing fun abruptly ended when the familiar aristocratic voice sang over their heads: "I'm sure Genesis Altessa would be flattered by her affections."

Selena tightened her lip, but Rahim glared at Silver, who strolled over to their campsite with an opened book levitating above his outstretched palm. "Why do you look so smug?"

Silver ignored him; he approached the weary Thor and bowed before giving Selena the same courteous salutations. "It is such a marvelous day for a stroll." Selena couldn't help but notice his book and that he was also a fan of Genesis; however, his pages were crossed out and scribbled on with notes.

Rahim stomped over to him, but Silver refused to flinch. "What was going on between you and that strange man?"

Silver only shrugged. "I threatened him, and he retreated."

"What about that dragon we saw in the shadows? It could have chased after us."

Raising an eyebrow, Silver remained undeterred with a stoic expression. "If there was another dragon, can I assume it didn't give you any trouble?" Rahim's face seared with rage, but instead of replying, he ushered Selena away so that the two could look at the map, but Silver stepped between them. "Umm, Selena or Andric, would you care to know how I was able to keep up?"

Only Rahim was unimpressed, and he rolled his eyes. "Oh please, no one cares."

"I figured that at least Liongod would like to know how a simple *human* was able to keep up with a dragon, with you being the latter half."

Rahim looked confused, but Selena clarified, "He just called you a dragon's ass." Thor's scaley lips curled into a sneer. Nostrils flaring, Rahim made a fist, but Selena's stern voice stopped them stone-cold before he and Silver could deliver blows. "Enough."

The two paused; Silver and Rahim pointed to each other and said simultaneously: "He started it."

Selena shook her head. "Rahim, this way, please." She motioned for him to follow but dismissed Silver when he approached too. "I'm sorry, but I need to talk to him alone." Ignoring the pained look on Silver's face, Selena pulled Rahim away.

Rahim grunted. "I know, stop fighting, but—"

She held up her hand. "You may not trust him, but I do." She paused when Rahim gave her a raised brow in confusion, unable to understand her faith. "I feel there's something familiar about him as if I've met him before. It's hard to explain."

Rahim's eyes lit up. "Are you getting your memory back?"

"I don't know, but I ask that you please believe me."

His eyes drooped to his feet, ashamed for his sudden rashness and outbursts. "I-I'm sorry. I don't want to lose you too. When I found out about mum…." Rahim trailed off. Selena couldn't help but shed a tear for Chaliss, too, the pain too fresh. "I can't lose anyone else. You may not be blood, but you're still the only family I have left, and I don't count that old git Rowan."

"You and Thor are my family too."

The two were interrupted when Silver made a painful noise. As Selena looked over, he lost his balance and fell; Rahim rolled his eyes as she rushed over, helping him to his feet. Silver dusted himself off while chiming, "Yes, I'm okay. I'm just eating the dirt."

Thor rolled to his stomach and clawed at the ground, watching the three interact in amusement. Rahim, doing his best to abide by Selena's wishes and dealing with Silver, stated the group would make camp within the valley. While Rahim pitched out their sleeping bags and Selena gathered firewood, Silver asked, "Then where does that leave me?"

"You can piss off." Rahim glared at him and wholly disregarded his and Selena's earlier discussion. He spun around and marched away, escaping Selena's smoldering and glazing emerald glare.

Silver, however, remained calm, his face a blank canvas, but Selena owed him an apology on Rahim's behalf. "Please, forgive him and pardon me." She curtsied but stopped and corrected her behavior by bowing instead and dismissed herself before Silver could assure her otherwise. She searched around until she found Rahim had stormed off towards the edge of the valley with the map, grumbling how far away Alfheim still was.

Thor jumped to all fours and stretched out his legs and claws as Selena walked past. **I would give Rahim some time and help him through his pain.**

He aided her by collecting sticks and, after gathering enough in a large pile, scooped them onto his harness while Selena lazily swung one around like a sword. *How can I?*

Be there for him.

Within minutes, thanks to Thor, he and Selena made it back to their campfire after gathering enough firewood that would last for a week. Rahim returned shortly after, still indifferent to Silver; he approached Selena, offering no apology to his earlier remark, and pointed to the map where it read, 'The White Plains.' "We're here," he slid his finger across the surface until finding the word 'Alfheim' written in bold letters, "I reckon it will take us about a week or two to reach the city."

Meanwhile, Selena grew distracted by Silver shooting tiny fireballs from his fingertips. His effortless use of magic made her feel envious, and the desire to learn the art took root.

Her stomach suddenly ached, and Thor stretched out his wings and claws after dumping his pile of collected legs where Rahim wanted to build a fire. His eyes flickered to a light shade of red: over time, Selena learned that the slight change in Thor's eye color indicated his mood. Red, for instance, usually meant he was hungry or anxious for a fight. **I'm going hunting and will return soon.**

Be safe.

I'm the hunter. You shouldn't waste your prayers on me but for my prey. He spread out his wings and launched himself into the air in one leap. Selena watched as his silhouette disappeared over the horizon.

Rahim mumbled as he pulled out a pack of jerky and handed it to her. "I made sure we didn't lose our things."

When Selena offered him a comforting hand, Rahim shrugged it away, and she sighed. "Thank you for getting my bag."

"Yes, I know. I'm the *bag* guy." He glared at Silver and gave a loud huff.

Silver turned his nose in the air. "I don't need your food. I can get it myself."

Their brewing animosity would soon explode, and Selena did her best to remind the two that the best way to reach Alfheim would be by working together. Yet, Rahim still stormed away as he cursed. As much as she loathed seeing him act this way, Selena would be waiting for him to talk about it when he was comfortable.

Ready to return, Rahim started a campfire, but Silver intervened, waving his hands. A few wooden sticks gathered themselves in the air and dropped right in front of Rahim into a neat pile. Silver then snapped his fingers, and the woodpile set ablaze. Rahim grumbled but gave a firm nod in a silent thank you.

Silver sat alone, appearing deep in thought with his nose stuck in his book, while Selena and Rahim drank and ate as the late afternoon wore on and the sun set over the horizon. Charcoal clouds hung oppressively low to the ground as they chased the chilling winds, and the two bundled within their sleeping bags; Silver remained indifferent to the cold weather.

Selena was intrigued; without looking up from his tome, Silver reached out his other hand and summoned a metal cube that would break apart and repair itself again. A dark aura wafted like smoke from the object as it floated above his palm.

Thor's soft flail of wings descended over their campsite as he returned from his evening hunt; already cleaned from the bloody mess, he curled himself near Selena and Rahim, draping his wings over the two and protecting them against the cold front. However, Thor couldn't pry his eyes away from his ruby harness, the gem gleaming from the dancing flames.

Yet, Rahim squirmed and glared out from his sleeping bag as Silver suddenly approached between re-adjusting his glasses. He eyed the man in white like a snake ready to strangle its prey. Ignoring Rahim's venom-spewing gaze, Thor lifted his protective wing, and Selena granted Silver a private audience and accepted his hand as he led her away from the campfire.

Silver stared at the sparkling diamonds scattered across the beautiful dark void for a moment. "You seem to be very interested in my magic."

"I won't lie. I have been since you and Kain saved me." Selena looked down at her feet. "I'm ashamed to admit that I'm a little jealous."

"You shouldn't be. I've had a lot of time to practice. Since we'll have plenty of time to reach Alfheim, I'm willing to show you what I know."

Her eyes sparkled like the twinkling stars, and she controlled herself from jumping in excitement. "Of course, I would love to—er, I mean, yes, Teacher."

Amused by her sudden eagerness, Silver clapped his hands together. "Then let's begin, my dear. First, I want you to look at everything around you. The four elements created everything you see: air, earth, fire, and water, existing in Niflheim and the very depths of Oblivion. Since the beginning of time, humans, elves, and dwarves alike have learned magic from the dragons and found the ability and will to use the created energies around us." Amidst Silver's instruction, Selena couldn't help but cast an admiring glance at Thor as he grew ensconced within his coils, but Rahim kept one eye fixed on Silver.

Silver continued: "The energies flow through every living creature, and we have learned how to use that force to manipulate the elements. Once you understand the original four, you can branch out and do anything. For instance, you could train yourself to casually see small glimpses of the future, teleportation, or breathe underwater—the possibilities are endless. There's also the forbidden magic, such as necromancy."

Selena shivered. "Is that what I think it is?"

"Indeed, yes: the art of reanimating corpses. The Council outlawed it in Armageddon, so I recommend staying away from that."

Selena shuddered as she reminded herself of the Lich and his abilities. "Is it possible to learn all of this?"

"Yes, although it is challenging and requires years of discipline. The dragon riders of the Force only know fire as part of their core training, but I want to help you learn more. However, if you wish to learn the others—and everyone is certainly free to do so if desired—you would have to study with the mages in Dragonspire or travel to the other kingdoms and find a teacher." His eyes turned to stone. "Magic has limitations, depending on your strength and endurance. Weaving the elements through your body and manipulating them can negatively affect you. You feel powerful when carrying that much energy within you, but you need a clear mind and understanding of your strength because one false move can mean the difference between life and death.

"Yet," Silver carefully explained, "I can sense that you have the power of the elements lying dormant within you. I hope that I can help you reawaken your abilities."

His lack of further analysis left Selena unable to contain her wildfire questions. "What do you mean by 'reawaken?' Does that mean I have the gift?" Her eyes widened as she couldn't contain her growing excitement. "Have I ever used magic before, and was I good at it, or was I learning?"

Silver held up his hands and gave her a nervous grin. "I can sense magical essences in everyone and everything. I-I don't know how good you were before, but all I can tell you is that you have used magic before." It was as if he avoided saying too much, but he refused to offer more information when Selena asked. Instead, he continued the lesson. "Since we're going to Alfheim, we will work with fire first. I want you to close your eyes and clear your mind; let go of all your self-doubt and negative emotions and focus on the energy surrounding you. Take it in and imagine it surging through your body." Selena smiled and did as he said. "First, I want you to imagine fire itself. Feel it as it flows through your veins and allow the energy to consume you. Breathe with it as it fills you."

She focused on his words and pictured a stable flame becoming a beam surging from the ground beneath her feet. Selena imagined it coursing through her body and heart; she suddenly felt hot as the energy rushed through her, waiting to be released. Instinctively, she thrust her hand forward, palm up, as she channeled the energy to her palm and fingers; her arm was about to burst into flames. Her eyes lit up when her concentrated power became fire: tiny embers crackling into the air, but she was happy to conjure them.

Silver expressed more excitement than she did, bouncing in his spot like a happy child. "Excellent."

"But they were small."

"I don't think you understand how long it takes to develop that concentration and channel energy like that. I'm very impressed, and I want to work with you more if you wish to continue." Selena smiled and nodded, grateful to his knowledge and offer of help. He stood next to her and began practicing. "Your movements are almost insignificant until you expel that energy from your body. Instead, it's through sheer focus and force of will."

"I understand." However, her self-doubt had returned.

Silver looked at her and stopped their lesson. "What's wrong?"

"It's nothing."

Noting her sudden behavior change, Silver placed his hand gently on her shoulder. "You are brilliant. Please, don't act so hard on yourself. I am here to help you, and I want to see you grow and be the best in Force. I know you can do it—you've already proven your potential." Selena was surprised to hear this from him, but his words made her smile. He grinned. "Let's continue, my dear."

Over the next few hours, even after Thor and Rahim fell asleep, Silver showed her more on what else she could do with fire, such as using breathing techniques to keep herself warm even on the coldest nights. He taught her another survival skill: Selena could clean her hands and body by killing germs with extreme heat whenever soap and water weren't available.

Through concentrated, intense breaths, her nostrils tickled from smoldering ember shards like a dragon ready to breathe fire, and her body instantly warmed as if she danced under the scorching sun. Silver praised her abilities as the flickering flames neither harmed nor singed her skin. "Curiouser and curiouser. Like a dragon, fire cannot harm you."

As the magic came easily, Selena learned how to manipulate the shape of her flames. Imagining Silver's arcane magic when fighting the Order at the Grand Exchange, her magic circled and encased her in a sphere, hardening into a molten shield. Silver even tested its stability by attacking it to see if she could hold it.

"You are learning exponentially faster than I anticipated. Excellent." He withdrew when satisfied with her prowess. "That's enough for now. You were amazing." Her molten fire shield disappeared, and Selena dropped to her knees out of exhaustion. Silver rushed over and helped her sit down.

Selena's heart raced hard as if she had been running. "It was exhilarating."

"I can't wait to see what else you can do. You're a natural."

After allowing her stiff muscles to rest, the two returned to their camp with Silver's arm underneath hers. Silver still wore his smiling expression as he commended Selena's brilliance; she blushed a little upon seeing his gleaming face and turned away, afraid if he noticed. "I know that we don't say it much," she began, "but we appreciate all you have done to help us. I know Rahim feels the same way, but if you could, please refrain from teasing—"

"I mean no ill will, but of course, I will stop."

The fire was almost out by the time they returned; Rahim stirred in his spot and mumbled some gargled words in his sleep. Thor was curled up on the other side, snoring, but he opened one eye as the two approached, the stones crunching underfoot alerting him immediately.

Assuring she was well to walk on her own, Silver removed his arm as she stumbled to Thor's side. "Sleep well, princess."

Selena's face burned hot, and her heart fluttered from his words. Silver had returned to his spot by the time she spun around, summoned his metal cube, and resumed reading his scribbled-out book. He only stopped to pull out a solid gold pocket watch and stared at its casing rather than opening it; though odd, Selena didn't question his behavior.

Thor unfolded a single wing and herded her close as she snuggled beside him within her sleeping bag. **I watched some of your lessons. You were amazing.**

Thank you. Silver said that it takes years of mastery to do what I just did.

Perhaps you were skilled before you lost your memory?

Silver believes so, and I feel like he knows more than he's letting on.

Do you think he can teach me as well?

Usually, dragons could master only a single element, but deep down, she believed Thor could learn more than just fire. *I don't see why you couldn't. Maybe we can learn together.*

Thor smiled and laid his head back down, wrapping her within his protective coils, and together, they drifted off to sleep.

CHAPTER 10: I'LL BE YOUR STRENGTH

The following morning hadn't lessened Rahim's tension and animosity towards Silver. Selena was unfortunately awoken to the sound of their squabbles before Rahim strutted away with his map and compass, pacing the campsite, hands shaking as he mumbled.

The irritated Thor explained, **He and Silver had been bickering with each other for most of the morning.**

I swear, sometimes men don't listen.

Thor snaked his head around, his blazing amber round-shield-sized eyes glaring her down to cinders. **Neither do you.**

Selena smirked. *Ladies don't have to listen, but they can give orders.*

Amused, Silver smirked when Rahim attempted to wage another verbal war but held his tongue and continued with his silent rampage. When Thor groaned and lifted his wing, allowing Selena free passage from his hold, Silver spun on the balls of his heels and gave her a huge grin. "My dear, would you like to learn a little trick in magic? It involves dark energy."

Her curiosity gripped her, and she nodded. Thor, however, kept his guard up; he rolled over on his stomach, tail sweeping across the dirt, creating dust clouds. Silver then took an unusual stance, like a puppeteer's. He crossed his extended arms, positioning his hands with his fingers arched like claws in the air. As Silver moved his fingers, Rahim's expression changed: his widened eyes grew, and a huge, ludicrous grin appeared on his face.

Thor lowered his head and kept his eyes fixed on Silver the same way a predator eyed its prey. A warning growl escaped from his scaly lips. **I don't like this.**

Through Silver's twirling fingers, Rahim clapped his hands together, eyes closed, as he tilted his head. "Oh, I love cute and fluffy kitties, and I just want to hug and squeeze them. I love them so much, especially the pink ones—I love the color pink. Little pink fluffy kittens for everyone."

Selena quivered at this performance as Rahim seemed possessed by a demon. With a smug smile, Silver lowered his hands, and Rahim snapped out of the trance; he clapped his twitching hands over his mouth. "What in Oblivion did I just say?"

Face fuming, Selena demanded to know what happened to Rahim; Silver calmly re-adjusted his glasses. "I briefly had Rahim under my control. However, I cannot change someone's personality, but rather bring to the surface what's hidden deep within their subconscious." The two looked over at the squealing Rahim as he swore between his clasped fingers. "Everyone has buried secrets. Rahim, for example, probably didn't know he liked kittens or even the color pink."

Rahim stormed over and pointed a single finger in Silver's face. "I do not like kittens."

"Well, which is it? Do you like kittens or pink? You need to make up your mind." Silver snickered as Rahim turned around and swore under his breath.

Thor growled as he dug his claws into the ground. Selena, in agreement, was not amused. "Silver, let him be."

His smile faded, and his hands clasped behind his back. "I wanted to show you everything I know. And besides, he was the one who started the argument." He flinched when her eyes grew tense.

Selena did her best to control her boiling anger. "That's not the kind of magic we should be using."

"My dear, you misunderstood me." Silver bowed and proceeded with caution. "I haven't used that kind of magic in a long time. That technique is forbidden, but I believe you should have the right to learn it if you must defend yourself. It's dangerous, as, during that moment, you are stripping the person of their free will and making them do your bidding; I would only expect you to use something like this against the Lich or his followers."

Selena turned away, regardless of Silver's harmless intentions; she still considered it wrong, even in self-defense. "Did you say that was dark energy?"

"Yes. Though not taught, two other elements exist outside the main four: light and dark. The only way to truly understand these two is to have full mastery and control over the four elemental magics."

She squinted at him; Silver jittered in place, anticipating her next question or statement. Perhaps, she thought, he was growing anxious and nervous for her prying too far, but she still asked, "I see that you've somehow found the time to master the arcane arts."

"Err, yes. I've had plenty of time."

Rahim was interested in what Selena was doing, and he marched closer to hear Silver's stuttering answers.

Thor arched his head over the group, chittering through the deep rumbles vibrating in his chest.

Selena crossed her arms. "How is that possible? You don't look much older than I am."

Silver bit his bottom lip and turned away. "Never mind that. We should—"

Rahim interrupted with a raised hand. "There's something this tosser isn't telling us."

His eyes darting between Selena's and Rahim's questioning stares, Silver smirked as he looked down at his feet, hands stuffed into his jacket pockets. "There isn't much to say about me."

"We beg to differ," Selena coolly said.

"I'm *not willingly* hiding anything." Selena's ears perked up when Silver emphasized his point; recalling how an unknown force prevented him from fully answering her questions prior, she wondered if Silver was afflicted with a curse. *But why am I not allowed to know?* "Now isn't the right time. I promise, when we have a proper moment, I will enlighten you three on the riveting tale that's called 'my life.'"

Silver flinched when Thor roared, wings extended. **If you want, I'll pin him down for you until he talks.**

I would leave him alone. Eventually, I will make Silver tell me himself.

Rahim grumbled and held a shaking finger to Silver's face, nearly touching his glasses, but Selena beckoned him away. Only upon her promise to pry for more information later did he relax and go back to studying his map. As the tense atmosphere began dwindling, Rahim finally announced their next course of action by traveling through the Hinterlands, the dangerous forest running along the base of the Mustang Mountains.

Even Thor grew agitated by this runaround. **Tell him that I will fly us straight to Alfheim once I'm well-rested. I refuse to walk through the forest.**

Rahim scowled when Selena reiterated Thor's idea but withdrew when Thor snarled at him. "I'm afraid that the Order might spot us if we're out in the open for too long."

Selena shivered. "But the Hinterlands are full of dangerous creatures."

"That's why we should stay near where the forest meets the plains. We should be fine there, but," Rahim sighed and cast a worried glance at the haunting trees, "You're right. Not only that, but I've heard that the forest is alive somehow, deceiving those who go in, and there's no hope for you if you get lost. People tell stories of monsters that lurk in the shadows that will snatch you if you're not careful: those who go in never come out."

"Never come out?" Silver raised an eyebrow. "Then where do the stories come from?"

Rahim made a disgusted face and pointed at the map to Alfheim. "Forget what I just said, but we'll be safe if we don't venture in too deep. We'll follow the Raging River until we reach the city gates."

As the trio made haste in packing their camp, Thor snorted while fidgeting with his harness before placing it upon his back for Selena to strap down. **I'm sure I'm scarier than anything we'll see in there.**

I could see you just eating them. The two laughed, but Selena couldn't help but look upon the Hinterlands with concern. *Still, I wouldn't want to test this eerie forest.*

Once Thor was properly saddled and their belongings strapped down, they made haste towards the Hinterlands. Though the emerald dream could be seen for leagues, Silver instructed Thor to maintain a steady pace that wouldn't tire him easily. "A speed of about twenty kilometers ought to do," he announced, "but do not hesitate to stop and rest if you need it, my draconic friend."

Thor only grunted but took Silver's advice; by his and Rahim's surprise, Thor coasted most of the distance, the wind to their backs. The trip took about a week with a few stops in between, which gave Silver an excuse to continue training Selena. With each lesson, Selena grew proficient to where Silver complimented, "you're far more advanced than any soldier I've seen." Rahim, however, remained indifferent and occasionally mocked Silver's instruction, but Silver ignored him for Selena's sake.

Finally, by the end of the week, they approached the Hinterlands with much-needed caution. The map didn't do the forest's size any justice; the trees looked as if they could swallow them within its depths at any second. The thick, lush ancient grove filled with pinewood; sunlight couldn't pierce its verdant shield, leaving the Hinterlands appearing desolate and life-less to the outside world. Like the bottom of the ocean, the emerald dream held its secrets.

The Raging River's clear azure stream appeared before the group after about an hour hike through the waving hills, its teal trickling along with the gentle breeze. Before Rahim could offer, Silver volunteered to scout ahead to ensure their surroundings were clear. Rahim snarled and rushed through the trees as he marched forward, his yells and accusations drowning from the thickening sward.

Thor continued watching where the two veered off, and he snorted and flickered his tail. **Is it wise to leave those two alone?**

Eventually, Silver and Rahim will learn how to work together.

You shouldn't have to play peacekeeper unless you intend to learn the magic Silver used on Rahim. Only then could I see them getting along. Thor's upper scaley lip curled back as he sneered.

Selena cringed and looked away. *That's not the kind of magic I want to use for entertainment. Something was unsettling about it.*

I wonder if you could take it further and control their actions completely. Selena shuddered at Thor's revelation and immediately thought of the Order; she assumed their pacts and oaths to the Lich gave him absolute command over their thoughts and behaviors.

As the pair waited for Silver's and Rahim's return, the sun slowly drifted towards the center of the sky; black shadows clung to the forest turf, its tangled heart giving a faint hollow echo beckoning them forward.

Thor snaked his head around and groaned, his forked tongue slipping through notched fangs. **I can't take much more of this. I swear by the Divines, I will tear the Hinterlands apart if those two aren't back soon.**

Selena's chest ached, but the two didn't need to wonder much longer; an ear-shattering explosion erupted close ahead, and an immense blast of fire nearby incinerated the trees nearby. She almost fell off her seat, but she gripped the reins until her knuckles turned white. *What was that?*

Thor rushed forward and through the flickering forest blaze with flames spewing from his clamped maw. As Selena screamed and held up her hands to protect herself from the wild embers, she remained unharmed; the fire kissed her copper skin like cool mist. Unsure how she came out unscathed like Thor, she dismissed her confusion as he tore his way through the tangled leaf and limb. The forest may be massive, but the lush grove didn't stand a chance for a mighty, rampaging dragon. Thor's ivory claws slashed through, and his paws stomped the foliage into the dirt. Selena's face drained of all color as she dared not think of the worst.

The wind swept past her face as Thor launched himself through the ash and bellowed a thundering roar that made the trees shake and quiver. As the pair crashed back down and caused the earth to tremble, they saw Silver standing before them with scorch marks covering his body and flames flickering from his charred hair. Meanwhile, Rahim hid behind a large rock nearby that barely hugged the singed circle.

Selena let out a breath in relief. "What happened?"

Unable to move and eyes still widened behind his blackened spectacles, Silver responded by blowing out a smoke circle. "I was making the campfire."

Rahim called out from the safety of his boulder, "You tried to kill me. I was almost roasted."

Silver shook his arms, and the fire's damage brushed away; his clothes now newly mended, hair cleaned, and he wiped his glasses clear. "Ah, *almost*, but I didn't."

Rahim stepped away from his shield, and his head kept whipping between Silver and Selena. "You should have seen the massive explosion."

"We did." Selena and Thor exchanged glances. "We thought you two were attacked by—"

"The Order?" Silver raised a brow, "Now, my dear, you shouldn't worry yourself over little old me."

Thor draped his head over her shoulder while Selena huffed. *It's very stressful. He certainly knows how to make things more dramatic.*

Indeed.

After ensuring Rahim was unharmed, Thor gently scooped him from the ground and assisted him onboard; Selena offered him a water-filled canteen before redirecting her group to continue their journey. Silver hopped aboard before Thor could help him up, using the stirrups to gain speed and altitude, clearing Thor's height effortlessly. Rahim turned away, and Selena wished he would keep his mumbled complaints and inappropriate comments to himself. Luckily, Silver kept his promise and didn't antagonize Rahim further.

Pine needles graced Selena's nostrils; although they remained close to the open field without risking exposure, the trees still blocked the lancing sunlight directly overhead, instantly bringing the atmosphere to evening temperatures. Yet, the air grew thick and humid, and the soft and moist ground squished beneath Thor's paws, the slimy stones slipping under his claws.

Thor's fiery eyes grew transfixed on the jumping catfish; he approached the riverbank and, with snake-like reflexes, snatched one in his mouth mid-air and gulped it down without chewing. Confused at first by its earthy taste, Thor caught several more before he was satisfied and swallowed many mouthfuls of water before continuing. **It's not as tasty as deer or sheep, but it's enough to satiate my hunger.**

Selena chuckled. *You and Rahim are both bottomless pits.*

Thor snorted and swished his tail as he walked away from the river. **I'm a growing dragon. One day, when I'm the size of a mountain, you will admire me.**

I already do, silly.

Several hours passed into the late afternoon before the four reached a bridge crossing the weaving river; Rahim broke the silence and announced taking a small break within a nearby small enclosure guarded by the trees and bushes. While he and Selena busied themselves in refilling their canteens, Silver dismounted and offered to use this small opportunity to Selena's advantage: continuing her magical instruction.

"If I didn't know any better, you seem much more excited about this than I am," she said through the squint of her brow.

"Of course, I am. It's not very often that I teach someone how to use magic. There was that one time, but it was a disaster. You're picking it up incredibly fast, and I want you to know everything." As Thor and Rahim stepped aside, Silver beckoned Selena forward. "You're developing an open mind, and now, I want you to take it a little further. Like the flame shield you made last night, you can also forge yourself a temporary weapon if you're ever disarmed. I want to see you make one." Rahim, however, kept disrupting her concentration as he spoke ill of her newly awakened talents. Silver's smile faded, but he bit his tongue, keeping the sarcasm to himself. "Don't worry about him, my dear. Not everyone understands, nor appreciates, what I'm teaching you. Focus on me."

On the other hand, Thor plopped on his stomach and crossed his forearms, wrapping his tail around his body. **I'm going to enjoy watching you.**

Please don't judge me.

Thor flashed his fangs and lifted his lips to smile. **Just for that, I get to judge you, starting now.**

Silver continued as he and Selena took opposite ends of their small training field. "Typically, younger minds lack the interest, concentration, and willpower to learn magic."

Sharing in Thor's and Rahim's inquisitive stares, Selena voiced what all three thought: "You speak as though you are much older than we are, and yet, you don't appear to be."

Silver bit his cheek as his nostrils flared, catching himself from almost making another mistake. "Err, enough of that, and let's continue. Pretend you don't have a sword or gun with you, and you need to fight in close combat. Show me how to summon an elemental weapon that you can wield."

Still figuring out how to catch him off guard, Selena concentrated, and flames ignited within her opened palms. Her blazes surrounded her and hardened into molten lava, but her orbed shield blocked out Silver's sounds and cheers.

Thor poked through her mental barrier and translated: **Silver is yelling about how you're using both fire and earth when he only taught you fire. Now, I'm curious: what are you?**

I don't know. It's coming to me as easily as being a dragon is to you.

At first amused, Thor then turned away. **Being a dragon....**

While he trailed off and fell deep in thought, Selena envisioned creating a tangible object to hold, and her face lit up when she stumbled upon an idea. She imagined her shield dissipating away, and it crumbled around her; the pieces then suddenly formed a ring orbiting her. As Silver, and even Rahim, inched closer with great anticipation, she closed her eyes and, with a deep breath, focused on the shards creating a rod. As they took shape within her hand, she exhaled a chilling wind that cooled it enough for her to hold. Silver watched in amazement as the pieces came together to form a sword with a dripping molten blade, the grip and cross guard frozen obsidian.

Silver's grin brightened the darkened forest as he explained how she used all four elements to craft her weapon; Selena shook her head, not understanding what he meant. "You used ice and air when you cooled your fire sword. Earlier, you used earth and fire to craft your shield." Suddenly, his smile vanished, and he placed a hand under his chin while quizzically staring at her, then clapped his hands. "You acted out of pure instinct. By the Divines, you make me so proud, and the Council will appreciate your talents."

Selena spun around to show the beaming Thor and Rahim her elemental sword, but Silver quickly and quietly drew his weapon from his sleeves. Her eyes drew to the gold etchings and the carefully carved dragon down the grip, and as his curved blade swung for her head, Selena immediately parried the attack. Rahim nearly jumped in but stopped when realizing he didn't have a weapon of his own. Thor, meanwhile, silently observed through the impatient tail flickers.

Silver paused and withdrew his war reaper scythe, the crystal rod pommel glimmering rainbows across the ground; the sinister curved ebony blade caught Selena's scowling expression when she expected a fight. She hissed. "What are you doing?"

Silver's sadistic smile made her skin crawl. "For research, of course." Selena gritted her teeth and tightened her hold, concluding he had been toying with her the entire time. Silver re-adjusted his glasses and placed one hand in his pocket. "I will let you deliver the first blow. This training for you is research material for me. I want to study and observe your nature. Even if you had been able to use magic before losing your memory, it's impossible to exhibit your current skill level in a short time frame. It's almost like you were *made* of magic." His voice remained calm as his twinkling ice-blue eyes pierced her emeralds, his glasses flashing from the evening sun setting behind her.

Selena attempted to meet Thor's gaze; he watched Silver like a hawk, but without showing the slightest concern, he didn't move. Neither did Rahim; instead, he complimented how Silver's weapon looked and appeared to be somewhat entertained. It was then she realized: "You planned this, and they're in on it."

Thor lowered his head in shame, and Rahim nervously whistled while twiddling his thumbs. Silver didn't openly validate her conclusion. "Shall we continue?"

Though she had never fought nor used a weapon before, Selena kept her sword steady before stepping in; readying for a strike, Silver made no attempts to stop her. Before she could deliver her first blow, he vanished in a plume of smoke. Selena abruptly stopped in mid-pursuit, and Silver reappeared behind her, using the rib to knock her down.

She face-planted into the ground, and her lava-dripping sword flew from her hand. The stoic Silver slid away, dug his weapon's crystal pommel into the ground, and leaned over the top with arms crossed. He yawned, growing bored of their duel. "Now, I'm wondering how I should properly conduct my study: perhaps I can perform experiments or dissect you. I've never done that before, so that could be quite interesting."

Selena wiped the dirt off her face and picked up her blazing sword, the liquid fire singing the ground from every drip of the blade; her anticipation for their fight rushed through her veins. Silver got into position but stood relaxed, his scythe dangling from his hand. Selena immediately knew that this wasn't right, and so instead of striking, she moved towards his side. He watched her from the corner of his eye and shifted his stance before she could blink and dashed forward. He used one hand to push her sword away and held his other to her chest. A blue aura appeared under his palm, creating a small explosion that threw her backward.

Laying limply on her back while recovering, she rolled on her stomach and pushed herself up, muscles weak and trembling. "W-what did you just do?"

Silver smiled. "I used your energy against you. Spirit magic, known as Aether, is magic in its purest form, eliminating the illusion of separation. You will reach enlightenment when you master the elements; you can even manipulate the Aether within your opponents, channeling the very life force flowing through your enemy's veins. You must keep an open mind."

His tone unnerved her, and Silver's merciless sneer pierced the evening sward. Yet, his grin faded, his gaze now blank and unchanged; Silver propped himself up with his scythe once more, predicting her next move.

His anticipation escalating, Rahim gripped his knees until his knuckles turned white. Through snarls and growls, Thor moved away from him and, his back arched like a hissing cat, inched to Selena's side; his pupils turned to slits and targeted Silver, who neither moved nor attempted to stop him. Selena's eyes filled with tears when Thor wrapped himself around her. *I'm hurt that you've been sitting aside this entire time.*

Thor extended his wings, wrapping her within his warm and loving embrace, and he snapped his fangs at Silver. **I had no idea he would take it this far, and I refuse to stand by any longer. I won't allow him to toy with you like a plaything.**

Silver merely shrugged his shoulders, indifferent to Thor's hostile behavior. "I'm sorry, Thor, but the plan changed. My experiment is to see her reach her breaking point." He then pointed at the snarling dragon. "This test involves you, too."

What is he talking about?

I should be the one asking you. When did he ask this of you?

I'm sorry, but last night, after you fell asleep, Silver told Rahim and me of his plans and asked us not to intervene. My dearest one, I had no idea he would push too far. His voice thundered with a sharp snap of his fangs: **This was not part of our agreement.**

Even as Thor's earth trembling roar echoed through the trees, Silver smiled once more. "Let's continue."

Thor's eyes gleamed like a venomous snake ready to kill. **I will be your strength, my dear.**

Pulling his weapon from the dirt, he charged full speed at Thor, who swung his tail, knocking Silver away. As he flung through the air, Silver flipped until he landed on his feet; with his reaper scythe at the ready, he launched himself upward, leaping high as the canopy's tangled branches. "I want to see your magic."

Curling into a ball on the sidelines, Rahim bit his nails as he watched the pair dodge; Silver landed hard on the ground, the force of his impact leaving a crater almost Thor's size and wafting billowing dust clouds. Thor readied his claws and fangs, but he blindly struck as Silver moved and teleported like lightning strikes; Thor couldn't predict where Silver wound up next.

Her wrath boiling like a rampaging dragon, Selena snatched her magma sword and focused channeling her energy; imagining her weapon as an extension of herself, she swung her molten blade, creating waves of fire slashing towards Silver. He vanished yet again and reappeared before her. The startled Selena flinched and stepped backward, but she rushed in for the strike after collecting her thoughts. Before Thor could snatch her away, Silver moved with inhuman speed, placing his blue aura imbued hands on both sides of her molten blade. His magic shattered her magma weapon like glass, and the aftermath sent her flying back.

Releasing a blood-curdling roar, Thor jumped to her aid and wrapped his wings around her. His maw widened as Silver slowly approached with heavy steps, a firestorm swirling in the back of his throat, ready to be unleashed. **Don't touch her. I will tear you to shreds if you do.**

Silver turned a blind eye to Thor's threatening posture but instead leaned over and placed a gentle hand on his neck; Thor didn't back away, but he herded Selena closer to his chest, ready to whisk her away at a moment's notice. As if his other personality had suddenly switched, Silver offered the two a kind smile. "Well done."

Selena was confused, pushing herself away from Thor's chest plate scales pressing against her body like cool metal. "Pardon me?"

Thor shared in her bafflement, but he didn't let up the snarls and growls, even as Silver explained, "You two will be fine—you're perfect for each other." His scythe disappeared in smoke. "I wanted to see how strong your bond was and if Thor was willing to do whatever it took to protect you. Her Imperial Majesty asked this of me: she wanted to test your relationship and abilities. However, I will admit that I am still curious about how you can learn magic so easily. I have a theory from a previous experiment of mine, but that I cannot tell you."

Rahim jolted from his spot once the situation cleared and approached Silver with hasty steps and a shaky voice. "If the Empress put you up to this, does that mean she knows what's going on?"

Silver clicked his tongue against his teeth as he re-adjusted his feathered trinket and buckles and strolled away. While Rahim badgered him about his connection to Her Imperial Majesty, Thor and Selena reconciled and made amends. **I must know then. Did Her Imperial Majesty anticipate the Council's plan, and does she know ours?**

Selena voiced out Thor's questions; Silver immediately stopped mid-strut, and his smile grew bigger upon spinning around. "As I serve Her Imperial Majesty, I'll just say that you have more allies than you realize. I must advise you and Thor to keep moving forward with your plan to join the Force, as the Empress is fully aware of your intentions. She currently awaits our arrival and is eager to meet you two."

I'm a little impatient myself, as she seems to know so much about me, about us.

Thor dipped his head in agreement. **The fact she's extended all this effort in keeping us safe is good enough reason to trust her.**

"Once we get to Alfheim, there is no turning back." Silver reached down to her with a friendly hand. "What say you two, Andric Liongod and Thor?"

She heartily accepted it. "Aye, we'll keep pushing forward then." Smoke wafted from Thor's nostrils as he released a series of chirps and clicks.

"Very good. Also, if you don't mind, I would like to stay close to research my possible theory that could help train future dragon riders. If I'm correct, we can use this to our advantage."

Attempting to wrap her head around what he meant, Selena dusted herself off after springing to her feet. "I only ask that you don't toy with me in the future."

"Of course, please forgive me, for it will not happen again."

They spent the remainder of their late afternoon and early evening resting before reaching Alfheim in the morning. Silver once again chose not to eat while Rahim was stuffing his face. In the meantime, Selena sat with

Thor by the roaring fire with an open book, reading about the different dragon breeds—courtesy of Silver. Together, they skimmed over passages and lists, learning and identifying the various species they've had the pleasure of meeting thus far. Vulcan, for instance, was a Fire Ridgeback.

The black dragons she saw soaring over Helshire with war supplies were the Onyxian Steelbellies, whose scales were dark as the void, and their hide and underbellies hard like steel—hence the name. Selena found the name of the blue dragon flying over the Grand Exchange: the Cerulean Iceclaw, master over ice and water.

Underneath mentioned the Blackland Steelwings, a breed similar to Thor's design, but the coloration and proportions didn't match: obsidian scales set against blazing crimson wings that could cut down trees. Yet, it was the only dragon class with a bone mask that Selena could see, but Thor shared no other resemblance.

Next on the list: the Aracania Venomtooth, rare in Armageddon, was an acid-spitter highly prized in the Force. Per Silver, the only one discovered in the Empire was General Araneus' dragon, who he named Aracania for her kind. "Be prepared to meet them, as they will be your superiors."

Thor nudged the page with his snout when Selena read about the earth dragons: the Viridian Longwings. **That was Aster's breed, Mr. Kingsleigh's dragon. I hope to see them again in Alfheim to introduce you properly.**

Selena smiled, and she flipped to another page detailing more about the Dark Knights and the Mythic Flight; the dragons were powerful guardians of their corresponding element, and no other breed could match their strength. Their clutch of eggs was all that remained of the flight after the war, currently under lock and key within the Council's headquarters until such a time came to find appropriate handlers.

Next listed an extraordinary breed: Divinity Dragons. Hailing as gods among mortals and known as the 'King of Dragons,' the Divines created their species to maintain peace and banish evil from their realm. Divinity Dragons wielded many abilities others couldn't: masters of all elemental magic, lifting and curing any disease, and the power of resurrection to be used only once. The Mythic Flight feared and respected their kind for their elemental mastery, as Divinity Dragons were more powerful than the guardians combined.

When Selena asked Silver more about Divinity Dragons, he looked up at Thor from his book before answering, "Only one can exist at a time, but there is no way to identify unless they've fully realized their power. As far as I know, there are no records of a Divinity Dragon in absolute grandeur; otherwise, they could easily be mistaken for another breed. Trying to distinguish one is folly."

"Do you have any idea as to Thor's breed?"

Silver's eyes remained focused on Thor, now squinting as he began to ponder. "I haven't the faintest idea. His is a species I've never seen before, like a mix between the Fire Ridgebacks and the Blackland Steelwings. We'll see what they say in Dragonspire."

Thor's eyes lit up from the passage, chittering in delight upon discovering these mighty dragons. **Even if I'm not any of these breeds, I still want to learn the other elements.**

I have a feeling you can.

However, her skin prickled when she grew consumed by an unbearably dark aura wafting through the whispering trees. Selena couldn't find the strength to move or scream with the oncoming dreadful presence threatening to devour her.

As she rolled away from Thor's side, he immediately sprang up to all fours, wings unfurled as he took his protective stance over her. Rahim paused in between bites of jerky, confused by Selena's and Thor's odd behavior; Silver, however, understood at once, and he prepared to cast magic, lightning writhing around his hands. The dark whispers grew to an ear-shattering shrill, and the air suddenly chilled; Selena used the technique to keep herself warm through steady, heated breaths. Emerging from the trees was a group of twenty robed cultists from the Obsidian Order, their silver masks gleaming in the moonlight.

The other three prepared for battle while Rahim backed away and hid behind Selena and Thor for coverage. Selena summoned a fire orb floating above her palm, ready to erupt upon her command. Thor reared back upon his haunches, wings spread and claws ready; Silver summoned his same scythe used earlier in the duel, eyes darting from one cultist to the other, hissing, "Last time, I thought I made myself clear."

"The Obsidian Order will never falter as long as the Dark Master commands us." The leader with the crescent moon scar stepped forth, and Selena finally saw him for who he was; she was appalled to see a young man serving the Lich, as he didn't share the resemblance as the demonic fanatics following him. His dark blue midnight eyes contrasted his ghostly pale skin, messy jet-black hair iridescent in the moon's shimmer. Upon his neck was a chain with a pendant of Death, a seven-headed dragon with ten horns.

The trembling Rahim poked his head around Thor's hind leg and pointed at their dragon while bravely, though foolishly, asking, "Do you honestly believe you can win against a dragon and us?"

Accepting Rahim's challenge, a roar like thunder shook the trees. A golden glimmer zipped across the sky at such an alarming speed that it made the air scream; Selena didn't see what it was. However, hearing the snarls and the beating wings made her realize it was the same dragon from the Grand Exchange. Thor's eyes locked on the gold shimmer whizzing back and forth, preparing himself for a fight. A pit dropped in Selena's stomach; she knew Thor would be no match against the colossal dragon.

The Lich's right-hand man sneered. "You will come back with us. The Dark Master is so longing to see you after taking his dragon."

Upon his command, the group swarmed in at once. As Silver, Selena, and Thor joined the fray, Rahim grabbed Thor's saddle straps dangling from his back and pulled himself on board. Thor paid no attention to the struggling Rahim as he focused on crowd control; he swiped his claws and swept his thick tail across the ground. As the Order switched from magic to gunfire, Thor took this momentary advantage and struck at them like a snake, wrapping his mouth around two at a time. Thor shook their bodies like a ragged doll between the erratic barrage of bullets and tossed them aside before tearing through another pair.

While Thor distracted one group, Selena immediately went to a defensive stance and created her fire shield. The Order's conjoined firepower of magic and bullets bounced against her orb, but her magic suddenly grew unstable as cracks spiderwebbed across her magma barrier. Gritting her teeth, Selena waved her hands, plucking strings of fire from her cracking shell and focused on forming the strands into a ring around her. She drew more energy, allowing it to expand outward. Noticing her growing fury, Thor and Silver dodged, and Selena's blazing circle exploded, knocking their enemies away in one swift movement, giving them a moment of respite.

Her flame shield dissipated into smoke as she collapsed to the ground, her vision blurry. Yet, after her magic knocked them away, the demonic cultists vanished into the shadows and reappeared, encircling the group with their remaining forces. Silver dashed through the forest, using the same technique from his and Selena's duel; lightning erupted from his palms while twisting their Aether energy, and a beam of light pierced his enemy's chest like a massive ice shard. One by one, Silver teleported and reappeared, killing one demon after another with this tactic.

However, one devotee broke from his formation with a summoned black bow pluming with dark energy and pointed a nocked arrow at Selena's head. While she stumbled back to her feet, unaware of her impending doom, Silver intervened; he thrust his glowing ice-blue hand through the assassin's chest, and the archer's body exploded upon Silver's touch.

As Rahim peeked over the saddle's edge, Silver called for his attention. "Leave now, before that dragon comes. I will stay here to lure the rest away."

Selena's vision cleared as Thor followed Silver's orders; he hovered before snatching her with his claws and began the steep climb skyward with a sweep of his wings. Dust billowed around him from the take-off, and the three were suddenly airborne. Selena reached out for Silver from Thor's clawed cage, crying and screaming to save him. However, Silver continued yelling for the trio to flee, and Thor and Rahim turned a deaf ear to Selena's pleas.

Thor snarled when the golden glimmer shot over the treetops, and the three finally saw the dragon in all its terrifying glory: a Sunbeam Shieldtail. It was at least twice the size of Thor with golden scales like polished armor plates. Many horns covered the dragon's jawline until they met with the curved horns near its crown. The silver parchment-textured membranes flapped like sails from a ship, the sky yielding and quivering to its magnificence.

Rahim's throat clamped shut. "Please, mister dragon, don't eat us."

The dragon's golden eyes fixated upon Thor, and its fangs separated, letting forth a deadly torrent of fire blasting towards the three. Thor tucked in his wings and dove to dodge the inferno, twirling around the trees, making haste towards Alfheim.

However, the dragon didn't give chase; it hovered for a moment with its wings still stretched out. Then, with a snap of its fangs, the golden dragon steered itself around and made its way towards the swarmed camp, fading within the thickened verdant sea.

When it was clear that the golden dragon had abandoned its pursuit, Selena, with hot tears straining her face, ruefully watched Silver disappear in the trees as the trio soared higher heavenward. However, a serpent-like dragon with scales as white as snow appeared through the lush, and the forest glowed from its blazing azure inferno.

CHAPTER 11: ALFHEIM

The trio flew through the long night, the silent and gloomy atmosphere becoming nearly unbearable. After ensuring they were a safe distance away, Thor finally assisted Selena back into the harness. While Rahim did his best to offer words of comfort, Selena sulked into her seat and leaned against one of Thor's horns, somberly looking back for any sign of Silver's survival. Though the mysterious white dragon fended off the Order, she wasn't sure if her mind was playing a cruel trick on her, as neither Rahim nor Thor saw it.

If you thought you saw a white dragon coming to rescue him, I believe you.

Selena felt offended. *Are you mocking me?*

Of course not. I only wished I saw it, too.

Rahim wasn't sure how to approach and offer comfort in her time of need. Their exchange grew awkward as he placed a hand on her shoulder, and his words sputtered from his mouth. When he failed to lift her spirits, Rahim withdrew and studied his map; Selena appreciated the effort when his and Silver's animosity still lingered.

When the awakened sun rose over the mountains, the grand ivory city of Alfheim was within aerial view; Rahim suggested walking the rest of the distance to avoid provoking the guards and the Force. "It would be best not to draw attention to ourselves until you two are safely enlisted. They may not like seeing a random dragon flying over." Selena and Thor couldn't argue with Rahim's logic, and Thor made his slow descent upon a clear dirt path when they were close to the city gates. If the watchtower guards had spotted them, Selena assumed there would have been an alarm, but the city continued peacefully.

Rahim held the map out before him, keeping them on the trail that would soon lead them towards the main gates; however, the trio paused when a tall figure appeared down the path, and Thor immediately growled with claws and fangs ready. Yet, the figure paid no mind to the awaiting hostile welcome; as it drew closer, its features became more distinct, and Selena recognized it as a fox walking like a human.

Meeting Loki and learning that some animals could speak was different from seeing one walking upright on two legs. However, as the fox approached, Selena and Rahim noted she was an elven woman wearing a baneful red fox mask. Her long, slick crimson dress glimmered in the dawn's shimmering rays, matching the brilliance of a deep ruby held by a wooden claw topping her walking staff clacking against the rock and dirt with each stride. Upon seeing the woman's gem, Thor grew self-conscious and vigorously polished his harness ruby to match her gleaming stone.

A fair elven maiden whose slender features poised with such grace that a human couldn't compare, she donned a unicorn hair woven dress of black and red. She had twisted her thick, fire-kissed hair into a single braid, decorated with golden chains and tiny jewels gleaming against her crystal pendant and dragon tooth necklace.

Selena wasn't surprised to meet one of Alfheim's elves, as they originally built the ivory city many years ago. Originally enslaved by the dwarves, the elves rebelled and sought refuge where Alfheim stood today, but many of the old mines still lay scattered around the mountains where the dwarves forced the elves to work.

The elf woman bowed as she hung the mask over her pointed ear and smiled; her bright green eyes burned like her flaming hair. "Salutations, and welcome to Alfheim. May I ask what brings you, travelers, to our fair city?"

Her calm and gentle tone reminded Selena of a tiny bell twinkling from a distance. Thor eased his growls and let his guard down while helping Selena and Rahim dismount, allowing them to introduce themselves adequately. "My companion, Thor, and I are reporting for duty," Selena stumbled as she searched through her shirt pockets until finding the forged documents and showed them to the stranger.

She took one look at the papers before accepting Selena's tale without question. "Ah, I see. You were already assigned a dragon then, Mr.—?"

"Liongod, Andric Liongod at your service." Selena bowed. "I rescued Thor about a month ago before receiving my orders for the draft. We both agreed it would be fitting if he joined with me as my partner." Selena gave the stranger a polite gesture that Silver taught her as a greeting by pressing a balled hand into her other open palm and bowed; Thor snorted, tail twitching, but he lowered his head, eye still fixed on the fox lady.

"It's a pleasure to make your acquaintance, Liongod. I am Neith Anahita, advisor to Her Imperial Majesty. And you are?" she asked Rahim.

His voice cracked against his dry throat. "Rahim Branwen, but I'm not joining the Force. The Order destroyed my home, and I was hoping to seek refuge here."

"That is very grave news indeed, and I offer my sincere apologies and condolences for your loss, Rahim. Of course, Alfheim is always open to those in need." Neith's glittering eyes scanned over the three, and she grinned.

Selena said, "We are grateful for your hospitality."

"May I escort you three inside the city? It's not too far of a walk, and the guards would grow uneasy seeing an unreported dragon waltzing freely around the city." She gave Thor a jerky nod. "I pray not to have given offense, Thor."

He snorted but dipped his head. **No offense taken, and I understand.** Selena repeated his words, and when Neith was satisfied, the three followed her upon her signal after releasing a long sigh in relief that she didn't question their fabricated story. Thor chirped and twittered as he whipped his head around, marveling at Alfheim's endless wall. **I can't wait to see what the city is like, and hopefully, that will be the last we will see of that golden dragon and the Order.**

I pray for our promising future.

She held onto high hopes the Obsidian Order wouldn't be so daring to attack them within the secured city; however, her stomach sank when Thor mentioned the legitimacy of the ongoing rumors. **I also pray the Lich has no plans for Alfheim.**

Selena replied sadly, *The reports are hard to refute, as everyone anticipates a battle.*

While Neith was busy sharing details about the city, Selena's eyes caught what appeared to be one of the abandoned dwarven mines; the decrepit and rusty cavern built into the hills was sealed tight by a massive metal door. Neith paused and added when noticing Selena's curious gaze. "It's one of many deserted and non-operable dwarven ruins and mines scattered across the Empire." Her eyes glazed over as she stared at the ancient ruin. "Many treasure hunters have sought them out, but they never return. It would be unwise to explore." As Her Imperial Majesty's advisor beckoned the group forward, Selena watched it disappear into the trees as they continued towards Alfheim.

The ancient grove began to clear, and the bright sunlight flashed in their eyes; even Thor lifted his wing to shield his face from the sudden glare. When their vision came into focus, the group stood before a proud, tall white wall of stone and marble, stretching on forever in both directions. Two statues of Xyaxon—as a lion—with deep rubies in their mouths guarded the massive gate, watching as Selena and her friends passed through. A colossal shield paired with a long sword hung overhead as two dragon busts mirrored each other on both sides, their tails twisting around the blade.

Neith asked the three to wait and approached the gate; she held up her staff, signaling the two guards standing post along the wall, asking permission to enter. After a few moments of silent anticipation, Selena heard the metal chains creak, and the door lifted from the dirt, pulling the earth as it ascended. While the awestruck Selena, Rahim, and Thor gazed upon the city's grandeur, Neith grinned and hummed. "Welcome to Alfheim."

Gracing the group with its majestic appearance was a giant metropolis ivory castle—Rune Citadel per Neith—built boldly on a mountain within the city's center; winding stone steps writhed around the massive citadel, leading to its immense towers stretching for the heavens. Thor kept his size in mind when trotting down the busy cobblestone roads, his claws clicking against the pavement; he was courteous in keeping his wings tucked to his sides, but the locals still couldn't help but stop and admire the gold and crimson dragon. Horse-drawn carriages rolled by occasionally, the clacking hooves rattling down the streets, carrying the more aristocratic audience.

Per Neith, Alfheim opened their gates to those seeking refuge, no matter their race. As expected, many of the denizens were elves, but Selena occasionally saw humans and dwarves among the populace. She admired seeing the diversity in skin shades; she was the only person of color in Helshire Village, but Alfheim was a rainbow. Contrasting Neith's delicately porcelain hue, the many residents strolling by came in various colors and tones, regardless of their race; even Rahim looked around excitedly, and Selena guessed he had never been to Alfheim before.

Shadows drifted overhead; three dragons soared towards Rune Citadel, and upon closer examination, Selena gasped when she saw the general's Aracania Venomtooth leading two Onyxian Steelbellies. Aracania's black hide, smooth as a snake's, and four-spined bat-like wings were dotted with green and light purple spots; purple fins trailed along her masted sharp spines along her spine and tail. Her lean face was devoid of any horn decorations, save for two on her head and a set on her jaw corners. She kept her three razor claws retracted in mid-flight, sharp enough to rip a man clean in half. Daintier than Thor and the two Steelbellies following, Aracania was still superior in weight and size, large enough to carry a small crew of about fifteen adult men. Her leaner frame made her more agile and acrobatic while airborne, which she now exhibited gracefully with her aerial show.

Aracania snaked her head around as she passed over and looked at Selena and Thor with great interest. Her rider, assumed to be General Araneus, leaned over his seat and gave the three a firm salute before leading the two Steelbellies away. Neith waved at the three passing dragons, and the group continued their course. "After you meet with Vidar and Her Imperial Majesty, General Araneus and Aracania will be your superiors. Once you two officially join, Liongod will report to Captain Bel and Captain Altessa at four-thirty in the morning. Thor, you will be with Aracania, as she trains all the new dragons in aerial combat, so please, mind your manners."

Curious and intrigued by one of the names, Selena asked Neith, "Is Captain Altessa by any chance related to Genesis Altessa?"

"Yes, I believe he is." Neith grinned; Rahim smirked and made silly faces at Selena, whose face glowed crimson in embarrassment.

As she led them towards the Fire Temple—a sanctuary at the base of the metropolis mountain—Neith continued explaining, "As the largest city in the Empire, Alfheim is the capital of Armageddon, separated into seven districts by the stone walls you see all around us: Market, Imperial, Dragon, Garden, Memorial, Sky, and Dragonspire. Currently, we're walking through the Market District." Selena learned that the Imperial District consisted of Rune Citadel within the city's center. Beyond the wall near the North Sea, the Dragon District housed the soldiers and provided proper accommodations for dragons. The wealthy families lived in the Garden District, while the lower classes remained in the Sky District. Dragonspire was its own jurisdiction, accommodating the scholars, mages, witches, and wizards. Neith said: "You can reach its towers by taking the giant bridge from the Garden District. We occasionally send our soldiers there who wish to further their education in the arcane arts."

In the middle of Neith's explanation, Selena noticed a large black and grey clock towering above the walls standing boldly in the setting sun. Mounted on top was a sculpture of Death, the seven-headed dragon with ten horns—the first head had four horns while the rest had only one. Its long tail arched around the clock's face while standing guard, its snouts facing outward; the main head with four horns overlooked the common rabble.

Neith paused and joined Selena in examining the grim-looking spire. "We call it 'the Pyre.' We built it to soothe the spirits of the fallen soldiers from the One Hundred Years' War—it stands tall in the Memorial District, where the dead rest."

Unable to tear her gaze away, Selena asked, "Why is it called 'the Pyre?'"

The clock tower answered her question and began its slow and steady chimes, waiting before screaming the next when the first was still dreadful in everyone's ears. It was like someone uttering one word repeatedly, making the hair on Selena's neck stand on end. Rahim's face turned pale, and Thor dipped his head in respect for the fallen; Alfheim listened to the Pyre shout, "die," seven times.

Neith led the trio away and towards the Fire Temple steps when the Pyre finished its last dreary chime. Its grey stone structure stood glumly after hearing the depressing clock; even the two Xyaxon statues standing guard grew cold. "Here, Vidar will meet with you and Thor to formally welcome you into the Imperial Air Force," Neith began as she spun around by the steps, "but Rahim, please follow me. I will show you your new living arrangements, courtesy of Her Imperial Majesty, where we will provide food and other living necessities."

Hesitant to meet the man she secretly hoped never to see again, Selena bowed. Thor, however, unfurled his wings, catching the sunlight within his fiery membranes. **I will strike him down where he stands if he refuses our enlistment.**

Easy, my dear one.

Rahim remained indifferent to Thor's hostile body language as he thanked Neith for Her Imperial Majesty's generosity in providing housing arrangements. Neith grinned as Rahim and Selena shared their farewells, and the two left Selena and Thor waiting on the marble steps. "Until we meet again, Andric Liongod," Neith said through the gleam of her eye and gave her a sly smile; Selena wondered if Neith knew of hers and Thor's ploy, but the advisor played her part well.

As if on cue, when Neith and Rahim vanished through the flowing crowd, Selena's ears twitched when she heard Vidar calling for their attention. She spun on the balls of her heels; Thor's low growls and snarls rumbled like his purrs and hums, but he controlled his building fury when the plump half-elf Vidar casually left the temple and stepped down the stairs, followed by two companions, one whom she recognized as Ashur. Ashur's pointed chin and gaunt cheekbones brushed against the wide collar of his formal attire mirroring Vidar's: dark red waistcoat with black and gold trimmings and buckles, black breeches, and polished hessian boots. His black hair slicked past his pointed ears; thick slanted eyebrows gave him this intimidating aura as if he were always angry. Around his neck, Ashur wore an obsidian dragon tooth necklace like Neith's.

Their third acquaintance donned in a midnight blue cloak stood in the shadows, face shrouded under the cowl. Streaks of silver-tinted locks flowed from under the hood, but the stranger didn't attempt to meet Selena's questioning gaze. Selena assumed her to be a woman, judging by the flowing matching dress with gilt-plated designs like graceful vines from a rose garden.

Vidar cleared his throat. "You two were the last recruits to arrive."

It took Thor nudging her arm to pull her attention away from the cloaked woman, and Selena bowed over her balled fist. "Please excuse our delay, but we arrived as quickly as possible."

Vidar squinted at the pair with his beady, piercing, icy eyes before extending his hand. "May I see your papers?"

Selena immediately straightened up and pulled out the forged documents with trembling fingers. Gritting her teeth, she silently prayed to the Divines that Vidar wouldn't question the legitimacy of her paperwork. Ashur cast the two a venomous glare as if he were a snake ready to strike, but he held his tongue. The stranger, however, readjusted her stance with a slight head-tilt upward, just enough for Selena to see her narrow jawline.

Vidar yawned after one quick scan and grew bored reading before handing them back; she and Thor sighed in relief. "So, Andric Liongod, we appreciate you coming here on such short notice. Neith informed us how you already have a dragon before leaving to meet with you two."

I knew it, Selena thought, *Neith is helping the Empress on our endeavor.*

Thor fluttered in his spot. **Most agreeable.**

Vidar continued, disregarding their slight deviation in behavior. "Though I cannot ignore rogue dragons roaming the Empire, it's never been heard of that one would consider paring with a mortal outside Council regulations. I wanted to hear more on the details on how this came to pass."

Although she rehearsed the story many times in her head, she stumbled to find the right words. "Please forgive me, for it is a long tale." With Thor's help, Selena spun their fabricated account, detailing Vidar and his two associates how she rescued Thor a month prior from a terrible creature that injured him, leaving nasty gashes in his legs and chest. Meanwhile, Ashur's crimson eyes pierced their tense narrative, and Selena feared he saw right through them. Again, he remained silent.

Curious, Vidar examined the two. "In the Hinterlands, you say."

Ashur's cold and threatening voice shattered the tense air. "Very brave of you indeed, Andric."

Keeping her emerald eyes fixed on the coiling snake, Selena continued: "To pay back his debt, Thor vowed to join me, and we agreed to enlist together." Upon finishing her tale, Thor's nostrils flared, but he bowed.

Vidar put a hand on his chin, still not wholly convinced. "Hmm. What do you make of this, Captain Bel?"

Selena silently cursed her luck that he would be one of her commanding officers; Ashur sneered, and she saw his upper lip twitch. "Strange this came to pass, as the Council holds all the dragons and their eggs under tight control." Thor instantly snarled, sweeping his tail across the steps; Vidar and Ashur flinched and stepped back to avoid his wrath, but Thor withheld further. Selena couldn't help but smirk.

While Vidar and Ashur were preoccupied with maintaining a safe distance away from Thor's brewing rage, the strange woman spoke; her gentle, warm voice could make Niflheim weep. "Captain Bel, feral dragons are quite common, and Thor could have been an abandoned hatchling. It wouldn't be the first to happen."

"Hmm. I suppose that would make sense." Vidar lazily replied; Ashur scoffed.

The woman ignored Ashur's boorish behavior and continued: "Despite Andric coming across a feral dragon in the wild, the two agreed that the best way to keep their bond was to serve the Empire. They could have easily gone rogue themselves, not to mention it would save the Council from wasting coin in providing another dragon from their archives."

A greedy glimmer ignited in Vidar's eyes, and Selena secretly scowled. "Then, I wanted to thank you two for your loyalty to the Empire. You will report to your bunker tonight, and tomorrow, the real training will begin." After clearing his throat, Vidar reluctantly approached Thor, but the dragon growled through clamped fangs.

Best he moves his hand away before I bite it off.

Soothing him gently, Selena demanded Vidar, "What are you doing?"

"Moving your dragon to his new quarters. You two need to begin your separate training." Selena hissed through her teeth, ignoring the stranger's gestures, signaling her to stand down. When she still refused, there was a furrow in Vidar's brow as he squinted at her, utterly puzzled. "Liongod, indeed you must know that soldiers usually aren't assigned to a dragon until after nine weeks of basic training. Given your extraordinary circumstances, Aracania needs to work with Thor separately until you finish."

The woman intervened when it was clear that Selena would not heed her warning. "Aracania will ensure Thor's comfort, Liongod. She and General Araneus have prepared his quarters, where Thor will have plenty of space and food. We raise fodder specifically for dragons to hunt in a penned area near your barracks."

Still unconvinced, Thor became her voice of reason instead. **I will go, only because I don't want to cause trouble with Vidar and his friend.**

If they mistreat you in any way—

Don't worry about me. I will be fine. However, if these foul gits mistreat you, I will burn this city to the ground. Thor snarled at Vidar as the half-elf reached for his reins but made no attempts to pull away.

I pray it won't come to that. After saying their farewells, Thor reluctantly followed Vidar down the road, tail still twitching.

Captain Bel, as he began taking his leave, scowled at her. "I will see you later this evening, *Liongod.*" Selena's smoldering eyes met his sneering gaze, but he left her with the stranger, devoid of further discussion.

The woman made a step forward with her head bowed. "I understand your apprehension given your circumstances, but I ask that you and Thor trust me for the time being." Confused, Selena spun around just in time to see the stranger lift her cowl. The sun blazed against her silver hair and tinted eyebrows; her delicate face glowed with the same copper-kissed shade as Selena's skin color. The lovely elven maiden's piercing blue eyes were magnified by the hue of the sapphires set within her golden crown. Selena's face drained of all color upon recognizing her royal host, and she immediately dropped to her knees.

And yet, a sense of familiarity washed over her, as if she had met this woman prior. Selena wasn't sure if it was a memory flashing through her mind, but she recalled herself as a little girl within this person's warm embrace. The woman's voice broke her thoughts and trance.

"Please, forgive me for failing to introduce myself earlier. I am the Empress of Armageddon, Aryl Aurora."

CHAPTER 12: THE INITIATION

Quivering, Selena feared she had disrespected Her Imperial Majesty; every uncomfortable second grew more unbearable than the last. "No, please forgive me, Your Imperial Highness. I had no idea."

"No, the fault is mine and Vidar's. He and Captain Bel failed to show the proper etiquette, let alone the introductions."

When Selena relayed the information to Thor, he was as appalled as she was; he expressed his desire to meet the Empress when the time would allow it formally. When Her Imperial Majesty gave her permission to stand, Selena nearly tripped over her feet, but she collected her bearings. "I'm surprised at the Council's utmost disrespect. Standing before someone of your stature will make anyone tremble in fear, and I pray I haven't insulted you, Your Imperial Majesty."

The Empress gave her a small, sad smile but completely disregarded her statement. "Liongod, you could never disrespect me. Rather, I can't tell you how happy I am to know that you and Thor made it here safely."

"We had some assistance, Your Imperial Majesty."

"Yes, I know. I ensured yours and Thor's safety without detection."

"Your Majesty, may I ask how is it that you know so much about us? Why risk so much on our behalf?"

"Of course, you may ask. However, I cannot answer that now. I fear our conversation isn't private, so please exercise extreme caution in the future." When she saw Selena's unsatisfied expression, the Empress reached into her cloak and pulled out a sealed rolled-up piece of parchment with an official wax stamp. "Do not open this until you are alone. It's for *your* eyes only." Selena bit her bottom lip; reluctant at first, she accepted the scroll and hid it under her shirt, treating the exchange as if it were clandestine. "Please, do as you're told for now unless I tell you otherwise. You and Thor must lay low, but you two should be fine." She gracefully strode past, head held high, and pointed at an awaiting carriage across the street. "That will take you to where you need to go. Until we speak again, my dear child."

Selena bent the knee to Her Imperial Majesty once more; pleased with their meeting, the Empress marched back to Rune Citadel.

As the blood-red sky loomed over the city, the dwarf-driven carriage drew closer to her destination down a quiet alley within the Garden District: Norrington Hall. Its many windows glowed from the fading sun; in awe, Selena saw numerous houses and manors throughout her trip, stretching far and wide across the open grassy fields within the wealthy territory. She could see the drawing room was brightly lit, and candlelight dimmed from the many bedroom windows: whoever lived here anticipated and expected her arrival.

After sending the coachman away upon drop off, Selena dusted off her clothes and approached Norrington Hall with heavy strides. Yet, before she had the chance to send a footman to alert her arrival, the front door swung open, and her heart sank to her stomach. Captain Ashur Bel's piercing bloody gaze nearly struck her down as he beckoned her inside.

Selena was given the grand tour of the august Norrington Hall, so named after Captain Bel's late father. As an only child, he inherited the estate once he became of age, shortly after Lord Norrington's untimely passing. "My manor is used in service for the Council. Her Imperial Majesty intended that you rest here shortly before reporting to the barracks," Captain Bel sternly scowled. "Quite unprecedented, but Vidar and General Araneus allowed it in your unique case." As he sized her with his eyes, he huffed. "I expect you have no skills."

Offended, Selena kept her tongue in check. "I will have the pleasure of proving you wrong."

"We shall see, and never forget to address me as either 'Sir,' or 'Captain.' Is that clear?" When Selena growled, Captain Bel's heated voice grew intense, "Mr. Liongod?"

"Yes, sir."

"That will do for now."

However, the visitation was cut short when Selena noticed three young girls sitting around a crystal ball in one of the many bedrooms. Captain Bel explained the three had the gift of visions, where they could focus and foresee images through a looking glass, allowing them to witness events happening in different parts of the world. During his account, Selena couldn't help but notice how their snow-white hair contradicted their supposed age, and she questioned if they were children at all.

The first, whose hair swept past her knees, donned her evening satin blue gown, extravagantly trimmed and decorated with lace and ribbons. Her sister —Selena assumed the three were triplets—tied her hair with a red ribbon, matching the color of her embellished dress. Lastly, the third, clad in green fashion, adorned her hair with a series of braids meeting in a single, thick ponytail. Their cold, pale faces matched their cumbersome expressions reflected against the glass orb.

Captain Bel ruefully introduced the triplets as the famous Oracles: Nona, the one in blue, Cassandra, wearing red, and Morta, donning all green. "They serve the Council—you will do well to avoid them as they will not waste their gifts on mere fortune-telling."

When the dinner bell rang downstairs from within the kitchen, he excused himself, briefly leaving Selena alone with the three sisters. Intrigued and curious, Selena nearly overstepped her boundaries by asking the triplets many questions regarding her past, but they interrupted her. "We will not answer your questions, Liongod." Baffled and her words lost, the Oracles added in unison: "When you find what you seek, the dragon will finally awaken."

"What in Oblivion does that mean?"

The Oracle triplets only giggled as they continued focusing on their looking glass.

When Captain Bel returned, he ordered Selena to follow him to the dining area, where supper and evening tea was served. Much to her surprise, the captain had two other guests staying with him for the moment to dabble more in the arcane arts and potion making through the Oracles' instruction, though they weren't recruits for the Force. She recognized Myrrdin as the first visitor, and the second was a young girl around their age, dressed in a sky blue evening gown: dark brown hair sweeping past her shoulders, freckles dotting her nose and arms. Her beautiful teal blue eyes lit from the dining table's flickering candlelight.

She smiled through her flushing pink face when Selena introduced herself. "It's a pleasure, Andric. I'm Niamh Wood. I've heard so much about you from Captain Bel and Myrrdin."

The two proceeded to enlighten Selena of their current arrangement with the Oracles, and soon, they expected to work with a third apprentice: Rahim was to begin in the morning. Much to her delight, Neith brought Rahim safely to the manor, where he could stay for as long as he worked with the Oracles. "Where is he?" Selena asked, hoping to visit him.

"Oh, he went to sleep a little before you arrived," Niamh said, "his spirits greatly lifted after Neith escorted him here, and he took his supper to his room."

Selena's heart soared to hear Rahim was doing well. Yet, as Niamh's and Myrrdin's conversation grew profound, a name was brought up that caught Selena's attention. "While here, I would watch out for Azrael," Niamh began her warning, "he and his dragon, Doragon, arrived shortly before you and Thor. The pair came out of the blue, just like you two."

Myrrdin bit his bottom lip. "That bloke isn't all bad."

"No? Bullocks. His troubled childhood gives him no excuse." Selena and Myrrdin stared at her, appalled by a young lady using inappropriate language. Ignoring their troubled expressions, her rants concerning Azrael's terrorizing behavior towards her and others grew with her temper.

The kitchen bell twinkled again, and Naomi, Captain Bel's chambermaid, arrived, interrupting their conversation upon serving dinner: roasted venison and vegetables, smoking potatoes with melted butter, and a platter with assorted fruits and cheeses. However, the captain remained absent from their dinner, and Selena preferred it that way.

Even with the captain's lack of company, the Pyre didn't fail to cast a gloomy spell over their banquet as it announced another hour had passed. Upon further inquiry, Myrrdin explained that Vidar initially approved the construction of the clock tower after the war. Confused by his longevity, Myrrdin clarified, "Elves and dwarves can easily live for hundreds of years. Even Her Imperial Majesty has ruled over Armageddon for damn near three centuries. As a half-elf, he could easily live to be half a millennium or more." Before Vidar took over, the Council was initially founded by Aydin Jormungand before the war; a good man and leader, a series of misfortunes led to his downfall. Losing his title and power, Vidar eventually took control, and Jormungand vanished without a trace. "Nobody knows what happened to that poor bugger," Myrrdin finished.

Selena suddenly grew distracted by Thor's snarls and growls. **Please tell me you're safe, my dear.**

Of course, I am. Why?

I feel a dark presence nearby, but I don't know what it is nor why it's here.

Selena whipped her head around, confused; when she reiterated that all was well, Thor still assured her that the aura was near. *I pray you're not paranoid.*

Nonsense. I know this feeling all too well.

Selena's skin prickled when Captain Bel's scornful voice shattered the dreary atmosphere, and she half-suspected him to be the evil looming in the area. "That's enough filling his head with stories. Liongod, General Araneus is growing impatient, and so am I. It's time for you to follow me."

As Selena said her farewells to Niamh and Myrrdin and grudgingly followed the captain out of Norrington Hall, he sternly said, "What you're about to endure can never be discussed with anyone outside the Force. The initiation is a ceremony testing your willpower, a sacred ritual performed since after the war." Captain Bel sneered, and when he believed Selena couldn't hear, he muttered, "You will most likely die." Her face became white as porcelain, and her feet froze to the ground; she only moved when the captain ordered, "Make haste, Liongod."

Flickering lampposts lined the eerily quiet streets, guiding the two towards the Dragon District. Believing that Captain Bel was possibly going against orders, Selena asked, "Is Her Imperial Majesty aware of the initiation?"

"Of course, she is, and so is the Council. The other recruits have finished their trials except for two last-minute stragglers like you—they are waiting."

The North Sea mirrored the pearl-grey clouds and glowing blue moon hanging over the Dragon District. The crisp cold smell of pine needles rose from the Hinterlands, gracing Selena's nostrils.

A vast field beyond the wall displayed the main building: four towers connected by tall, thick stone walls, framing a massive courtyard. Captain Bel led Selena to an imposing hall that rose from the nearest tower. The courtyard was cluttered with training equipment. Wooden targets and fake dummies lined up across the field for sword practice and archery, with a shooting range far beyond the courtyard closer to the back wall. Rows of large stables fit to house dragons lined the seaside, built upon heated flagstones for the dragons' resting places. A rainbow of scales murmured happily, stretching over the stones within their quarters. Swaths of the field beyond the barracks, close to the Hinterlands, were dedicated to the feeding grounds: wrought-iron fences penned the well-tended massive herds of cow, sheep, and pig.

Selena noticed two pathways by the doorway upon entering the musty hall: the right led to the soldiers' barracks through a spiraling staircase, but Captain Bel brought her attention to the locked metal door on the left. The two marched down the long and damp corridor until reaching a small medieval dungeon where two young men dressed in casual attire waited. She assumed them to be brothers due to their physical alikeness: lightly tan-hued skin, brown hair, matching amber eyes, wearing white cotton shirts with a dark red vest, white breeches, and leather shoes.

As Selena took her position beside the recruits, Captain Bel sauntered towards a tall, stone basin surrounded by three small wooden goblets on the ground. Thick black liquid filled the dish, its foul odor unbearable, making her skin crawl.

"We see you were late too," one commented; Selena sheepishly nodded.

Captain Bel cleared his throat. "This sacred ritual began with the One Hundred Years' War. As we were nearly overwhelmed by the Lich's demonic forces, the Council decided only to recruit the very best. Our soldiers have grown stronger over the years: to resist the demons' dark magic, we must drink the blood of our enemies."

The horrified trio trembled; Selena knew demon blood was poison, and she suddenly understood Captain Bel's snarky remark. Before she could fire her opinions of this barbaric ritual, the recruit beside her said, "W-won't this kill us?"

Captain Bel's lips twisted into a sneer. "It's a noble sacrifice we must make to resist the Lich and his army. Yes, not everyone can withstand its effects, and many have died during the initiation. However, we've also grown stronger."

The two young men looked at each other with glossy eyes, but Selena was the one who asked, "And what if we refuse?"

"Then you will die by my blade as per the Council's order. Once you begin the initiation, there is no turning back."

"What will happen if we die from the demon blood?" the third recruit asked.

"We will see that you receive a proper and honorable funeral, as we have done for countless others."

The three exchanged glances, and when Captain Bel was satisfied by their lack of further questions, the recruits proceeded forward in a single file. One by one, the captain filled their cup with the poison and handed it over; Selena received hers last. When Captain Bel gave the command, the first two enlistees nodded to each other and reluctantly took their first sip collectively. Selena, however, had yet to bring the black ooze to her lips. When the captain gave her a fierce glare, she closed her eyes as a few tears trickled down her face. Without another moment's hesitation, Selena took a quick drink from the goblet.

The black liquid tasted vile as soon as it touched her lips, reeking of death and decay. When she could no longer withstand its rancid flavor, Selena pulled her cup away. However, thus far, the three remained impervious, and they released a communal sigh in relief.

Selena caught herself grinning, but it quickly faded when she saw the smirk sneaking across Captain Bel's face. She dropped the goblet, and her head spun to the sudden shrieks of pain from the brothers. The two bent over, heaving up a nasty piled mess, holding their stomachs as their eyes rolled into the back of their heads.

Selena panicked, but she began to feel ill too. The taste started coming back up, and she hunched over as she retched blood. Her body burned as if she were on fire, and her muscles convulsed as she fell into a violent seizure; Captain Bel remained indifferent to their cries of excruciating pain. Every muscle in Selena's body began tearing itself apart; her vision grew blurry, and an ear-shattering ring left her deaf to what was happening around her. Suddenly, the shapes and colors melted away, leaving her in absolute darkness. An evil presence preyed upon her mind, and a shrill from the grave called her name; she was about to die.

Her body trembled from the pain, and as she collapsed, her mind began swirling into Oblivion.

CHAPTER 13: THE MIDNIGHT DUEL

Her ears resonated louder than a dragon's roar, but the constant ring slowly lessened as the minutes passed. Selena's blackened vision melted away, and the dungeon scene returned with a flash of blurry light.

Currently laying on her back, as her muscles finally relaxed and she could catch her breath, Thor's thundering voice shattered what remained of her thoughts. **Thank the Divines you came back.**

I....

Throat parched and cracked, Selena numbly reached forward, but her arm collapsed over her chest. Her racing heart nearly exploded. She tilted her head only to see Captain Bel standing in a corner and arms crossed behind his straightened back. He ignored her pleas for water, keeping his eyes transfixed on the brothers.

Selena rolled to her stomach, fighting her aching muscles, careful to avoid her messy vomit pile. As her ears finally cleared, she saw that one recruit wouldn't stir. His brother loomed over, shouting and screaming for him to wake, but Selena turned away. Her strength finally and fully returning, she stood up in between deep breaths and wiped the bile staining her mouth.

Seconds later, footsteps echoed down the corridor, and two men donned in black cloaks surrounded the body. The first one barked: "We just finished burying the others, Captain Bel."

"We have one more for the House of the Dead."

As the surviving brother swatted the caretakers away, Selena dashed over and held him back. He struggled and fought against her as the robed men carried his brother's body away. "No, you can't take Alexander. The Force was our only chance for a new life. We had nothing back home."

Captain Bel shook his head but offered no words of comfort for this loss. "He will receive an honorable funeral."

The initiate broke free of Selena's grasp, falling to his hands and knees as he sobbed. She joined his side with pain and understanding, and the two mourned in silence. After giving the two a few moments, Captain Bel ushered them out of the dungeon and back to the main hall. Awaiting their company was a tall, young elven man donned in a dark red coat with tails embellished with gold buttons and buckles; the wide collar showcased his white waistcoat contrasting his black breeches and hessian boots. Selena noted the many medals fastened to his jacket, marking his high rank within the Force.

Captain Bel and the highly decorated official exchanged pleasantries, and Selena's eyes widened when the captain introduced this man as General Araneus Morleth himself. Achieving his rank at twenty-four, he was considered the youngest war general in history. He wasn't as fair in complexion as most elves, but the alikeness to Alfheim's denizens was evident upon his narrow face; his maroon hair christened with silver streaks couldn't hide his pointed ears, nor his deep purple eyes.

He gave a quick salute to the recruits. They returned the same gesture, and Selena quickly addressed her commanding officer as she bowed, "Andric Liongod at your service."

As the general's eyes peered to the second, Selena nudged the recruit's arm. "Erik Bjornson, sir."

"Bjornson, I've heard of you. Your father was an honorable man. It's a pleasure to have you join us today. My condolences for your loss—Alexander will receive the same honor as those who have died fighting to protect the Empire. Captain Bel, have they recited the oath?"

"Sir, not yet."

"Then I will start." He placed his right hand over his heart and raised his left. Selena and Erik did the same. "Repeat after me. Upon my honor, I solemnly swear loyalty to Her Imperial Majesty and obedience to the officers of the Imperial Air Force." Selena's lips trembled as they repeated the words. "That I will bear true faith and allegiance to the same. May the Divines judge me and strike me down if I fail. Long live the Empire."

General Araneus gave the two a brief tour of the base to see the dining hall and the steam baths. During their trek up the tower stairs towards the barracks, he explained that the recreational room below was only for their lazy afternoons after finishing the day. "As my last recruits, I assign you two as bunker buddies. That means you will share a bunker and watch and support each other. You must be fully dressed in uniform and down at the courtyard by four-thirty in the morning for roll call. You will display any footwear in a perfect, imaginary line under your bed. I also want to see your laundry bags hung over the foot of your bed to keep the mildew problem at a minimum. I've assigned a chest to your bunker with two sets of keys; use it to lock your gear. You won't believe how many of my recruits have gotten into trouble for leaving their things unsecured, so develop the habit now.

"Basic training will be the hardest nine weeks of your lives, but you two will make fine soldiers," the general continued, "you can either like or hate me, but you will obey your trainers and me. After basic training, Bjornson, you will be assigned a dragon."

Erik stumbled over his feet as the three made it to the endless main hallway leading to their quarters, but he quietly replied, "Yes, sir."

General Araneus peered at Selena over his shoulder. "You're an extraordinary exception, Liongod. Pray don't disappoint Aracania or me."

"Thor and I will work hard, sir."

"Very good." The general paused after fishing out two keys and unlocked a door. Selena and Erik trudged inside across the squeaky floorboards towards the bunk bed with small, lumpy mattresses and clean linens folded on top; moonlight lanced through their high window that they could only reach from the top bunk. True to the general's promise, a locked rusty chest sat in front of the bed with its key on top. Gracing the walls were shelves stocked with different-sized training uniforms next to a single desk with a brightly lit lantern.

The two inspected their new quarters, and General Araneus gave Erik one key. "I will keep the other duplicate. When you are not in your room, I expect you two to lock this door. You only get one copy, so entrust one person to keep it safe. I expect you two ready and down on the training field with your brothers for roll call by four-thirty in the morning." General Araneus ordered.

Erik and Selena gave him a salute. "Yes, sir."

The general then pointed to the shelves. "Since we couldn't get you two appropriately sized, we had extras for you to choose."

"Thank you, sir."

Before he left, General Araneus announced, "Lights out," and closed their door.

As Selena grabbed the lantern and rummaged through the garments, Erik grumbled and handed her the room key before scrambling up the bunk's ladder and collapsing onto his newly claimed bed.

I wish I could help him. After finding baggy clothes to hide her womanly figure, Selena set them aside on the desk. Remembering she still carried the scroll given to her by the Empress, Selena unrolled it after making herself comfortable on the bed and read:

"Please, forgive me for the lack of formality, but this is the only way I can communicate with you without drawing attention. As you and Thor know, be wary of Vidar, but if you two remain hidden in the Force, the Council cannot touch you.

"Give my regards to Rahim. Loki recently sent word that he and Chaliss are safe in Nuvak for the time being; Neith had already extended the news to Rahim. Know this: you two aren't alone. You have allies."

Selena's heart raced with joy from the news; she smiled and understood Rahim must have been so happy. Yet, her impatient dragon poked and prodded her mind until she finally acknowledged him. **You've been ignoring me since the initiation.**

I'm sorry. I didn't mean to, but I was focused on General Araneus' instruction.

Aracania had already finished introducing herself earlier. Her rider could have been as courteous instead of keeping you all night.

When Selena heard Erik snore, she rolled the letter and held it over their small trash bin as she burned it with an ignited flame from her palm, the ashes drifting like snow. *There was a death.*

I heard.

As Selena unwrapped the cloth that flattened her chest, she added, *I still thought I was about to die. The other two didn't react as severely as I did.*

It doesn't matter; the point is you're alive.

She shuddered slightly with her following question. *What would you have done if I did? Would you have moved on to another?*

No. I would have lost my mind and found a way to off myself.

I would never want you to—

Thor hastily interrupted. **That's what I would have wanted. When I spoke with Aracania, she explained if you had died from the initiation, they would offer me the courtesy to join you in the afterlife.**

No—

I would have accepted it in a heartbeat.

The dreary conversation turning south fast, Selena couldn't help but shed a few tears if the reverse happened, and she ultimately said, *I would gladly accept that honor, too.*

She felt the warmth of his love envelope her. **Join me at the seaside.**

The general said it's lights out.

Then sneak out.

Careful not to wake Erik, Selena tip-toed across their rickety floors, maintaining the stealth ability of a mouse as she avoided the patrolling guards. Finally, she dashed across the open field towards Thor's quarters, but he was already flying to meet her halfway.

His giant shadow loomed over her, and he made a slow descent, hovering by beating his wings forward and backward. When Selena approached, Thor landed upon his haunches, wings still unfurled. His back bare of his harness, Thor's whole body gleamed from his evening bath in the sea and a fresh coat of oil, courtesy of the caretakers tending to the dragons. He snaked his head down until his snout gently bumped her forehead. **Please, let's not talk about death anymore.**

Of course. Selena then shared with him the good news of Chaliss' survival.

That is wonderful. I feel relieved, and I'm sure that you do as well.

And Rahim.

Thor extended out a single paw for her to take; as soon as she stepped within his grasp, he curled his talons before gracefully sweeping himself heavenward, his tail slithering off the ground. He took her high through the endless diamond sky above the barracks and the glistening North Sea. Selena had missed the air blowing through her face, the feeling of being weightless in the sky.

Thor steered around until they soared above the line of stalls housing the dragons. Selena had hoped Alfheim would provide better accommodations, but the dragons' quarters weren't much better than the ones from the Black Pub. *You deserve to rule over a diamond castle with a pile of treasure to guard, my dear.*

I would like to see if the Council could make better arrangements in the future. Thor's line of thought trailed off as he ticked away different ideas flashing through his mind. **We could always propose these changes to Vidar. What do you think?**

I will try to request an audience with him as soon as I'm able. It wouldn't hurt to try and see what he says and what they can afford to do.

Selena leaned against his claws as the wind swept past her face, enjoying their peaceful communion; she spread out her arms and closed her eyes, pretending that she was the one with opened wings. Thor's spirits lifted from her resolve, and he soared closer to the twinkling stars glistening over the ivory city. However, as soon as he circled back to the mainland, Selena suddenly felt the weight of despair press upon her shoulders.

Thor stopped abruptly when a golden flash zipped above the Hinterlands. Through the sinking pit in her stomach, Selena ruefully watched the oncoming silhouette of a massive dragon rushing towards them, set for a collision course.

No.

I will rip them apart. Thor growled and hissed through clamped fangs. Plumes of smoke writhed around his nostrils as his chest expanded from the sudden deep breaths, and he unleashed a thundering roar.

Peering through his clawed cage, Selena saw the same young man hunting them down astride the wretched Sunbeam Shieldtail that had been terrorizing them. Her face became white as a ghost, and the two sent chills and shivers down her spine. The pair reminded her of Death himself.

The boy's heartless expression was full of hatred and malice, his ashen skin nearly glowing in the moonlight. His black hair covered his ears, thick eyebrows resting over his cold, icy eyes. Over his right eye was the dreaded crescent-shaped scar Selena never wanted to see again, nor his necklace of Death.

His dragon seemed to wear the same face. It curled its upper lip as flames flared from its serrated fangs. Its metallic scales glowed like the smoldering sun, even at night. The dragon snorted when confronting Thor and Selena again and extinguished the flames from its maw.

The two enemies floated before them like a golden ghost waiting to strike.

The boy's lips curved into a sneer when he and Selena locked gazes. "So, you're one of the last-minute recruits?"

"We don't know you, nor do we care to know you." Selena's gut wrenched. *Why would he and his dragon be out in the open instead of disguised? Unless—*

"I'm surprised by you. I thought that you would have at least learned some manners if you're planning on hiding within the Force."

"Who are you, and what do you want with us?"

The boy looked bored and leaned up against one of his dragon's horns. "If you must know, you can call me Azrael." He then patted his dragon's thick armor-plated neck. "He is my partner, Doragon."

When she immediately recalled Niamh's story about Azrael and Doragon, Selena felt like she was spiraling out of the sky and into Oblivion's endless abyss. *He and Doragon are masquerading as recruits as well.*

While Thor kept his eyes locked on Doragon like a wolf stalking its prey, she asked, "What did you and the Order do with Silver? Is he—?" She couldn't finish. Thor shared her sentiments by giving Doragon a few half snarls.

Azrael only shrugged. "Dunno. Maybe he is, but maybe he isn't."

Thor half-opened his maw to show off the ferocity of his fangs, and Doragon did the same. Thor didn't back down despite the golden dragon's advantage of size. **I will tear him apart and peel off his luster-less scales one by one.**

No. Let's get out of here and report this to General Araneus immediately. She tightened her grip on Thor's claws as her heart nearly burst from her chest, and Thor steered himself away.

However, Azrael and Doragon raced past them again before Thor could make his descent. "Going so soon?"

After the two dragons exchanged air-piercing snarls, Thor dropped to the ground and landed near the trees on the beach. However, despite his massive bulk, Doragon was a fast flier. He made a nosedive with eyes locked on Thor and nearly toppled him, but as Thor evaded, keeping Selena safe within his claws, Doragon swiped at him once before backing down.

When Azrael ordered Doragon to stay back, Thor deemed it safe to release Selena from his talon confinement. However, he still herded her close with a protective arm; eyes turned into slits as flames plumed from his maw. Though she would pose no threat to Doragon, Selena still ensured to remain beside Thor to protect him; she spread out her arms as if to shield him from Doragon's wrath.

Azrael, however, remained calm and ignorant of her wasted efforts as Doragon reluctantly helped his companion dismount; Azrael stuffed his hands into his pockets with his head tilted. "Congratulations on passing the initiation. I'm surprised you didn't die like all the others—I was looking forward to being invited to another funeral."

"You've been following us since Helshire Village." When Azrael burst into laughter and Doragon opened his maw wide enough to swallow her whole, her anger boiled and would soon erupt like a volcanic explosion when she realized they were wholly responsible for the settlement's fate. "You two burned it down."

Azrael casually shrugged, uncaring that she caught him. "Kudos to you. Too bad your mother didn't make it."

"*Matu* is safe far away from here," Selena sternly retorted, her blazing eyes ready to incinerate the two.

"So, not your mother then. It makes no difference to me, but I can't allow you to leave here and report me. But if the word were to slip out about you and Thor—"

He's blackmailing us, Thor growled and bared his fangs again.

We could always do the same to him and Doragon. What kind of game is he playing?

"I've been longing for this moment, as you two have evaded me for months. You're just a child and a girl, no doubt."

The two had her and Thor cornered like scared rats; Thor lifted his wings to make himself look more intimidating, and Doragon did the same. Selena feared that Doragon would strike them down at any moment as he leaned back on his haunches, tail thumping against the ground.

Azrael laughed. "Wait until the Council hears about this. A girl disguised as a boy in their ranks—you two would be executed on the spot."

"And if the Council were to find out about you being one of the Order, you and Doragon would be, too."

"That does put a damper on our relationship, but I'm willing to take that risk." Doragon's lips curved into a sneer, matching his rider's smug expression. Thor dug his nails into the ground, preparing to attack and anticipating Doragon's preemptive strike.

Azrael jerked his hands in her direction before Selena could move, summoning fire waves slashing her down. Rolling across the dirt, Selena gritted her teeth but immediately stood up once the flames disappeared and took a defensive stance, creating her magma shell to protect herself. Azrael took a step back when he realized what she could do and smiled. "So, you can use magic. I was beginning to wonder." Doragon roared, and before lunging at Thor, Azrael ordered him to stop and stand aside. "Do not interfere."

Thor bared his fangs, but Selena asked him to do the same. **Are you sure?**

Yes. This fight is mine alone. Do not attack unless Doragon does first.

Azrael got into a more relaxed state, and his hands hung low. As he flickered his fingers, blue energy spheres erupted from his palms, and two spirit pistols took form within his grasp; he aimed both guns at her. Selena bit her inner cheek until she tasted blood. "You know how to use Aether."

Azrael's eyes widened in genuine shock. "Where did you learn that? Oh, let me guess: Silver, yes?"

"You two must be acquainted somehow and not as enemies. Is Silver part of the Order, too?"

Instead of answering, Azrael fired one warning bullet over her head. Understanding that he wouldn't back down from their duel, Selena plucked strands of fire from her shield and created a sword with a curved blade. She cooled the grip, hardening to obsidian, while magma dripped from the weapon.

Azrael began firing; the spirit bullets pierced right through her shell. After the second shot, the shield shattered like glass, leaving her defenseless. "How is that possible?" Selena asked.

"Aether is much stronger than any single element. The only way you could stop me is if you knew how to channel spirit energy, but all I see is a weakling."

Selena gripped her molten sword through clenched teeth and dashed forward, her blade aimed directly for Azrael's chest. Unfazed by her oncoming attack, he held up one pistol and shot at her weapon, destroying it to pieces that floated like ash drifting to the earth. Yet, while he was distracted, Selena reached behind her back with her free hand, pulling a blazing dagger out of thin air; Azrael's widened as he was caught utterly unprepared by her second strike. Selena side-stepped him before he could recover and wrapped one arm around his neck while holding the dagger to his throat.

Azrael swallowed hard as he dropped his Aether pistols, and the guns vanished in a plume of smoke. "I won't lie, I underestimated you. I won't do that again." Doragon roared and flew down to save him, but Thor blocked his path; the two dragons were about to exchange a flurry of claws and fangs, but Azrael ordered Doragon to stand down.

Sweat dripped down her face as she pressed the flaming blade deeper into his skin. "I will let you go if you leave us alone." Azrael looked down at her dagger and blew on it like a candle. It turned to smoke and vanished, and Selena quickly stepped back.

Soon, the barracks were in an uproar: the dragons from the stalls growled and roared, irritated by being woken up in the middle of the evening, and a group of five patrol guards ran down the beach with weapons drawn.

"Halt! Put your hands up, now," one sentry demanded. Selena and Azrael exchanged unpleasant expressions as the guards surrounded them with pointed guns. Thor and Doragon carefully inched towards their handlers, smoldering eyes locked on one another.

Captain Bel wasn't far behind; he emerged from the shadows, piercing eyes threatening to lance the two for breaking curfew. After explaining to the city guards they were new soldiers, the sentries lowered their weapons and stepped back. The captain leaned down and glared at the two handlers. "What in Oblivion were you two and your dragons doing out of bed this late at night?"

"Nothing, we were just...." Selena trailed off. Pain swelled within her chest as she wanted to tell them about Azrael and Doragon, but she bit her tongue. Looking at Azrael from the corner of her eye, they stared at each other with such disgust, but the two were in silent agreement. "We were training." Selena looked down at her feet.

"Training this late? That's reckless. Is this true, Azrael?"

"Aye." It looked like Azrael wanted to say more, but he sucked in his cheeks.

Captain Bel scanned the two before spinning around to face their dragons. "Doragon and Thor, take your riders back to the barracks and return to your stalls afterwards. General Araneus will not hear about this, but he will receive a full report if this happens again, and I will take disciplinary action. Am I clear?"

"Yes, sir," Azrael and Selena said simultaneously.

"Good. Dismissed."

As Captain Bel and the guards left the beach, Azrael spat at the ground before mounting his dragon. "Have fun in the morning." Doragon snarled, and the pair flew away.

Thor nudged her arm, his heated gaze still fixed on Doragon's fading figure. **I will go after Azrael if he hurts you in any way.**

He won't. If he does, the Council will immediately know, and so will the rest of the Empire. He won't take the risk. She collapsed into his paw, and Thor carried her back to the barracks, the two finally able to savor the night's quiet ballad.

CHAPTER 14: THE VENOMOUS SERPENT

Swallowed and swirling within the void, Selena panicked; her mouth filled with the vilest taste that ever plagued her lips. Shaking and trembling, she curled into a ball, shaking and quivering from the sight of her crimson tainted skin.

An ear-shattering shrill from beyond the grave screeched through her mind: "I can give you death. I'll show you that it's so much easier to give up and fade away into nothing...."

The dark presence vanished, and the void melted like spilt oil paint. Selena's eyes burst open, and she stood within Hinterlands before the giant metal door leading to the abandoned dwarven ruin. She instinctively tried to open it, but the sealed closed door wouldn't budge. Unsure of what made her want to open it, the mysteries and secrets concealed within were more than she could bear. The unknown was frightening but also captivating.

The door burst open only when she backed away, and the black void swallowed her.

Selena's muscles ached when the Pyre awoke her, her heart beating fast like it was about to explode; the clock chimed three in the morning.

Eyes fluttering open as her vision focused, she collapsed back into the sheets and pillows and nearly fell back asleep until she shot up, remembering she was in the barracks.

My dear.

Her heart fluttered like a bird hearing Thor's voice after enduring that nightmare. *I'm up.*

Good. Aracania is already parading across the field with her wake-up roars. Though faint, Selena's ears picked up her cries.

Good luck, my dear.

You, too.

Erik was still asleep, but she ignored his snores and the pain burning her body as she went to the desk with her clothes and, after wrapping her chest and the mark on her hand, she changed into her training uniform. After tying the drawstrings of her baggy pants, she paused when Erik moaned from his top bunk when he heard her shuffling around.

Selena climbed up the ladder and shook his shoulders. "Erik."

"What?" he mumbled and rubbed his eyes. Before Selena could speak, he pushed her hands out of the way. "I'm up." The two slid down the ladder, and when he changed, Selena faced the corner and tied her boot laces together as an excuse to give him some privacy. Face burning, she focused on locking her belongings in the chest, but Erik ignored her shame.

Even though he didn't say, Selena knew what ran through his mind. The lines under his cold and grim eyes gave it away; he hardly slept. She couldn't imagine being in his shoes, hoping to find a new beginning with possibly the only family he had left. All she could say was, "If you need to talk, I'm here."

Erik huffed and threw his old clothes in the sack hanging from his bed. He shuffled out the door, and Selena followed; the two melded with the tired crowd marching and yawning down the corridor and towards the courtyard.

The brisk, cold air kissed against her cheek; though it was springtime in mid-Azniine, Selena's breath turned to fog as the group of about thirty recruits trekked across the frost-tipped grass. She carefully looked around to see if Azrael had joined their line-up, but he wasn't anywhere to be found. When she asked Thor about Doragon, he confirmed his absence, too.

Those two couldn't be bothered to show, yet they're supposed to be recruits like us.

Hopefully, they'll face a court-martial trial.

As they lined up single-file, General Araneus appeared from the shadows as the Pyre read four-thirty, followed by Captain Bel and someone Selena thought she would never see again. Her smile brightened up the darkened courtyard. "Silver."

As if he heard, Silver immediately signaled her out and gave her a sly smile as he continued walking beside Captain Bel, head held high and hands clasped behind his back, donning the same uniform as his partner, but in white with blue and gold trimmings. It was then that Selena realized he was Captain Altessa, which explained his vast knowledge of magic, dragons, and Alfheim's customs.

Selena eagerly poked at Thor's consciousness. *Silver is Captain Altessa. He's coming out to introduce himself now with Captain Bel.*

Thor hummed in delight. **I had a feeling Azrael was only bluffing—that is fantastic news, and that explains so much.**

I'm wondering if he's a handler. Have you seen and met his companion yet?

I've met Jade, Captain Bel's companion, but I haven't seen Silver's. Perhaps he doesn't have one?

But I thought all soldiers had dragons.

Maybe not everyone does.

General Araneus stopped and faced the new group. Before he spoke, Aracania soared overhead with her flight of new dragons, with Thor among them. Thor took a moment to look down until he saw Selena among the lineup and gave a series of chirps and clicks in approval before continuing his course.

Once the dragons passed over, General Araneus began: "Welcome to your first day of basic training. I'm warning you now that today will be the hardest. This group of recruits is the smallest we've ever worked with, but all of you will make fine soldiers for the Force. Allow me to introduce you to Captain Ashur Bel." As he gestured towards him, everyone bowed in respect; Ashur extended the same courtesy. "And to Captain Silver Altessa, our newest achievement." Silver took a bow as well. "Some of you may have difficulty doing so, but you will obey their every order. You will be surprised by how many have faced a court-martial for not following that simple rule. I will expect you to uphold the oath you made after the initiation." Selena turned to face Erik, who looked down at his toes, ignoring her gaze.

Over the next few minutes, General Araneus went over the same rules he had discussed with Selena and Erik the night before. After he finished, he gave one final salute before stepping away, leaving Ashur and Silver in charge.

"I'll continue from here," Ashur growled to Silver and took his place. Silver moved out of the way but glared at his co-captain as if he wanted to object. "By the end of your nine weeks with me, you will all come to hate me, but you will learn discipline and respect. I will grind you into the ground, so you will know how worthless you are. You are not dragon riders yet—you will have to earn that respect and right, and we will start by learning obedience. If any of you move by the time I return, I will see that all of you run the entire perimeter of Alfheim. Do I make myself clear?"

"Sir, yes, sir," everyone shouted at different times.

"I can't hear you."

"Sir, yes, sir," all the recruits responded again in unison, their voices roaring and vibrating off the stone walls.

Silver looked as though he were about strike Ashur down himself, but he held back. The two spun away to leave the group in the frigid cold. However, Selena faintly overheard their conversation. "Don't you think that's harsh?" Silver asked crudely.

"I understand that this is your first day as a captain, so I will forgive you for not seeing it my way."

Silver's voice rose with his brewing wrath. "This is barbaric, and you know it—leaving them out in near-freezing temperatures. Do you want them to die of hypothermia?"

"It's nowhere near cold enough, and you will learn your place, *Captain.*"

"But your behavior is even colder. We're supposed to start them off with drills, per General Araneus."

"They will begin drills after we teach them a lesson. It's to show them respect, diligence, and obedience," Ashur paused before sneering, "they will understand that they are just lowly pawns for the Council's wars."

Silver stopped abruptly and looked back, catching Selena's eyes before walking away. However, while the recruits shivered, she remembered his previous training; she wallowed within a summoned warm embrace through deep and steady breathing. Flames plumed from her nostrils upon exhaling like a dragon ready to breathe fire, and the cold no longer bothered her.

Selena looked at the others shaking in their boots, and Erik raised a brow at her incredible skill. She turned her head this way and that before whispering instructions to him on what she had achieved. He possessed enough skill to use magic, and when no one was looking, Erik brought his hands to his mouth and, after a few attempts, replicated her technique by breathing tiny embers to warm his palms. One by one, Selena whispered her instructions down both sides of her lined formation, and the intelligence spread like wildfire. Some recruits could accomplish the feat, while others couldn't; those with the aptitude huddled close with the unsuccessful bunch and shared a small open flame hidden within their clasped hands in case Captain Bel watched.

Selena couldn't tell how long they stood outside: minutes turned to hours. The new soldiers looked around, but they maintained their warm basal temperature through periodic breathing techniques, and Selena couldn't help but smirk at defying Ashur's barbaric instructions. The sun peeked over the horizon, and the young recruits no longer needed to use the skill; the formation filled with whispers of gratitude, "Thank you, Liongod." Then, the Pyre chimed six in the morning.

Finally, the formation heard footsteps behind, and the whispers immediately stopped. Selena's eyes followed Ashur's sneaky movements, and he carried a vast sneer as if he believed he won their respect. "I see all of you are still here, just as I ordered. Perhaps you have what it takes to make it through the training." He pulled out a whistle draped around his neck and blew hard to get everyone's attention. "All of you will now head back inside for hygiene care and clean your room. When you finish, your breakfast will be waiting for you in the dining hall; then, you will report back here ten minutes before the Pyre chimes again. When you return, we will begin drills. You are dismissed from my sight."

As the formation scattered, the recruits continued muttering about "Liongod's brilliant skills" and "Liongod told that foul old git what's for." When they passed her, each one said thank you, and Selena's face beamed with satisfaction for making Ashur look like a fool. Silver must have overhead, as when he and Selena locked gazes on the courtyard before she marched inside, he smiled proudly.

They all had less than an hour to complete their morning tasks; Selena rushed through to finish on time. Unfortunately, she had to remake her bed several times to ensure her sheets weren't crinkled and all the corners were underneath the mattress. Erik also had some trouble; it was more difficult doing it from the top bunk, so Selena volunteered to help him.

The two hurried through their breakfast of cornmeal and salted crackers with small pieces of assorted berries. Upon finishing, the recruits returned to the courtyard ten minutes before five, where Ashur and Silver continued with further instructions. Most of their days, they explained, would be busy practicing drills, as they were important in keeping the group together in times of combat and ensuring everyone was always battle-ready.

It was a rough start: Captain Bel taught them the command flanks as they marched around the training grounds, but the sluggish group moved in different directions and tripped over one another through his yells. On the other hand, Silver stood behind him, smoldering eyes blazing from behind his spectacles. Anytime he attempted to give a command, Captain Bel immediately asserted his dominance by shouting out contradicting orders. After several hours, Captains Bel and Altessa ordered the soldiers to head towards the sparring field next to the shooting range.

However, Silver trailed behind, allowing Ashur control, and eventually caught up with Selena. "You were bloody magnificent, and that tosser still believes he taught you all a lesson."

She smiled. "I had a great teacher; let him keep believing that. It's so good to see you, Silver."

"It's Captain Altessa now," he said and winked, "don't let the others hear you address me otherwise, and you are a great pupil. I couldn't ask for a better student."

Selena blushed from the compliment. "Oh, yes, of course, Captain. But I thought something terrible had happened to you."

"I've told you before to not worry about me."

"How did you escape? I saw a dragon before we left."

Silver nervously chuckled and scratched the back of his head. "A dragon, you say?"

Selena's smile faded as Silver was again keeping secrets. "I could have sworn I saw one saving your life. Was that your companion? Are you a rider too?"

"The Order didn't stand a chance against me, and no, not at all. Captain Bel is, however. His partner, Jade, is an Imperial Pearlscale, an uncommon breed, and he likes to keep to himself. Unfortunately, Jade shares the same attitude of despising others and tends to stay away from the public eye—you may or may not get a chance to see him."

Disappointed by his sudden drift in conversation, Selena couldn't imagine Captain Bel ever having a dragon of his own; she supposed their companionship fitting as the two deserved each other. She knew the Imperial Pearlscales were more regal in appearance, and like Aracania, the strikingly white dragons possessed the rare ability over venom that ate through flesh, bone, and even metal.

Silver maintained reluctance in answering how he managed to escape; Selena wanted to press the subject further but understood this moment wasn't appropriate. Instead, he said again, "Now, we should probably get going before Ashur has a heart attack. The Divines forbid if he ever does." He pretended to make gasping noises while clutching his chest as they followed the other soldiers; Selena nudged his arm to make him stop, but she laughed too.

The new soldiers circled the large sparring area as Captain Bel made his way center field, holding a sword. Behind him was a large, old barrel carrying many long, wooden sticks.

Silver broke away as Selena took her place among the formation, and she twirled her head around to see Thor and the other dragons again but to no avail.

Captain Bel smacked the side of his barrel to get her attention. "For those with a dragon, you are not allowed to communicate with your partner. In the future, the dragons will be wearing a special amulet preventing communication—a masterpiece that I call the Silent Vow if I say so myself. It's an invention made by the scholars and mages for the Council. If I catch anyone distracted or in a daze, you will answer to me." Ashur's heated gaze made Selena's blood boil; she knew he antagonized and called her out specifically.

That can't be true. I just spoke with you earlier. No response. *Thor?* Her dragon still didn't reply, and her dread threatened to crush her. *No....*

Even Silver looked horrified by this design, but Captain Bel continued: "During these nine weeks, we will train all of you to fight with a sword, a firearm, and a bow, as part of your formal curriculum. We will also teach you how to be self-reliant, where you will learn how to make and take care of your weapons, how to survive if ever stranded, and so on. Afterwards, you will get to choose your specialization. A true soldier is versatile, and it is also the tradition that you use our forge to make your weapons upon advancement, as they will be an extension of yourself.

"Sword fighting is a crucial and essential practice that you must learn. All the dragon riders know how to use a blade. Today you will learn the very basics of how. Everyone, grab a stick from the barrel behind me. We will not use actual swords yet, as we don't want any accidents here." Her legs felt like lead with every step she took as the recruits got in line to grab their weapon while Captain Bel continued: "Everyone, find your bunker buddy and partner up. Once you do, you two will line up and face each other, like so." Captain Bel barked again as he and Silver modeled his command; the soldiers followed suit. "The first rule in sword fighting is to relax. It is easy to tense up in combat, but it's crucial to let your body stay loose. It is also traditional that you always begin by showing respect to your opponent by giving a bow at the beginning of each match. Observe."

Silver and Ashur gave the demonstration and held up their wooden swords as if they were in an actual duel. Captain Bel stepped forth and swung his weapon in Silver's direction with finesse and grace. However, Silver blocked his attack and knocked Ashur's sword clear from his hands through a twirl of his blade. Some young boys snickered, and Silver smiled.

However, Ashur narrowed his eyes; his face beat red from this humiliating defeat, and he pointed to those closest still laughing. "What are you laughing at? Twenty push-ups from you three—count them out."

"The rest of you practice disarming your partner," Silver called out to keep the training moving, but his icy stare was ready to strike Ashur down.

"Yes, sir," the rest of the recruits shouted and hastily followed his orders. Ashur gnashed his teeth before snatching his weapon off the ground but didn't interrupt Silver's instructions.

Erik motioned for Selena to follow him as they took their place among the line of soldiers already practicing. After ensuring they had enough space, they attempted to take the same stance as Silver and Ashur before striking each other with their sticks.

Selena saw Silver approach from the corner of her eye, but Erik struck her upper left arm amidst her distraction and mumbled. "You're supposed to disarm me."

Face burning with shame, she apologized for her distraction; Silver observed her form from afar and dashed to her side, switching to a more relaxed stance. "You need to keep your balance. That's the second rule. Because with that, you can strike or parry without getting hit."

"Yes, sir."

Her shame grew, but Silver wasn't bothered. "Look down at my feet. Try to keep them at shoulder's width apart, and when you move to strike your opponent, ensure that your feet are spread and not close together. When you do parry an attack, keep the blade close and try to predict your opponent's movements and attacks so that you can counter them." Selena repeatedly practiced the stance that Silver showed her until he was satisfied with her form. Hers and Silver's initial duel played through her mind, but Silver pretended it never happened, possibly to continue their ruse. Though she was naturally proficient, Selena closely followed his instructions.

After about an hour of going through their training swordplay, Selena learned that there were thirteen basic rules to remember. Silver went through the entire list during their session. "Captain Bel and I will be going over them with you throughout basic training. By your last week, you will have them all memorized." Silver smiled and winked. Meanwhile, Ashur observed Silver's training methods without saying a word, scowling from his claimed corner, but he didn't interfere.

After the lesson, the soldiers practiced drills again for the rest of the day, having only a small break for lunch. They had fifteen minutes to eat their meal of salted pork, a few fresh vegetables of carrots and peas, and more hardtack. They were finally dismissed around five in the evening to catch up on their chores, wash their clothes, relax, and prepare for the next day. Her body ached as she stumbled out of the training grounds, and all Selena could think was how to endure the next nine weeks.

She perked up as she saw Neith's fox mask gleaming over the flowing sea of recruits dispersing to their leisure activities. Her Imperial Majesty's advisor moved with haste and purpose as if she were on a mission. She called for Selena's attention with a message from Rahim and left after delivering the letter; since Loki was still in Nuvak tending to Chaliss, Selena assumed Neith had accepted the messenger role for now. Tearing it open, Rahim requested to see her in about an hour at Norrington Hall.

Marching back to Captain Bel's estate, Rahim, the Oracles, Niamh, and Myrrdin waited outside the front gates, but they didn't see her approach. Instead, Rahim and Niamh were caught in a deep, heated discussion regarding a young lady named Maria, a friend Niamh had invited over for evening tea with Captain Bel's permission. Somehow, Rahim wholly convinced himself that Maria was a vampire; Selena tried not to laugh, as his claims made her immediately remember Kain.

Niamh wasn't amused. "Rahim, there are no such things as vampires."

"Yes, there are. I know of a secret group called the Shadow Templars—assassins who serve Her Imperial Majesty."

Niamh rolled her eyes but immediately saw Selena and waved her over. "Andric, it's so good to see you again."

When she joined their group, one by one, they asked her many questions about what her first day of training was like, and of course, she was more than willing to oblige. Selena offered Rahim a hug to commemorate the good news regarding Chaliss' survival, and his face made the whole sky light up like the morning sun. "Silver is here as well, and he's a captain, no doubt."

Rahim was surprisingly happy to hear of Silver's safe journey to Alfheim. However, at the very mention of his name, Myrrdin's eyes pierced the crowd, but no one noticed his sudden change in expression. Rather, he promptly excused himself and rushed down the street. The others commented on his odd behavior, but the triplets watched Myrrdin vanish with glum faces.

After gossiping about Myrrdin's near theatrical performance, Niamh suddenly looked behind Selena and gestured towards a new face whom Rahim began cowering from, and Selena assumed the approaching young lady to be Maria. Though Rahim's allegations held no merit, Selena couldn't help but slightly wonder, given Maria's more morbid appearance: black hair as beautiful as the night decorated with a blood-red headband, extenuating her deep violet eyes and fair complexion.

She had already switched to her black evening gown, decorated in pink lace and red ribbons; the hem flowed and danced with every step she made as Niamh properly introduced her to the group. Rahim, meanwhile, continued casting disapproving glances through his furrowed brows.

When Niamh finished, Maria eyeballed Selena up and down with a quizzical look. "You're the one who everyone is talking about then?"

Her low, soft voice tinted with sadness and despair didn't excuse the insulting remark; Selena's eyes flared with sparks. "Pardon me, but how is that to appropriately address someone?"

Realizing her mistake, Maria recoiled from Selena's smoldering words. "Please forgive me. I shouldn't have been so forward. Rumors have been spreading about a new soldier arriving with a feral dragon. That's the first time anyone has heard of it, aside from Azrael's case. Rogue dragons don't exactly take to civilians."

"Thor is different, and I've earned his loyalty."

"I'm sorry, please don't take offense. If anything, I'm happy to see that not all wild dragons are the same and that Thor trusts you completely."

Despite Myrrdin's untimely absence, the group joined together for evening tea in the parlor—save for the Oracles, who excused themselves to continue their work for the Council in secret. Rahim kept one eye fixed on Maria; however, he even relaxed after Naomi served scones and biscuits, and Rahim casually exchanged pleasantries with the two ladies.

Selena dissolved her spoonful of honey in her green tea while Niamh continued peering at her in secret. Yet, though she didn't see it at first, Selena noticed Niamh's odd behavior around her specifically. When Niamh blushed and turned away, Selena's face turned a light shade of pink when she picked up subtle hints.

After the sun completely disappeared from the sky, Maria announced her need to leave and exchanged farewells with everyone. However, she muttered in Selena's ear, "May the Black Fox hide you."

Hearing someone else refer to Gundisalvus by his secret code name made Selena shiver, and she instantly wanted to know Maria's connection to the ill-fated man. But Maria had already left Norrington Hall, returning to her home within the Sky District.

While Selena was dazed and confused by Maria's secret exchange, Rahim murmured to Niamh, "I need to have my wooden stakes ready in case she sneaks into my room and drinks my blood."

Selena's nostrils flared as she retorted with her head still turned away, "She's not a vampire."

"It doesn't matter to the stake."

Turning a deaf ear to Niamh giggling at their banter, Selena announced it was time for her to return. She and Rahim shared their goodbyes; she wished to avoid Niamh's amorous display, but when Niamh offered to walk her to the Dragon District, Selena found herself standing on a precipice and eventually agreed. After being trapped in an eternity of uncomfortable silence during their trek, Selena asked, "How long have you and Maria known each other?"

"For as long as I can remember. I know Maria looks like she might bite, but she's a lovely person."

"Good luck in trying to convince Rahim otherwise." Selena laughed.

Niamh grinned and cleared her throat. "Are you and Rahim together?"

Selena almost tripped over herself and, without warning, burst out laughing, enthralled and entertained that someone mistook them for a couple a second time. Regardless of her disguise, Selena guessed that others didn't seem bothered by what they perceived to be their amiable relationship. Niamh, however, failed to see the humor in her question. "Of course not. Rahim is my brother."

Selena raised a brow when Niamh took a breath of relief; she wondered if her original notions were misconstrued, and perhaps Niamh had taken to Rahim instead. "Oh, I just wasn't sure. You and Rahim seemed very close and…." Her voice trailed off, though it was as if she wanted to say more. Selena gave a crooked smile, but when Niamh saw her expression, face blaring red, she immediately spun on her toes and marched back to Norrington Hall. "It has been a pleasure, Andric."

Selena watched Niamh skip back to Captain Bel's manor with a mystified brow. "What was that all about?"

Immediately upon her return to the barracks, Selena relaxed after supper and finished her remaining chores. Twilight seemed bleak and dull without Thor; she had attempted to see him earlier, but the patrolling guards caught her sneaking from her bunker.

Captain Altessa got involved and dismissed the sentries, only to reassure Selena that their separation was for the best right now. When she still wouldn't accept his answer, Silver carefully added, "Remember when I told you that those in Dragonspire could help identify his breed? They're currently working hard to test his abilities whenever he's not training with Aracania."

"Is it necessary for him to continue wearing that Divine awful amulet?"

Silver's tone had softened. "I apologize, my dear —that wasn't my decision, but the Council's. It won't be for too much longer, I promise."

After it was lights out, Selena instead snuck into the steam baths to wash after the soldiers were in bed. Though she could have done the alternative through controlled burns to kill the bacteria, soap and water were much more soothing.

The following day, Selena immediately awoke when she heard the Pyre strike three in the morning, the sky still pitch black. She forced herself to stay awake, knowing that Captain Bel would punish her if she failed. Selena then let herself roll off the bed and got on her hands and knees. Getting herself into the standard push-up position, she did ten to wake herself up. After finishing her morning stretches and exercises, she reached for her clean shirt and trousers.

She heard Erik stir in his bed as he drove himself up. Although he had been quiet since the initiation, Erik still found a way to get through the day, and Selena did what she could to be there for him.

Like the day before, the recruits filed a single line, and as the clock read four-thirty, Ashur and Silver walked onto the training field. Instead of standing out in the cold for hours, the captains immediately instructed the soldiers to march and practice plank orders. They improved considerably since yesterday, with minor errors.

When the Pyre struck six, the routine was the same: clean their bunkers, hygiene, and breakfast. Fortunately, their room wasn't too messy; hardly any cleaning was needed other than just making their beds. Yet, Azrael still hadn't shown up for basic training, and Selena wondered if he and Doragon had been involuntarily discharged. *That would be a relief if Thor and I never saw those two again.*

After meeting again in the training courtyard, a contingent of heavily armed guards stood single-file behind the two captains, weapons and shields ready. Their intimidating presence made the group pause briefly before Captain Bel urged them forward. When Selena looked at Silver, silently questioning what was happening, he raised his hand, telling her to wait.

Captain Bel announced: "Today is going to be a little different. We will learn about some of the dangerous creatures you may encounter on the battlefield. Today, our added security is for your protection because you will meet one face to face." A sharp gleam flashed across his eyes, and Selena suspected foul play. "The Oracles helped us track down this creature in particular—"

"We're here," Nona interrupted, arriving from the main hall with Cassandra and Morta following close.

Cassandra continued, "Be prepared for a big surprise—"

"That the Council planned for you." Morta finished, holding a glowing bottle of liquid gold, but her eyes targeted Selena from the crowd; Selena wondered if this was a warning, and she grew tense.

Captain Bel grinned at the triplets, and Selena's throat swelled when he thanked them for gathering the venom sample. "Do any of you know what this is?" When he received the consensus as no, Ashur frowned from their lack of knowledge. "This is Marcupo venom, a common ingredient used by assassins in most poisons."

Captain Bel waved his free hand, and a large, thick book with a black cover appeared in a puff of smoke above his outstretched palm. The tome's pages flipped open like a deck of shuffling cards until it stopped: a giant black snake with a red crest at the top of its head appeared on the page. Selena held her breath and recognized it as the same creature that hunted Gundisalvus in her dream.

The picture came to life as it popped out of the page, the miniature animation moving independently. "The Marcupo is closely related to the Mameleu, a large and highly venomous snake species native to Runefell. It is the fastest moving land snake, over five meters per second. This beast is infamous for delivering multiple strikes, injecting large amounts of toxic venom that spreads rapidly within the bitten tissue. The unusual composition of toxins in the venom causes severe envenomation and death much faster than any other snake in the world. Neurological, respiratory, and cardiovascular symptoms quickly manifest, usually within minutes. However, it is common to deliver dry bites as a warning."

Even a dry bite could tear your arm off, given the size of its fangs. Selena shuddered.

"Another interesting fact is that the Marcupo is attracted to the smell of its venom, even as it flows through its prey's veins; the substance tends to make it react more violently. Untreated Marcupo bites have a one hundred percent mortality rate.

"Aside from dragons, this snake species has the longest lifespan of any known creature—the oldest reported specimen lived to eight hundred in captivity." Captain Bel closed the book, and it disappeared in a cloud of smoke. "The Oracles helped us track its whereabouts, as they're rare in Armageddon." As if on cue, a gentle hiss echoed from the shadowed tower; as the Oracles stood back, four guards broke from formation and marched with Captain Bel towards the dungeons where the initiation took place. The group waited in uncomfortable silence for a few moments until they heard the crack of a whip and chains rattling.

The hall's massive doors burst open, and a giant snake slithered out from the darkened building with incredible speed, wearing a thick steel collar around its neck tethered to a thick metal chain held by the four guards that accompanied Ashur. It was blind in its claw-marked scarred left eye, the same from her dream about Gundisalvus' murder.

Though far-fetched and mostly unlikely, Selena immediately drew the conclusion: *I believe Ashur was the one who used this poor creature to kill Gundisalvus.* She gritted her teeth and clenched her fists.

Some recruits ran away as the guards struggled to hold the snake back. The other sentries joined to help their struggling brothers in arms, but the Marcupo gave the chain one final tug, and the contingent fell forward, dropping the shackles. Selena had to keep herself from screaming as the desperation to run crept upon her. However, she remained put and steadfast, even as the massive snake went after her directly, leaving a trail of dark, purple blood dripping from its opened slash marks upon its back.

Silver growled, but Selena stopped him from interfering when she noticed the Marcupo slowing its pursuit. Its scarlet eye met her emeralds, and it finally halted, ignoring the trembling soldiers hiding behind the scattered training equipment. A long, slippery red forked tongue slithered from its bared fangs dripping with golden venom, tickling her cheek. It studied her as it pulled away with no intent to harm, but when Captain Bel emerged from the hall and cracked his whip against the snake's back, the Marcupo immediately spun around and hissed at its captor.

As the snake stirred its tail across the dirt, Selena tripped when it swept underneath her feet. Another lash made the creature cower and slither away, giving the guards a chance to collect their bearings and fortify their strength at grabbing and holding the chain. This time, the snake didn't pull away.

Selena's heart ached. "Why did you capture this poor creature—only for its venom? Typically, snakes won't harm you unless you mess with them."

When she spoke out of term, everyone held their breath and stepped away as Captain Bel glared at her; Silver, however, sneered but remained on guard if the situation turned hostile. "The Marcupo is one of the deadliest snakes in existence."

Ignoring everyone whispering how she spoke out of term, Selena met Captain Bel's spiteful glare and looked back at the recoiling snake as the guards escorted it back to the dungeons. "Just because the Marcupo is venomous doesn't make it evil. Instead, it's been abused and neglected. What you're doing is completely barbaric— you're the venomous snake." She pointed at him instead. The recruits slowly peered from their hiding spots, and after witnessing the serpent's harmless interaction with her, they whispered amongst each other in agreement.

Ashur looked like he was about to strike her down; even Silver stepped forward to intervene, but Ashur didn't move. "Liongod, you will give me one hundred sit-ups and push-ups, and then you will clean the entire courtyard by yourself for speaking out of line." He sneered. "For one full week, you'll be assigned to kitchen duty, and following lights out, you will meet me here on the courtyard where you will run laps until I dismiss you."

Silver spoke up and marched right over to Ashur with a raised fist. "Bullocks! Liongod will do no such thing —he's right, and animal cruelty is punishable by law. I will see that General Araneus is aware of your cruel methods."

"You're stepping out of line, Altessa. As your superior officer, whatever I say goes, and you will do well to remember your place—"

"We are the same rank, so therefore, you're not my superior. Endangering the recruits and animal abuse, not to mention—"

Selena had enough and stepped forward. "Thank you kindly, Captain Altessa, but your defense won't be necessary." She met Ashur's glaring and perplexed expression. "I will gladly serve my punishment, *sir.*"

CHAPTER 15: BITTER WORK

Her week of punishment went by quickly as Selena distracted herself with all the ways she could exact revenge against Ashur for his maltreatment. Silver had offered multiple times to get General Araneus involved, or even Her Imperial Majesty, but Selena declined. "What kind of an example would I make if I didn't accept my punishment?"

Silver continued arguing. "You shouldn't have been punished in the first place."

Her kitchen duties involved serving and cleaning up after all three meals, and she wasn't excused from showing up for drills and regular training. Silver had slipped her a stamina potion that restored her depleted energy before meeting Ashur on the courtyard for laps. "This will make you feel like you've had a full night's sleep; I will not watch him try and kill you. Knowing him, he won't release you until it's time to begin drills."

Selena was thankful, for Silver was right; she wouldn't have survived the first night, as Ashur made her run in an endless circle around the courtyard's perimeter, not releasing her until it was thirty minutes before roll call. Luckily Silver's miracle elixir gave her the energy of ten dragons, and she breezed through her punishment like a champion.

However, what nearly broke her was when Neith delivered a message straight from Her Imperial Majesty when her taxing week finally ended: she was not to see Rahim or the others until she completed basic training. Silver was furious, as he was also forbidden to interfere and interact with her. "But I'm one of your trainers. This mandate is an outrage! I will march myself straight in there and tell her like I told Ashur—" His voice was immediately cut off after storming out of his office and slamming the door shut through his rampage, leaving Selena confused and melancholy.

Unfortunately, combining her growing nightmares involving the mysterious metal door and the Empress' mandate, Selena began lagging in physical fitness. Despite completing Ashur's punishing week, her growing depression was enough to dampen and stall her basic training progress and determination. She excelled in the arcane arts, surpassing even the master mages within Dragonspire, but she always finished last with laps and the obstacle courses—not even Silver's stamina potion could cure her dreary aura.

Erik's obligation as her bunker buddy meant he had to run back and help her push forward. Though she had won the respect of the others, Erik's attitude grew hostile over time; she knew he was irritated, and he certainly wanted to run her face into the dirt. Yet, she still picked herself up to keep running, with Erik following and grumbling. "Maybe you should just quit. Magic alone isn't enough."

Ashur took every opportunity to humiliate and punish her when running laps around the courtyard; as she tripped in the mud fresh from the morning shower, he walked over and spat on the ground. "Even I couldn't whip you into shape. You are weak and a disgrace to the Imperial Air Force. If you have any respect for us, then you will pack up and go home by morning." Yet, she persisted, still unable to see Thor and Her Imperial Majesty refusing to accept Silver's pleas to lift her orders.

By the end of Selena's first month, her unit trained with bows and firearms for the first time, each recruit with their setup: apples laid on a wooden plank balanced over a rock fulcrum. The two captains demonstrated the exercises by stomping their planks, the fruits flying into the air, and before the apples fell, they shot arrows through their cores, pinning them to a target sitting dead center of the field. The young men lined up to their stations and did the same, but as expected, many arrows didn't touch the apples, let alone their targets set to two hundred yards away.

Silver jeered and mocked his partner. "Perhaps another teaching method?" Ashur growled at him and yelled at those closest to face his wrath.

Selena was not doing well, either. She continued losing control over her arrow, and the apples fell before she even fired. Ashur made every attempt to humiliate her at failing publicly, but Silver had enough; eventually, his orders superseded Ashur's, and he finally got General Araneus involved regarding Selena's abuse and mistreatment. Captain Bel was forced to take a leave of absence until further notice before the Pyre struck noon that very same day.

While General Araneus and Aracania dealt with Ashur and Jade, Silver had permission to dismiss them early. As if to celebrate their well-earned victory, Selena and Erik made their way towards the on-site recreational center near the dining hall: a large smoking lounge with a few old and torn couches and three large wooden tables with decks of cards and board games available. The two passed by a heated chess game surrounded by a betting audience.

Yet, the others were busy fiddling over newspapers, whispering, "The rumors are true," and, "The Lich is organizing an attack against Alfheim."

"When do you think the battle will happen?"

"I dunno, but it looks like soon—weeks, maybe."

Selena had invited Erik over an empty table to play cards, and he muttered: "I don't have anything else better to do."

Not allowing his gloom to dampen her spirits, Selena attempted to make small talk while fighting past his cynicism. "What game do you want to play?"

He only shrugged as she shuffled the cards, but Selena's heart stopped when she saw Azrael strut by, head up high. He waltzed through after his month-long disappearance, oblivious to the severity of his crimes against Her Imperial Majesty and the Air Force for avoiding training.

She nearly slammed the cards down until Erik asked her, "What are you playing at?"

"What do you mean?"

"You come out of nowhere with a dragon already before joining the Force. You're gifted with magic, but you can't ever keep up with the rest of us when it comes to physical work. Are you purposefully not even trying?"

"That's not true, and you know it."

"I must keep watching you—always running back to help because that's what I'm supposed to do. Captain Altessa never yells at you, but he wants me to be your keeper. Why even be here? Why don't you go back home?" His burning words left her in cinders, and a tear trickled down her cheek. She wiped it away before Erik saw it, but he already realized his mistake and immediately apologized. "I shouldn't have said that."

"No, you're right, but I can't go back home. I have to stay for Thor; otherwise, the Council will take him away forever. I must do this for him."

"If you cared that much about your dragon, you would try harder." Erik looked as though he wanted to say more, but he held his tongue. Instead, he turned away.

"I'm already doing my best—"

"No, you're not. You're down on yourself. If you want to protect him, you need to work harder and push yourself more. You're playing the Council's game now, and we're just pawns. If you lose, it's game over for you."

Selena knew he was right; his words hit harder than being run over by a locomotive. The two made silent, mutual amends for past hostilities, but before they could begin their game, one of the bulkier recruits sitting on a shredded couch nearby, Volt White, shouted her name. "It's Liongod. What brings you in here?" She ignored his taunts as Volt's face turned red, and his nostrils flared; even Azrael's head whipped past the gathering crowd, and he scowled. When she didn't respond, Volt got riled up more than usual. "Do you think you're too good to answer me?"

Please, walk away, she thought.

He jumped up from the couch and, before Selena could prepare, lunged for her, grabbed the hem of her shirt and yanked her up in the air. The others surrounded Volt as his ogling audience, but Erik looked shamefully down at his hands. "You think you're too good for us with your magic tricks? I bet I could break those scrawny bones of yours."

Selena swallowed hard. "I would rather know magic than be an empty-headed muscled neanderthal."

His face was now the same color as a tomato; he surprisingly released her shirt until pushing her back. "Looks like Volt will have to teach you a lesson."

Erik whispered, "Liongod, leave while you can. He's twice the size you are."

Ignoring his advice, Selena tightened her fists but quickly relaxed her muscles, refusing to back down. Volt cracked his knuckles as the others swarmed the two, chanting, "Fight," repeatedly. As he delivered the first blow, Selena stepped to the side, keeping her hands behind her back. Volt stumbled and fell forward, his pride nearly shattered by the negative comments and boos from the spectators. He swung another punch as he stood up; Selena watched where he struck and avoided every blow without hitting back, dancing around Volt.

Growing weary, Volt attempted to hit her once more, but Selena finally reached out and grabbed his wrists. While maintaining eye contact with him, she balanced herself on one leg while using the other to swipe him from underneath; he lost his footing and fell backward. Realizing what she did, she immediately backed away, but the soldiers burst into cheer and crowded around her as if she were a hero; Selena and Azrael locked gazes briefly, but he dashed out when the others were distracted.

However, her celebration was cut short when she heard Captain Altessa's voice echoing from the entrance. "What's going on here?" Immediately, the boys cleared away, leaving Selena and the defeated Volt for Silver to see. Volt immediately stood up and dusted his robes off before he and Selena offered a salute. Silver's eyes blazed over each soldier as he approached. "What happened? Explain yourselves."

Selena attempted to speak, but Volt interrupted her. "I wasn't doing anything when Liongod attacked me, sir. I-I dunno what I did to provoke him. I didn't do anything, I swear."

"That's rubbish! Sir, he attacked me and—"

"Attention!" Everyone brought their heels together and stood up straight without another word. After a moment of silence, Silver eyeballed the two accused and immediately called forth Erik. "Bjornson, what say you? What happened here?"

Erik cleared his throat. "Sir, Volt attacked Liongod on sight. He was only acting in self-defense."

"Do you swear on it?"

"Sir, yes, sir."

"Are you lying to me, soldier?"

"Sir, no, sir."

Satisfied, Silver turned sharply on his heels and faced the trembling and sodden Volt. Without warning, Captain Altessa punched him so hard in the gut he heaved over and vomited blood. Selena looked away, and Silver pointed to the boy closest to the retching Volt, ordering, "Take him to the infirmary, now."

"Sir, yes, sir." Not wishing to test the captain's patience, he helped Volt to his feet, and the two shuffled down the hall.

"The rest of you are dismissed, except for you, Liongod. This room is out of order for the night." The area emptied in seconds, but the last to leave was Erik; he and Selena exchanged glances before returning to their quarters. Silver cleared his throat when they were alone and stretched out the hand that struck Volt. "I'm sorry you had to see that."

"It's fine. Thank you, Captain." She bowed, but he stopped her.

"No, that's not fine. Ashur may be suspended, but none of my soldiers should behave that way—they know better." He gave her a tiny grin. "I knew you didn't start the fight. I needed a witness to testify for you in front of everyone; Erik is a good buddy to you."

Selena smiled and nodded. "Yes, he is. But sir, if I may."

"Please, go on."

"I know I'm falling behind everyone in physical training. I want to tell you I will fix it and work harder to protect Thor." Her voice cracked like glass. "Is he doing all right? I haven't heard anything, and I doubt Her Imperial Majesty would be of any help after her recent order."

"My heart breaks for you two, but from what I hear, Thor is doing well for the moment—he had another growth spurt. He's damn near the size of a three-leveled house now—we've had to augment his harness, as he can easily carry a crew of twenty, perhaps more. However, we know he misses you dearly."

Selena couldn't stop her eyes from shimmering. "Does Thor still have to wear the Silent Vow, even though Ashur is suspended?"

"That was the Council's decision urged by Ashur's argument, but I'm currently fighting to have that wretched amulet removed."

Her face flooded. "I promised Thor to see if the Council could upgrade the dragons' quarters from mere stalls to more fitting and deserving accommodations."

"That is a lovely gesture, though Vidar may not be so willing at the present time."

"I told Thor I would still try. I want to fight for him, but I have nothing to show." She sighed and wiped her tears. "They still haven't identified his breed yet, have they? I don't mean to complain like a child, but why does our separation have to drag on?"

Silver's face turned paler than usual. "You have every right to be angry. I've been fighting in your stead because this hasn't been fair to you or Thor, though I fear Vidar and the Empress deem me difficult. I don't care because they need to hear it, even if it makes their ears bleed. As for their progress, I'm afraid I don't know. I could only suspect that the experts are being cautious." Silver saw the light vanish from her face, and he placed a gentle hand on her shoulder. "I promise that my associates are hard at work, and I will send word as soon as I hear anything. Please, allow us one more week."

"I appreciate you advocating on our behalf. Thank you, Captain." Concluding that her best chance to see Thor again was by excelling in her training and agreeing to the conditional allotted time, Selena then asked, "Could you please help me improve as a soldier?"

Silver's face lit up, and he smiled. "Of course, my dear. I could never say no to that." His grin vanished. "I'm sure you've heard the rumors, as everyone is talking about it."

"It's settled then. The Lich is preparing to attack Alfheim soon."

"Yes. The Oracles alerted the Council last week with this confirmation once the Lich finalized his plans. Not to worry, though. We'll make it through." It was unorthodox; she forgot all manners in their moment as she reached out and embraced Silver. The gesture took him by complete surprise, but he returned her embrace. "I believe in you."

Over the following weeks, as promised, Silver trained with Selena one-on-one in the courtyard well past five in the afternoon after the others had left; the two spent some evenings well beyond lights out in building new skills. Silver ensured to bring enough potions to help her endure the countless sleepless nights, and Selena was ready to begin.

Determined, Selena worked hard day after day, night after night, until an hour before roll call. After accepting Silver's stamina restoration elixir in the mornings, she rushed to the steam baths and got ready for the next day. Selena had spent every evening running laps and through obstacle courses until beating the required time. Eventually, she surpassed other records, becoming the fastest in her unit.

Through Silver's guided instruction, Selena ensured mastering her shooting skills; once she figured out her aim and grew comfortable with various firearms, she fired bullseyes with every shot. Consequently, her abilities behind the bow developed hand-in-hand with her use of firearms, though Selena's timing needed work: she would release her arrows prematurely before the apples reached the air. With Silver's continued patience and advice, she learned how to time her shots, and by mid-evening, Selena finally pinned the fruit to the target's center.

Selena also pushed herself past exhaustion as she and Silver dueled every evening over the next month through sparring matches with sticks until Silver was confident enough to move forward with swords. Her self-assurance grew with her already hidden skills, as Silver made previously clear from their first contest. After familiarizing herself with the difference in weight, she quickly grew accustomed, and eventually, Selena was as proficient as Silver, and their duels came to a draw.

By the end of her eighth week, Selena surpassed everyone within her unit. She ran laps at record speed and always finished first through the obstacle courses; Selena put her team to shame when demonstrating her improved skills throughout the weeks, even Erik. He surprised her when he said, "Thor should be proud of you." However, Selena noticed his growing gloom, and Erik had become quieter than usual; it was the first she heard him speak in weeks, and Selena was greatly concerned.

When Silver rounded up the soldiers near the sparring field before the Pyre struck five, he congratulated each one for surviving the first eight weeks of basic training, with only one more to go. "Next week on the sixteenth of Xol, everyone except for Liongod will have the privilege of being assigned to a dragon egg. The Council has set aside a clutch of eggs, and their shells have already begun to harden; the new dragons will hatch within a fortnight, so stay focused and keep up the excellent work. Long live the Empire."

Before the group fully dispersed, Selena believed she saw Ashur lingering in the courtyard shadows, watching and observing, but the moment she turned away and looked back, he was gone.

That same late afternoon, Selena invited Erik to join her on the trip to Alfheim's famous library; he abruptly declined her offer, only responding with a series of groans before wrapping himself in his blankets. She ruefully left their bunker when Erik refused to answer anymore.

Her trip to the library within the Imperial District was less than relaxing, as Selena's thoughts continued buzzing like angry bees over Erik's sudden decline in his mental health. Yet, her trek was still precisely the vacation she needed from her weeks of bitter work. She wasn't necessarily disobeying Her Imperial Majesty's orders, as she didn't intend to reunite with Rahim and the others. Silver preserved his argument with the Empress to give Selena more freedom as basic training was nearing its end, but she persisted that isolation served Selena's best interests. She had lost all respect for Her Imperial Majesty and hoped never to confront her again.

After sending away the coachman upon taking the carriage into town, Selena stopped in awe as she approached Alfheim's massively grand library of marble and stone; a colossal dragon statue displayed on top, wings unfurled and its tail writhing around the spires.

Yet, she looked over at the grim clock tower as the Pyre's deathly shrills announced another hour. Selena flinched when she thought that one head had moved, and she broke out into a run up the library steps, bumping into the flowing crowd of those leaving and entering, whispering about the upcoming battle and how the Empress and the Council were in a frenzy preparing against the Lich's gambit. One tall gentleman donned in a black cowl zipped past with a small cup, and as Selena spun around, he slammed against her side, and the liquid he carried splashed all over her. Instead of apologizing, he rushed away and vanished across the street.

Infuriated, Selena looked down at her soaked shirt and groaned, now needing to change. Hesitant, she sniffed her stained clothes, catching a sweetened whiff. Cursing her luck, she called for another carriage back towards the barracks before it became too sticky. The coachman ferried her past the gate leading to the Dragon District, and as the carriage dropped her off, her ears picked up a faint hiss from a snake hiding nearby. Not thinking any of it, Selena quickened her steps towards the barracks, but her heart raced when she next heard chains rattling.

As she broke into a full sprint, the noises were near-deafening, and Selena suspected foul play when she concluded that the stranger's accident was intentional. When she saw the vision-impaired Marcupo slither from behind the closest barrack tower at lightning speed, Selena knew that Ashur was the one who set this treacherous deed into play.

Maybe it was false hope, but she prayed that Thor would break his silence. *Please, answer me. I need you now.*

No response.

Sweat dripped down her forehead, but Selena wanted to try and reconcile with the giant snake; however, she gritted her teeth when she recalled that the Marcupo grew violently aggressive upon smelling its venom. Even now, the giant frenzied snake, hood flared like a cobra, didn't slow its pursuit; the blood-lust was written upon its only good eye. She pushed and shoved her way past the guards patrolling the fortress, who, confused at first, quickly took up arms against the racing snake, but the creature zipped past before the sentries could retaliate.

The snake's long tongue slithered out of its mouth; Selena felt a cold shiver run down her spine as it touched her hair. She spun around a corner and pressed herself against the wall to hide in the shadows. Luckily, Selena received a moment of respite as the Marcupo stopped and sniffed the air with its tongue, ignoring the crowd-filled screams and yells as the soldiers rallied. Selena held her breath and kept quiet, beads of sweat dotting her forehead, teeth clattering. The snake paused, tasted the air once more, and hissed when it finally found her. Selena wasted no time running away; the snake screeched and resumed its hunt.

Selena didn't account for the rocks ahead and tripped, falling face-first into the grass as she peered over her shoulder to judge the distance between herself and the snake. The Marcupo gained inhuman speed, but Selena still jolted to her feet and began using magic. However, the snake was too quick; its dragon-like maw opened wide, and one of its smaller fangs coated with dripping venom stabbed her forearm just as she punched blasts of fire.

Its single fang pierced through her arm like a sword penetrating flesh. The snake recoiled before its maw clamped shut, but the venom had done its damage; it rushed through her veins, and Selena's body convulsed and ached as she collapsed upon the grass. Her blood-curdling cries rang louder than that wretched clock tower as she trembled and suffered from muscle spasms, and her sight grew blurry.

Please, Thor….

Her vision faded fast, and as the Marcupo recoiled, preparing for another strike, a pair of massive talons appeared overhead, pushing the giant snake away. Thor, weighing nearly twelve tons and the size of a large luxurious house like those from the Garden District, swooped in with a flurry of beautiful fiery wings catching the sun's rays like stained glass windows.

Still, the snake's size was comparable to Thor's new growth; it struck back, but Thor swatted it away, leaving deep gashes into its thick tree-trunk-sized neck.

The loveliest sound in the world returned, twinkling within her thoughts: **I'm here, my dear, and I will never leave your side again.**

As the Marcupo made its multiple strikes, Thor tore through its scale armor, careful to avoid its venom-drenched fangs. However, the snake screeched as it found its opportunity and latched onto Thor's neck, sinking its fangs deep.

No!

Through ear-shattering snarls and growls, Thor shoved it away and opened his mouth, unleashing a beautiful, steady torrent of fire blazing like the sun.

Her body grew limp, but Selena still smiled upon seeing his developed skills; when all that remained of the snake was a pile of ash, Thor began succumbing to the deadly venom, and he collapsed near her, the earth shuddering from his massive weight. Black smoke plumed from his nostrils as he tilted his head to meet her horrified gaze.

I love you.

His eyes fluttered, and she faintly heard Silver yelling in the distance. Before her vision completely faded, Silver arrived with an elixir that he quickly administered to both her and Thor; Selena fainted.

When her eyes flickered open again, Selena was lying in a cot with metal rails within a white, sterile room. Niamh, Rahim, and Maria leaned over one side while Silver sat on a stool, swishing two different colored medicinal potions together in a single vial. She met their gleaming smiles, and they released a collective tense sigh when she finally awoke. Yet, her throat swelled, and her muscles occasionally contracted; Selena saw her injured arm wrapped tight.

Before Rahim could stop her, Niamh leaned over and, without warning, gently touched the side of Selena's face. Flabbergasted, Selena pulled away from Niamh's touch. "Oh, I'm so sorry. I was just…." Niamh's voice trailed off, but Rahim tightened his jaw but didn't speak; Selena didn't consider why he was so anxious.

Content to see her awaken, Silver hopped from his seat and gently held her eyes open as he lifted her chin towards the light lancing through the nearby window, satisfied to see her pupils contracting normally. While Rahim kept casting shadowed glances at the ashamed Niamh, Silver brought the mixed vial to Selena's lips. Without thinking, she immediately took a huge gulp but spat out the extremely bitter concoction. "Did you expect wolfsbane to be sweet?" Silver asked.

Selena wiped her mouth. "Wolfsbane?"

"It's a flower and the only known antidote for Marcupo venom."

"Is she going to be all right?" Rahim blindly asked. Silver immediately scowled at him for his mistake in referring to Selena as 'she,' jeopardizing her alias.

Niamh and Maria exchanged confused glances. "Err, s-sorry, I was—"

"It's fine." Yet, she shared in Silver's disappointment.

As Selena reluctantly and ruefully took another sip of the elixir, Silver pressed a warm, wet towel over her forehead. "Andric will live, thank the Divines."

Niamh seemed none the wiser; however, Maria had a sudden crease in her brow when she eyeballed Selena up and down, the blankets and sheets nearly outlining her feminine shape. It was then that Selena realized her alias had been compromised, but when she mouthed the question to Silver, he shook his head.

He leaned in and whispered, "All medical staff are under oath not to disclose any personal information." When Selena didn't seem convinced, Silver added, "They're my private doctors whom I've worked with and known for years. You're fine."

Selena gripped the handles of her bed rails, and she carefully poked at Thor's drifting and slumbering subconscious. Worried about his lack of response when their mental link was re-established, she asked, "And, sir, what of Thor? Please, tell me he's all right." Her voice nearly broke when the harrowing memory replayed itself. The weight of the world lifted from her shoulders when Silver smiled and nodded. "He learned how to hold a steady flame. I saw it."

"Thor is extraordinary, to say the least." Silver immediately clamped his mouth shut as Selena and her friends leaned forward to hear what else he had to say. Instead, he shook his head and said, "Thor will be fine, but he's currently on bed rest, like you. He wasn't too severely injured, thank the Divines. The venom, however, was the main cause of worry, but you two got the antidote in time."

Silver then delivered some fantastic news after he was satisfied that Selena had enough of the wolfsbane potion: Her Imperial Majesty finally renounced her previous order. Selena was free to mingle with her friends like before, and the Council agreed it was time to do away with the Silent Vow. "It was impeccable timing: I removed the neckpiece when Thor suddenly urged us to follow him."

Selena hissed as she sat up and gritted her teeth when expressing her suspicions of Ashur's involvement. "It all played out too perfectly; I know he set me up."

Rahim, Niamh, and Maria gasped; Silver's eyes became sharp as a two-edged sword. "I wouldn't put it past him, but we need solid evidence against Ashur if we're to report him to General Araneus and the Council. In the meantime, please, get some rest." Silver grinned. "You and Thor have so much to discuss."

CHAPTER 16: THE DIVINITY DRAGON

As promised, Rahim, Niamh, and Maria were granted visitation rights during the remainder of Selena's recovery, courtesy of Silver and General Araneus. The three were delighted when Her Imperial Majesty renounced her decree, though Selena still couldn't help but wonder why the Empress meddled in her personal affairs.

Per Rahim, Ashur's manor closed its doors to him, Niamh, and Myrrdin since the suspension, but Silver invited them to his property: Dragonstone Estate. "I'm never at home, so you three are more than welcome to stay for as long as you need," he began, "However, please mind my alchemy lab tower: it's strictly off-limits." Rahim and Niamh were grateful, but Myrrdin immediately declined Silver's generous offer before abruptly leaving in a great hurry. While Selena, Maria, Niamh, and Rahim commented on his rude behavior, Silver glared at him through a furrowed brow in suspicion, but he never voiced his opinions.

Selena spent the next few days recuperating within the infirmary, though she was anxious to leave when Thor finally awoke. *I love hearing your voice again.*

As do I, dear one. Aracania and the others have kept me busy with my studies.

I've been working hard, too. She sighed when the guilt set in for failing to deliver her promise. *I haven't had the chance to talk to Vidar about making the appropriate accommodations to your living arrangements, but Silver has been advocating on your behalf.*

Silver has been keeping me informed, but.... Thor's voice trailed off. **The Council has been refuting his arguments. Silver assured me he would not rest until they agree.**

I'm so sorry. There must be something we can do to change Vidar's mind.

I believe the Council will eventually do something about it if enough of the dragons complain. Still, I appreciate you not forgetting.

When they cleared Selena to return to the barracks, the dragons lined up outside the fort to welcome her back with triumphant roars. She recognized Vulcan with Gromm and Beck among the formation, giving her a firm, warmhearted salute. Of course, the three knew of her ruse but have kept their oath to Her Imperial Majesty. "Good to see you finally about, Liongod," Gromm said and grinned.

Next to them was Aster, the Viridian Longwing she and Thor first saw at the Grand Exchange. Aster stood to Thor's shoulders, but his wings stretched slightly longer, his species having the longest wingspan to body length ratio than other dragons. Standing beside Aster's side was his rider, a Mr. Kingsleigh. An older gentleman donned in a curled brim top hate and a long, twisted mustache, Mr. Kingsleigh tucked his lime green neck scarf into his collar and adjusted his jacket buckles before bowing to her. "Aster and I have had the pleasure of meeting your fine companion before returning to Alfheim," he said upon shaking her hand, "Though I must say, he is quite the extraordinary creature, talking about wanting to read books and such. My dear Aster never showed such interest before, but Thor has been quite the influence."

Selena took pride in this news. "Dragons are brilliant beings; I've read to Thor as often as I could since he hatched, and I believe it helps contribute to their intellectual prowess."

Mr. Kingsleigh looked at her, perplexed, but all he could say was, "Ah, yes."

Thor stood next to them in grandeur, donning a solid gold chain set with rubies around his neck, gleaming against his crimson scales. When he caught her admiring his new trinket, Thor twittered and chirped. **Aracania gave this to me for protecting you, my dear.**

That's beautiful. I'm so happy to see you with such dazzling treasures. Her grin grew. *I was ecstatic to see you breathe a steady flame.*

Thor hummed as he flexed out his claws against the cool dirt. **I was able to do more than that during our isolation, my dear one.**

What do you mean?

I promised to let Silver explain it.

Aracania stood in front, wings unfurled, finally introducing herself properly, wearing a gold torque set with royal topazes around the base of her neck. She lowered her head to meet Selena's open palm and chittered upon her touch. After dismissing her flight, Aracania bowed to the pair before joining General Araneus. The two met with Silver, who watched from the hall entrance, and the three fell deep in discussion about what Selena could only assume; however, the three continued peering at Thor and her.

Thor wrapped a massive protective arm around and herded Selena close. When General Araneus and Aracania flew away from the fortress together, the grinning Silver called for their attention as he dashed over. "Not only did they believe you two were ready to start training together, but…." He lost his voice as his smile grew. "Perhaps we should discuss this over tea, my dear— all three of us."

The two were invited to evening tea at Silver's manor, Dragonstone Estate, near Dragonspire, a modest establishment but still an august house exceeding Norrington Hall's splendor.

After Selena helped Thor attach his new chain to the recently modified harness—the leatherworkers lengthened his buckles and straps—the two flew together for the first time in about two months. Thor purposefully flew in circles above the ivory city, taking as much time that could be spared before meeting with Silver. Though the flight was still too short, Selena enjoyed and wallowed in Thor's warm company.

Near the giant mage's tower were endless acres of lush land surrounding a small and well-stocked lake bordered by fresh pines. The water mirrored Dragonstone's noble towers of white stone, the tallest spire housing Silver's forbidden alchemy lab.

Thor's shadow drifted over Silver leading Rahim and Niamh across the mossy flagstone path and up the front steps; after a brief exchange with his footman, Rahim and Niamh were beckoned inside as Thor landed on his haunches near the front marble water fountain. As soon as he helped Selena dismount, Thor began examining his reflection in the flowing water, flickering his tail and unfurling his wings. He then looked at his rubies and polished them with a closed fist until satisfied with their new gleam. Selena and Silver laughed, but Thor ignored them as he turned his head, inspecting every possible angle from his rippled mirror.

You're a mighty dragon building a treasure trove to guard.

You saw Aracania's jewels.

I think yours are better. Yet, Selena couldn't help resisting looking at her reflection, though she didn't recognize herself. She was no longer a frail and delicate young woman; she bore both a young maiden's beauty and a similar ruggedness as the other young men, built with lean muscle on her arms and legs.

Silver approached and patted Thor on his neck. "You're welcome to hunt anywhere on my property, as its occupants have been left alone for far too long." Thor snorted and brushed his snout against Silver's shoulder in gratitude before accepting the offer; he flung himself skyward towards the trees beyond the lake and vanished below the thick canopy.

Silver invited her inside, and Selena made herself comfortable within the parlor with Rahim and Niamh; Rahim noticed their odd behavior, Niamh's light smiles flashing at Selena, whose face wouldn't stop blushing as she turned away. The awkward exchange paused after the tea was served, and Silver finally answered Selena's burning questions, beginning with pulling out an old tome from the nearby bookcase.

Silver's fingers danced across the pages until he found what he was looking for and pointed to a listed familiar dragon breed that made the group's eyes widen in awe. "Do you remember this breed?" Selena and Rahim barely had the strength to nod, unable to tear their gazes from the title reading, 'Divinity Dragons.' Niamh, however, was lost and confused, but Rahim promised to tell her when the timing was more convenient.

"You don't mean to say—" Selena met Silver's blazing grin, and her jaw nearly dropped to the carpeted floor. "But you said it was almost impossible to identify one."

Silver raised a finger to the air. "Ah, *almost.*"

Rahim anxiously grabbed a crumpet, anticipating Selena's conclusion; eventually, Selena asked, "Are you sure?"

Silver slid the book across the oak coffee table before standing again and pacing the room. "We still don't know what breed Thor hails directly from, as any dragon could carry the Divine's blessing. It's a way to hide their nature from the world, protecting themselves from those targeting them and willing to misuse their powers. I still stand by my original hypothesis that, for his physical species, Thor is a cross between the Blackland Steelwings and the Fire Ridgebacks, but one thing I know for certain is that he is a Divinity Dragon."

My dear, is this true? Instead of directly answering, Thor hummed, his deep voice twinkling across her thoughts.

"That's incredible, but why did it take so long to confirm this?"

"As I've said before, it's complicated to identify one. As the scholars were stumped figuring out Thor's unique design after managing to hold his flame, Thor baffled us more when he began using ice, as we knew he wasn't an ice dragon. Then, he somehow started using wind and earth and other abilities none thought possible. That was when we realized his extraordinary nature, but upon reporting this news to the Council, Vidar wanted Thor to remain in Dragonspire until further notice." Selena's expression turned distraught, and Silver added,

"However, I made a compelling argument for allowing you and Thor to train together, which would help you two grow powerful for the Force. Only then was Vidar persuaded differently."

"Please, do not make Thor wear the Silent Vow again. I will not stand for that in the future," Selena firmly declared after setting her teacup down.

"I promise I will have no part in using that barbaric enchantment."

When Rahim and Niamh finished their tea, Silver urged them to follow him to their new rooms. Meanwhile, Selena took it upon herself to search through his many bookshelves gracing the drawing room until stumbling across a hefty tome with Gundisalvus' complete works. Yet, her heart stopped when she heard a terrible, snarling voice. "Not you again, Liongod."

She ruefully turned around, and her face became ghastly white to see Azrael scowling at her. "What are you doing here?"

He sneered at her demanding question, but his smile disappeared, and Azrael gave her a stiff bow. "I'm a guest here."

"Why in Oblivion would Silver invite you to his estate?"

"You should ask him." His dark blue eyes darted to the book she carried and changed the subject. "I saw your battle against the Marcupo, and I have to say that was pathetic. You'll never finish your training nor succeed against the Lich."

Selena gritted her teeth. "That creature nearly killed Thor and me."

He clicked his tongue against his teeth and stuffed his hands into his pockets. "You two should have been no match, but I suppose I was wrong. It looks like I don't have much to worry about."

"What do you mean?"

"I don't have to worry about you reporting Doragon and me to the Council. You and Thor aren't even fit to be part of our ranks anyway. You two will likely quit by morning, and soon, Doragon and I will resume our hunt."

More confused than angry, Selena dared to ask, "Why are you telling me this?"

"To torment you. You two will be watching and waiting until we're ready to attack from the shadows."

"Rubbish. How can I be so sure you didn't already report us to the Council?"

"You can't be sure of anything anymore, but I will say this: Doragon and I may not be the ones you should worry about," Azrael said before walking away.

Biting her inner cheek until she tasted blood, she went to return the book she pulled out until browsing across another titled, *Myths and Symbols.* Curiosity pulling her in, Selena began skimming through, hoping that she would find the answer regarding her mysterious mark. Most of the symbols etched in the pages were ones she already knew: the dragon's head was the sigil of the Empire, and Gundisalvus' signature symbol of a black fox head. To her dismay, her search led to another dead end. However, several small, folded parchment pieces clung to the book's back cover. Selena read through handwritten cursive journal entries dating over two hundred years ago upon unrolling the paper; the first read *'Seventh of Stardusk, 1375ED.'*

Her eyes soared over the random collection of notes talking about fascinating symbols throughout history; the second page cataloged a few hand-drawn sigils, and her eyes brightened when she saw the one from her hand within the list. The caption, *'Royal Family Crest,'* was written beneath the mark.

Then Her Imperial Majesty would know. Why is this etched into my hand?

Next to the drawn symbols was the word, 'Revelation,' with a sketched reaper scythe. Selena knew that Revelation was Death's weapon, a soul-eater blade. While researching Ragnarok, she had come across the name before, but the sickle wasn't as famous. Though believed to be a legend, Selena knew Revelation must exist if Ragnarok was real: the two weapons helped balance life and death.

As Selena continued reading the following notes, her eyes scanned across randomly written inconsistent phrases. One caught her attention, reading, *"Revelation shall be the only hope for man,"* and, *"He's always watching, but the Lich can't see me. No one can see me."* Shivers trickled down her spine, and she read another, *"The dragon-born will decide the world's fate."* Concluding it was more than a coincidence, Selena knew she had to ask Silver about how that would be possible. Yet, after turning to the last note, she came across an astonishing entry about Divinity Dragons, referring to Genesis Altessa's research of an extraordinary find. *"A Divinity Dragon in existence, such a beauty. No one shall know what it bears, but Genesis even proved it true: a Divinity Dragon had laid her clutch of only two eggs, one incubating the chosen one not born of man. Such marvelous discoveries! The Lich will fear for his existence, and I must keep this secret safe—yes, safe."*

When she heard Silver's footsteps approach behind, Selena slammed the book shut with the notes and thrust it back in place upon the shelf. "Selena, are you all right? By the Divines, you look like you've seen a ghost."

"I-I don't know. I hardly know myself."

As Silver's eyes darted to the recently returned book, its spine not entirely aligned with the row, he deeply sighed, preparing himself for Selena's brewing questions.

After confirming Niamh and Rahim were busy getting ready to tuck in for the night, Selena demanded more answers, to which he stuttered and stumbled through as best as he could. "Azrael is an odd fellow, but I guarantee he and Doragon mean no harm." Suddenly, Silver's head whipped around as if he were ensuring the two were away from prying ears. "We are currently being watched, but I can guarantee yours and Thor's safety: Azrael and Doragon are informants disguised as members of the Obsidian Order. They've been secretly feeding us information about the Lich in return for… *personal* gain."

Rude to pry further, Selena still wanted to know the pair's motives for willingly working with Phantom Dust, as she assumed him to be unpleasant. She dug her nails into her palms when Silver couldn't elaborate. "If Phantom Dust won't allow you to help me, I will find him myself and make him tell me. I believe I deserve every right to know who I am."

"Yes, of course, but I'm afraid D has a terrible habit of vanishing for long periods, only appearing when something goes wrong."

"I will find a way to make him show himself." She then lifted her left hand and confirmed her knowledge behind the symbol's story. "Is that true?"

Silver bit his bottom lip, attempting to hold back the curse waiting to sew his mouth shut; based on his expression, Selena knew it to be true. "That mark isn't commonly known outside Alfheim," was all Silver could say without activating the spell.

"I assume you're not allowed to tell me why I have it." Silver could only shrug, and Selena slowly grew agitated, not at him, as it wasn't Silver's fault, but her determination to seek out Phantom Dust escalated. Instead, she tried one final attempt by asking, "Is it true that Divinity Dragons can lay eggs incubating other creatures?"

"I—" Silver's lips immediately zipped shut, and Selena's breaths quickened as she grew more confused by this implication. When Silver took a few deep breaths and was allowed to move his mouth again, he held up a hand but fell deep in thought before speaking. "It's *fascinating*, to say the least; I never said they *could* or couldn't."

"So, the stories I've heard about this unknown entity born from a dragon are true," Selena concluded. Silver tightened his lips but didn't deny her statement; Selena worded her following assertion negatively in hopes of breaking the curse's rule. "Then, there is no book that could tell me more about this dragon-born."

Catching on to what she was doing, Silver's face brightened like the dawn's light, and he pulled out an old, leather-bound journal and a delicate scroll sitting upon a row of books. "I want you to have these from my collection—they were passed down from my family to me." Carefully accepting both gifts, Selena went to open the journal, but Silver stopped her. "Please, wait until you return to your quarters. You will find them both quite fascinating."

Selena's face brightened at his meaning when he winked, and she hugged the texts close to her breast. "Thank you for telling me what you can."

As Silver escorted her outside the manor, Thor announced his upcoming return, but before Selena ventured off the steps, Silver said, "No matter what, my dear, remember this: a life lost can never be brought back again. Countless others—mages, scientists, and scholars alike—have tried reconstructing life but failed. Although they can recreate the physical-chemical makeup of a body, no one before has ever successfully brought back the dead."

Selena twirled around to see Silver had vanished when she approached the water fountain. Only when she peered at the evening sky did Selena see a brilliant white wing-less dragon slithering across the diamond-adorned nether like a snake, its sky-blue locks dancing with the wind like a horse's mane and snow-white scales glistening in the moonlight.

That was when she realized it: *Silver is a dragon.*

CHAPTER 17: THE WELL OF SOULS

Thor returned from his evening hunt after Silver disappeared over the horizon, and during their brief flight back to the Dragon District, Selena regaled him with all she had learned. However, when she gave the news regarding Azrael's and Doragon's secret alliance, Thor shared her resentment. **It doesn't matter if they're supposedly allies. I will strike them down if they continue tormenting us.**

Silver trusts them, but I don't know if I ever will.

You don't have to trust them. Thor landed within the vast courtyard and scooped Selena from his harness. **If what you say about Silver being a dragon is true, that would be interesting. I've never heard of a human transforming into a dragon.**

We've read about shapeshifters before—even Loki has a similar ability. I wouldn't be surprised if Silver were one, too.

Maybe. Thor snaked his head down and sniffed the journal and scroll. **I will be anxiously listening.**

Selena dashed towards the main hall when Thor launched himself upward, returning to his quarters. After racing into her apartment, she paused when noticing Erik scribbling on a parchment with a quill. Selena called his name, but he ignored her as he kept writing. She set Silver's gifts aside on her desk and offered to play a game with him. "I know it's been rough, and perhaps it can help pass the time." Erik paused to contemplate her offer but shook his head and resumed. "Is there anything I can do? Will you be all right?"

He finally spun his head around and met her gaze with a small smile Selena had never seen from him before. "I'll be fine." Slightly taken back, Selena returned his smile and gave him a thumbs-up; he gave her the same gesture and continued his task.

After ensuring his wellbeing, she lit up a lantern and dove into her blankets with the ancient and delicate scroll opened first. Thor confirmed he was tucked in for the evening, and Selena began reading about how technologically advanced the dwarves were compared to the other races, abandoning the ways of magic to build alien machinery.

Throughout history, scholars and explorers discovered strange metallic artificial devices combined with magic stones for uses unknown in deserted ruins and mines scattered across Armageddon. Originally built during the elves' enslavement, the dwarves sealed the entrances with large, metal doors before abandoning them entirely, concealing whatever creations they had inside from ever being discovered. The recent discovery made by Gundisalvus unearthed new dwarven technology near Alfheim: a device that collected starlight to predict future events. However, the dwarves transcribed the readings in the Elven Language, a tongue forgotten save for the few who studied dead languages.

How fascinating. I would love to see one.

That ruin we walked past on our way to the city was probably the one discovered by Gundisalvus.

Selena finished the scroll and opened the journal over her lap. Scribbled on the inside cover was 'Genesis,' and the journal contained notations on magic and alchemy principles much more advanced than she had ever read. She understood some of it, but most of the content read like a formula with written side notes. *It sounds like mixing magic with human life.*

The taboo magic involving human experimentation was illegal and punishable by death. The next page read of foxes, demons, and other creatures that could trace magical essences from leagues away, while others gave off auras that attracted demonic and undead forces.

What do you suppose that means?

I don't know but keep reading.

Upon continuing, Selena eventually found a piece of parchment creased neatly within the book. She unfolded it and read telepathically to Thor: *"Normally, a life lost can never be brought back again. I've watched countless others—colleagues and scholars alike—try and fail, and no one has ever successfully brought back the dead, but I believe I'm about to make history."*

Selena only paused when Thor continued moaning and snarling as he worked himself up in a frenzy, desperately trying to recall forgotten memories regarding this spine-chilling information. Yet, he urged her to continue.

"Near the time of the One Hundred Years' War, Her Imperial Majesty was with the stillborn child; the grief-stricken Emperor and Empress did all they could within their power to bring their daughter back, but there were consequences. The Council somehow discovered their

desperate attempts, and the Emperor is now in Mortemholdt. Her Imperial Majesty was spared but grew ill after using illegal magic—she can no longer bear another child. I could not heal her sickness, and it is slowly killing her with no known cure, but I believe my recently finished project can bring back what they lost."

Thor began humming in the back of her mind.

Interesting. For some reason, I'm starting to remember now....

Remember what?

I believe....

With haste and eagerness, Selena's eyes raced across the page held by the parchment notes, and her heart nearly burst from her chest when she saw the royal family sigil drawn on the bottom. The following entry contained more notations about the formula from the beginning.

"After many long years of research, I have finally created the Well of Souls that will bring back the dead, and its first test subject will be the stillborn Crown Princess. Once I begin the first stage, I must move immediately to phase two once there's a detected heartbeat: transferring the infant within the Divinity Dragon mother I recently discovered before laying her clutch. My new alchemical formula should allow me to only move her safely without human transmutation—I've already sent my research notes to Varathka Gundisalvus. I must act fast."

Hands trembling, her lips quivered over the following words: *"Their Imperial Majesties picked out a name for their daughter if my project works: Selena."*

My dear one.

No... no!

The blood drained from her face, and her heart raced from the possibility—no, not chance, but fact. *That's not possible. That can't be... no!*

She rushed to the next page to prove herself wrong, but to her dismay, the journal only confirmed her origin. *"The experiment was a success: I figured out how to safely transfer the child into another incubating egg within the dragon immediately after discovering a heartbeat, and she lives again. The Divinity Dragon now carries two developing eggs where the child will be nurtured and stabilized by the mother's constant magic stream.*

"After she lays her two eggs and passes on her blessing by offering a prayer to the Divines, unfortunately, she will die, but there has only ever been one Divinity Dragon in existence at a time—such extraordinary creatures. I don't know how long it will take before she lays her eggs—months, maybe even years—or how this will affect the child, but she will live.

"The Divine mother dragon has finally laid her small clutch after several months and passed her blessing to both eggs. I'm not sure what that will mean for the child, and I will watch over them. The mother dragon departed to find her final resting place within Shadowgreen Grove. May the Divines welcome her, for she brought the new Divinity Dragon and the reborn child into this world.

"Dragons can take years before finally hatching; otherwise, they can remain within the shell for however long they choose, as they draw sustenance from the world's Aether to sustain themselves indefinitely. Divine Dragon blood runs through this child's veins, and I suspect she may have received the Divines' blessing like her egg-mate."

The following few pages were small notes documenting how the two eggs fared, and while still grasping her identity, Selena instantly understood Silver was Genesis Altessa. The author wrote the journal entries in the same hand over a two-hundred-year time frame, including the one recording her birth:

"Twenty-first of Xol, 1575 ED: It could still be a while before the dragon hatches, as its shell has yet to harden, but the child's egg has begun cracking. I assisted with her birth, and after picking her up in my arms and cleaning the membrane off, she opened her eyes and cried for the first time. At that point, I knew she would live, but there was something wrong. Her parents were elves, but the girl was reborn as a human; the process also etched the royal family sigil into her left palm. I need to look at my formulas to figure out why these mistakes happened, but this child is a miracle for now. To show Xyaxon praise for my project's success, Her Imperial Majesty fashioned her daughter a new surname: Selena Liongod."

Selena Liongod, you're the Crown Princess, the first-ever born from a dragon and brought back to life. I remember now, my sister.

She leaned against her pillow, her eyes shimmering and face flooding as her mind refused to grasp her past news. Her Imperial Majesty's gestures and unwanted involvement struck Selena down like a lightning bolt, but her heart tore through her chest when the Empress—her mother—wouldn't confront her with this information.

With Thor's constant reassurance, she calmed down and read through a few more entries written in different handwriting documenting her early life, including her development in using magic. She had a family all along and smiled a little, tears falling down her face; she read entries from her mother, but there was no other mention of her father. She re-read the texts several times before sadly accepting he was either still imprisoned or—

Dead, she said. Selena gave up and moved on to the last page dated the week before the new year and read:

"Twenty-third of Moonstar, 1591 ED: I lost everything. The Lich ravaged and destroyed my research, the lab, and the Well of Souls I spent several hundred years building. He stole its only success and the Divinity Dragon egg. I've failed, but I will help get them back, no matter the cost. The Empress is pleading with the Council to rescue the child as I write this, but we haven't mentioned anything about the dragon's egg to Vidar. They may never let us have it back, or worse, they may destroy the egg in fear that the Lich corrupted it. Who knows what the Dark Master will do once he has her blood?

"I was arrogant and foolish; I shouldn't have taken her in as my apprentice for her safety, but she was brilliant. Amazing with magic, but she radiates energy. Because of my careless behavior, the Lich found out about her and the surviving egg. If he bathes that egg in her blood, the hatchling will become the Destroyer of Worlds, corrupted in shadow and darkness with only one purpose. I pray it's not too late."

She immediately shut the book and tossed it across her bed as she cradled herself. Her brain stuttered as it took a while for her thoughts to catch up, and she withdrew into the sheets.

Selena.

She couldn't answer as the tears continued pouring down her cheeks like a steady stream; unlike Thor, the journal didn't trigger the return of her memories. Yet, Selena was trapped within her mental chaotic brewing maelstrom. Thor continued pleading for her attention, but Selena's words failed her. *I....*

Please, don't shut me away.

She buried her face into her hands to catch her tears, but Erik ruffling around from the top bunk interrupted their discussion. At first, Selena quieted down, guilty for accidentally waking him. However, her heart suddenly shattered like their window.

My dear, what's happening?

Ignoring him, Selena threw off her covers and noticed their broken window; immediately, she dashed to get suited for battle, believing the fort was under attack. She called Erik's name, but she received no answer, and his covers didn't budge. Selena clambered up the ladder, and her face turned ghastly white in horror when he wasn't in bed; only a note was left on his pillow. She pushed through the shards of broken glass from the window large enough to fit her entire body through; Erik was down below, on his back, laying in a pool of blood.

Seconds later, the ear-shattering alarms shouted across the facility, and every soldier and security guard raced to the courtyard in battle-ready gear with weapons drawn. Dragons roared from the seaside and zipped towards the fortress in three v-shaped formation groups, with Aracania leading the front.

Selena rushed down below with lightning speed, pushing and shoving through the fray and blitz; she forced her way into the courtyard until she found Erik's body. When she saw he wasn't breathing, she got down on her knees to start chest compressions through panicked crying.

"What is going on here?" Silver called out, but his face turned white when he saw the scene. He grabbed Selena's arms and pulled her away, but she fought against him to continue. "Liongod, stop! It's too late."

"No, I won't give up; I can still save him." Selena strained against his hold, even as Silver tightened his grip. She kept hearing Thor reach out with a gentle and pained voice during her struggle.

Let him go.

No!

Aracania ordered her groups to remain in position when confirming they weren't under attack, and the dragons hovered aloft, watching the dreary and somber scene below. Thor carried the right flank in her group, and his eyes met Selena's briefly among the pell-mell crowd.

Her strength finally waning, Silver turned to a nearby guard and ordered to clear the area. As the sentries rounded up the grim-stricken soldiers, Silver yelled through the chaos, "Where is Azrael?"

Selena's face swelled with tears, but she whipped her head around as Azrael casually strolled through the dispersing crowd like the grim reaper, stoic and indifferent. General Araneus followed him, hastily marching to the horrific scene, gesturing for the stragglers to leave and return to bed; Selena's ears rang as he ordered Silver to remove her from the scene. "No, please, I can save him—"

"Captain, please escort Liongod back to bed, now."

She attempted to break free again, but Silver had her locked in his arms; he hoisted her to her feet and forcibly walked her back to the main hall. Eventually, Selena gave up fighting his grasp, and when they were clearly out of sight, Silver brought her into a hug. She could no longer hold back her tears, and she dug her face into his jacket, muffling her sobs.

General Araneus stood next to Azrael and asked, "Time of death, please."

Selena glared at Silver, silently asking why Azrael was called to declare the time of death when he wasn't a doctor nor coroner. Instead of offering her an answer, he tightened his hold. Nevertheless, Azrael didn't gaze up at the clock; he knelt and reached out to close Erik's eyes. "Two minutes past midnight."

The Pyre read eight minutes past; Selena realized Azrael had cited the immediate time when Erik first jumped from the window and committed suicide.

As the caretakers from the House of the Dead and higher-ranked officers prepared Erik's body for the embalming process, Selena sat alone in her bunk after Silver had escorted her back, wallowing in grief washing over her like an ocean wave.

Thor's gentle voice poked at her consciousness: **I'm right here.**

I know.

Eyes full of tears, she climbed back up to Erik's bunk, snatching the note he had left behind. It was the letter he had been working on when Selena last spoke to him.

"I'm sorry, Liongod. Since my brother's death, I have lost everything dear to me. We had no home or family left since the Order destroyed our village in the Air Kingdom. We had hoped for a better life here in Alfheim, but I lost all the will to live after Alexander. Thank you for the last few weeks of your optimism and for putting up with my moodiness.

"A moment is all we are, and the world may not care if my light vanishes from the millions of bright stars still twinkling. I will join you now, brother."

"I care," she whispered through shimmering eyes and folded the note with trembling hands. The Council's war preparations brought pain and suffering throughout the Empire, and now Selena wasn't sure if defeating the Lich would bring peace. She constantly replayed her last interaction with Erik and blamed herself for not staying with him, not recognizing the signs, nor his silent cries for help. The weight of the world rested on her shoulders as she failed him like the other lost souls.

She didn't stir when she heard knocking, and the door swung open. "Liongod," she heard General Araneus say, "I am sorry for what happened, but I must ask you some questions."

"Sir, I'm not sure if I'll have the answers you're looking for."

"Anything at all will help. What exactly happened before the incident?"

Her lips quivered as she recounted their final conversation, and Selena waved his last message when she finished. "He left this behind."

After snatching the note and scanning it over, General Araneus nodded and folded it into his jacket pocket. "We will need to keep it for our records. Erik will receive an honorable funeral and join his brother. Sadly, this is more common than you think, but I have already arranged a new bunker buddy for you." He spun around, and Azrael appeared in the doorway with his bagged luggage thrown over his shoulder. Selena sprang to her feet, ready to fight, but Azrael turned a blind eye to her sudden hostile behavior. "You two will be assigned together from now on; time for bed and lights out." General Araneus closed the door, leaving Azrael and Selena alone.

"Is this a cruel prank? If so, I'm not amused."

Azrael ignored the heat coming from her voice, and he threw his bag over the top bunk. "I didn't ask for this."

Disregarding Silver's defense for Azrael and Doragon, Selena wanted to scream and strike him down, but she couldn't. Instead, she fell to her knees, crying. Unmoved by her tears, Azrael leaned against the wall, watching as if he were bored. When she finally caught her breath, Selena scowled at him. "Tell me why you're really here. Is it so you can finally capture and take Thor and me to the Lich? I don't care anymore, so why not be done with it already?"

"No, I'm not doing that. If anything happens to you and Thor while we're still here, you have other enemies within the city. I won't have any part of it unless you break your end of the deal."

"I don't understand."

"I honor all my bargains. I will uphold my oath to you if you keep yours to me."

As much as Selena wanted to argue more, she loathed his strangely moral nature; yet, to her knowledge, her alias hadn't been compromised, and the Council hadn't suspected her disguise. "I still don't trust you," was all she could say.

"I never asked you to." He stopped for a moment before continuing. "Also, you shouldn't blame yourself for Erik's death. It was bound to happen sooner or later, and it was probably his time."

Enraged by his lack of sympathy and sensitivity, Selena was ready to unleash her brewing wrath. "He had plenty of time here." She withdrew her remark, but her nostrils still flared against her reddened face. "What gave you the right to announce his time of death?"

"My skills are between me, the captain, and the general. You've earned no right to know." Ignoring her draconic fury, Azrael peered over his shoulder at the journal Silver had given her. A low grumble escaped his throat, and his eyes burned. "Where did you get that?"

"It's mine." Selena grabbed it and held it close to her chest.

"Easy, I wasn't going to take it from you, but I wouldn't leave that thing lying around."

Selena glared at him in suspicion. "You know what's in here, don't you?"

"I can only assume, but journals are meant to keep secrets." Azrael climbed to the now vacant spot on top and curled up.

Are you two done arguing?

Did you hear all that then?

It was hard not to hear. Come outside.

Selena made her way out with great care, escaping the barracks after all the lights were out. As she reached the beached dragons' quarters, Thor flickered his tail and opened his arms for her to sprawl and lay on; he wrapped her within his protective coils, continuously reassuring her that it wasn't her fault. Still, she said, *I'm so sorry, Erik. I couldn't save you.*

You didn't know that he was in that much pain, and you tried your best.

Selena tilted her head back and looked at the burning blue and green sky, unable to understand how the stars continued sparkling and the earth kept spinning. *Why should life keep moving forward after what happened?*

Because it has to, we must live for those who couldn't keep going on. Thor snaked his head around, his blazing eyes attempting to meet her teary eyes. **You and I have to keep moving forward. Erik would have wanted that.**

Selena's shimmering emeralds met his comfortingly warm gaze. *I know you're right, but why do I still feel this way?*

Because you care, that will make you a good ruler one day.

A ruler? I don't want the throne.

It's your birthright as the Crown Princess.

To Oblivion with my birthright. Selena believed knowing her past would bring her peace, but instead, she felt trapped in a make-believe fantasy world.

While she grew ensconced within Thor's coils, her eyes grew fixated on the trees blowing in the distance, wondering how she could move forward for Erik; when Selena recalled the scroll Silver gave her, her thoughts flickered with an idea like a newly lit candle. *I know how we can make this right by Erik and keep going.*

How?

Since we know the Lich will attack Alfheim soon, I want to find Ragnarok and use it to fight against the necromancer.

Thor snorted and flexed out his claws, taking clumps of dirt with each pass. **You're mental. One, that's dangerous, and two, we don't even know where the sword is.**

I may be mad, but I believe Ragnarok is near Alfheim. I want to speak with the Oracles for confirmation.

Why do you think it's close?

Gundisalvus was fascinated with ancient dwarven ruins, and he discovered the one outside the city before he died.

Thor yawned and tightened his arms around her more. **Hmm. Then hopefully, the Oracles can help us. However,** he nudged Selena to her feet and arched his neck towards the weeping heavens, **let's ease Erik's soul with our promise.**

Facing the flickering stars, Selena gave one final salute to Erik's passing spirit. Thor leaned back on his haunches, wings unfurled and unleashed a mighty roar, the world quivering from his requiem. With his massive maw opened wide, Thor released a steady stream of fire blasting across the sky like a shooting star.

The following day during their weekend break, Erik was given a proper funeral in the Memorial District within the House of the Dead. Everyone from their unit paid their respects, and before Selena left, she dug through her pockets, pulled out the deck of cards she and Erik played with, and set them on top of his stone casket.

She marched from the cold marble hall towards an awaiting carriage across the busy street, unaware and not recognizing Her Imperial Majesty waiting near the cemetery. Her sudden twinkling voice made all the remaining color drain from Selena's face. "It's a pleasure to see you again, Liongod." It had been two months since making her acquaintance, and Selena still snarled before spinning around with an automatic bow, not daring to share eye contact. The Empress paused when Selena straightened, her gaze still glued to the ground, focusing on keeping her lips sealed. She refused to let her tongue be a loose cannon. "I'm sorry to hear what happened," Her Imperial Majesty finally said after the two stood in awkward silence.

Yet, the tense atmosphere steeped. "Erik's service just finished."

"I see." The Empress looked skyward, silently admiring the metal-hued clouds swirling overhead. "After all you've endured, from the snake attack to this, I wanted to ensure your wellbeing." Selena's throat clamped shut, but she struggled not to lash out in anger; even Thor occasionally intervened to soothe her brewing fury. "Your safety is of the utmost importance—"

Selena could no longer hold back. "I would have been a whole lot better without your interference, *Your Imperial Majesty.*"

Selena, back off. She ignored him.

The Empress tilted her head but gave a small smile instead. "Come, walk around Alfheim with me. I want you to tell me what you've learned."

Her Imperial Majesty pretended her comment didn't happen, and Selena ruefully joined her side, hands clasped behind her back as the Empress strolled ahead. "There isn't much to say, I'm afraid."

"Eight weeks of basic training, and there isn't much to share?"

"I'm sure Captain Altessa has given you his report, along with seeking many audiences—"

The Empress whipped around before the two reached the edge of the street. "I was ensuring your safety, my dear child. I had hoped by eliminating all distractions that you would remain focused on your studies without jeopardizing your plans."

"I believe you mean *your* plans. I don't need anyone to keep me safe, Your Imperial Majesty, and I was doing just splendidly without your meddling." The Empress looked as though Selena had struck her across the face; with tears swelling in her eyes, Selena inched forward and whispered so the public couldn't hear, "I'm sorry, but I'm so angry that you've withheld everything from me, Mother."

The Empress' face became like porcelain: pearly white with a fragile expression. "You know."

"I know who I am now, but I will continue hiding, just as you wish."

Her Imperial Majesty's face softened and, with an already cracked voice, said, "Do you think this is what I wanted for you? What *we* wanted?"

"I don't know, and I wish I could at least ask my father, wherever he is, or Phantom Dust." Selena stepped back and bowed before her mother could say more. "Good day, Your Imperial Majesty."

Selena returned to Norrington Hall after the carriage dropped her off and sent the footman to fetch the Oracles while exercising caution to avoid Ashur. To her relief, they didn't turn her away, and the footman hastily left. Moments later, the triplet sisters strolled down the flagstone paths, their gleaming white hair still decorated according to their names, chanting together, "Hello, Liongod."

Selena bowed. "Always a pleasure. I'm glad the former captain hasn't lashed out at you three after his suspension."

The Oracles exchanged glances. "Captain Bel has been missing for the past month," Morta said.

"He vanished right before General Araneus began his investigation," Cassandra added.

"And we haven't seen him since he banished Rahim, Niamh, and Myrrdin from the estate," Nona finished.

"Ashur must be hiding something, or else he would have willingly pleaded his case with General Araneus and the Council. But you three are still here."

Morta said: "Norrington Hall is currently in service for the Council, and therefore, we can use it as long as we need to."

Cassandra folded her hands in front and followed with, "We offered Rahim, Niamh, and Myrrdin refuge when the Council seized Ashur's assets, but they refused to return."

Nona bowed and finished their synced explanation, "Myrrdin has also disappeared since Captain Altessa opened Dragonstone Estate to the three."

Selena recalled Myrrdin's odd behavior whenever Silver was around; she couldn't understand the animosity between the two, and Silver was also at a loss. However, she remembered the reason behind her visit, but the Oracles disrupted before she could voice her questions. "We know why you came." They grinned.

"Then I suppose I'll skip the chatter. Do you know how—?"

"Yes and no," the sisters began with unified voices, "It's not easy to predict the future because the outcome can always change from the actions you make now."

"Of course, I understand. Based on our current course of action, however—"

"You may or may not win this battle." The Oracles' constant interruption made Selena's face burn in irritation; their vague inclinations didn't help, either.

"Will you three please stop doing that? I can't think or talk straight." The triplets snickered, but they withheld further remarks. "I suppose I'll change my question. I believe I know why the Lich is planning his assault on Alfheim: he's after Ragnarok, and I'm convinced it's hiding in the abandoned ruin outside the city. Please, can you tell me if I'm heading in the right direction?"

"Hmm. We can, but we don't have to."

"Why?"

The Oracles inched forward together and leaned in. "If you're already confident, do you *really* need us?"

"I could be entirely positive, but that won't make my notions correct—a confirmation is all I ask."

The three shared a sneaky sneer before finally saying, "You'll find the ancient device within, resting beneath the starry skies."

CHAPTER 18: THE SHADOW EMPEROR

The Oracles returned inside, and Selena made the brisk walk back towards the street, now with a clear set purpose; however, before she could call for a carriage, Niamh marched towards her with Rahim chasing her heels.

"I told you he would be here," Niamh sternly announced, but Rahim's face turned bright red when he reached up and grabbed her arm. "Let go of me."

Rahim quickly pulled away. "No, please, leave him alone." Selena's eyes continued darting between the two, at a loss, but Rahim waved her down and mouthed the words, "Leave."

When Selena failed to heed his warning, Niamh pried her arm away; Selena immediately stepped back as if she were about to run. "I heard about the funeral, and I'm so sorry. When I knew you were there for the service, I went to see you, but I saw you storm away."

"Niamh, stop," Rahim began, but she silenced him.

Face gleaming red, Niamh continued, "I wanted to ask you something, Liongod."

"Ask me what?"

"I know it would be hard for you since you're in the Force and… I-I know your sole duty is to protect the Empire."

Rahim inched closer, waving his hands in huge wiping motions, telling her to say no, but Selena said, "I don't understand." Niamh looked as though she wanted to scream. Instead, she wrapped her arms around Selena's neck and kissed her cheek when Selena moved her lips away. Rahim tripped over his feet, and an awful noise escaped his mouth; Selena didn't know what to do but immediately pushed away. "What are you doing?"

Niamh suddenly realized her mistake and apologized for her impulsive behavior, collapsing into Selena's arms. "I-I'm so sorry. I like you, Andric, and I-I was hoping that maybe…." She couldn't find the strength to finish.

Selena was at a loss for words. However, she blushed and helped Niamh to her feet. "I do like you, but as a friend. I don't want to lie to you," she paused when her thoughts immediately drifted towards Silver, "but I've taken to someone else. That doesn't mean we can't be friends." She flashed a small smile.

Niamh's eyes widened as more tears trickled down her face, but she wiped them away and nodded. "I'm sorry for that. Of course, I would like to be friends." She gave Selena one last hug before running back the way she and Rahim came.

After collecting himself from the initial shock, Rahim shuffled his feet, placing a hand on Selena's shoulder to help him stand upright. "You know, if Niamh knew who you were, then—"

Selena glared at him. "Then what? She can't help it. Would you still be against it if she liked me knowing I was a girl?"

"Not at all. It's just...." Rahim lost his voice as he looked back at her fading figure turning a corner. "I like her."

She instantly recoiled and withdrew her harsh words, but the moment Rahim confessed his affections, Selena's face began burning when her mind raced to Silver. She hadn't realized her growing fondness until Rahim noticed her blazing expression, and all she could say was, "I know the feeling."

"What do you mean?"

"I'll tell you later." Ignoring him, and instead of a carriage, Thor offered a flight. His shadow zipped over the two within moments, and Thor scooped them from the street with a single paw before soaring back to the Dragon District. He glowed and chittered in delight when Rahim praised his mighty size, as he hadn't seen Thor since they arrived in the city, and added an "at this rate, Thor will be the size of a mountain."

As the two looked down at Alfheim from Thor's clawed cage, Selena finally said, "What I said to Niamh was true—I've also taken to someone."

Thor snorted upon hearing her news, and his head curled back in shock like a snake about to strike. Rahim's eyes widened as he began asking who it was, but his lips sealed shut when he realized it was Silver. "That's madness; he's your superior."

"Do you believe I don't know that?" she sighed. "After all the time he and I had spent together, it just grew —"

Rahim hastily interrupted. "I know that's not allowed."

"That's why I will never talk about this again."

Thor, however, was displeased. **I don't remember you mentioning this to me before.**

Because I'm ashamed, and I know he doesn't feel the same.

His tone turned gentle. **Perhaps he does—given his status and situation, Silver is only being cautious.**

It reached late afternoon when the trio arrived at the cliff overlooking the North Sea, per Selena's request to watch the sunset in solace. Thor gently dropped the two before excusing himself for his evening hunt and launched towards the feeding pen.

Clouds billowed and rumbled over the horizon, but Selena wanted to enjoy the day's last rays of sunshine before the storm. Standing over the edge of the precipice, Selena observed the sea's still surface, smooth as glass; the calm and peaceful scenery made her want to step over and allow the water to wash away her worries.

As Selena sat down, knees drawn to her chest, Rahim spun in place as he enjoyed the view away from the city. "Dragonstone is nice, but nothing beats this." He laughed, but his smile faded when Selena was caught in a trance. "Please don't tell me that tosser is upsetting you."

"No, he's not, and stop calling him that. I would be a little grateful he opened his home to you and Niamh."

"Err, sorry. I swear, I'm grateful."

The two watched the sunset over the horizon while Thor still gorged himself on sheep; when Selena's thoughts finally cleared, she shared her recent experiences and discoveries, from confirming Ragnarok's whereabouts to learning who she was. She finished her tale when the sun dipped over the peak, and Rahim's jaw dropped to the ground as he sat next to her. "I like the sound of using that legendary sword against the evil necromancer. Let's get it now."

"Not yet. We would have to hide it once we found it or risk it falling into the wrong hands."

Rahim's face brightened. "What about giving it to Silver? He could keep it at Dragonstone."

"I won't endanger him and Niamh. We're better off leaving the sword for now until we need it."

"I suppose." Rahim sighed in disappointment but eventually agreed with her logic before enjoying the news of her Divine and royal nature. "All this time, you're the Crown Princess and the one from the prophecy, the dragon-born." His head whipped around to see Thor picking his claws clean. "He's your half-brother, then. To think we have two Divinity Dragons in existence—I'm sure Silver was thrilled with the way he goes on about dragons."

Selena bit her bottom lip as she clasped her hands around her knees. "He's Genesis Altessa." When Rahim expressed his confusion, she explained how she came to her conclusion; even Thor paused to pay attention to their conversation, although he already knew when they read the journal.

"That would be wicked if he was. No wonder you're so infatuated with him," Rahim nudged her shoulder, "now he can truly be your *beloved*."

Face burning in embarrassment, Selena peered over her shoulder in fear that Silver overheard, but all she saw was Azrael strolling over with his hands thrust into his trouser pockets. Circling overhead was Doragon's golden gleam; Thor fixated his gaze upon his once-feared adversary, but now the two dragons matched in size. He jumped to all fours, wings extended, ready to pounce upon Doragon, but he ignored Thor.

"Speaking of tossers," Rahim grumbled, but Selena shushed him, hoping Azrael would stray away. To her dismay, he snickered when seeing the two and trekked over as Doragon landed behind him upon his haunches.

Azrael approached with his arms crossed. "What's this? Calling people names, are we?"

"We don't want any trouble," Selena said through her teeth.

Doragon hissed and snarled, but Thor quickly swept himself skyward in one leap and zipped towards them. When Doragon saw him make his descent, he backed away with low growls but acknowledged Thor as the alpha; his eyes caught the gleam of Thor's golden chain and his string of rubies, but Doragon didn't let up.

When Azrael inched forward, Rahim jolted to his feet, but Selena stood up and met Azrael's temper. "What do you want from us? We haven't done anything to you."

Azrael ignored the interaction between the two dragons, even as Thor stepped closer, anticipating an attack against Selena. Doragon swiped at Thor's front legs, and the dragons almost lunged for each other if Selena hadn't asked Thor to back down. Instead, the two watched each other like hawks, snarling through clamped fangs.

"Do I need a reason for anything I do? You think you know everything and can read people like a book." Azrael reached up and grabbed her shoulders, forcing her to step back. "You know nothing about Doragon and me, nor what we've endured." Rahim reached out to pull Azrael back, but Doragon was faster; with snake-like reflexes, he swept his tail across the ground, shoving and tripping Rahim. Thor retaliated by launching for Azrael, but Doragon stood in between, and the two massive dragons rolled around behind their handlers through a snarling flurry of claws and fangs, leaving deep gashes in one another.

Selena struggled to break free, but Azrael was stronger. She could use magic to fight him back, but Azrael was better with the craft. She won their duel last time because she caught him by surprise; even with her training, she was nowhere near his skill level to use Aether.

After collecting his bearings, Rahim resumed his effort to rescue Selena, but Azrael didn't waver until she stood right on the cliff's edge. He sneered as he shoved her once more. "I hope you can swim." Selena lost her footing and fell over when Azrael backed away; Rahim pushed past and reached out to grab her hand, but she slipped through his fingers.

The water below her was steady and calm, ready to embrace her. The cold, hard impact against its glossy surface was like a thousand needles piercing her body at once, and the shock of the drop slowly made her lose consciousness.

After diving in after her, Silver wrapped one arm around her and swam back to the surface. Stoic-faced, he carried her back to shore, and Selena coughed up the salty seawater as her vision cleared.

Azrael and Doragon were nowhere to be seen, but Thor circled overhead, his skirmish settled for now; Rahim ran over and hugged her when Silver helped her stand. "Thank the Divines. I gave Azrael a proper beating for what he did."

Before her buzzing thoughts cooled, Silver spun her around with trembling hands to make eye contact. "Why did you face him alone? Why didn't you call and run for help?" His voice cracked like it would break any moment.

Thor landed near the two and roared. **He's right. I should have ferried you two away when I had the chance.**

Completely undone, Selena pulled away. "Why are you mad at me? What do you want me to do, crouch down and let you guys fight my battles for me?"

"We are all trying to keep you safe."

"You told me that Azrael and Doragon wouldn't harm Thor or me. Was that a lie?"

"No," Silver sternly said, "but now, he will answer to Phantom Dust."

"I don't believe Azrael will listen if he hadn't already. Why would D appear now?" When Silver couldn't answer, Selena stepped forward and whispered, "Why do you care about keeping me safe? Is it to protect your greatest achievement, Genesis?" Silver took a step back as he studied her through furrowed brows. "So, it's true then. It made sense when I read the journal."

Thor growled as he snaked his head around. **Selena, back off.**

She ignored him, and Silver pinched the bridge of his nose. "Yes, I'm not trying to hide it anymore—I'm Genesis Altessa."

Selena paused, her eyes glossing over like a frozen lake in winter. "What are you then, a dragon? Is that how you've lived this long?"

"No, but that's beside your initial concern. Yes, you are important and my magnum opus, but that's not why I want you safe—"

Her flowing tears betrayed her; his words ripped Selena's heart to shreds when realizing her affections were deeper than his. "Then what other reason is there, to hide me? That was certainly my mother's only concern. I don't even know who my father is, and if he's still alive, he probably doesn't want me back either."

"Don't you dare—"

When Rahim attempted to join in on their heated discussion, Silver glared at him. "Okay, I'm sorry. I will ask later after you two finish arguing."

"This isn't a joke anymore, Rahim. None of you understand all I've gone through." Selena didn't expect either to respond; Thor snarled and reached over to grab her, but she slipped through his claws and ran in the other direction, ignoring their pleas for her to stay. Thor readied himself to chase her down, but Selena heard Silver ask him to stay before pursuing her himself, calling for her attention.

The sky turned black as soon as she made it back to the barracks. Thanking the Divines Azrael hadn't returned, Selena dove into the blankets, jumping and flinching from every ear-shattering thunder roaring overhead.

Her door suddenly squeaked open, and she heard Silver's footsteps strut across the floorboard. "Liongod."

She yelped when the thunder cracked again. "Please go away."

"What are you doing under the blankets?" She quivered as the desperation to run away crept closer, but Silver placed a hand on top. "Are you afraid of the thunder and lightning?" When Selena didn't answer, he sat on the bed with great care, wrapped his arms around her, and pulled her close. "I'm sorry I never realized how alone you truly felt. Thor and I will always be here for you."

*****

The torrential rain lessened; Azrael sat within Doragon's coils on the cliff overlooking the sea, growling through his teeth while complaining about Selena and Rahim. Undone, Doragon hissed at him to stop. **You do understand Phantom Dust won't be happy.**

I don't care anymore. He picked up a nearby stick and threw it over Doragon's tail, yelling at the sky.

Her very nature makes you angry, yet you helped with the Well of Souls.

Azrael escaped from Doragon's protective golden coils and began pacing. *I should have never helped Silver.*

Bullocks, this dark world needed two Divinity Dragons. I hate tormenting them, but I followed you. I wish you would leave them alone. Besides, Doragon nodded to the recently healed deep gashes Thor gave him, **I believe he will kill me next time. He already outweighs me, and I will not adjust my size anymore.**

He growled but lowered his head in defeat, disregarding Doragon's ability to shape-shift as Azrael's spirit beast guardian. *Maybe you're right.*

Of course, I'm right. I still regret burning the village.

The two lingered in silence, allowing the air to cool from their hot tempers. Azrael sighed. *Perhaps I despise how she seems hopeful and forgiving even when others don't deserve it.*

Like you? Don't you think you deserve forgiveness?

Azrael thrust his fists into his pockets and peered at Doragon from over his shoulder. "No, I don't deserve forgiveness. Not after all that I have done."

"Don't worry. We're not as forgiving." The voice startled him and Doragon, and Azrael spun around to see Kain Vanguard leaning against a tree. His crimson eyes pierced the darkened veil, contrasting his pearly-white vampiric fangs. Off in the distance, Silver raced towards them in a fit of rage, face burning red while screaming rambling nonsense Azrael couldn't understand; a trail of dust clouds billowed from Silver's stampede.

Kain yawned and stretched out one hand, waiting until Silver was near. He snatched the captain's jacket collar and yanked him back, but Silver dragged his feet across the dirt, attempting to pull away. "You bastard! How could you do that to her? I will kill you myself if she doesn't."

Kain tightened his grip. "That's enough."

"No, it's not. This twat is going to pay. Let me kill him, just this once."

"There's no way I can let you: D gave me that right."

"Absolutely not. He disobeyed D's orders—*I* will have that privilege." Silver tugged his collar from Kain's curled fingers and marched to the indifferent Azrael, but Doragon growled and snarled between tail flickers. "I will have you court-martialed for this."

Azrael scoffed and turned away, but Silver grabbed his shoulder and spun him around. "Do you not care about protecting our two Divinity Dragons?" Silver's nostrils flared when Azrael ignored him. "Don't you remember helping me with the Well of Souls?"

Azrael scoffed. "That was a mistake." Doragon snarled in disagreement, but his companion turned a deaf ear.

Silver fumed as words fired like bullets. "Mistake? How dare you? Our job is to make sure that its only success lives—think of what we could accomplish, like using her genetic makeup to our advantage. Azrael, have you seen how easily she can channel magic and how amazing she is?"

"I don't give a damn—"

Silver ignored him. "She has the blood of a dragon running through her veins, and I think she has a hidden ability because of it."

Now Kain was interested. "What do you mean?"

"I don't know, but I've never been wrong before."

Annoyed, Kain shoved Silver aside and marched over until his face was a small breadth away from Azrael's: "You will not go against D's orders again, but I believe he'll remind you soon."

Azrael snarled back and spat on the ground, but he didn't argue. Silver leaned in close when Kain stepped aside, disregarding Doragon's maw pluming with smoke and embers. "If you don't, the next time you hurt her, by the Divines, I will kill you myself. I don't care what you are." He then stormed off.

Doragon wrapped a protective arm around Azrael and held him close to his chest before launching to the stars in one leap. Kain watched the pair disappear before joining the angry captain. "What was wrong with you back there?"

Silver snorted. "I don't know what you mean."

Kain reached over and grabbed his jacket again. "Stop being a prick for once. You're getting way too protective." Silver kept his head down, and Kain's eyes widened. "If you tell me of your affections for the girl, I will vomit."

"That's none of your business."

"No, but that's D's concern. I don't know how he will take it."

Silver slowly hung his head in defeat. "It doesn't matter."

"Yes, it does." Silver shrugged, and Kain threw him back. "Dammit."

"Do you think I meant for this to happen? After all the time I've spent with her, and getting to see how wonderful and perfect she is—"

"I don't want to hear any more." Kain sighed and rubbed his temples. "Does she know?"

Silver looked towards the North Sea once more. "It's probably for the best she doesn't."

Kain raised a fist like he was about to strike Silver but only extended a finger and pointed at him. "Don't do anything stupid." He then marched off. Silver dug his hands into his pockets and stood there for an eternity. He looked up at the stars and smiled.

*****

When the thunder and lightning ceased, Selena was comfortable enough to emerge from her hiding place; sitting in Azrael's bed, she propped her head up with her arm against the windowsill. Despite their animosity, she remained vigilant in watching for Azrael's return, with only Thor to keep her company.

How are you feeling?

I'm better. I'm sorry for how I acted.

I understand, but I wish you would have talked to me instead of Silver.

Are you getting jealous?

No, never.

You're so full of it, but I'm sorry I didn't talk to you about it.

Hmph. Apology accepted, and….

And I won't shut you out like that again. I was just so upset, and I wasn't within reason.

I know.

Their conversation was interrupted by the soft flail of wings from above. A dragon's shadow glided across the ground towards the top of the barracks. She then saw Azrael running down the training field, and she immediately knew that the dragon was Doragon. *I believe Azrael is in trouble.*

Good for him.

Now is not the time to be sarcastic. He might need help.

I'm not helping him. He and Doragon can rot in Oblivion for all I care.

Azrael ran until a few chains shot through the air, wrapping around his ankles. He tripped, falling face-forward into a pile of sharp rocks, nicking and bloodying his face. *He's under attack. I must help him.*

After what he did to you?

Yes.

Ignoring Thor's protests, Selena began climbing out her window but stopped when she saw a mysterious man walking towards Azrael. Doragon wailed from his perch and crouched down; Selena wondered why he didn't save his companion. *How could this man scare a dragon?*

The man wore a regal red jacket with gold buckles and trimmings, its collar brushing the underside of his chiseled cheekbones. His mask of black and white sent a cold chill shivered down Selena's spine; he made heavy strides towards the imprisoned Azrael, holding the three chains binding him loosely in one hand.

Azrael rolled over to face his attacker, who stopped and lifted his hand. The chains unwrapped themselves from Azrael's ankles and disappeared underneath his jacket sleeve. The man leaned on one knee beside Azrael, but their conversation remained inaudible; Selena leaned further out the window to hear. "You must control your anger. Her Imperial Majesty and I gave you strict orders."

Azrael wheezed and spat blood. "I already dealt with this from Silver and Kain." He forced himself to stand and summoned his spirit pistols, and to Selena's surprise, the man didn't stop him. Before Azrael could fire a single bullet, the stranger, still on one knee, flicked his wrists, and a large, tangled mess of metal shot out from his sleeve, wrapping around Azrael like angry snakes strangling their prey. His spirit guns shattered like glass.

The Chain Master then waved his hand up, and the shackles followed his command, slamming Azrael into the nearby stone wall. While the man watched, Azrael howled in pain and hung his head low in defeat. The man scoffed. "You're weak in this form, from your anger." With another flick of his wrists, the chains withdrew, dropping the undone Azrael to his hands and knees. The stranger leaned in to whisper more in his ear, and Azrael only glared at him.

He finally stood up and backed away, allowing Azrael to flee. Doragon shuffled around on the rooftop before taking to the sky, swooped down, and snagged his rider with his claws before the two disappeared into the night.

Thor's snarls echoed across her mind. **Well?**

Azrael is fine, but this Chain Master badly injured him.

I like him better already. Hmm.

What is it?

I remember him before I hatched from when Gromm and Beck rescued us: Phantom Dust.

Her eyes locked on Dust, and she jolted outside to catch him before he withdrew back into the shadows. *Now is my chance to confront him.*

To her surprise, Thor agreed. Phantom Dust marched off the courtyard through the side arches and towards the Hinterlands, not peering behind as Selena pursued him within the darkened veil. The brisk night wind cut across her body, but Dust remained undeterred through his long strides; suddenly, Selena's walk turned into a quick jog when he disappeared through the thickened trees. *Where could he be going?*

Thor's humming and chittering carried like the wind in the leaves. **Be careful.**

The ancient grove's enchanting evening ballad pulled her into its dense verdant embrace, and eventually, she reached a small moonlit meadow, but Dust was gone. She swore under her breath but heard footsteps approaching from behind. Her skin began to crawl, and her heart caught in her throat; Selena spun around and came face to face with the towering Chain Master.

His mask's eye sockets were like the void as he met her terrified gaze. Selena backed away as he approached, and Dust's stoic tone chilled the atmosphere. "You shouldn't be wandering around unarmed."

With her fear and paranoia rising, she started summoning a weapon for herself. Before she finished, he grabbed her hand while it was in midair. Her breath quickened, and her heart was about to explode; Selena knew, at that moment, he had her at his mercy and could kill her. He didn't stir. Engraved on the very top of his mask was a symbol of the black fox, and Selena raised a brow as she squinted. "As I've said before, it's unsafe to wander around unarmed."

Dust released her hand; meanwhile, Thor began asking how their encounter went, but she didn't have an answer to give. Selena stepped back but was shocked when Dust pulled out a small, dark green leather bag. "What is that?"

"It's an ingot: dragon bone melded with steel. I smelted this myself to save time, already perfect to begin shaping."

"You're a blacksmith, too."

He nodded. "I used to be, professionally. I find that dragon bones are much better to mix with steel than unicorn horns. From this, you can make the sharpest and finest weapon that will neither dull nor break—you could cut through the thickest of metals and pierce armor in one slice. Use it well."

He offered her the bag. She was reluctant but cautiously accepted his gift; she slipped her hand inside and pulled out a perfectly smooth and light-weight brick, gleaming with a copper-tinted ivory hue. "Thank you."

Dust turned sharply on his heels as if he would leave but stopped. "Mind your manners to your mother. She loves you dearly."

Selena shamefully looked down at her feet when she recalled their nasty exchange as she returned the ingot to the bag. "I swear to be in the future. Thor told me you're trustworthy, and there is one more question I hope you can answer."

"I believe Silver had already told you more than you were supposed to know. He has a terrible habit of talking too much, and I'm afraid you'll be wasting your time with me."

"Please, answer just one question, and I will leave it alone forever. Who and where is my father?"

It was an uncomfortable silence before Dust could say, "He's dead. The Council killed him a long time ago."

Selena felt her heart squeeze. "I think you're lying."

His eyes shattered the darkness. "Think what you will."

He walked away, but Selena ran in front, preventing him from leaving. "You've taken charge of my protection, but for what reason? I need to know—"

"Know what? What good will come of this? I don't have time to explain, and I'm already behind with my plans. Good day."

He strutted off but what Selena said next made him stop dead in his tracks. "Were you ever going to tell me the truth? What's more important than answering my question, Father?"

The Shadow Emperor immediately spun around. "What did you just call me?" It sounded more like a plea than a demand.

"So, it's true then. Why did you tell me that my father was dead?"

"I am, according to the Council." He paused and studied her as if she were a strange creature. "I will admit, you're incredibly bright for someone so young."

Selena wanted to scream, hit a tree, lash out, hug him, and run away. Tears streamed down her cheeks. "Why did everyone want to keep it a secret?"

Dust held out both hands, palms facing up. "To protect you. I don't have another answer or excuse, sadly."

"That doesn't give you, or Her Imperial Majesty, the right to keep that from me. Days ago, I had no idea who I was, and I'm just finding out that I'm the Crown Princess and a dragon. Silver was the only one with the decency to tell me anything." Dust ruefully looked away, and Selena inched closer. "Please, make time to explain."

Caught in great anticipation over his answer, he finally agreed. "You deserve to know. We never made the best decisions. Your mother and I aren't perfect, but we feared the Council would have found out if we revealed ourselves to you." He paused as his eyes shimmered behind the mask. "I can't tell you how devastated we were when you were stillborn. Your mother and I tried to do everything to bring you back, but we did treasonous things that night. The Council somehow found out and immediately ordered me taken away and executed but spared your mother. Meanwhile, Silver had finished his project and offered to help."

"The Well of Souls."

Dust nodded. "I managed to escape Mortemholdt before being taken to the guillotine and was on the run for quite some time before Vidar declared me dead. I had to stay away from Alfheim, and the only way I could contact your mother was through letters.

"After Silver's success and for the next two hundred and sixteen years after, I got a letter from your mother through Loki every week about how you two were doing so that, in some small way, I was still involved. The Council knew nothing about you or the Well, but somehow the Lich did. He took all of Silver's research notes, destroyed his project, and kidnapped you and Thor's egg. Rescuing you and your dragon was our first and only priority.

"We only wanted to keep you and Thor with Chaliss temporarily until we resolved the situation, but we decided to let you live there when we learned you had no memory of us. You were happy, and so was your new companion. Your caretaker was kind and generous to care for you as one of her own, and so we compensated her well, and she hid her wealth to avoid suspicion."

Selena's eyes glistened. "Why didn't you and Mother come back for us? Didn't you want us anymore?"

"Of course, we did—your mother and I loved you more than anything, but we wanted you to live a fulfilling, happy life away from strife. I can't tell you how painful that was for us." Dust clinched his fists. "However, we had to intervene as soon as the Council decided to take you away. You weren't supposed to meet Silver and Kain, but we were secretly around. We planned on rescuing you two, but you and Thor had already fled."

"And Helshire Village was gone." Selena's nostrils flared when her fists trembled at her sides. "Then why did you finally return to Alfheim?"

"Because I wasn't happy when I found out what Azrael did. I know Kain and Silver almost tore him to shreds, but he needed to hear it directly from me."

"I don't understand. Azrael and Doragon have been following and tormenting us, not to mention what they did to Helshire—how do you trust them?"

"It was never their intention to harm you, and as for the village...." Phantom Dust turned away as his voice trailed off. "There is no excuse for that, and I pray for those whose lives were lost in that fire. Azrael has a complicated past." Selena was not wholly satisfied, and he sighed. "I will let him explain it when he's ready, as it's not right for me to speak in place of others." The tense air steeped. "You probably hate and despise us."

"You're my father. All I've ever wanted was to know my parents." She didn't know how to feel: happy, sad, angry? "Please take off your mask."

Dust hesitated. "Do you want to look at the face of a dead criminal?"

Selena shook her head and touched it, but Dust immediately grabbed her arm. "I want to see my father."

They stood in uncomfortable silence. It felt like an eternity, but he finally nodded, released her hand, and lowered his head. She investigated the empty sockets of the mask to see his eyes; she swallowed her fear and pulled it off. His hollow deep blue eyes set against his chiseled and narrow pale face, filled with grief, perfectly pairing with his black hair swept behind his long, pointed ears like raven feathers catching the moonlight—a thin braid wrapped with tiny, gold chains dangled beside both sides of his jawline. Selena dropped the mask and, without another thought, embraced him as the tears began swelling.

Dust staggered, but he hugged her back. Selena tightened her hug and sobbed into his jacket. "How could you two have left me? I appreciate Chaliss and all she did for both Thor and me, but I needed you—I needed my parents. I understand why you two did what you had to do. But why do I still feel this way?"

"Your mother and I love you more than anything. Even as I was in prison and on the run, I thought about you two every night and how much I missed you both. I swore I would never let harm befall you two again. We will take back Armageddon from Vidar one day. The Council has been trying to usurp the imperial family, but we will end it."

CHAPTER 19: THE BATTLE FOR ALFHEIM

The following few days flew by since confronting her father for answers, but Selena hadn't seen him since; she understood he had to maintain his guise, just like she had to with hers.

As much as Selena welcomed the sweet solace, she worried Phantom Dust had taken it too far with Azrael. When her bunker buddy had finally returned, he barely acknowledged her existence. Instead, he crawled into bed and slept throughout their weekend.

Yet, Selena was anxiously looking forward to the promised training with Thor. As her ninth and final week of basic training was nearly complete, everyone from her unit was fitted for custom armor orders by the dwarf blacksmiths, and they would complete their pieces by their last day on the fifteenth of Xol. Meanwhile, she and her fellow brothers built upon their previously learned skills, learning how to cooperate as a team. During field training and their fifteen-kilometer march back to post, Selena remembered Erik and Alexander, wishing the two could join their well-earned victory.

Selena had mentioned the dragon bone and steel ingot to Silver after meeting him in his office after training, explaining that she wanted to make a sword; he happily exclaimed, "You will have a fine weapon yet." However, she was hesitant in sharing her discovery regarding Ragnarok; when she did, Silver's face turned paler than usual, and his head zipped back and forth to ensure no one eavesdropped. "The Oracles told you this?"

"Yes. Why?"

"They usually don't answer questions from anyone outside the Council. Hmm." He placed a hand to his chin as he fell deep in thought. "If what you say is true, you can't tell anyone else about it."

"Other than Rahim and Thor, you're the only one I've told. I had hoped to use it against the Lich—"

Silver's voice suddenly turned cold and stern, like his ghostly expression. "Absolutely not. You could get yourself killed. Leave Ragnarok alone or risk your imminent demise: only a Divine can handle that sword." He pointed to the glossy ingot Selena showed him. "Don't worry. We will forge you a suitable weapon that the Lich himself will fear."

When she first shared the news with Thor, he only snorted. **Where did your father get the bones?**

Err, he didn't say, but he never struck me as a dragon killer. When Thor still wasn't wholly persuaded, she added, *I don't think he would have killed a dragon without a good reason, or perhaps they're from an already dead dragon.*

Enough. If it's truly better than steel, I pray this will be the finest sword ever crafted.

Upon their final day, Silver presented each cadet with their new armor: dragon head-shaped helmet with scale-plated chest pieces and greaves. After meeting their new dragon partners tomorrow, he announced that the blacksmiths would work with the graduated soldiers to forge their desired weapon and pick a combat specialty. Silver then dismissed the new soldiers to spend the remainder of the day with their families. Instead of taking the much-needed break, Selena asked to begin some exercises with Thor later before forging herself a new weapon.

After briefly meeting with Rahim, Niamh, and Maria for morning tea and breakfast at Dragonstone, Thor, magnificently blazing the large ruby from his newly fitted harness, made his graceful descent. He readjusted his golden chain set with the smaller string of matching sparkling rubies before plucking Selena off the ground and placing her on the saddle seat. During their short flight to the training courtyard, Selena quickly changed into her steel and unicorn horn armor as Thor landed, lightweight metal forged to withstand the heaviest blows: one revolver and a pistol belted to her waist, and her new round shield strapped over her back.

Aracania was busy commanding several groups before and after taking flight; they practiced different aerial maneuvers and formations once airborne. Trainers down below used magic, creating large hoops set around at different angles in an obstacle course to fly through. If any dragon made a mistake and missed, they would have to try again.

While their dragons were occupied, the soldiers busied themselves with archery and sharpshooting through the instruction of Colonel Theron Cyres, an elf whose skin tone was a dull shade of dark maroon, contrasting his light sea-green hair. Though he donned the typical military apparel, a golden crown of twisted leaves and vines decorated his head, matching his gilded fang-shaped earrings. A seasoned instructor, Cyres was one of the few experts in magic besides Silver, his talent hailing across all four elements. Since Silver handled training recruits, Cyres would be Selena's new superior starting next week.

He strolled past Gromm and Beck, the brothers laying on the ground with rifles, shooting at their targets with quick precision. Azrael stood nearby, firing real pistols; he only paused after Colonel Cyres passed by and peered at Selena as Thor came near, not flinching from the dragon's warning snarls.

That is the first time we've seen him train.

Thor snaked his head upward. **Doragon, too.**

As Aracania's formation soared overhead, the pair saw Doragon managing the right flank. He barely swiveled his head enough to see them, and to their surprise, Doragon dipped his head in greeting before resuming his training.

Silver waited for the two in the middle of the field, grinning ear to ear. "You look like a proper dragon rider." Selena's sense of pride for her achievements displayed across her face.

Aracania's group finished their final lap before she was satisfied and dismissed the dragons for the day. Doragon raced to the field, landing beside Azrael, who holstered his weapons. Silver, meanwhile, watched them like a hawk.

Thor's muscles tensed and tightened, but Doragon eased the tension by lowering himself towards the ground, wings unfurled and one paw extended outward. Immediately, Thor relaxed, and his growls ceased; Selena hoped this marked the end of their feud, but Azrael still wasn't happy. Satisfied, Silver dismissed them, and Azrael raised his hand in a salute before turning sharply on his heels. Doragon straightened up while casting an admiring gaze upon Thor's exquisite jewelry, and he became airborne with one massive leap with Azrael scooped in his talons.

Aracania swooped in, hovering aloft; her head bobbed up and down, followed by a series of clicks and chirps that Selena interpreted as commands. Thor responded likewise and joined her in the sky, floating through beating his wings forward and backward. **She says to prepare yourself as well.**

Very good.

Colonel Cyres joined Silver and watched as Selena figured out how to securely strap herself to the harness with carabiners, allowing her to use both hands without holding the reins constantly. After removing her shield and slipping her arm through the leather handle, Thor shook and spun in circles, testing her safety belts; Selena confirmed all was well.

Upon Aracania's wing signal, Silver waved his hands in circular motions, summoning a series of fire rings dangling in mid-air, positioned all around the courtyard's edge. When Aracania roared, Selena gripped her revolver, and Thor raced towards the first elemental hoop. Thor's agile acrobatics were on par with Aracania's, despite his massive bulk; graceful like a swan but with deadly precision like a hawk, he dashed across the courtyard obstacle course at record time, flying through each flaming ring without fail. Aracania chirped in approval when he finished, but Silver recreated the lap with new hoops, and this time, Colonel Cyres assisted.

As Thor rounded towards the first ring, Cyres unleashed lightning tendrils zapping from his fingertips; Selena instinctively held her shield to counter, reflecting and directing his magic skyward. Each hoop was like an earned prize as the pair fought off every attack between rings; when Cyres switched to using flames, Thor exhaled a torrential stream of ice shards lancing the ground like giant crystal spears, extinguishing the fire. Both instructors dashed away from his attack, and Thor was free to finish the course.

Impressed, Colonel Cyres continued attacking with magic streams, switching from one element to another. Thor continued at it for hours until he demonstrated his other abilities with wind and earth. Selena was proud of his outstanding skills until Cyres misfired, striking her with a torrent of flames. As Thor snarled and dove away, Selena assured him she was unharmed. When Thor landed, and Selena dismounted to reassure Colonel Cyres of her wellbeing, Silver was the only one grinning. Selena understood Silver's lack of concern. *Mortal magic cannot harm a dragon, my dear.*

That still didn't stop Thor from thoroughly inspecting her until he was satisfied. **Dragon or not, I will not stand idly by if you somehow got hurt.**

Their training ended when Selena heard someone calling her last name. This time, Neith, wearing her red fox mask, pushed past the line of soldiers marching to the dining hall after Cyres dismissed them. Selena removed her charred but undamaged helmet and waved Neith over. The two exchanged pleasantries and bowed before Neith handed over a sealed parcel. "It's from the Council," she warned and left as quickly as she came.

While Selena fumbled with the parcel, Silver wondered aloud, "I hadn't seen that messenger of hers in a long time. I hope Her Imperial Majesty hadn't replaced that fox."

Selena squinted at him after unrolling Vidar's message. "I'm assuming you mean Loki, and it may be because you did something to him. As to what, I could only imagine."

Her fingers fidgeted while she read the official letter; Selena couldn't understand why the Council wanted a meeting with her and Thor at the Fire Temple at eight in the morning. Silver and Cyres were confused but reassured the two that this couldn't mean disciplinary action, or they would have reported directly to General Araneus and Aracania.

Yet, Selena remained unconvinced, and her anxiety grew. *What if the Council found out about us?*

Thor snaked his head around her. **I don't believe so; otherwise, they would have taken immediate action. Rest easy, my dear one. Soon, we'll know the truth.**

Selena arose before the sun, and, careful not to wake Azrael, she dolefully dressed in her best uniform: black jacket with gold clasps, buttons, and trimmings, complete with her finest breeches and polished hessian boots. She slipped on her formal gentleman's gloves, easily concealing her mark. After combing her recently cut hair back in a sleek shine, Selena dashed through their fort and past the dining hall, too nervous to eat.

You should, Thor said, **I always feel better after eating.**

But you're always eating.

Thor hovered above the courtyard as she marched outside, cleaned and scales brilliantly oiled. Instead of the harness, he proudly wore his ruby set chain as a badge of honor. After scooping her off the ground into his paw, Thor propelled himself up and over the gates, sweeping himself higher with long, slow wing beats. The two flew at an arch, and before Selena could fully enjoy the flight, Thor descended before the Fire Temple.

Each step felt heavier than the last as she marched through the door. As Thor was the size of a three-leveled house, instead, his head slithered through the doorway; he clicked his nails against the marble stairs with impatience.

An altar stood in the very back with three sculptures of the Divines behind it: Xyaxon stood in the middle, Death to its left, and Ulrich, the Emerald Dragon, to its right. The eyes of the lion were rubies, while the eyes of Death were sapphires, and Ulrich's were emeralds. Painted above the ceiling was the depiction of the three beasts in a cosmic battle with one another. Lit candles trailed the edges of the long, crimson carpet stretching from the door to the altar.

A lantern flickered in the doorway leading to a massive war room with a long, oak table, surrounded by a large group murmuring over a map with pinned flags marking specific locations. General Araneus leaned over with two hands on the table, studying what Selena assumed to be battle plans. Next to him was Vidar Helios peering to what the general pointed at with Captain Altessa and Colonel Cyres towering over the two. Standing to the general's other side were the Oracle triplets and Her Imperial Majesty, the Empress.

Be careful, Thor warned, but Selena had better control over her emotions this time; Silver broke away from the discussion when she approached and escorted her over to greet the others. Even when she reached her mother, Her Imperial Majesty still smiled, and Selena bent the knee.

Vidar offered her a handshake and clapped both hands over hers. "Impeccable timing, Liongod. We summoned you and Thor here because we're preparing for battle."

"What battle, sir?" After offering her a seat, Silver resumed their topic of discussion that, to Selena's fear and dismay, bore troubling news of confirmed rumors.

"The battle for Alfheim is upon us," General Araneus clarified, "The Lich has amassed an army of about thirty thousand and is en route towards Alfheim. He rounded up those nasty Orc creatures, Trolls, and other horrendous beasts willing to serve." General Araneus glumly looked over to the Oracles. "How much time do we have?"

The sisters said together, heads facing downward: "The morning of the nineteenth at the tolling of the bells." They looked up when Selena felt her heart beating faster, trembling in terror and excitement that would soon fade. The Oracles gave her a secret sneer that only she saw, and Selena suspected they were encouraging her to begin her pursuit for Ragnarok soon.

General Araneus snarled in frustration from the little time given as he looked at Silver and Cyres. "Our scouts have reported they're traveling by dragons ferrying vessels. So far, they've counted about ten, but I reckon there will be more. They've been traveling by night to avoid detection until now." His eyes flashed at Selena, who had remained silent. "Normally, I wouldn't send fresh soldiers directly into the line of fire without a dragon, but given yours and Thor's extraordinary and fortunate circumstances, we need your assistance."

"Sir, we would be honored to serve, but Thor and I just began aerial combat training, and I don't have a weapon yet—"

"I'm afraid it's already been decided. Liongod, you and Thor will report to Aracania later this afternoon to begin preparations. As for a weapon, I'm sure Captain Altessa or Colonel Cyres can supply an appropriate one for now."

Selena gave a firm nod, and a salute with no further say on the matter. "Sir, yes, sir."

"Very good. Dismissed."

Silver nodded to Colonel Cyres, confirming he would be the one to make the accommodations; he broke away and escorted Selena out of the temple once Thor withdrew his head from the entrance. She expressed her desire to make her sword. However, the temptation to find and use Ragnarok for her own steeped, and she mentioned it once more to Silver, who only warned, "That sword has only brought misfortune to those who seek its power. You will be corrupted and destroyed. Please, I beg of you, leave it alone."

She huffed, but she agreed, for Silver's sake. However, Selena secretly decided to look for it when she had a clear window; Thor also expressed his agreement by saying, **We'll find it, but if Ragnarok becomes too dangerous, I will destroy it myself.**

I find that more than agreeable.

Instead, she switched back to the subject of making her weapon. Though she could craft one through magic if the need arose, Selena needed to have one readily available. "It takes longer to summon an elemental weapon than to unsheathe one that's ready," she explained. "Will I have enough time to forge my sword?"

Silver squinted at her. "I could help you speed up the process and make one with magic—"

"I would rather do it traditionally. I believe perfect weapons are forged through blood, sweat, and tears —not magic."

Silver scratched his head. "I don't know. With the Force caught in a frenzy, Aracania may not allow you to leave her sight, and the process can take a while."

"With your sleepless draught, I can work on it tonight while Thor and I train with Aracania during the day."

Silver's face brightened. "I believe I still have another vial; you will have your sword by morning."

Selena shared his enthusiasm. "Then we have a plan, Captain and Master Alchemist."

He smiled and bowed; Selena placed a gentle hand on Thor's muzzle and propped her forehead against his snout, a silent communion between rider and dragon.

From Thor's deep rumbled purrs and chitters, he said: **We will go to battle, but we will receive the tribulations, sorrow, and triumphs from the aftermath.**

CHAPTER 20: DRAGONHEART

After Thor ferried the two to Dragonstone and dropped off Silver, the pair immediately reported to Aracania through the chaotic blitz and pell-mell preparations. Once they arrived, she began the long, grueling hours of formation and combat training. Selena and Thor were tasked to hold the left flank of Aracania's group. Given Thor's massive size, his unique breath abilities, and accounting for Aracania's vulnerability, she assigned him near the front to protect her while she led. Doragon picked up the right side, and the two nodded in mutual understanding. Azrael, however, still avoided Selena's gaze.

The groups practiced drills while staying in formation, and though Selena and Thor hadn't had the chance to learn yet, the two barreled by learning different flag signals, such as when to fall back or unleash a breath attack. Though Selena had a difficult time, Thor understood and memorized without difficulty. **Don't worry; I'll help you remember.**

It would be much easier if we all shared a mental link.

Even though we can, once we choose our partner, we dragons will never accept nor open our thoughts to another. We'll get by with this alternative.

Aracania didn't permit rest until the sun dipped below the horizon, and only upon her dismissal were the soldiers and dragons released. Thor left briefly to eat; however, as Azrael and Selena returned to their bunker, he bowed before gathering his evening wear and retired to the steam baths.

After grabbing the ingot from their shared locked chest, Selena returned to the courtyard to see Silver had returned with his promised sleepless elixir. One drop to her lips was enough to rejuvenate and awake her like the morning sun, and she announced, "I'm ready to begin."

Silver led her near the massive warehouses beyond the training field's arches to their training stone forge built with bellows—bags of supplied charcoal piled next. He explained most weapons and armor were imported from Rhumbek; Alfheim received shipment hours prior with readied supplies, leaving some of their forges unused.

However, Selena gasped when a mysterious cloaked figure emerged behind the unlit furnace. Fearing it was possibly the former Captain Bel, Silver reassured her all was well; he sneered when the Shadow Emperor stepped forth, mask-less this time. When he and Selena embraced, Dust said, "I understand I'm taking a huge risk, but I couldn't stand idly by when Silver and Azrael told me of the upcoming battle. Your mother and I don't want you to be a part of this."

Silver's eyes danced between him and Selena as he held up the dragon bone steel ingot. "You, sir, implied otherwise by supplying the perfect metal and offering to help forge her sword—"

Dust snarled, but Selena interrupted before he could snap at Silver. "It's okay, but Father, Thor and I have to do this or face court-martial and worse."

"We could keep you two safely hidden. Your mother and I would rather give up the throne than see you fight against that necromancer. We did everything we could to rescue you from him, and now you'll be thrown back into his clutches."

She gave him a small smile and looked up as Thor flew overhead upon returning from his meal and landed beside the large forge. "I can't run away forever. This time, Venexus will face the might of two Divinity Dragons." Silver and Dust flinched and recoiled upon hearing the Lich's actual name, but Selena was amused, unyielding to the power of fear.

"If you're ready to fight," Dust said finally, "let's ensure you have a proper weapon."

While he and Selena worked together to prepare the forge, Silver examined and admired the perfectly smelted ivory bar gleaming like gold. "I knew you used to work for a blacksmith before you were crowned Emperor of Armageddon, but your skills are unmatched—this is the finest ingot I've ever seen, given how difficult it must be to meld dragon bone and steel together."

The Shadow Emperor scoffed at Silver. "Genesis, you seem to forget I became the finest blacksmith in all of Armageddon and took over my master's shop. It was difficult—only dragon fire was hot enough to smelt and fold the two together, free of impurities." Dust looked up to the chittering Thor and nodded. "We will need your fire soon, dragon."

Silver's face turned red, looking as if he would whistle like a boiling tea kettle. "Don't call me Genesis; it's Silver."

Dust merely shrugged, turning a cold shoulder to his near explosive anger. Selena, on the other hand, looked at her father in awe. "I would love to learn more about you and Mother."

Much to hers and Silver's surprise, Dust grinned. "I promise when we have more time, as our history is a long tale. Rest assured; I will guarantee your new sword by morning."

Thor laid to the side as Silver, Dust, and Selena immediately went to work, eyes fixated on the three like a cat ready to pounce. Dust took numerous measurements of her hands and arms while asking questions about her preference for a one or two-handed sword. Once Selena announced one-handed, he asked for her opinion on design while warning that "its usefulness in battle is worth far more than its appearance." After showing her different advantageous shapes, Selena settled on a simple leaf-shaped blade with a dragon bone steel curved cross guard. When Dust and Silver began drawing up ideas for the grip and pommel, Thor suggested a jeweled design with a ruby to match his scales and gems.

Once satisfied, and after arranging the charcoal appropriately and Dust asked nicely, Thor happily released a small and controlled stream of flames to light the forge. The dragon fire needed only a few minutes to burn the charcoal to an evened bed, and when Dust declared it ready, Selena placed the nugget into the forge. Upon Dust's signal, Thor spewed a steady torrent through closed fangs, his roaring pillar making the metal bar glow cherry red. Closely following her father's teaching, Selena removed the dragon bone steel with a pair of tongs and placed it upon the anvil, and Dust followed by a series of quick blows from the hammer.

Selena returned the ingot to the forge when the heated colors faded, and Thor bathed the lumped metal with fire again. The three repeated this strenuous drawing-out process as the night wore on. Dust eventually broke off a smaller piece for the cross guard to use later; she, Thor, and Silver watched in admiration as he demonstrated his hammering technique, working the sides, edges, and tang into shape. He paused to occasionally inspect the raw sword's width, length, and thickness before continuing his craft. Selena watched as every blow he made miraculously transformed the already perfect ingot into a deadly blade thirsting for battle.

Halfway through the evening, Phantom Dust finally stopped and deemed his workpiece satisfactory after one final assessment, the incomplete and rough blackened blade eager to serve its purpose.

He allowed the blade to air cool for a while before bringing it to the nearby workbench next to a set of grinding wheels, and Dust spent the following couple of hours explaining the process to Selena and Thor while refining the blade with files. However, Thor half paid attention as he busied himself polishing his necklace until the gold and rubies sparkled from the fire's light. Meanwhile, Silver mixed fine-grained clay, charcoal ash, and powdered perlite in preparation for the quenching process through Dust's instruction.

When Dust finished filing, he announced to Selena before she could ask about the next step, "I will take care of the rest from here."

As he smothered the blade's edges and spine with Silver's blend, he waited until the clay hardened before laying the sword flat upon the smoldering coals. Silver clarified when he noticed Selena's look of confusion, "This is a greatly anticipated step, as you hope the blade won't shatter from the first quench. Your father doesn't want to risk losing the sword."

Dust slowly pulled it towards his hip while pumping the bellows, and as it escaped the dragon fire, he turned it around and repeated the step. After ensuring the edges were imbued with an even orange color, Dust lifted the blade from the coals and, through perfect timing, plunged it into the nearby trough, thick steam clouds wafting from the sizzling water.

Phantom Dust returned it to the fire, bringing the sword to the same low heat, and quenched it a second time; Silver leaned close and whispered in Selena's ear, "This is the mark of a true master blacksmith. It takes a fine eye and many years of experience to time the second quench without making the sword brittle."

Though typically it could take days or more to polish the blade, Dust completed his handiwork within hours, revealing its true hidden rose-tinted ivory beauty, the marbled metal marking different layers of steel mixed dragon bone.

Once Dust was satisfied with the perfect shape and carved middle grooves, he and Silver worked to prepare the hilt. It took Silver no time to gather all the pieces and transmute a large, perfectly cut deep ruby by combining and converting smaller gems from a tiny bag he carried. He crafted a perfectly smooth piece of oak for the hilt and, after fitting the tang, wrapped it in polished black shagreen from sharkskin. Dust, however, spent the next several hours working and shaping the smaller piece he had saved earlier into the desired curved cross guard, and he lined the scabbard with matching colors to the blade: glossy, rose-tinted ivory Silver designed with magic.

Phantom Dust had delivered his promise and finished his masterpiece by the time the Pyre chimed four in the morning. After fitting the perfectly cut large ruby within the dragon claw forming the pommel, he inspected and approved the solid but flexible blade, sheathed it, and handed the dragon bone sword to the awe-struck Selena. "This is the finest weapon I've ever made. Use it well."

Thor snaked his head over the three to inspect the finished piece and twittered in satisfaction. **Your enemies will learn to fear your blade and wrath, my dragon sister.**

"I will cherish this forever. Thank you." Upon heartily accepting the gift, the sword shimmered as it whistled upon unsheathing; light as a feather and an extension of her hand, the blade vibrated as if alive. Its rosy glow glinted with the dragon fire used to forge it, appearing ready to unleash a deadly inferno.

Selena gave it a few swings until her father urged her to test its strength against a nearby boulder. Doubtful, she made a single, diagonal cut, and the giant rock cleaved in two, like a heated knife slicing through butter. Amazed, she inspected her blade; the metal remained unscathed like a flawless diamond.

Silver gave Dust a smug grin as he crossed his arms. "D, my old friend, you've outdone yourself."

Thor lowered his head and nuzzled the ruby pommel. **A fine weapon like this ought to have a name. Don't you agree?**

Yes, I believe you're right, but I'm terrible with names.

Hmm. I think it should have 'dragon' in there somewhere. It seems only fitting.

When Selena looked at the gem and back at Thor, the very concept that the ruby symbolized how she would always carry him within her heart gave her the idea. She held up the sword, its point aimed for the heavens, as she faced Silver and Dust and announced, "I name thee Dragonheart."

Both Dust and Silver smiled from her chosen name. "A perfect name, indeed," her father agreed.

Immediately after saying farewell to her father before he withdrew back into the shadows, Selena and Thor rushed to join roll call. Aracania rounded and rallied her dragons and soldiers to begin the next day's preparations.

The two endured drills and practiced real combat scenarios like the day before and were only dismissed when Aracania was satisfied. With no further news of the Lich and his army, and as their window of opportunity continued shrinking, Selena grew restless. She and Thor wanted to find Ragnarok soon, either the evening before or during the battle.

After finishing another long and grueling day with Aracania, Silver invited the two over to the sparring circle to practice with Dragonheart. She passed by the others training with their partners, but Silver offered to become her opponent.

Thor circled overhead and landed by the archway with his wings still unfurled, the evening sun barely catching the gleam of his scales and jewelry. After hearing Thor's chirps, clicks, and roars, the other dragons soon joined him, including Aster, Vulcan, and even Doragon. When Doragon called for Azrael, he broke away from the dispersing crowd and joined his dragon's side, watching and waiting for the upcoming duel with great curiosity.

Silver summoned his reaper scythe and readjusted his glasses. "Do not hold back, Liongod. I want you to throw everything you've learned at me." After the two bowed, Silver immediately began attacking with both melee and magic attacks; he didn't go easy, as he used all the elements to his advantage. Instead of matching his speed and attacking back, she propelled herself around the field by summoning concentrated flames from her palms. When an opening presented itself, Selena unsheathed

Dragonheart, and as she lunged forward, Silver parried her attack, blocking her sword with his sickle.

He sneered and pushed her back, but Selena wanted to see how far she could go; she instinctively imagined herself being hard-headed and stable, like the earth. She slowly lifted her hands, and the ground rumbled before erupting skyward, creating a sturdy wall. Silver dashed over, punching it down, but Selena slid to his side when the rocks crumbled. Envisioning the surrounding Aether energy that could be manipulated, including Silver's, she lifted her hand. His eyes widened when realizing what she was about to do and teleported away. However, just as he did, Selena immediately spun around and knocked him out of stance by tripping him with her leg.

Silver caught himself and regained his posture, but he couldn't stop smiling. "Very impressive. You predicted what I would do, and you knew where I would attack next. How did you do that?"

At this point, Selena realized she and Silver had attracted a large audience of both dragons and soldiers; even Aracania had joined and was watching with sparkling amethyst eyes. "I don't know how to explain, but I thought I had visualized all our Aether energies. That was how I saw you move from here to there, even though you teleported." The crowd gasped in amazement; Azrael's eyes widened, and his face drained of all color, but Doragon leaned down and exhaled warm smoke over him, tousling his already messy hair.

"That's amazing—even I still have trouble doing it." He ran over and lifted one of her arms, examining her like she was his greatest discovery. "I'm looking forward to seeing what else you can accomplish, though I suspect you have yet to awaken your full potential."

"What do you mean by that?"

Silver bit down on his tongue when he noticed their adoring audience and nervously scratched the back of his head. "Perhaps we will save that discussion for another time, Liongod. Ahem. Let's continue."

The two dueled until the sun completely vanished below the horizon, and it only ended once Selena shattered Silver's weapon with Dragonheart upon a single swing. Realizing her mistake, she apologized profusely, but Silver clapped. "My scythe is just a conjured weapon. I can quickly summon it again, but you, my good sir, have bested me." He bowed upon admitting and conceding defeat, and the crowd cheered for Selena's unmatched skill. The dragons applauded by clicking their nails against the rocks and chirping in delight.

The soldiers were dismissed for the evening, but Azrael was the last to leave. He approached and bowed in respect. "It looks like I've underestimated your skills and prowess yet again. I never expected you to figure out how to use Aether on your own."

"But I didn't use—"

"You did in a sense. If you can see our energies, you can use Aether." Azrael nodded and marched away, leaving Selena bemused and confused, as that was the friendliest exchange the two had shared.

The eve of battle was a deadly silence. Silver invited Selena and Thor over to Dragonstone for evening tea, allowing her to reconvene with their friends, though Selena hoped this wouldn't be the last time she would see them.

During their flight, they saw dragons patrolling the perimeter of Alfheim, watching for the Lich's army that was soon to come. Archers lined the walls, passing by crewed catapults supplied with piles of boulders, oil pits, and brightly lit braziers. Earlier that day, the civilians had evacuated to a heavily furnished underground bunker with enough food, water, and other resources to last for years in case of a global emergency. However, Niamh, Maria, and Rahim still wished to see her one last time before joining the others.

Her hand automatically went to her sword, and a terrible notion dawned on her: eventually, she would have to face the Lich and his legion of the undead. Selena accepted her role, of course, but her stomach churned as the dreaded moment inched closer. *And we still don't have Ragnarok yet.*

We will find a way. We may not even need to use Ragnarok against the necromancer. Your sword is deadly enough.

It's not just that. We must get the sword before he does. If the Lich finds it, then....

As Thor landed by the water fountain and helped Selena dismount, he said, **The Lich won't find it. He's had so long to search, and I doubt he would get it before the battle.**

I don't want to let the Lich hurt or threaten anyone else ever again. I will make a difference.

Thor curled around the fountain as Silver dashed outside and welcomed Selena inside. Niamh, Rahim, and Maria sat in the parlor, sharing earl grey tea with lemon and biscuits. They happily accepted Selena's new company, and the four indulged in casual conversation while Silver brewed her green tea with a side of honey. After he served her, however, Silver retired to his alchemy tower for the moment, leaving the group to resume their party.

Her worries soon melted away, and she laughed and smiled as she stirred the honey before sipping; she showed off her new sword that the three coveted and praised its masterful and beautiful design.

Yet, Rahim broke the ice when he pointed to Maria and said, "Andric would love to hear more about you. Tell him."

"Tell me what?"

Maria shifted uncomfortably in her seat, and she threw her clasped hands down into her lap. "I dunno if I should."

Rahim gulped down his biscuit and tea. "Liongod is a huge fan, believe me."

Maria's eyes sparkled when she met Selena's curious gaze. "All right, but I must warn you that I haven't told anyone else this. My mother always said I should be ashamed, and she even dropped our last name, for she feared persecution."

However, before Maria could finish, Rahim grew impatient and said bluntly, "She's the great-granddaughter of that Varathka Gundisalvus fellow."

Selena nearly dropped her teacup in shock, but Maria shushed the jeering Rahim. Suddenly, Selena understood her comment about the Black Fox from months ago but was unsure why. Niamh, however, didn't react, and Selena wondered if she already knew.

Maria pleaded, "Please, don't tell anyone, as Armageddon isn't too fond of his name."

Selena, however, set her tea down and immediately bowed before her. "It's such an honor, and I had no idea. Why did you mention the Black Fox?"

"Because Rahim told me of your interest in Ragnarok and my great-grandfather's work; I thought I could hint at my connection."

As amazed as Selena was, she was still baffled, for she thought his family line ended when his daughter, Marceline, passed away. However, Maria clarified that "before my grandmother died, she had a child at a relatively young age. I believe she was as old as I am now, and my mother was also named Marceline for her."

Selena grinned and met Rahim's wide-eyed expression. "There's something I want to tell you, too."

Rahim's smile faded when he realized what she was about to do and waved his hands in an x-shape. "Don't do it."

Her thoughts rumbled from Thor's warning growls. **Listen to Rahim. Don't.**

Selena continued ignoring the two. "But you and Niamh have to swear to me that you won't tell the Council."

"If you haven't noticed, I despise every one of those old gits. I'm sure that whatever you want to tell me can't be any worse than what I've confessed already."

Niamh also agreed. "Nor I trying to kiss you, I suppose." Her face immediately burned bright, and she went back to sipping her tea.

Still ignoring Rahim's and Thor's warning, Selena finally said, "I'm not who you think I am." While explaining her guise—and avoiding the topic of her Divine nature and royal bloodline—Rahim plugged his ears and shouted so that Niamh and Maria couldn't hear. However, Niamh placed a hand over his mouth, and they listened to her confession.

As she finished, Niamh's face turned cherry red when she realized she was attracted to another young lady, and her head swiveled away. Maria, however, wasn't nearly as shocked, but her widened eyes sparkled from the flickering candles. "Well, that is a huge shock, but honestly, I've had my suspicions. I didn't say anything because it wasn't my business and for obvious reasons."

Rahim jumped to his feet and pointed an accusing finger at Maria. "How could you possibly know that Andric was a girl?"

Maria remained indifferent and calm. "Unlike most people, I pay attention to small details. I must say, you've played your role well to fool the Council and everyone else."

"Have your opinions changed of me? Niamh?"

Still blushing, Niamh shook her head and flashed her a quick smile. Maria offered her a handshake instead. "It's nice to meet the real you, Selena Liongod."

Once Niamh overcame her embarrassment, she stood up and curtsied before going upstairs and returning with a suitcase. She and Maria decided it was time to join the secret underground bunker before the upcoming battle. "May the Divines watch over you and Thor," Maria said, and she and Niamh marched away from the estate.

Rahim, however, stayed put, and Selena urged him to follow their example. "I don't plan on running and hiding now." He sighed. "I half-expected you to tell them about you being the Crown Princess and a dragon, but I still don't think that was the best idea in telling them you're a lady."

"They deserved to know that at least," was all Selena could say.

Though Rahim may have been more at ease, Thor was still skeptical. **I hope you haven't jeopardized our ruse, my dear one.**

I don't believe so. I trust Niamh and Maria.

Silver still hadn't returned, but Selena gave her regards to the footman before joining Thor by the fountain. Rahim followed her, and when the manor's doors closed, he asked, "You're going after Ragnarok, aren't you?"

Blind-sighted by his abrupt assumption, Selena could only shrug, as she wasn't sure if the moment was now. "Thor and I are still figuring that out, and we cannot leave on the eve of battle." Thor slid his head across the pavement and opened his blazing eyes, smoke wafting from his nostrils and clamped maw. Yawning and stretching as he stood up, he plucked Selena from the ground and planted her on his back.

"Then go *during* the battle," Rahim resolved. "They'll be too busy fighting out there to notice."

Selena strapped herself down with the carabiners. "Believe me, they will notice."

I think Rahim has a point. I believe if we slip inside the dwarven ruin during the battle, it will take the others a while to realize we're not there.

But we're assigned directly beside Aracania. She will see us missing.

As soon as we find a break, that will be our chance.

The Council would put us on trial for treason if we went against orders. However, if the Divines find it agreeable, we will seize the first golden opportunity.

CHAPTER 21: THE SIEGE OF THE NORTH

The tolling of the war bell disrupted the peaceful dawn of the third morning, and the Imperial Air Force flew into a frenzy. While Azrael tightened his bracers, Selena's hands trembled as she donned her official armor, and she strapped Dragonheart and her shield over her back. She grabbed a pack with provisions, such as her spyglass, compass, map, her Force issued revolver, a water-filled canteen, and flares in case of emergency.

As soon as the two were ready, she and Azrael raced through the fort with the other battle-ready soldiers. By the time they reached the dragons, Aracania had her groups already in formation and ready for flight. Doragon and Thor—in harness with strapped supplies including ammo, extra flares, two spare canteens filled with water, beef jerky with hardtack, and blankets—chirped and chittered upon seeing their riders.

Though the ground crew had already secured his saddle, snug against Thor's warm belly, Selena anxiously fiddled with the straps until he groaned. **I'm fine. Stop fussing over me.**

I'm sorry. I just want to make sure.

You're trembling. We'll be fine.

What if we can't stop the Lich from getting Ragnarok? At this rate, we won't have time to find it before he does.

We're two Divinity Dragons, and we will rain fire upon our enemies. The Lich should be afraid of us.

Thor extended his paw and hoisted Selena over his back. After she belted herself to the seat and tightened her carabiners, Thor unfurled his wings and quickly shook the harness, and Selena confirmed the straps held. The other dragons in all three groups did the same; the excited Aster, who upheld the rear left flank of Aracania's formation, nearly bucked Mr. Kingsleigh off the saddle before being adequately strapped down. "By the Divines, you act like this is your first battle." Aster looked down shamefully, and Mr. Kingsleigh withdrew his comment and stroked his neck.

Colonel Cyres and his companion, Onyxria, a female heavyweight Onyxian Steelbelly, took the lead in the second formation beside Aracania's. Vulcan seized charge of the right flank behind Onyxria, and Selena waved and saluted to Gromm and Beck. The Steelmane brothers acknowledged her gestures and returned to their preparations with Beck cleaning his revolver and Gromm ensuring enough ammo.

However, much to Selena's dismay, Silver wasn't amidst the pell-mell crowd as neither dragon nor human, though Colonel Cyres wasn't concerned. Instead, the third group was led by an Imperial Pearlscale, its strikingly white hide as smooth as a snake's skin. Two long tendrils the length of its neck flowed in the breeze. Donned around its neck was a solid gold torque set with sapphires; the deep color magnified the hue of its sea-green eyes that pierced Selena's emeralds.

Its frill decorating its jawline flared and trembled, and Thor snarled upon seeing the dragon. **That's Jade.**

I assumed, though I was hoping to be wrong.

Jade hissed and unfolded his massive wings but didn't step out of place. Thor responded with a warning growl, but Aracania snapped at the two, ending their quarrel. **He blames us for Ashur's suspension and disappearance,** Thor said, **I don't understand how they can still allow Jade to serve when his rider committed treason.**

As much as Jade is like Ashur, he shouldn't be condemned for his handler's sins. However, I figured Jade would have been suspended, too.

He was for a while, but Aracania recently cleared his return. Thor still snarled in between his tail flickers but turned away when Selena begged him to leave Jade be; he instead focused on comparing his golden chain to Jade's jewelry set, but Selena reassured him his treasures were worth far more.

General Araneus marched forth with a helmet underneath an arm and united with Aracania, ensuring all was in order. As soon as Aracania helped him into the saddle, she signaled with her wings to take flight. The riders put up a great deal of noise as the dragons rose into the air, echoing throughout the covert. Doragon's blazing presence in his gold-silver brilliance overshadowed Aracania's slick and shimmering black and purple hide. Thor's crimson and golden gleam radiated with the morning sun's rays, casting flecks across the ground as the dragons beat up into the sky.

As the Pyre's war bell finished its last ring, the three groups positioned themselves above the wall, hovering aloft, waiting for any sign of the enemy. The archers below got into position, bows taut and arrows nocked. Giant boulders dipped in oil sat in piles beside the already armed standard catapults and trebuchets near blazing braziers. The eerie silence welcomed the glistening morning sun slowly rising over the horizon. When she noticed a flying object soaring towards them some distance away, Selena pulled out her spyglass and identified it as a fireball.

The blazing meteor collided with Alfheim's wall, destroying one of the catapults nearby. Not too long after, another comet rained upon them, and the Lich's army was soon drawn insight: from their perspective, the ferrying dragons flew in unison like a murder of crows. They were positioned accordingly, the larger weighted dragons above while the smaller ones swarmed underneath, shielding the transport vessels.

As the flight drew closer, Selena counted their fifty-and-more dragons compared to their twenty-five, the full might of Her Imperial Majesty's Air Force. Each ship from the enemy carrier valued close to a thousand soldiers apiece. The Lich's numbers far surpassed their initial estimate of thirty thousand; however, on Aracania, General Araneus sent up the first flag: *Engage enemy at close range.*

As the formation leaders took their separate battalion and, once the dragons chose their targets, they struck out immediately. Thor's eyes locked on an outlying transport dragon, a heavyweight riderless Blackland Steelwing; to Selena's surprise, its unwaning strength continued pushing towards the city. As its eyes fixated on the approaching pair, it paused mid-air without faltering from its heavy load. The smaller dragons guarding the Steelwing scattered like fleeing cockroaches as it reared its head back and exhaled another fireball soaring straight for Selena and Thor.

Thor folded his wings abruptly and made a steep dive to avoid the fire blast, but the Steelwing was relentless, unleashing a deadly volley of pure fiery destruction. Swiveling his wings and through a few mighty wing-strokes, Thor weaved through the inferno storm; one meteor launched towards them, and the two were set on a collision course.

However, before Thor could switch direction, Selena unbuckled herself from the harness, and, upon unsheathing Dragonheart, she dashed along his spine. Instinctively calling forth air magic, she jumped in the air, blade held high. Once more, she envisioned its energy, and Selena swung her sword at the dragon's fire as the fireball drew close; she repelled the attack, countering ten-fold, directing the blast into the transport dragon. Before the Steelwing could disengage, Selena's redirected offense struck it from the burning sky in a series of explosions, its vessel dropping with its body.

As she briefly floated while Thor swiveled around and focused on catching her within his claws, Selena pointed out their next target. Thor halted himself in mid-air while he dropped her back into the harness, and he beat up quickly once Selena strapped herself back in. **Please, don't do that again.**

I will only be that reckless if it means using its attack against it. Only a dragon's magic can harm another dragon.

Then you can do that without leaving the saddle.

While Thor worked on making contact with the next transport, Selena's eyes darted to Aracania for any signs of distress; facing another Steelwing head on, she had already reared her head back like a snake, green acid and poison boiling within her open maw. The other dragons beside her slowed their wing beats as General Araneus signaled: *Fall back.*

Once her formation cleared, Aracania unleashed her deadly spray of poison and venom upon her target, her acid concoction burning and eating through the shrieking Steelwing and the handles of its metal ship. When Aracania's fangs clamped shut, General Araneus sent a flag to Jade's formation: *Clear to engage the enemy.* Jade snarled, but his eyes locked on an oncoming struggling heavyweight transport, a Crimson Deathwing—a rare species with powers over fire and earth—the only breed aside from Divinity Dragons that could use more than one element.

As Jade folded in his elegant wings and dived, the smaller dragons protecting the Deathwing dashed towards him in pursuit. Jade came to a brief halt as they zipped past; through swift and heavy wing-strokes, he was now flying directly for the carrier. He reached its unprotected underbelly with acid boiling from the back of his throat, and Jade spewed his flesh and metal-eating spray. The acid burnt through both vessel and dragon; Jade immediately dashed away as his target plummeted with its talons wrapped around the ship.

When Jade returned to his formation, Colonel Cyres and Onyxria made headway, aiming for the closest carrier, a Typhoon Wraithclaw, a mottled drake of light green and yellow colors, and a master of wind. The pair exhibited forty-plus years of combat experience as they wily won past the defending smaller weights, skillfully taunting them away until Onyxria found the perfect opening. While she and Cyres distracted them, Cyres signaled: *Flank to starboard.*

As soon as Onyxria made another pass with the small defenders focused on her, Thor made a steep dive towards their exposed target, nearly caught unaware by this transport's unexpected crew and careful to avoid the retaliating Orc riders. The hideous creatures were all like Selena had imagined; they towered over her like giants with stone-cold thick grey and light green skin, giant ivory tusks erupting from their huge underbites, scrunched ugly faces plastered against their bulbous skulls.

Even as they prepared to cast magic, ignoring Thor's protests, Selena jumped off with Dragonheart at the ready and sliced through one clean in half as she boarded the enemy transport. The surviving Orc spell weavers conjured arcane weapons, but Selena was too fast, striking each one down with lightning-speed swings from her sword. However, one managed to break away from her deadly dance; it picked up a thick, heavy chain and began swinging it in circles above its head.

Selena turned around and blocked off its initial strikes with her shield, but the creature soon disarmed her, the chain wrapping around her body like a boa constrictor. She struggled to break free but looked up when Thor's thundering roar made the sky tremble; as Onyxria and Cyres successfully took down the defenders, Thor swooped in and engaged the Wraithclaw in melee combat of fangs and claws.

The Wraithclaw's sudden jerks and jolts bucked the surviving Orc overboard, its thick leg tangled in the slowly tearing carabiners that couldn't support its massive weight for long. Selena was next; she hit the saddle's edge before the dragon relaxed finally. Its chest muscles began to swell and expand, but Thor clawed at its widening maw to disrupt its wind attack, and he dashed overhead, plucking Selena from the now loosened chains as the Wraithclaw jerked and pulled away. The dangling Orc's straps snapped, and its body dropped like a boulder sinking in the ocean.

Thor swiveled his wings and turned around through tightening his chest muscles. When he unleashed another roar, he summoned a meteor shower raining from the blood-red sky, its blazing fireballs striking the Wraithclaw and its vessel down to meet their explosive demise. Colonel Cyres gave Selena and Thor a salute, and Onyxria roared triumphantly; as the four returned to their organized groups, General Araneus sent the flag: *Prepare volley.*

Thor returned to his position, and the dragons created more space between them as they prepared their coordinated breath attacks against the first line of the incoming carrier swarm. They paused to hover as their powers built and brewed, the transport dragons unyielding, and General Araneus sent up another flag: *Commence fire.*

In unison, Her Imperial Majesty's dragons reared their heads back with their abilities boiling and wafting from their open maws—Aracania and Jade inched further forward to avoid injuring their comrades from the back-spray. Once the carriers were close, the allied dragons unleashed their combined elemental might, a deadly rainbow display of absolute raw power.

Aside from size, the dragons were organized by element: the two acid-spitters in front—except for Onyxria, master over lightning—the fire breathers next, followed by ice, then earth. The Force lacked wind dragons, but now Thor was more than capable of switching abilities if Aracania needed. Yet, for the moment, Thor belched his torrential conflagration upon the transports and their defenders; their deadly conjoined flare of breaths struck them from the sky in one sweep.

However, as they won past the line of battle and the allied dragons ceased their fire, Selena's expression changed as she saw an endless wave of carrier dragons rising over the field from a great distance. Thor, however, snorted and tensed his wing muscles, eager for another battle; Selena wished she could share his enthusiasm. *The Divines help us.*

Numbers do not win a battle.

The day continued to wear on as the formation groups held the transports back, preventing the vessels from making landfall. The dragons grew visibly tired as the sun began setting, their wings laboring and struggling to remain aloft. When nightfall descended, the carrier dragons halted pursuit towards the city and landed by the Hinterlands with their ships. Aracania inched a little closer and snarled; General Araneus pulled out a spyglass, and once he confirmed that the Lich's army had stopped, he sent up the signal: *Ceasefire.*

Her Imperial Majesty's dragons returned to Alfheim, except for two scouts on high alert circling the city. The archers remained as vigilant as a hunter stalks its prey, prepared for when the vessels made landfall, but they had yet let loose a single arrow, the catapults and trebuchets untouched but ready to launch.

As the three formation groups reconvened to the fort, Thor's muscles burned as he strained his wings, and he landed ungracefully near the Fire Temple's entrance, the force of his impact making the earth quiver. He groaned when Selena unbuckled herself from the harness and asked for assistance in dismounting, but he scooped her in his claws and set her down before wrapping himself within his tired coils. She managed to take two steps before collapsing on his arms, Dragonheart slipping from her exhausted and trembling fingers.

Selena's ringing ears picked up the faint sound of someone calling her name, and she had enough time to turn around before Rahim nearly toppled over her. Her eyes fluttered open as she fought the urge to sleep. "What are you doing here? You're supposed to take shelter with the others."

"I snuck away before the guards sealed the bunker: I had to ensure you and Thor were all right.

Besides, I believe our window of opportunity just opened." Rahim's face lit up, and Selena jolted forward when she realized what he meant. However, she looked over at the exhausted Thor, who only groaned when she mentioned the idea to search for Ragnarok.

This chance may be our last, my dear one.

Thor yawned and swept his tail across the pavement, creating dust billows with each pass. **I will eat and get some water first.** He lazily stood up on his wobbly and burning legs, stretched out his wings a few times, and launched himself skyward in a swayed flight.

After quenching her thirst by draining her canteen, she and Rahim talked about their plan to leave during the ceasefire, but she worried about going against orders. They would be labeled deserters and possibly charged with treason if General Araneus found out; however, the needs of the greater good came before hers and Thor's duty to the Imperial Air Force.

When Selena expressed her concerns, Rahim reassured that "once we win this battle and drive that evil necromancer away with Ragnarok, you and Thor would be celebrated as heroes. Besides, that captain of yours will put his title on the line for you."

She still hadn't seen Silver since the day before the battle, and she hoped all was well with him. Once Thor perked up after eating four sheep and three large cows, he returned and made his descent through the soft flail of wings. **I'm ready, my dear one. Are you sure about doing this?**

I'm sure. There's only one way to end this battle: we must find Ragnarok.

Rahim was adamant about joining their venture, not pressured by Selena's dissuasion. She glared at Thor as he dropped Rahim over his back, but he reassured, **I think you worry too much.**

I don't want Rahim getting hurt or us. Selena sighed after Thor helped her into the harness, ensuring Rahim was securely belted in his seat before strapping her carabiners. *Let's just find Ragnarok before anyone wonders where we went.*

We'll answer to General Araneus later after we defeat the Lich. Thor shook his shoulders, the harness still holding tight, and, after stretching out and folding his wings several times, he made heavy wing-strokes to lift his still tired body off the ground, but then Thor soared over the city wall. The full moon's radiant light cast a silver glow over the land. Thor moved swiftly and silently towards the beckoning emerald sea, careful to avoid the enemy camp not too far ahead.

Yet, Selena's skin prickled as Thor dove through the canopy; the forest looked and felt different at night. The restless trees were like slumbering guardians, the wind blowing fervently through their leaves as they made their way through tangled limbs. Even the trickling Raging River grew still and silent; she feared the forest itself would attack them for disturbing its peaceful slumber.

When Thor found a meadow close to the path Neith used to escort them to Alfheim, he landed haunches first, careful not to get tangled in the verdant mess. Because of his size, it was impossible not to disturb the ancient grove; his wings caught and snapped through the thick branches as he tucked them into his sides. After Selena declared they were close, Thor helped the two dismount, and the trio continued forward on the dirt trail on foot.

Thor remained indifferent to the haunted forest, but Selena and Rahim shivered as the Hinterlands grew darker, black shadows adorning the lush, green turf. The trees thickened and rustled restlessly, and Rahim squeaked like a mouse, pointing ahead while claiming to have seen a pair of enormous yellow eyes watching them. Although Selena hadn't seen them, she did hear the shrill of a child's laughter echoing through the moonlit beauty of the forest clearing.

"I don't feel like being monster food today," Rahim whispered.

"I don't think anything would eat us." She gulped and pointed at Thor, trying to convince herself to be strong, but her efforts remained folly. "I'm more afraid of him than anything else we would see in this forest."

Thor snorted, ember shards escaping from his smoke-filled nostrils. **These forest creatures should fear me.**

Rahim bit down on his nails as his head continued whipping around to the distant wolf howls. "Do you hear that? A wolf pack called the Aynu live here, and they can shape-shift into humans."

"Don't be ridiculous." Yet, Selena's hand immediately went straight for Dragonheart when the howls continued bouncing through the trees. She only withdrew her draw when they faded, and the world grew quiet once more.

Their trek didn't last long; the two paused when Thor stomped ahead, snarling through closed fangs. **I believe we're here.**

Selena and Rahim raced Thor through the clearing, and her eyes scanned over the shiny, metal door sealing the entrance to a massive, stone structure built into the waving hills. *Yes, this is it.*

She ran towards the ruin's entrance, large enough to let a dragon of Thor's size pass, and worked on prying the sealed-tight door open, but to her dismay, it wouldn't budge. Thor snorted and herded her and Rahim to the side as he charged forward with his horns and rammed the door until it swung open. Once Thor backed away, Selena and Rahim tip-toed and peeked inside but only saw darkness with wafting clouds of steam escaping. She and Rahim exchanged confused and terrified glances, and Selena unstrapped her shield and unsheathed Dragonheart. "Let's find Ragnarok together and stop the Lich once and for all," Selena resolved.

Rahim nodded and gave her a tight-lipped smile. Thor snarled, stuck his head inside, and unleashed a mighty roar, warning the ancient ruin that its final hour was near. When it didn't answer Thor's threat, assured, the trio ventured through the cloud of steam.

CHAPTER 22: THE GUARDIANS OF THE CAVE

The cavern was not what Selena had thought it would be if she could even call it that. Instead, the ruin led them through a long and open corridor of stone and metal lined with pipes gracing the walls, pumping steam into the air sporadically. The Raging River trickled within the cave and collected underneath the giant catwalk the trio walked carefully across. A few burnt urns sat in the corners of the entrance, covered and buried partially in dirt mounds; the forgotten ruin was from another world not belonging to Armageddon.

"What is all of this?" Rahim asked as he peered over Selena's shoulder.

Thor sniffed every nook and cranny as he treaded carefully, occasionally releasing a low growl and rumble, his nails clicking against the stone floor. Selena placed her hands on a copper pipe, the metal vibrating as it drew steam from the flowing river. "This place looks like it has been here for hundreds of years, yet their inventions still seem to work. They must be much more technologically advanced than we thought, but the dwarves in Alfheim never mentioned anything like this."

Rahim shuddered. "That means we need to stay alert. I'm not sure what could be in this mechanical mine."

He lingered behind, but Selena sprinted ahead to stay with Thor as they trekked up a steep incline, her six steps to his one, vigilant to avoid broken copper and steel parts scattered on the ground. They only paused upon hearing a hiss, and a steam cloud wafted in their faces. Grinding and clanking of metal echoing down the halls made her heart race, yet Selena was amazed to see that none of the pipes or copper gates plastered into the walls carried any rust. Despite the lurking awaiting dangers, a spark of curiosity and a sense of adventure swelled within her breast. She was determined to find Ragnarok and defeat the Lich once and for all, and her motivation kept her moving forward.

Thor abruptly paused, however. He sniffed the air and quickly snapped his fangs between growls and snarls, tail flickering as he clawed at the floor. Rahim quivered from seeing Thor's hostile reaction and pressed his fingers to his lips. "I feel like something is watching us."

Selena gripped Dragonheart as she inched forward, but Thor's head swung around. **Don't move.**

Too late in heeding his warning, she felt her heart caught in her throat as her foot suddenly sank into the ground with her following step. Thor roared and immediately wrapped an arm around Selena, herding her close to his chest away from the activated trap. The path behind remained clear, but Rahim pointed at the ground leading to the dead-end ahead; a piece of the camouflaged metal floor ejected long spikes and quickly soared upwards into the ceiling, leaving a large square-shaped black pit.

As the trio slowly inched towards the edge, an ear-shattering shrill escaped the abyss, and two massive burning orange eyes peered at them from the darkness. Thor moved the terror-struck Selena and Rahim away with his tail when suddenly, a giant snake matching Thor's size with dark greenish-grey scales slithered from the hole. Unlike a Marcupo, the creature's venom-drenched fangs, like tusks from an elephant, radiated with an eerie pearly glow. The colossal snake's spined-hood flared like a cobra's as it watched them like a hawk. The terrible stench of rotting flesh lingered around the creature's presence.

Rahim dashed behind a nearby pile of rocks and busted urns. "W-what is that thing?"

Selena gulped as her hand trembled around Dragonheart's hilt, and she unsheathed her weapon. "I-I believe it's a Grootslang. Very similar to the Marcupo, but it will still try and kill us either way."

Thor stood in front of Selena and Rahim with wings fully unfurled as the primordial snake inched closer, its topaz-like eyes fixated on his lustrous scales and necklace. The Grootslang fully emerged from the abyss, and the spiked platform slowly descended from the ceiling and covered the pit, retracting its sharp barbs. As soon as the floor became whole again, the walled dead-end quivered and crumbled, revealing a giant golem crafted of golden and silver metal parts gleaming cherry red like a heated ingot in a forge. Its eyes began glowing yellow from its human-bust spiked helm, the gears turning within its heavily armor-plated torso.

It slowly lifted and moved its titanic limbs, and the guardian golem trudged forward, lifting its massive, bladed arm to push away the rocks and boulders through swiveling its upper body. Steam exploded and plumed from its armor, and the guardian released a fire breath over

Thor's head like a dragon. The Grootslang hissed and shrieked as the flames faded, and the snake leapt forward to meet Thor's flurry of claws and fangs.

While Rahim stayed away from the two snarling beasts, Selena focused on dodging the golem's slow but powerful swings, careful not to get close to its inflamed body. As soon as the titan threw another blow, Selena dodged as its bladed arm struck the ground, sparks flying from metal clattering against stone, and slashed Dragonheart at its torso; the clash of dragon bone steel on metal rang in the air. The golem staggered back but regained its balance as Selena repeated her maneuver, waning its steamed vigor.

Concurrently, Thor resisted the urge to aid Selena's fight as he avoided the Grootslang's massive fangs soaked and gleaming with venom. The colossal snake swung its long, sword-sharp tail that could slice through Thor's blood-diamond hide. He anticipated each strike and batted the snake's head and tail away before delivering deadly blows with his claws. However, the Grootslang paused when it couldn't break through his defenses, and its slit eyes fixated on Selena as the mechanical colossus knocked her away. She slid across the ground on her back, Dragonheart flying from her grasp; the giant snake suddenly changed targets and pursued her instead.

Before Selena could prepare for the snake's incoming strikes, Thor reared up, wings extended, and as he unleashed a mighty roar, a myriad of massive rock spears manifested above him and shot straight for the Grootslang. The snake screeched and writhed with pain as the earth shards pierced and penetrated its body and soon fell limp upon the sharp stone stakes, its black blood pouring and dripping to the ground.

Yet, the metal guardian behemoth breathed fire for the Grootslang's loss and stomped towards Thor in retaliation. Selena jumped to her feet and snatched Dragonheart, but Thor stood in front; maw opened wide, he unleashed a deadly torrential diamond storm of ice and frost that extinguished the titan's flames and crusted over its heated armor. Thor stepped forward, still holding his crystallized breath, and the golem eventually succumbed to the dragon's icy stream. Steam spewed from its limbs and head, and the guardian stumbled backward, collapsing in a clunk of metal before shutting off.

Only after ensuring the two creatures were dead did Rahim finally emerge from his hiding place and begin praising the two. Thor licked away the icicles sticking to his teeth and gums, but he snorted and held his head high. However, his pride diminished when Selena rubbed her back and arms; minor bruising and scrapes, but she reassured him and Rahim, "They're nothing serious."

Rahim quivered upon looking at the Grootslang's impaled body. "I'm afraid to know what else is in here."

After reassessing their slight injuries, the trio resumed through the crumbled wall that hid the mechanical titan, discovering a new hidden passageway that went deeper inside the ruin. Selena and Rahim jumped across the scattered rocks and boulders, but once the two cleared the way, Thor squeezed his entire body through the opening, making it bigger and nearly causing a cave-in. Yet, the ceiling held, and Thor successfully made it through.

Selena looked back at the inanimate colossus and shuddered upon its elaborate construction, possibly the peak and highlight of dwarven technology before the ravages of time. *I bet you all I have the dwarves set up these traps and creatures to protect Ragnarok and their starlight reading device.*

Thor only growled as he focused his slitted eyes down the darkened, twisted corridor. The three passed by broken metal pieces with scattered gem shards littering the ground; ahead was a locked room filled with discarded ore and ingots—a mixture of gold and silver bullions—behind a thick, steel gate. Thor briefly paused, inspected the hidden and secured treasures, and began pawing at the gate, sticking his muzzle through the wide bars. Selena's redirection failed; growing impatient from the gate's resilience, Thor backed up and charged forward with his horns aimed at the lock. Unable to withstand his might, the gate bent and buckled as he tumbled through, and Thor swept it away as Selena and Rahim cautiously peered inside.

Thor's eyes weren't the only ones sparkling from the trove; Rahim stepped lightly over the hunks of metal and picked up a smooth, gold bar covered in dirt. "I bet this alone would make me richer than the Empress herself." He immediately stopped as he met Selena's inquiring gaze, fearing he possibly insulted her mother. "Err, I mean—"

"Don't worry about it." Her hands went to her hips as Thor began shoveling the bars and ores into his saddle without delay.

Do you think your father could make me some jewelry from these?

I'm sure he could, but we need to find Ragnarok first. Thor paused and shamefully looked down at the last gold bar, but Selena quickly added, *I promise when the battle is over, I will ask Silver and my father to help build you a treasure trove, my dear one, and then we can set aside the remaining silver and gold in a bank vault for safe keeping. How does that sound?*

I am willing to wait until after the battle, but why can't I keep and guard the rest?

You would make the other dragons jealous, and if they saw your new wealth, they and other treasure hunters would attempt to steal from you. Thor snarled and curled his protective claws over the solid gold ingot. *However, by locking them safely in a bank vault, your fortune will be waiting for you whenever you need it.*

His growls slowly faded as he scooped up the precious bullion and dropped it in his saddle before finally agreeing. Selena and Rahim climbed up his arms and arranged their heavy yet, rewarding haul, totaling fifteen bricks, in an organized pile before securing them with spare straps and belts; Thor, meanwhile, focused on his gold and ruby chain.

The gleam in Rahim's eye vanished when he asked, "Wouldn't we get in trouble for not reporting this sudden influx of wealth to the Council or your mother?"

Selena finished tying down the leather straps and sighed. "I don't know, but quite frankly, the Council doesn't need to know, and I don't believe my mother would give a damn. Thor at least deserves this." She smiled when he chirped and chittered in glee; Thor moved and twisted around when she gave the word, and Selena ensured the precious hoard remained in place.

"Don't forget me," Rahim pointed at himself, "I think I've earned one bar."

Swiveling his head, Thor snorted but gave a firm, jerky nod upon seeing the gleaming pile. **I suppose he can have one, but only one.**

Fair enough.

Rahim clapped his hands once and clicked his tongue against his teeth. "That means we'll have to find a safe place immediately after the battle before locking them in a bank vault. I'm sure Silver can help."

Selena nodded. "Dragonstone it is, then."

Satisfied, the group left the pillaged and broken treasure room; as they trekked further down the dark and damp corridors, Selena heard trickling water ahead. The halls began widening with each step until they stumbled upon a large, steamy area with a pool split in half by a massive copper pipe bridge. Moonlight lanced through the stone ceiling cracks, reflected by the churning and swirling water. To their dismay, they had to choose between two separate side-by-side paths across the pipe bridge. Thor assisted his riders from the harness, and they approached their choices with heavy consideration. Rahim placed a hand under his chin, and his face brightened when he pointed at the left passageway. "This way."

As he mentioned for the pair to follow, Selena ruefully asked, "Do you know where you're going?"

"No." He disappeared around the bend while Selena was still busy reconsidering their options, but soon she wasn't given a choice when an ear-shattering crash and scream bounced off the stone walls. She and Thor ran to his rescue.

The passage came to a dead-end, but they reached the edge of a massive pit where Rahim had fallen below and twisted his ankle. Selena leaned on one knee before the edge and disappointedly shook her head. "You never cease to amaze me."

Through painful groans, Rahim looked up at her in spite and rubbed his leg. "I don't see you coming up with any ideas."

"The injured should remain silent."

Rahim's mouth opened a little but couldn't offer another comeback. "If you must know, there is a hidden passageway near where you two are standing." When Selena and Thor backed up and saw the camouflaged corridor of stone and rock, Rahim added, "Who is the oblivious twat now?"

As Thor plucked Rahim from the pit and placed him within the harness, Selena approached the hidden tunnel when she heard an eerie and haunting howl whistling in her ears. "It's pulling me in," she whispered and met Rahim's astounded expression. "I believe we'll try your way."

His beaming face was enough to prove his point, but he uncrossed his arms. "I'm never right. Why do you think I am this time?"

"I have a hunch." A flame flickered upon her open palm as she waved her left hand, and she guided the two down the dark and swerving corridor.

Thor snaked his way through Rahim's discovered passage and snarled as he barreled forward. **I feel it, too: Ragnarok is close.**

Though the tunnel greatly accommodated Thor's height, the passage began narrowing as the three pressed onward; when he had enough, Thor swiped once at each side, and the rock scraped away to widen the path. As he trudged along, he pushed and shoved the piled debris until they dissolved into the ground, keeping the area clear of clutter.

You never cease to amaze me, Selena observed, and Thor's chest vibrated as he purred like a cat.

As they advanced further down, the darkened veil grew thick, and Selena could only see her faintly lit hand. She fed her flame, but Thor snarled as he released a long and steady fire stream, his blaze glowing red, orange, and yellow across the walls. The exit was just ahead, and the three dashed towards it until stumbling upon an atrium of stone and metal devoid of all light built within the Mustang Mountains.

The natural amphitheater was large enough for Thor to fly freely; he stretched out his wings and extinguished his fire with a snap of his fangs. As his light faded away, blue gemstones trailing along the walls dimly illuminated the two-layered staired atrium. Captivated in wonder by the crystallized lamps, Selena released her flame as she and Thor inspected the azure display.

Rahim pointed ahead when he spotted their exit across the way, and after Thor assisted Selena in boarding, he stretched out his wings and glided over the large, opened center. However, he suddenly paused mid-flight when a loud bone-shattering shrill vibrated from the dark corner close to the door. Thor snarled and growled in response, warning whatever creature awaited that he was just as dangerous, but Selena couldn't stop her heart racing; she pulled out both Dragonheart and her shield, anticipating the creature's unyielding contest.

The shriek faded, but the shadowed corner escaping the blue crystal light suddenly glowed from hundreds of peering, yellow-slitted eyes. Thor was the only one not intimidated, but Selena and Rahim cowered against the bullion pile.

The many eyes blinked at different times, and suddenly, a creature with the head, front talons, and wings of an eagle and a lion's body, tail, and back legs stepped forth, a formidable gryphon matching Thor's size. Selena identified the gryphon as the legendary All-Seeing Argus when noticing its eagle head covered in many eyes. "One hundred, to be exact," she clarified, reciting from past texts.

"Why would anyone be daft enough to get close and count?" Rahim asked, but he covered his ears when the Argus screeched again and launched itself in the air towards them.

Selena warned, *Its swiftness even rivals the winds. Be careful.*

I'm a dragon, am I not? I am the master of the sky, not it.

Thor reared his arm back and swatted the creature away with a mighty swing, slamming the many-eyed gryphon back down. Realizing that Selena couldn't convince Thor otherwise, Rahim quickly strapped himself within the harness as an airborne battle between the two creatures was inevitable. Selena, however, was determined to give Thor the upper hand, and she realized what she had to do.

The Argus recovered; it flapped its long, feathery silver-tinted wings and zipped to meet its adversary. As the gryphon was upon him, Thor quickly extended out his rear leg and kicked it hard within its chest; while it was dazed, Thor slashed with blinding fury, his talons leaving deep gashes in its maned neck. The creature recoiled, giving Selena enough time to slide down Thor's shoulder, and when the Argus closed in again, she made the leap of faith with Dragonheart held high and landed upon its back.

Not losing her bearings as half of the creature's eyes swirled and locked on her, it bucked and jerked; through gritted teeth, Selena aimed her sword for its wings and, before the Argus performed a barrel roll to toss her overboard wholly, she sliced its shimmering wings off in one clean cut. The creature came crashing down through the spurts of blood pouring from its severed limbs, writhing and twisting in howls of pain and agony as it hit the ground. Selena free-fell briefly until Thor caught her with an opened paw, and he landed upon his haunches in the middle of the atrium, still holding her close to his jeweled chest.

Once its amputated feathered wings completed their slow descent, the griffin eventually got to all fours, shrieking through its boiling wrath. Thor relinquished his hold over Selena as the Argus recuperated enough and charged for him. As its beak attempted breaking through his armored chest scales, Thor grabbed its muscular body, digging his claws into its flesh and slashing upwards towards the neck and eyes.

The tormented screams threatened to shatter the blue gems lighting the atrium, and the gryphon wriggled itself free from Thor's deadly and bloody hold. Yet, it wouldn't give up the fight and began attacking in a blind rage. It lunged for Thor again with claws and an opened beak, but Thor met it with opposition; his fangs and the gryphon's bill snapping against each other made Selena cringe. She saw poor Rahim holding the saddle's edges in fear of his straps breaking from the battle of the beasts.

Instead of interfering and risking being ripped to shreds, she got into position to cast magic; inspired by Thor's beautiful display to use other abilities, Selena imagined the surrounding earth: stable and solid. Feeling the nearby rocks, embracing their strength and vitality, she dug her fingers through the stone and ripped it from its place. Twirling the broken pieces between her fingers, she waved her hand, and the rocks levitated momentarily before the shards fired into the creature's eyes like bullets.

The Argus shrieked as it pulled away from Thor and pawed behind its head. While Selena rapid-fired rock shards at the creature by waving her hands, Thor stood up on his hind legs, forearms close to his chest, paws opened. When he unleashed a thundering roar, he summoned a burning orb of light within his claws, its magical waves sweeping the atrium in concentric circles, each more powerful than the last.

The gryphon shut its eyes from the blinding light and retreated as the intense energy grew; Rahim remained behind Thor's neck, blocking and shielding his gaze. Selena, however, discarded her amazement and took advantage of the opportunity. She trekked through the energy waves threatening to push her back, but she continued her unyielding march until she approached the screaming Argus, but it made no effort to defend itself. With all her might, she held up Dragonheart and decapitated the creature with one clean slice, its head rolling and splashing through a puddle of its blood away from the body.

The atrium suddenly turned eerily quiet save for the light orb's pulsating hums, and then Thor released his magic. **It was an enormous feeling I wanted to unleash.**

You're amazing.

Rahim trembled as he peered over the saddle at the dead All-Seeing Argus. "I swear, you two with your magic." He huffed in irritation. "Sorry, I hate cowering down during a fight."

"Hopefully, we won't have to anymore," Selena assured.

"No, what I mean is that—oh, forget it." When he refused to elaborate, Selena sighed and cleaned off her sword. Thor scooped her within his claws and flew towards the upper platform leading to the exit, the trio anticipating what else awaited them beyond the massive metal door.

However, Selena and Thor agreed that their search was nearly at a close. *It's like I can sense Ragnarok's presence.*

I feel the same. Thor released her before the door and nudged it with his snout; he issued a series of chirps and twitters as it cracked from a light touch. **Not much farther, now.**

Nodding, Selena pushed it open.

CHAPTER 23: RAGNAROK

The three felt desperate to escape as the endless void within the following room threatened to consume them. It was a realm of emptiness and fear.

Selena felt alone, and she shuddered as a cold whisper brushed against her ear. The darkness was enchanting; it was like a haunting ballad pulling her deeper inside. Then came to her ears a sound like a ticking clock; her heart was beating hard against her chest. She felt her paranoia rise as she trembled, her breath quickening as she reached out to touch Thor. She wanted to scream but couldn't find the strength; the emptiness would swallow her cries, and she would be left in sepulchral silence.

Her anxiety faded when her fingers brushed against Thor's rough hide, and Selena relaxed. Rahim, however, remained indifferent to the chilling and supernatural atmosphere. "I can't see shite."

Selena waved her hand, and a small flame appeared in the middle of her palm. Holding her hand up like a candle, she looked around as the darkness melted away, revealing a sizable spherical stone chamber that could welcome several dragons protected by a metal-covered dome. Selena's fire reflected against a massive gold and silver orb standing before them, but before she could observe it, Thor spun around when his eyes caught a lever strapped between two gears on the floor beside the entrance. **My dear, over here. What do you suppose this does?**

I don't know, but let's find out. Without another thought, Selena pulled the lever.

An ear-shattering screech of grinding metal pierced the air, and the ceiling dome shifted, its casing opening at the center and folded downward, revealing the night sky through thick, tempered glass. The beautiful stars were like candles wafting in the heaven sea as the moon hung directly overhead, light lancing through the vaulted ceiling and illuminating the strange gold and silver object Selena wanted to inspect.

The device was a colossal arch emblazoned with mirrors sitting upon a raised platform of metal and glass. Selena treaded lightly up the stairs leading to the machine, discovering a glowing crystal orb displayed on a small pedestal directly below the arch, gathering a faint light beam from a smaller gem hanging beneath the mirrors. Even Rahim was interested as he peered from behind Thor's neck for a better look. Recalling Silver's scroll detailing such a contraption, Selena took some time to examine every angle and appreciate its glory. *But how do we make it work?*

Thor reared up on his hind legs and climbed onto the platform, observing the focus crystal's faint energy line. **I think you should cast magic at it.**

Why?

Crystals give off energy. Perhaps if you directed magic at it, it would feed its energy line, and the stone will power the device.

Remembering how the dwarves combined magic to power their technology, Selena had a hunch Thor's idea wasn't as far-fetched as initially anticipated. *I'll give it a try.*

When Selena repeated what Thor suggested to Rahim, he laughed. "Just shoot magic and hope that it works, right? Leap before you think." Taking a step back, Selena held out her hands and directed a steady stream of fire at the large crystal. As the gem glowed brighter, the energy line pulled from the small jewel magnified in strength, and rays of light beamed from the large crystal and reflected off the mirrors. The second quartz fastened within the arch collected the light from the mirrors and projected the energy onto the stone wall behind them.

Selena and Thor ran behind the machine to see what image the crystal created, but to their dismay, the device wrote words in the Elven Language on the back wall. *A fantastic discovery, but I wish I knew what it read.*

Even if we don't find Ragnarok, maybe we can figure out how to use this to our advantage and defeat the Lich.

But it's in the Elven Language. We don't know how to speak it, let alone read it.

There must be a way to translate it.

Rahim leaned closer as he observed the writing on the wall. "I wish Niamh were here. She began learning the language, but…." His voice trailed off when he attempted to remember any information she may have told him that could help translate.

While Rahim busied himself with the transcription, dark whispers hissed through Selena's ears, and she turned around to see a hidden altar within the machine's looming shadow. As she approached, she caught a gleam of a blade sheathed within. Thor snaked his head around and growled when he saw the altar, too, yet Rahim was the last to notice. "Something about darkness, but I'm not sure—" He yelped when Thor quickly spun around, disregarding the machine's possible warning.

Selena sheathed Dragonheart as she grew entranced by the strange black metal—she knew it wasn't regular steel—its smooth blade emanating a peculiar purple glow, magnifying the pommel's black stone, cut like a perfect diamond. The hilt carried an unusual design, an armored guardian with a lion headdress helmet and six wings creating the cross guard, three on each side.

Thor's low snarls vibrated from his chest. **For Xyaxon's Divine sword, Ragnarok looks sinister.**

Her heart began to race as she reached out to touch Ragnarok, despite Thor's and Rahim's warnings to back away. She was this close to it, just a mere breath away. The legend was true; it was right there, almost as if it were mocking her. By the Divines, she found it. So tempted to grab it—but she had a moment of clarity as she withdrew her hand, afraid of what would happen if she did. Conquering her fear and the sword's spine-chilling call, Selena closed her eyes and reached forward.

Expecting the worst to happen, her eyes fluttered open; she already had her hand upon the cold weapon. Her breaths quickened as she wrapped her fingers around the carved hilt and easily pulled it from the altar, the unsheathing of metal whistling from the light draw; Ragnarok fit in her hand like Dragonheart.

Rahim's eyes widened as he released a sigh of relief when Selena remained unaffected and fell back against the treasured ingots. "By the Divines."

Thor snorted, but his eyes remained transfixed on the wicked blade. **You're foolish, as well as you are brave.**

Selena was unsure of what to do with the sword after dealing with the necromancer; she thought to take it for herself at first, but she knew she couldn't control whatever power it contained. She then thought maybe destroy it so that no one could use it; even if she sheathed it back into the altar—as only a Divine being could draw it—its existence would continue stirring turmoil and conflict. No matter her solution, it would have to be immediately brought to her mother and father, or Silver, to decide its fate.

However, she suddenly froze in place as a cold feeling consumed her. Her desperation to run away arose, but Selena dug her nails into her palm as her body swayed; her heart throbbed in her throat, and her vision grew blurry. When Thor noticed her behavior, he immediately snarled with fire and lightning pluming from his clenched maw and arched his back like an angry cat. The confused Rahim cowered into the harness, his head whipping in circles to find the dark source. Selena's mind echoed with sinister laughter that slowly evolved to a deathly shriek.

She dropped Ragnarok and fell to her knees, the sword's purple aura growing brighter as she gasped and coughed. The air turned into frost nipping at her skin. Her body trembled, and she felt like she had plunged into one of her nightmares. The laughter sounded eerily familiar, pulling on the strings of what little sanity she had left at that moment. She felt as if her insides ripped to shreds. Selena clutched her chest. *Is this from the sword?*

When she had a moment of respite, she looked up to see her dragon growling and snarling at a robed figure standing near the entrance. The man completely ignored Thor's hostilities and approached Selena as she recovered and grabbed the Divine sword; when he lifted his cowl, she relaxed when she recognized him as Myrrdin. "Where in Oblivion have you been?" Selena asked, "How did you get in here?"

Myrrdin's eyes occasionally flickered over at Thor, whose unexplained brewing aggression swirled like the flames wafting from his serrated fangs; Myrrdin's indifference unnerved even Rahim, who continued muttering under his breath, "Something doesn't feel quite right."

Myrrdin finally said, "I had to follow and warn you three when I saw you traveling through the Hinterlands."

Selena squinted at him as she tightened her grip around Ragnarok. "Warn us about what?"

"All of you are in danger. Come with me, and I'll take you somewhere safe."

Thor's eyes remained fixed on him like a wolf stalking its prey, but Selena ignored his behavior. Yet, she couldn't shake the odd feeling creeping along her skin as his voice began carrying the same shrill tone that plagued her nightmares. "You shouldn't have followed us," was all Selena could say.

Myrrdin's eyes suddenly sparkled and gleamed with sinister intent when he saw Ragnarok, but he tore his gaze away. "I saw the Lich's massive army for myself—we honestly don't stand a chance against his power. Resisting him would be futile, and the only way to save Alfheim is to surrender."

"What in Death's name is this twat going on about?" Rahim asked, and Thor unleashed a sharp snarl that made Myrrdin take a step back. "Don't listen to him."

Thor reached over with a shielding arm and pulled Selena away. **Who is this boy, and how is he acquainted with you and Rahim?**

His growls and snarls escalated when Selena recounted their initial meeting. *Why are you acting this way?*

Something isn't right. The dark presence we felt isn't from Ragnarok.

Then where—?

"Is your dragon okay?" Myrrdin asked, interrupting their thoughts. "Has he grown mad from Ragnarok?"

Thor's low grumbles turned into menacing growls, and Selena finally understood. **You know it now: He's the Lich. Myrrdin is Venexus himself.**

Myrrdin suddenly brought his hands together and began uttering a prayer in the demonic language. He looked up and gave a heartless and vicious smile when he finished, his eyes now glowing red. In that instant, his form changed, growing remarkably large. His face became concealed behind an eerie white mask with black holes for the eyes and mouth, slight chips lining the edge as if it would crumble away any moment. His ghastly, frayed white skin tightly hugged the features of his narrow skull, set with dragon horns tearing through the black linen folds of his voluminous cloak, black poison dripping from his sleeves. What terrified Selena the most were his horrific crimson-glowing eyes peering through empty eye sockets.

Thor brought Selena and Rahim away from the dreaded necromancer, but five cloaked figures from the Obsidian Order draped in shadow arrived in a plume of smoke, circling the trio. The Lich's all too familiar dark voice pierced the shadowed curtain. "It seems you saw right through me, dragon, but no matter. I would have spoiled all the fun if I kept up this charade any longer."

Selena held Ragnarok in defense through Thor's protective hold when she noticed the Lich's minions stepping forward, but they didn't attempt to attack. "Stay back," she growled, her voice cracking like glass.

Amused by her senseless vigor, the Lich gave a deep-throated laugh. "If it weren't for me, you wouldn't have found Ragnarok in the first place. Oh, yes. Since the One Hundred Years' War, I've known its whereabouts, but only one of Divine birth can pull it from the altar. Now, at last, it's finally mine."

Thor roared as he flexed his free claw, and Selena hissed through her teeth. "You led us here, and you've been reading my thoughts and haunting my nightmares."

"I've been reading your thoughts since the day you were born, or should I say, born again. Thank you for acknowledging those wonderful dreams—they were a gift from me. Those about Gundisalvus himself made you such an easy target as you were so fond of his books. He may have been a great general and battle tactician to have defeated me, but his writing and ranting about Ragnarok led to his easy downfall. My loyal servant killed him all those years ago for revenge, but Gundisalvus was valuable after all.

"My gambit was ready for you, Liongod, and it played so perfectly. The Divines certainly have a sense of humor, for your Divine nature was what I needed to obtain Ragnarok finally. As I've planned, everything led you directly to me in the end. It was so easy for me to gain your trust since our direct encounter at the Grand Exchange." The Lich's glowing eyes flashed over to Thor. "Though I must say, I'm incredibly disappointed by your continuous rebellious behavior, young dragon. You were supposed to serve me, not some mere *child*."

Selena and Rahim dropped to their knees with hands covering their ears as Thor unleashed a deafening roar. **I am not your dragon, necromancer, nor will I ever be.**

The Lich only sneered. "You can repay your insolence and disobedience, dragon, and save her pathetic life. You two would be so valuable to me; imagine the possibilities of what we can do with her blood. Great power lies dormant within you two, and I can show you how to unlock it. Join me, and together, we can change this world into one that is worthy and rule as gods more powerful than the Divines themselves."

Selena's face fumed with rage at the offer; Thor's roar made the cavern tremble. "We will never join you."

"Oh, but I sense your ambition, Liongod. The very desire to grow strong in the ways of magic rests within you. Give Ragnarok to me, and I will show you how to unleash your dormant, cosmic powers. All it takes is your blood, even just a single drop."

Her hands shook as she, much to her shame, slowly considered the Lich's offer. While Thor and Rahim continued urging her to ignore his lies, Selena imagined all she could do if the bargain stood true: she could rebuild Helshire, bring back lost lives, and create world peace—

As the Lich gently extended a ghastly, skin-frayed hand, Selena immediately brought Ragnarok to her chest. "No, you can't tempt me."

"You still know nothing. Why throw away my offer to protect this filthy, corrupted world? Open your eyes to the truth, Liongod: everyone you knew selfishly used you in their game. Look at the Council—do they try to maintain order and make Armageddon better? Vidar and the others are even more corrupted than I am." He paused, allowing his words to steep. He chuckled when he saw Selena's betrayed look of trepidation spreading across her face. "Wouldn't you rather live in a perfect world, free of war, death, and suffering? Give me Ragnarok, and I will give you that wonderful tableau, a world worthy to exist."

Selena was the only one who counted his words; the Lich was right, to an extent, of course, but she resolved that the world was balanced; it could neither be truly good nor evil and no force in the universe, not even the Divines, could change that. "You liar. Even if what you said is true, we deserve a second chance. Everyone can change." Thor roared in agreement, and Selena pointed Ragnarok at the necromancer. "We will do what we can to protect everyone and save the world from you."

"Then your soul to Oblivion just like the rest of them." Chanting in the demonic language, the Lich waved his skeletal hands; vaporous mists of black and purple coiled around him as he summoned two weapons: one-handed reaper scythes like Silver's. Yet, their different designs had eerie intent, lustrous long curved blood-colored blades protruding from the snaths' mounted skulls covering the attachment rings.

As Thor unleashed the brewing firestorm erupting from his maw, the necromancer vanished and reappeared behind the starlight reading device, provoking Selena to chase after him. She slung her shield over her left arm and raised Ragnarok with her right, falling for the taunt; Selena escaped Thor's protective hold and dashed towards the Lich to engage him in melee combat. **What are you doing? Get back.**

Please, keep Rahim safe.

Thor's roars vibrated off the dome glass as he galloped to her aid while Rahim flattened himself against the saddle. Knowing they had no chance of subduing the rampaging dragon, the Order vanished out of Thor's way in smoke, only to reappear behind their Dark Master.

Like in her duel with Silver, she worked in predicting the Lich's movements, ducking just as one blade slashed towards her head, but Selena had never faced a dual wielder before. He purposefully missed the first strike, and while she was distracted, the Lich sliced at her backside with the second. Before she could move away, the scythe scraped and broke off parts of her armor, a large cut flayed across her back, dying her metal plates crimson. As Selena collapsed to her hands and knees, Thor charged after the Lich with his horns, but the necromancer teleported once more; he reappeared further away and suddenly lowered his weapons. "Oh my—we're expecting company," he said slyly.

As Selena used Ragnarok to prop herself up, ignoring the warm blood dripping down her skin, she heard familiar voices echoing from the entrance. *That sounds like Silver. He's back.*

Thor's snarls continued bouncing off the machine as he approached Selena, wrapping her within his coils. **It sounds like he's not alone, either.**

Even Rahim was happy to see Silver dashing through the door, but he recoiled upon seeing his unfamiliar accomplice, Kain Vanguard, ruefully following the captain with hands stuffed into his pockets. The two bickered like children over the current situation until Kain eventually said, "Another damn mess I have to help you clean up."

"Isn't taking the fight to the Lich your forte? After all, his undead army is like your kind—"

Kain growled and snapped. "Being a vampire isn't the same, and those damned soulless creatures are not my kind." He and Silver paused when they saw Thor guarding the injured Selena as she clutched onto Ragnarok, and their gaze slowly shifted towards the Lich, who leered at them in triumphant amusement.

When Silver noted Rahim's surprising involvement, he nodded to Kain; following Silver's direction, he vanished within the shadows and reappeared behind Rahim in a spire of black smoke. As Rahim stuttered and quivered over the shock of meeting an actual vampire, Kain groaned when noticing his twisted ankle and hauled him over his shoulder, using the shadows to teleport back to the chamber's entrance.

"Stay here," he growled at Rahim before joining Silver, who administered his familiar healing tonic to Selena, closing the wound on her back. Though Selena was healed, her armor remained damaged, but she was determined to rejoin the fight against Silver's and Thor's pleas. Meanwhile, Thor's smoldering eyes fixated on the pacing necromancer, anticipating a surprise attack.

When Selena refused to back down, Thor's wrath grew to cataclysmic proportions; as his inferno squall bellowed and brewed from his mouth and began encasing his body, Thor prepared for another horn charge. Kain, Selena, and Silver dashed away when the dragon stampeded towards the Lich, but the necromancer calmly stood his ground and extended a hand. Chains made of shadow appeared in a plume of smoke and wrapped themselves around Thor and his snout, extinguishing his fire; he collapsed, the ground quaking from his massive weight. He struggled and squirmed to break free from his chained prison, but his efforts were folly.

No! Selena rushed to Thor's side, but the Lich vanished, reappearing before her like a lightning bolt, and attempted another slice to her arm. However, this time, Selena was prepared and blocked his attack with Ragnarok, the sound of metal clanging across the dome. The Lich's disguised indifference to her swiftness almost betrayed his apprehension as he miscalculated Selena's skill. However, his deep, shrill voice stayed cool and calm. "Your dragon cannot help you. His betrayal and insolence make him useless, like you."

Thor continued snarling and growling through the chains. **Don't worry about me, my dear. Back away from him.**

But—

I promise I will fight my way out of these chains. The necromancer cannot keep me like this forever.

When Silver rushed forward to pull Selena away from the jeering Lich, the necromancer said coldly, "Hello again, *Genesis.*"

Silver stood between him and Selena, his arms spread open to make a shield while Kain watched his back. "This isn't exactly how I imagined meeting you again, *Venexus.* Were you growing bored of your disguise already? I'll admit, prancing around as this Myrrdin fellow was clever, but I reserved my notions."

"At least I didn't keep my secret from the world long, unlike you." The Lich sneered and pointed at Silver with the skull upon his scythe. "Now is your chance to tell everyone, Genesis, what you are. Should I call you a shapeshifter or demigod?"

CHAPTER 24: THE DRAGON AWAKENS

Though Selena smirked that her suspicions regarding Silver's unique nature were true, Silver merely shrugged and grinned ear to ear when the Lich referred to him as a demigod. "Well, a demigod is just an ancient shapeshifter, so I believe I've earned that title." Even in the face of evil, Silver remained as sly as ever.

Kain pinched the bridge of his nose while Rahim had more of an erratic reaction to Silver's exposed identity. Thor, however, couldn't care less, as he focused on fighting against the Lich's magic to free himself of the dark bindings.

Venexus ignored Thor's vain attempts. "Your title and powers don't concern me. Tell me: how does it feel to know I can easily take away her life instantly? You'll live alone for the rest of eternity, knowing you couldn't do anything to save her. After all, she is the only living proof of your crowned achievement—the fabled dream of a madman slipping through your fingers." He paused when his crimson eyes darted to Selena, and her face became fragile like a porcelain vase when she felt his dark presence pressing into her thoughts. "Or, taking away the pain of a cursed love, affections never to be reciprocated."

Selena tightened her grip around Ragnarok, ignoring Silver's curious gaze; he suddenly pushed her towards Kain as the Lich summoned a large shadow ball pluming with black and purple smoke, and he released the magic. Silver, however, created a large blast of light that countered the dark attack. An explosion erupted from the collision and sent the allies flying across the chamber. The Lich's minions stepped forward, but he gave an order in the demonic language, and they returned to their stoic positions.

Silver growled, his hands ready to cast magic. "Your fight is with me."

"I don't think so. You and I are done here. The child—her blood—belongs to me. I need it to unleash my dragon's full power. He doesn't need to be in the egg for me to awaken the Destroyer of Worlds."

To Thor's dismay, the shadow chains continued holding, but he continued squirming and slamming his body against the ground. **I will never serve you.**

Selena didn't need to repeat his words, for the necromancer sneered at Thor's persisting defiance. "What do you call yourself, dragon? Thor? You've made yourself her pet, but you will concede and serve me in the end days. The time will come when I imbue you with the strength to kill a god. Her blood will awaken your true power, dragon—your days are numbered."

"Not if I kill you first." Selena roared like a dragon as she held up Ragnarok, but she and Silver flinched from the Lich's eerie laugh.

"Though I admire your bravery, Ragnarok cannot kill me. Nothing can."

Without realizing it, Selena remembered and recited the words she read from Silver's manor:

"Revelation shall be the hope of man. If Ragnarok cannot destroy you, Revelation will." She fixated a determined gaze upon the startled necromancer.

When the Lich looked over at Silver, he jeered, "You can search for the next hundred years, and you will never find Death's weapon."

Before Selena valiantly stepped forward, Silver gritted his teeth and charged after the Lich with inhuman speed, blasting fire, followed by ice mixed with the tangled web of lightning. As the Lich teleported away from Silver's wrath and continued taunting, Silver called upon his reaper scythe and rushed at the necromancer with it held high; the Lich held up one blade, and as Silver's weapon met his in a clash of metal, the Lich flew across the chamber. However, the two remained upright as the force broke them apart.

The zealots finally marched forward to protect their Dark Master when the Lich hissed; yet Kain stepped into the shadows and met the five minions when he resurfaced from a summoned misty spire. Kain gave them a toothy grin, but they were unfazed by his vampiric nature as they readied weapons and magic.

Rahim, on the other hand, quivered when he saw the fangs. He almost lost his voice, but he whispered under his breath, "I knew vampires were real."

Kain smirked. "Does Captain Vanguard of the Shadow Templars ring a bell? I don't believe you want to meet the same fate as your other comrades." His threat went unheeded as they marched forward; one fired a warning shot above his head, and Kain called upon his weapon: a two-handed morning star, its deadly sharp spikes ready for bloodshed.

The sharpshooter blasted a small hole in Kain's shoulder, but he only staggered while shaking his head and rotating his shoulder. "I hate it when you bastards do that.

It's annoying." The injury healed itself, and before they could flee, Kain held up his massive, spiked mace and smashed it into the gunslinger's skull. As the Order spread further out, Kain snapped his fingers, and three shadow doppelgangers appeared before the others, and one by one, Kain struck them down; Rahim whimpered from his terrifying display.

Meanwhile, Selena wriggled herself in the middle of Silver's contest against the Lich, but Silver continued pleading for her to step back. Selena announced when she was at her wit's end: "I will not stand and watch you fight my battle for me. The Lich is my fight."

Silver snarled through gritted teeth when he and the Lich broke away from another clash. However, he inhaled deeply and met her determined gaze. "I won't allow you to face him alone."

The Lich's mocking laugh interrupted their touching moment. "I will ensure a special place for you two in Oblivion."

After seeing how futile it would be to use magic against the Lich, Selena reminded herself to focus more on melee attacks. While she drew his attention by attacking head-on, Silver dashed to the side with his scythe at the ready, but the Lich was prepared. He countered Selena's attack and used his second scythe to block Silver's. Silver moved with the speed of a dragon, targeting every weak spot he could find, but the Lich was just as quick in blocking, if not faster. Their weapons clashed together in a flurry of blinding strikes, sparks of lightning and fire flying in random directions from each collision.

Maintaining a level head, Selena stomped forward. Her foot sunk into the ground, and a large, earth wall shot up in front of her. She made diagonal slices with Ragnarok, and the perfectly cut sharp pieces flung through the air, aiming to pierce the Lich while Silver had him distracted. However, to her dismay, the necromancer crossed his two weapons, protecting himself from the attack; the rocks crumbled upon touching his barrier.

Before Selena could unleash another strike, the Lich extended his hand through the dripping black acid from his cloak. The Lich glared at the two through his expressionless mask, and Selena and Silver ran towards the bound Thor, creating an arcane shield to protect them against the Lich's swelling, devastating attack. Meanwhile, Kain rushed to Rahim's side and dragged him through the door, back inside the atrium.

Following the Lich's demonic enchantment, he slashed his arm through the air, and black acid rained upon them, corroding and melting all it touched save for Silver's and Selena's steadfast magical barrier. Selena's chest ached when not even the dwarven device could withstand the necromancer's raid, and its glowing message faded; she feared that the machine's warning about the future would be lost to the ages forever.

Once the acid rain faded, Kain returned after ensuring Rahim's safety and joined their side, and the three ensued their fight with the necromancer. Selena couldn't help but commend the Lich's dual-wielding ability. It irritated her, regardless, as she had not been able to get in a single blow. Kain did what he could to help, but the necromancer quickly blocked every attack from all three.

Speaking once more in the demonic language, the Lich suddenly levitated in the air as he grew imbued with a purple aura, and giant, black raven-feathered wings sprouted from his back. He released his weapons; as they kept themselves suspended in the air, he waved his hands, and an invisible force threw the three across the chamber and away from Thor. The Lich taunted, "I will give you the privilege to be well acquainted with my minions."

Selena propped herself up with Ragnarok's untarnished blade. "I've already met your followers. What else can you throw at me?"

"Those foolish imbeciles are worthless, unable to accomplish simple tasks." The Lich glided across the ground and waved his hands once again. The room grew black from the shadows adorning the walls, and tiny, draconic-looking creatures emerged from the dark abyss, their bright red, circular eyes piercing the darkness like smoldering embers. "Those from the Obsidian Order have but one purpose: distracting the world while I move quickly and quietly throughout the lands. But now, you have the honor of meeting my demonic allies from Oblivion."

Selena clutched onto Ragnarok for support. Her heart raced as facing these shadow monsters tormented her worse than her nightmares. The glowing red eyes surrounded her as shrill, childish laughter stabbed her ears. Silver's, Kain's, and Thor's voices grew faint as they called her name, and when the Lich's black magic severed her connection to Thor, Selena felt wholly alone. She swung Ragnarok as the demons surrounded and lunged for her one after another. Each one she slew disappeared into the black mist, leaving behind a pile of ashes in its place.

The Lich, meanwhile, focused his other attacks on Silver and Kain, keeping them away from Selena trapped within the shadowed veil. Massive black vines emerged from the sleeves of his cloak, obeying the Lich's will as they sought the two. Silver danced through the tangled web of thorns, slicing and cutting each vine and branch, the dark magic shattering like glass from his weapon. Kain bashed and slammed his way to freedom, and when he was in the clear, he rushed towards the Lich, gnashing his vampiric fangs in frustration. The Lich pulled back, his twisted black forest breaking like ice, and resumed the melee offensive, slowly turning defensive as Kain and Silver retaliated ten-fold.

Concurrently, Selena remained determined as she ran through the darkness, slicing through each demon daring to attack. Gritting her teeth and tightening her grip until her knuckles turned white, she stood her ground with Ragnarok ready. Before the horde surrounded her, Selena envisioned the world's woven strands of energy, and Ragnarok's ebony blade glowed blue. Unable to contain the magic any longer, and as the demons pounced, Selena spun in place with Ragnarok pointed outward; the gathered energy unleashed in one concentric wave, obliterating the Lich's summoned allies and her shadow prison.

Silver and Kain watched her in awe when she returned; the Lich, however, snarled and growled as Selena made her way towards Thor. With the idea of using Ragnarok to free him, the Lich manipulated the shadows beneath her feet. They transformed into claws that latched onto her ankles; she tripped, and the black talons dragged her away. Thor's eyes turned to slits as his attempts to escape intensified, muscles tightening in his arms and legs as he gathered his strength. Though the Lich hadn't noticed, Thor's chains rattled as he slowly stretched them to their limit.

Selena wriggled around until she could slash Ragnarok at the shadow hands, and she rejoined the duel against the Lich. While the necromancer blocked Silver's attack with his first scythe, he aimed his second sickle at Silver's side; Selena rushed in with Ragnarok and slammed it against the crimson blade before the Lich delivered his deadly blow. When their weapons made contact, the impact force created cracks along Ragnarok's edge, spiderwebbing towards the cross guard.

Lightning writhed around the Divine sword, and as the Lich pulled away, Ragnarok shattered like glass, and pieces of it flew in every direction. The Lich hissed for the loss of the legendary weapon, and while Selena was stunned in shock, he snatched Ragnarok's hilt and impaled her in the stomach with what remained of the sword. Her armor couldn't withstand the broken ebony, sharp obsidian erupting like a volcano with every enchantment and spell.

The pain was unbearable. Selena's mind shattered with the sword, and she collapsed on the ground as the taste of metal filled her mouth, her hand frantically wrapping around Ragnarok's hilt and black diamond pommel. Silver rushed to her side and summoned his arcane shield, protecting the two from the elemental magic flaring from the fractured shards and shooting blasts and beams in all directions. The Lich and Kain caught the force of the impact and smashed against the walls. The chamber trembled like it was going to collapse.

Amidst the chaotic flare, Thor snapped off the chains binding his snout as he opened his maw with a thundering roar. As each of his shadow shackles broke off link by link, Kain swore under his breath and checked on Rahim, who limped from the doorway to see what was happening. After ensuring he could walk, Kain summoned a shadow portal that could only allow for short-distance travel to Dragonstone Estate, and Kain ordered: "No matter what, stay there."

Rahim gulped but nodded; he limped through as fast as possible, and the portal closed once he crossed over. Before he could join the others, Kain ducked when a large explosion erupted above their heads, crashing into the ceiling, and breaking through the glass dome. Debris from the destructive magic fell and destroyed what remained of the starlight reading device and the altar; the earth rumbled like the Mustang Mountains would soon collapse on them. The Lich concealed himself within an arcane shield protecting him from obliteration.

Yet, ignoring Ragnarok's wrathful devastation, Thor's breaths grew deeper and heavier, turbulent winds and dust clouds circling him in a rampaging maelstrom. His smoldering amber eyes flashed red like the furious flames exploding around his body, and as Thor roared, his fire grew, disintegrating the remaining bindings to ash. The Lich looked amused by his efforts; Thor took his stance and reared up as the flames spread. He roared, and the blast grew to an exploding shockwave, easing Ragnarok's cataclysm.

Silver's shield withstood Thor's wrath, but not the necromancer's: his magic bubble cracked and shattered like glass. When Thor released another destructive concentric wave, the Lich held up his hands and siphoned the attack, redirecting the flames behind him. Thor's blazing inferno danced off his hide as clouds swirled around him expanded upward. Bolts of lightning mixed with fire bellowed within his crimson squall, and Thor unleashed flaming meteors raining upon the necromancer. Still, the Lich remained unscathed from his magic, the fireballs passing through him like an apparition.

As Thor's rage subsided, he rushed over and wrapped Selena and Silver within his protective coils. The necromancer, however, praised Thor's growing abilities. "Young dragon, your powers are just beginning. You will soon unlock the gift I've given you before you hatched."

"I'm tired of hearing him talk." Kain reached down and grabbed one of the shattered pieces of Ragnarok. Holding it between his fingers, he chucked it through the air like a throwing knife, and it struck the necromancer's forehead, piercing his mask. The Lich's head jerked back from the force of the blow, and black blood oozed from the cracks.

Yet, the necromancer's shrill laughter made them cower. "Oblivion awaits my glorious return, and I'm growing bored of you. I will withdraw my army, so enjoy your victory, but I will eventually return. I *always* come back." He turned to dust as his words rang throughout the broken chamber.

Silver released his barrier and propped Selena up when all was quiet, his hands fumbling with the vial containing his healing elixir. However, his concoction couldn't heal her wounds this time, possibly due to Ragnarok's lingering power; Selena winced in pain from every sudden movement she made, and she spat out blood.

Thor snaked his head around her and Silver, draping over a shielding wing. **I won't let you go, my dear one.**

Her racing heart nearly exploding from her chest, Selena turned away when Silver brushed her hair from her face. "About what the Lich said before, I—"

Her aching dry throat stung from every word she forced. "S-stop." If he was referring to the necromancer unveiling her hidden affections, Selena feared to know Silver's answer.

"W-wait, I—"

Selena's lips trembled. "No. I-I want t-to remove t-this…. P-please help me…." Her voice cracking, she tightened her grip around the hilt, ignoring the black diamond's gleam from Ragnarok's pommel.

Low rumbles escaped from Thor's throat when Selena struggled with the broken sword. **My dear, let Silver help you. I know he cares about you deeply.**

Even Kain winced when he marched over, and he turned away. Silver, however, clenched his teeth as his eyes darted between her and the broken sword. "You'll bleed to death if I remove this."

Selena closed her eyes, squeezing out a single tear. "I'm bleeding... t-to death... n-now," she snarled. Her eyes flashed open as her nostrils flared, and her hand shook over Ragnarok's hilt. "Fine, I'll take it out...m-myself."

"But—"

Selena coughed up another messy crimson pile on the ground. While Silver figured out how to help her without risking further damage to her insides, Kain knelt beside Selena and wrapped his hands around the hilt instead. "I'll pull it out whenever you're ready, Silver." He peered at Selena and clicked his tongue against his teeth. "You just keep getting yourself into more trouble, Princess."

"The Divines... have a sense of humor."

"Are you still sure about this?"

Selena grew impatient and spat blood in Kain's direction. "Just do it!"

Kain lowered his head and laughed a little; he had come to respect her tenacity. "You have guts, kid. I hope I don't have to rip 'em out of you." He nodded to Silver. "I'm ready when you are."

Silver's hands trembled as he reluctantly left Selena's side and drew a large circle around her with a piece of chalk he had in his jacket. When he finished, he knelt beside her; sleeves rolled up and with a hand near the impaled site. Thor's eyes fixated on Silver as he growled and snarled as a warning. Silver met his smoldering gaze and reassured him, "I always know what I'm doing."

Kain rolled his eyes. "Must I remind you of how wrong you are?"

Silver ignored his response and waved his hands, the strange symbols he drew glowing gold. Ragnarok's broken hilt shook and rumbled within Kain's grasp, and Selena felt like her whole body was on fire, only to be quenched in cool water like a sword from the forge. Her flesh healed the gaping hole with each pull. Selena tried fighting away the pain, but it grew so intense when Kain and Silver were close to finishing. She cried and screamed and howled, begging them to stop, pleading for the pain to end.

Her vision faded, and her mind slipped away as Kain finally pulled out the rest of the broken sword; when Selena sank into a torpor, her eyes glowed, and her body swathed in light. Thor, Silver, and Kain quickly withdrew as she lit up like the morning sun. Thor's mind filled with whispers chiming like wind charms as he ruefully watched Selena's light grow. He snarled at Silver, believing it was his doing. **My dear, can you hear me?**

Yet, her voice was lost to him. The blinding light spread to every inch of the destroyed chamber until a sudden beam shot upwards at the stars and ignited the heavens. When the light faded, the three gazed upon a Divine entity standing before them in Selena's place: a turquoise spectral dragon thrice Thor's size leered over them with piercing, glowing emerald eyes that were unmistakably hers. She unfurled her colossal ethereal wings, celestial mist wafting from their edges; her crown-shaped horns gave her a regal appearance, like an empress or a queen. Gleaming like the twinkling stars was a massive smoldering ruby emblazoned upon her chest, shimmering from her Divine light.

In awe and wonder, Thor gazed upon her glory, but Silver and Kain dove behind the nearby debris pile when Selena roared. A ring of blue energy surrounded her, and as she flapped her majestic wings, she released powerful azure shockwaves expanding outward.

Thor remained unaffected by her growing fury.

Selena, stop!

Silver peered over his arm shield to see her gathered energy. "I think she triggered it. She proved my theory and awakened the dragon lying dormant within her—amazing."

After releasing one final blast, her eyes stopped glowing, and the dragon vanished in smoke, leaving Selena—human once more—unconscious in its place.

CHAPTER 25: THE DAY OF ETERNAL DARKNESS

Her head throbbed, and her eyes fluttered open to the infinite Divine sky drifting peacefully above. As she collected her thoughts and recalled what had happened, Selena felt her stomach and realized that Ragnarok was gone, and she no longer suffered from pain. Despite her moment of respite, she lunged forward and bolted to her feet when she didn't recognize her surroundings.

A burning aurora painted the sky. The iridescent clouds writhed around the colors like milky smoke, aesthetic and illusory. Sieves of mist caressed the sapphire blue stone pillars standing beside her. The realm's spectral gas gilded with eerie intent. Two silver ore moons hid behind the northern lights while a whirring waterfall trickled beside her smooth, rock and ice platform floating freely in the air. Its teal tear tracked the rugged face of the distant broken tower and plunged into the abyss below.

Selena then felt her stomach quench when she looked over the edge to see the endless drop below. She panicked and whipped her head to find a small, icy bridge connecting her platform to another with a castle made of glass. She last remembered a strange feeling of overwhelming power washing over her before blacking out, but now, she felt alone and even isolated from Thor's consciousness. "Hello? Is anyone here? What is this place, and what happened to me?"

A twinkling consciousness brushed against her thoughts: strong but kind, like if the sun itself could sing. "Don't be frightened, Young One. I have summoned you here so that I can warn you."

"Warn me about what? What is this place, and who are you?"

"This is my realm, Niflheim."

Selena froze as her heart felt like it was about to burst; she trembled and found herself immediately on her knees. "You're Xyaxon, one of the three Divines."

"Yes, Selena Liongod, it is I, Xyaxon. Like all other Divinity Dragons before you and Thor, you yield to us, and I brought you here to warn you: war, death, and destruction threaten your realm. The Day of Eternal Darkness draws nigh."

"What is the Day of Eternal Darkness?"

"The starlight reading device gave its prediction before its destruction. It's a solar eclipse caused by distortions in time and space that no one can prevent: the demons and undead grow stronger while we Divines weaken. The Day of Eternal Darkness was upon us ten thousand years ago, and Venexus had overthrown Death and took over Oblivion, making him stronger than you could imagine."

"But that happened so long ago. What does the Day of Eternal Darkness have to do with what's occurring *now*?"

"The eclipse will return by this upcoming winter solstice, and Venexus will use its power to finish what he began: to destroy your world."

Selena's face turned pale as the solstice was only six months away. "How do we stop it?"

"There is no stopping it. It has been foretold."

"Then why did you tell me this? I don't understand." When Xyaxon wouldn't answer, Selena was left alone with her thoughts. She began pacing, her eyes occasionally drifting to the wafting cosmos until she recalled her resolve to protect the world she made to the Lich. "No, I will not let that happen. I've always been told that we are free to choose our path, and I'm choosing to stop it." Xyaxon still didn't reply, and Selena eyed the castle across the ethereal bridge. She trudged carefully, reaching the delicate structure; its towers were smooth and glassy to the touch, stretching endlessly towards the vast, divine pool. "Hello? Xyaxon? Great, now the voice inside my head is ignoring me."

As if answering her frustration, Xyaxon said: "If you are to be the light that chases away the coming darkness, you must be a positive force for yourself. Expose your heart and face what you fear most. The closer you are to the light, the darker the shadows." A sound of clashing metal echoed in the air, and Selena spun around as Niflheim became shrouded in a dark curtain. Yet, a bright light glowed like the stars at the castle's entrance, and when Selena looked down, she saw her shadow moving independently. It pulled itself from the ground, tangible and animate like a real being, and walked over to her, armed with the same sword and shield as she.

It dashed across the platform and vanished into the darkness outside the light's range. The rays spread across the realm, and Selena pulled out her sword and shield, anticipating a surprise attack; she spun on the balls of her heels when her shadow lunged for her, their swords clashing.

After pushing her clone back, Selena held her shield up and raised her sword; she dashed forward when she believed to have the element of surprise. To her disappointment, her shadow followed the same tactic, and their blades crossed from the unsuccessful blow. However, Selena noticed how her doppelganger mirrored her changes in direction when she side-stepped it, the two circling each other in a delicate, endless balance.

She gritted her teeth and jumped up in the air with her sword, but the reflection copied her maneuver; the two fell back in sync when their weapons collided again. Her face burning with frustration, Selena threw blow after blow until she and her shadow were caught in a blinding flurry of clashing metal in a deadly yet symmetrical dance. Her opponent knew which exact move she would make, regardless of whether she mixed her strategy.

Selena clashed blades with her shadow once more, but the impact pushed the two fighters back. She felt drained and tired, yet, when pausing to take a breath, she noticed her clone did the same. When she straightened, so did her twin. "You're my reflection." Dragonheart hanging to her side, Selena walked up to her shadow and touched the hazy image. "I don't know what to do."

Xyaxon commanded: "Tell yourself that you're worthless. Tell your shadow that it means nothing and that it's useless."

"No."

"Why not? You're already doing this to yourself. Throughout your tale, Young One, you've convinced yourself that you're a burden and a tool. Do you think that?"

Tears welled behind her eyes. "No."

Xyaxon paused, allowing Selena to wallow in her self-created despair. "Is there something else you would rather say?"

Her emeralds shimmering like a frozen pond, Selena bit her bottom lip. "You're perfect just the way you are." Her shadow vanished in smoke and returned underneath her feet, inanimate.

"Well done. You're very wise for someone so young." The light orb disappeared, and the darkness surrounding Niflheim melted away. Selena sheathed her sword and strapped her shield over her back again before walking inside the barren keep. "Now, listen carefully. Venexus had initially planned to use my sword during the Day of Eternal Darkness to create a new reality without the Divines and where he will rule as a god. He needed both to harness incredible power, amplified by the eclipse."

"But I accidentally destroyed Ragnarok, so he can't use it anymore for his plan."

"Indeed. Young One, Ragnarok's existence within your world caused nothing but turmoil and strife. Its obliteration was for the betterment of all, so I thank you for that. However, I'm afraid the future of your world hasn't changed, and Venexus is still on the path leading to its end."

"How is that possible if Ragnarok was destroyed?"

"I'm afraid I don't know. I cannot foresee his strategy, but I know he will succeed if not stopped—Venexus will find another way, and you and Thor must defeat him before the long winter."

Selena's anxiety crept upon her as she began pacing. "I barely came out of that fight against him alive. I don't know how Thor and I can face him again, not without proper training."

Xyaxon's voice remained cool amidst Selena's heated thoughts. "Do you remember anything that happened to you before I summoned you here?"

Selena closed her eyes as memories of a Divine celestial dragon flashed across her thoughts like lightning bolts. "It was as though something overcame me like I was suddenly very powerful, but I couldn't control it. It felt like I stepped out of my own body."

"You have the soul and the blood of a Divinity Dragon. You possess the ability to transform into such, empowering yourself with their skills and abilities. You are most powerful in this form, but you need to learn control. If not, it will completely consume and destroy you."

"How? Why could I never use this power before?"

"When the Lich almost killed you with Ragnarok, he accidentally triggered and unlocked your ability. With complete mastery, you would be able to take on the dragon's state at will freely. Normally, only one Divinity Dragon is allowed to exist at present, but the demigod has found a way, as he always does. However, this fortunate accident is a blessing in disguise: the eclipse would also hinder Thor and you, but your combined might could still be enough to stop Venexus. We Divines are already weakened with that dreadful day drawing near and cannot interfere, but yours and Thor's existence gives the world hope. Now, open your eyes...."

Her eyes fluttered open, and Selena stirred within her bed; pain surged through her limbs. She winced when she moved her bandaged arms, blood staining the white linings of her bed and clothing. Dragonheart lay on the floor, partly unsheathed beside her round shield and the remains of her dragon armor torn and gouged with blood staining the metal.

Selena shot up from her bed when she realized she was in the barracks. However, she nearly fell off the bed when she thought she saw Death, but Azrael sat beside her. "What are you doing here?"

Azrael raised his brow. "We're bunker buddies."

Selena scowled, but she withheld any nasty remark that rose to the tip of her tongue. However, she relaxed when Thor slowly poked at her thoughts. **I was afraid I lost you, my dear.**

I will never leave you. I'm glad you're all right.

Of course. Doragon has been delightful company while I waited for you to awake.

Doragon?

He and Azrael are not the unmitigated asses we had assumed them to be.

Surprised by Thor's forgiving nature, Selena's voice nearly cracked when she and Azrael reluctantly shared, surprisingly, a civil conversation. Yet, he mumbled, "I would report to Captain Altessa in the morning. General Araneus and Aracania were very upset with you and Thor for leaving during the battle." When Azrael noticed her remorseful expression, he said, "Silver already made his report and defended your actions, and General Araneus immediately declared you two heroes."

"I suppose he can be very convincing."

"Despite mine and Silver's differences, he is someone you want on your side."

Selena studied him with a quizzical brow, attempting to understand his character change, but she discovered little. "I must know, why did you try and kill me before?"

"I wasn't trying to kill you. It was a front for—"

"No, I mean from when you pushed me off the cliff." Azrael suddenly turned quiet from her icy stare. "How could you do that?"

He turned away. "You weren't going to die."

"You always make subtle comments like you know when we're supposed to die. Even General Araneus trusted you to declare Erik's time—"

Azrael snorted. "You're almost as bad as the captain."

She gave up when he wouldn't answer her other questions, too tired to persist. Instead, Selena attempted to move but cursed her luck when her body locked up in pain. She looked under her shirt and saw a massive disgusting-looking scar across her stomach.

Thor said, **At least Silver healed you—everyone was so worried.**

Selena scowled. *There's no reason to be.*

Oh, by the Divines, there isn't. Rahim and I barely had a scratch on us. You were the one who was impaled and nearly bled to death.

I'll be fine, but there is something I need to tell you when we have time, perhaps tomorrow after I meet with Silver.

Thor chittered. **I may not have been able to speak with you, but I heard your dreams, my dear one. Perhaps Xyaxon wanted to share the warning with me as well—rest easy, and we'll talk more tomorrow.**

She had slept until the Pyre struck three in the afternoon, only waking up when Thor poked and prodded her enough times. Luckily, Silver was in his office, waiting when Selena finished getting dressed and changed her bandages. He didn't look up from the letter he was reading when she walked through the door, but he still greeted her by name. "How are you feeling, Liongod?"

"Better now, thank you." She sat in the chair in front of his long, oak desk, and Silver went to shut the door.

Yet, Selena's face glowed with crimson embarrassment every time she looked up at him, but Silver didn't notice; he sat on the edge of his desk and clapped his hands together. "I believe Azrael already told you, but I will confirm that General Araneus and Aracania have declared you and Thor as heroes in the Battle of Alfheim. Of course, they weren't happy that you two left during the ceasefire, but I submitted my report once we returned." He chuckled. "Thor was reluctant in relinquishing the gold and silver bars you three found, but I already locked them away for safekeeping until further notice. Not to worry, as the Council nor anyone else was made aware of your haul. I can only advise you three to be careful."

"They were more for Thor than anything. He had hoped you or my father could craft him more jewelry when there was time."

"Of course, and I promise we will in the future, but they're safe in a vault for now."

She looked down at her hands while twiddling her thumbs. "What happened to what remained of Ragnarok?"

Tight-lipped, Silver said, "The broken sword lies buried beneath the rubble; powerless, it no longer poses a threat." He stood up and clasped his hands behind his back as he bit his bottom lip; it looked like he wanted to say more. "Liongod, I—"

"Thank you, Captain." Selena stood up quickly and made haste towards the door, wiping away a single tear before he could see.

However, Silver marched over. "Please, wait." Selena paused mid-reach for the handle, but she still couldn't meet his gaze. "Please, before you go, I need to give you something." He only returned to his desk when she looked up, pulling out a sealed card decorated in lace and painted roses. Noting her confusion, Silver quickly clarified, "It's your birthday today, the summer solstice. This card is from all of us: your parents, Rahim, Thor," he cleared his throat, "and me."

"I-I didn't know it was my birthday. I suppose I forgot but thank you."

He handed it to her. "Even with the battle, we would never forget. Happy seventeenth, my dear." She examined the front and back of the card, and Silver added, "You and Thor are welcome to Dragonstone. Perhaps, later this evening, you two can join me where we can indulge in a more private conversation."

Selena tucked the card away into her shirt and nodded, looking at her feet. "We shall join you."

Once Thor finished gobbling his supper, he met Selena by the courtyard, harness-free; he found her charmed by the birthday card she had yet to open. He hovered briefly before gracefully landing on his hind legs one at a time, wings unfolding like a lady's fan. Like his shiny jewels, Thor's hide gleamed in the evening solstice sun from his bath and a fresh coat of oil.

Happy hatching day, my dear dragon sister, Thor said as he extended a paw for her to climb aboard.

Thank you. As Thor wrapped her in his claws and launched himself towards the serene heavens, Selena felt a familiar perception of a sensory experience—not of her and Thor flying together previously, but on her own wings. When Thor asked about her thoughts, all Selena could say was, *They're like memories as if I used to be a dragon.*

Or perhaps dreams but with the envy of soaring with wings not yours. Dragonstone's shimmering ivory walls were quickly within their aerial view; Thor made his descent near the familiar water fountain, and Selena sent the footman to inform Silver of their arrival. Once she had dismounted, Thor observed his reflection while fidgeting with his necklace. **I trust Silver in protecting those bars for me. I can't wait for new jewelry pieces.**

Selena smiled, but her eyes quickly dashed away when Silver rushed outside. Rahim, Niamh, and Maria peered through the doorway, but Rahim pulled the two back; the three scrambled within the parlor, doing what Selena could only imagine. When Silver saw she had yet to open her birthday card, he paused at the steps and frowned. "Wouldn't you want to read it?"

She fingered the card's seal. "I will later."

Thor lowered his head on the ground and nudged her back with his snout. **I think Silver is trying to tell you something.**

As she and Silver stood in uncomfortable silence, Selena briefly turned away to meet Thor's leering amber eye. She inhaled deeply. "Please, forgive my rude disposition. That was never my intention, but…." Selena turned around to see Silver observing her with a puzzled brow, and he stepped forward lightly. "I was afraid the Lich was right: I've grown fond of you since our first meeting, but I've convinced myself you never felt the same way." Her cheeks burned like fire, and her eyes darted down when Silver approached close. "Even now, I-I still wouldn't know what you could like about me if your affections were the same. I know I'm not very pretty, and all I'm ever good for is just reading."

"Don't say that." Silver's voice grew fragile. "You are beautiful, wonderful, intelligent, unique, talented, perfect; just everything about you—" He immediately paused when Selena's gleaming eyes perked up. "Kain warned me to back off, but it seems as though I can't. Please, I want you to see the card."

She quickly wiped away the few tears she couldn't stop from forming, and she opened the card with trembling hands. It read 'Happy Seventeenth Birthday,' on top, but her eyes lit up when she saw a book-pressed white rose clinging to the crease.

Selena gently picked up the flower, and Silver brought her into a tight hug. "Thank you for telling me," he whispered into her ear, "but, as you now know, the Lich is a liar. He will torture you because he knows you and Thor pose the biggest threat to him; no wonder the Lich was in such a taking to losing Thor."

Bristling, Thor said, **I made my choice, and it shouldn't concern the Lich in the least. I'm not the necromancer's dragon, and he has no grounds to object.**

Selena smiled when she repeated Thor's words to Silver. *Never fret, my dear. As you've said, you chose who you wanted, and you're wholly entitled to whomever you deem worthy.*

I will never let anyone take you from me.
Nor I.

Silver grinned upon seeing the riled-up Thor, and he ran his fingers through Selena's short chocolate-brown hair. "Does it bother you that I'm a demigod?"

"No, not at all. It sounds exciting, and I assume you've seen so much."

Silver's expression turned grim. "Being immortal isn't as amazing as you believe it to be, as you just *exist*. While you may not age, you watch everyone you know around you grow old and die. After a while, you begin losing your memory of anything you may have done or anyone you've met. You slowly grow mad as time presses on, realizing existence is pain."

"I-I couldn't begin to fathom."

"Honestly, it's a foolish endeavor—a madman's dream." Silver laughed, but he tightened his hold around her. "Most people have a difficult time engaging with a shapeshifter."

"I wouldn't." Her cheeks deepened in hue, and he chuckled. "Do you remember who you were before?"

Silver nervously chuckled. "Sixteen thousand years is a damn long time. I have vague memories of my past, but I remember being a young man who was a carpenter. I don't think I was much older than you were when it happened, maybe eighteen, or perhaps I was already in my twenties. I wish I could remember more, but it's been so long." She melted within his embrace for a few moments longer before Silver quietly asked, "May I kiss you?"

Her heart nearly stopped as her face burned crimson, ignoring Thor's snarls and irritated tail flickers, his sudden jealousy flaring as loose embers from his nostrils; without thinking, Selena said, "You may."

Silver slowly and gently touched her face, and the two met for a tender kiss. When she touched his cheek, their kiss became passionate. Yet, they only broke away when Thor growled and nudged his nose between them. **That's enough, you two.**

You've certainly grown jealous.

Silver lightly laughed through his red cheeks when he noticed Selena covered her lips with her hand; he took off his glasses and cleaned them with a pocket cloth. "Well, I'm sure I'll get an ear full from your father, but I could care less. I believe we've kept your party waiting long enough."

Thor watched Silver as if he were stalking prey when he escorted Selena inside the parlor. Rahim, Niamh, and Maria impatiently waited with a two-layered, attractively decorated chocolate frosted cake, with a dragon sugar sculpture as the topper. Celebratory desserts of this caliber were so expensive that only the wealthy could afford them; yet, Silver insisted, and everyone enjoyed the sweet confection melting with every bite when Selena blew out her candles in a single breath.

When Selena asked about his foot, Rahim moved it around until he winced. "Still hurts, but it's not too bad."

After finishing the cake, the small party enjoyed a delicious bowl of punch, one of the greatest pleasures after the grueling battle. Yet, when Selena inquired about her parents when the others were out of earshot, Silver regretfully informed that "Her Imperial Majesty was unable to attend, as her dealings with the Council kept her detained."

"What about my father?"

"I'm not sure. I mentioned the planned affair, but he never did say."

They finished with half of the cake remaining, and after ensuring the others wanted no more, Selena brought the leftover outside and offered some to Thor; he slurped it into his mouth in one lick. **That is tasty. Is there more?**

I'm afraid that's all there was, my dear.

Selena's smile widened when a familiar figure emerged from the pouring evening mist, and she saw it was her father, his mask slung over one ear. As much as she wished her mother could join, she still happily approached, and the two joined for an embrace. Chittering, Thor swung his body around and joined their cherry reunion. "I'm still amazed by how much you've grown." Thor nudged Dust's open palm in greeting. "I apologize on behalf of your mother, but she couldn't attend."

"Silver already explained, and it's all right."

The two turned around when Silver strolled by, leaving the gleeful Rahim, Niamh, and Maria celebrating without the main guest of the evening. "Thank you for joining us, Your Imperial Majesty."

The Shadow Emperor lifted his hand and shook his head. "No formalities, please. Not out here—I've been taking enough risks lately."

"It's your daughter's birthday; well worth it, I'd say." Silver mentioned towards the front door. "Would you care for some punch? I used brandy this time."

"No, thank you, as I can't stay for much longer." He gave a faint smile that Selena was only allowed to see. "I'm afraid I didn't have time to find a gift, but—"

"I have Dragonheart," Selena happily interrupted, "a lovely gift you made for me. I'd say that counts."

"Very well. I'm glad it has served you well." He sighed and placed a heavy hand on her shoulder. "Your mother and I were so proud of you when Silver and Kain told us of your battle and how you never gave up against the Lich. He's afraid of you and Thor—that's why he's extending all this effort."

Selena's glowing face suddenly faded when Xyaxon's warning rang across her thoughts like the Pyre's grim chimes. *I must tell them about the eclipse.* The once happy birthday celebration turned dreary quickly when she carefully delivered Xyaxon's omen, leaving them stricken and dismayed. While her father fell into quiet contemplation, Selena said, "The winter solstice is six months away, and I know that Thor and I must figure out how to control our powers to have any chance at stopping Venexus."

Dust gave a jerky nod towards Silver. "If you have any ideas, now is the time to speak."

Silver grabbed his chin and looked at the trickling water, puzzled. "I don't know the answer, but we will figure it out together. When we do, we'll have two Divinity Dragons waiting."

Selena nodded when she and Thor met each other's determined gazes. "We're coming for you, Venexus."

Thor stood upon his haunches and unfurled his wings as his chest swelled, and he unleashed a thundering roar that made the earth and heaven shake in fear, warning the necromancer his days were numbered.

*****

Lights flickered among the stooped, guardian trees behind Norrington Hall, and a ghostly gleam passed through their branches, descending steadily towards the estate's mirrored pond.

The tree-tops bent and yielded to Jade, who pushed through the wide clearing, his wings pinned to his sides, and nearby was the sound of muffled footfalls. His elaborate sapphires and gold caught the moonlight, alleviating the radiance from his strikingly white scales; Jade's emerald eyes shimmered like his gems in the darkness.

He swiveled his head to the sound of hissing snakes, and the former Captain Ashur Bel trekked along the pond's edge with a companion: a woman donning a prestigious sleeve-less military uniform. Jade quietly snarled from the shadows as the woman looked eerily like the one responsible for his companion's suspension from the Force. Yet, he saw the differences: her long, platinum blond hair drifting past her waist, purple eyes sparkling against her copper-toned skin, and cobra tattoos on both shoulders.

Jade slithered across the grass and joined the two as they approached. Ashur stroked his head while reading a leather-bound journal with one hand. "I knew you weren't who you claimed to be, *Andric Liongod.* I have proof that will condemn you and your accomplices to the gallows." Ashur closed the book and paused to face his companion. "Thank you for finding this, and the Dark Master knows Azrael is a traitor. Your next task awaits, Medusa."

*****

SOAR THROUGH

THE ARMAGEDDON TRILOGY

By C.D. MULLER

Don't miss out on these exciting adventures!

About the Author

C.D. Muller (also under the pen name Crystal Summers for romance) was born on December 9th, 1990. Of her love of *Harry Potter*, she discovered the magic of writing when she was fourteen.

She graduated from Patagonia Union High School in 2009 and attended college to study Computer Science and Programming. She participated in community events, such as writing plays for her local theaters and hosting author presentations for elementary classes.

Her husband's death heavily affected Muller's writing and art. She almost gave up on both but used her talents to help her cope with depression and anxiety. She currently lives in Tucson, AZ, with her new husband, newborn son, and three cats. For more information, go to https://crystaldsummers.com for updates and her social media.